TABLE *for* ONE

WEATHERHEAD BOOKS ON ASIA

WEATHERHEAD BOOKS ON ASIA
Weatherhead East Asian Institute, Columbia University

LITERATURE
David Der-wei Wang, Editor

Ch'oe Myongik, *Patterns of the Heart and Other Stories*, translated by Janet Poole (2024)
Vasily Eroshenko, *The Narrow Cage and Other Modern Fairy Tales*, translated by Adam Kuplowsky (2023)
Dung Kai-cheung, *A Catalog of Such Stuff as Dreams Are Made On*, translated by Bonnie S. McDougall and Anders Hansson (2022)
Jun'ichirō Tanizaki, *Longing and Other Stories*, translated by Anthony H. Chambers and Paul McCarthy (2022)
Endō Shūsaku, *Sachiko: A Novel*, translated by Van Gessel (2020)
Paek Nam-nyong, *Friend: A Novel from North Korea*, translated by Immanuel Kim (2020)
Wang Anyi, *Fu Ping: A Novel*, translated by Howard Goldblatt (2019)
Kimura Yūsuke, Sacred Cesium Ground *and* Isa's Deluge*: Two Novellas of Japan's 3/11 Disaster*, translated by Doug Slaymaker (2019)
Tsering Döndrup, *The Handsome Monk and Other Stories*, translated by Christopher Peacock (2019)

HISTORY, SOCIETY, AND CULTURE
Carol Gluck, Editor

Yoshiaki Yoshimi, *Grassroots Fascism: The War Experience of the Japanese People*, translated by Ethan Mark (2015)
The Birth of Chinese Feminism: Essential Texts in Transnational Theory, edited by Lydia H. Liu, Rebecca E. Karl, and Dorothy Ko (2013)
Kojin Karatani, *History and Repetition*, edited by Seiji M. Lippit (2012)
Natsume Sōseki, *Theory of Literature and Other Critical Writings*, edited and translated by Michael Bourdaghs, Atsuko Ueda, and Joseph A. Murphy (2009)
For a complete list of books in the series, please see the Columbia University Press website.

TABLE *for* ONE

STORIES

YUN KO-EUN

TRANSLATED BY LIZZIE BUEHLER

COLUMBIA UNIVERSITY PRESS   NEW YORK

Columbia University Press wishes to express its appreciation for assistance given by the Pushkin Fund in the publication of this book.

This publication has been supported by the Richard W. Weatherhead Publication Fund of the Weatherhead East Asian Institute, Columbia University.

COLUMBIA UNIVERSITY PRESS
Publishers Since 1893
New York Chichester, West Sussex
cup.columbia.edu

Library of Congress Cataloging-in-Publication Data
Names: Yun, Ko-ŭn, 1980– author. | Buehler, Lizzie, translator.
Title: Table for one : stories / Ko-eun Yun ; translated by Lizzie Buehler.
Other titles: 1-inyong sikt'ak. English
Description: New York : Columbia University Press, 2024. |
Series: Weatherhead books on Asia
Identifiers: LCCN 2023042657 (print) | LCCN 2023042658 (ebook) |
ISBN 9780231192026 (hardback) | ISBN 9780231192033 (trade paperback) |
ISBN 9780231549622 (ebook)
Subjects: LCSH: Yun, Ko-ŭn, 1980——Translations into English. |
LCGFT: Short stories.
Classification: LCC PL994.96.K65 A61213 2024 (print) |
LCC PL994.96.K65 (ebook) | DDC 895.73/5—dc23/eng/20231017
LC record available at https://lccn.loc.gov/2023042657
LC ebook record available at https://lccn.loc.gov/2023042658

Printed and bound by CPI Group (UK) Ltd, Croydon, CR0 4YY

Book and cover design: Chang Jae Lee
Cover image: *Mr. Zebra* © Choi Dahye

CONTENTS

1. TABLE FOR ONE

The customer comes in alone. The owner is a bit slow-witted and asks, "How many in your party tonight?" This is a family-style barbecue restaurant, though, so you can't really say she's slow-witted. Two servings of pork belly, a bowl of rice, a bottle of soju. Nothing too unusual, but for the order of a woman who came in alone at 7:00 p.m., it is sort of strange.

The woman drinks half a glass of soju for every three pork wraps, using both hands to have a quiet meal. Flipping meat with tongs, cutting it with scissors, grabbing it with chopsticks, putting it in her mouth with her hands—a typical way to eat. Even so, she feels uncomfortable, trapped by the gazes of those around her. The table, covered with one set of silverware, is like a boxing ring. The woman sits alone and faces the fluttering stares. The curious spectators throw a left hook, a right hook—the woman's only way to defend herself is steadfast eating. Sometimes, she too takes aim. In the empty spaces of the barbecue joint, gazes collide and then disappear like smoke.

The meat hardens into charcoal on the hot grill. At the rate the woman is eating, she won't be able to finish her food.

More than half the order of the woman who came alone at 7:00 p.m. remains on the table. She probably asked for one extra serving of pork so that she could eat the first. At a barbecue restaurant selling only servings of two or more, one portion of the woman's meat is left to turn into charcoal. At 7:30, her meal ends.

Did she really have to have meat? Some might ask that. For a solitary dinner of pork belly at 7:00 p.m., it would have been easier to stop by a butcher on the way home from work than a bustling barbecue restaurant. But the woman has her reasons. Just as I, staring at her, have my reasons.

Staring at the woman is as embarrassing as eating pork wraps alone, but avoiding eye contact with her during the thirty minutes of mealtime is hard. If the woman lifts her soju glass, I lift mine; if the woman fiddles with her napkin, I do as well. And if the woman lifts her gaze and looks straight ahead, I have no option but to do so, too—because I'm staring at a wall as I sit, and on the wall hangs a large mirror. The only thing I can do to avoid her is to keep from staring at the mirror too long.

If not for a flyer I'd chanced to discover, the restaurant would not have become my chosen venue for practice and study. At two hundred thousand won for three months, I could have joined a gym, learned yoga, or bought expensive health products like red ginseng extract and gamma linoleic acid, but I chose to invest in a more pressing need. I enrolled in a course to learn how to eat alone. If I could develop a healthy stomach and an open-minded spirit in three months, like the flyer had said, wouldn't that be the most efficient way to spend my money?

Before enrolling, I had to pass a physical examination. It wasn't a detailed exam, just a consultant measuring my pulse and blood pressure and looking at my pupils and tongue to determine if I could immediately enter the class. After a basic conversation about my health—consisting of questions about instances of poor digestion, what and where I'd been eating when that happened, what I usually did about it, whether or not I exercised regularly—the consultant jotted something down on a piece of paper. The handwriting was difficult to read, like a doctor's.

"Hmm, okay, okay," the consultant said. "Cases like yours, Inyeong, are very common. It seems like you have a slight case of nervous indigestion, but that's not a major problem. We do this check as a sort of precaution. There's no need to push yourself, you know."

The consultant said that he had always had indigestion from eating too quickly when he ate alone, but after he'd graduated from the course himself, the issue had gone away.

"If you're curious about the structure of the course, it's divided into steps," he explained. "First there's a written test, but it's just common sense—you'll pass without a problem. To give you a heads-up, solving practice exam problems will help you prepare better than memorizing information. After the written test, there's twenty hours of skills testing—this consists of five steps—and after that, if you pass a ten-hour practical exam, then you'll receive a certificate of completion. Usually 15 percent of students pass the first time."

"Fifteen percent? That seems awfully low . . ."

The consultant smiled widely upon hearing my words. At the end of his mouthful of straight teeth, a lone gold tooth shone like a star.

"Of the 85 percent who fail, more than half sign up again. Surprising, isn't it? But that's typically how it goes. The course has the appeal of a triathlon. To explain a bit more clearly, I haven't seen anyone disappointed about wasting their money, even if they don't pass the first time. Even if they don't pass on the first go, they can feel in their bones how their lives have changed. There are even a lot of parents who've heard about this place from word of mouth and decided to send their children here. It's because the kids' personalities are improved. Generally speaking, it happens to all of them. Let's see, how many months should I sign you up for? If you pay with cash, we'll give you a 10 percent discount. Yes, yes. Okay, now, if you could just fill out this form on the back of the information card. See this one line about your resolutions? Eating alone is ______. If you could just fill in the blank space."

Eating alone is <u>tiresome</u>.

I thought of the descriptor quickly, but it really was the best-fitting word for the sentence. Eating alone is the most tiresome thing. No, maybe even frightening. To be clear, it wasn't eating alone so much as going into a restaurant alone. I'd lived by myself for two years, but eating alone at home was comfortable. The problem was when I ate out. Every Sunday night, I began to dread the upcoming Monday, but not because I'd have to go to work. I was worried about lunch hour for the next week.

My coworkers all disappeared at lunchtime. They flocked together somewhere, leaving that one remaining person no option other than to pop into restaurants on their own. I was that person, and I'd already spent the past nine months like this, five days a week.

It wasn't like this at first. The first few days after joining the company, I'd gone to nearby restaurants with my coworkers for lunch. However, barely a week passed before I was separated from the rest. As soon as it was lunchtime, all the workers swarmed together and left. I, too, hurried to organize my space and get up from my chair, but no one waited for me. The next day was the same, and the day after, too. It seemed that the reason for my exclusion wasn't simply that I was too slow.

The first day I was excluded, I went to KFC and ordered two chicken tenders, a Zinger burger, and a diet soda, eating everything in thirty minutes. It wasn't too awkward. I wasn't so timid that I couldn't eat a hamburger alone, and besides, my mind was too busy for me to feel awkward. As I chewed my Zinger burger, I wondered why in the world I had been left out. Was it really a problem that I'd gotten up from my seat one or two minutes late?

The same thing happened the next day, despite the fact that I'd gotten ready early. The others rose from their seats leisurely, or went to the bathroom. After hesitating for a bit, the most natural thing I could do was press the elevator button to leave. I went to Dunkin' Donuts as if I were running away. There, I filled my stomach with a cup of coffee and two donuts. As I took my first bite of donut and first sip of coffee, potential reasons appeared like the word of God. Was the issue that I hadn't been friendly enough to my colleagues? Should I have gone up to them and suggested, "Let's go eat?" I thought about my coworkers, but I couldn't come up with an answer. There wasn't really anyone *more* friendly or *less* friendly than me. After I swallowed one of the flavorless donuts, I realized that tomorrow I'd have to find something else to eat. Paris Croissant and Starbucks had menus that would fill my stomach, but I couldn't spend months continuing this way.

At some point, my lunch menu moved on to kimbap, ramen, and noodles, and eventually I was able to eat a proper restaurant meal of kimchi soup with rice, surrounded by other office workers. Kimchi soup soon expanded to bean paste soup and beef stew and chicken soup with ginseng. However, because there was a limit to my movement and menu choices during the lunch hour, I mostly circled between the same restaurants. When I went back to KFC, I realized that eating alone the past week had been a mistake. I'd clearly taken the wrong path. Had I been too social with someone my coworkers avoided—maybe the manager? Or the department head? Someone else? Could that have caused this disaster? Anyhow, thinking there was a specific reason for my exclusion was much preferable to realizing that there wasn't.

Lunch hour always ended with time to spare. From ordering my food to paying the check, I was finished in twenty minutes, thirty at most. Throughout the entire meal, I had only one thought in my mind. Was there a predetermined amount of time that one had to eat alone in their lifetime? If so, I was fast filling my quota.

Those times when I couldn't wait a full hour and went back to the office ten or fifteen minutes early, I returned to my cozy seat, shadowed by three partitions. Before I could even digest my lunch, the regrets would pile up. Why didn't I just eat a kimbap here? I'd tried that, of course, but lasted only about four days.

When I went to lunch alone, I avoided restaurants within a five-hundred-meter radius of the office. As my feet took me far, far away, my eyes scanned the windows of the restaurants I passed. I looked for restaurants with people eating by themselves, or devoid of customers entirely, walking, looking, walking, looking, until I found the winning place. I considered the cuisine only after going in. People eating alone worry more about stares from others than they do about menu options.

Searching for a restaurant near my office with few or no customers was like trying to buy a house on a low budget. Like homes that are affordable but lack charm, quiet restaurants on a road busy with office workers served terrible food. After I moved my class time to my lunch hour, I no longer had to worry. The materials we practiced with were meals in themselves, so attending class at noon took care of lunch as well. It seemed like a lot of other people had the same idea, because lunchtime was much busier than the other class sections.

Monday, Wednesday, and Friday at 12:10. Students followed the lectures from behind tables instead of desks and held chopsticks instead of pens. The instructor strolled casually between the students and corrected their posture and expressions one by one. In order to return to work on time after forty minutes of class, I had to hurry, but it was still better than going back ten minutes early.

Step One—coffee shop, bakery, fast-food joint, snack bar, neighborhood Chinese restaurant, food court, restaurants near my class, cafeteria

Step Two—Italian restaurant, large Chinese restaurant, traditional Korean restaurant, family restaurant
Step Three—wedding, first-birthday party
Step Four—barbecue restaurant, sushi restaurant
Step Five—unforeseen circumstances

Going by the sequence laid out in class, I'd barely passed step one, but living like this didn't pose any major obstacles. Any street had plenty of step-one options. However, sometimes you want to eat meat, or sushi, and eventually you grow tired of avoiding restaurants just because they're filled with large groups of customers. I attended class three times a week without fail and quickly rose to step two. Step two was different from the start. All by myself, I had entered a realm of restaurants in which the first thing I'd be asked at the door was how many people I was eating with.

"If step one was breastfeeding, then step two is soft baby food. You can't begin by eating rocks. If you get the hang of baby food, your stomach and mind will be a little more comfortable."

The instructor's statement was more of a formula than a suggestion, an incantation more than a formula. Not weekends but weekdays, not lunchtime or dinnertime but the hours in between—target those times. Target corner tables rather than those in the middle. Seats at the bar are also good. Hang your coat or bag on the chair facing you and take advantage of tools like a book, earphones, a cell phone, or a newspaper. Become a regular customer and befriend the owner or waiters. Befriending the cook isn't a bad idea, either. When going to a nice restaurant, call ahead and reserve a table for one. If you make a reservation, no one will pay attention to you. If possible, avoid going out on couples' days like Valentine's Day, White Day, or Christmas Eve. Instead, take advantage of niche times like holidays such as New Year's or Thanksgiving, when restaurants will be empty. All of these guidelines are meant to free solo eaters from the attention of others. Overcoming their stares is the ultimate goal, but if that's difficult, then avoid them entirely for the time being. They stare at me because I stare at them. If I don't look at anyone, then I don't know who's looking at me.

For students hoping to kill two birds with one stone by eating lunch during class, the organizers had paid special attention to the type and flavor of the course materials. The materials fee was separate, but considering that it included lunch three times a week, it wasn't too bad.

"Today we'll be having steak," the instructor said. "Steak is a good choice because it requires use of both hands, but it's inconvenient because it makes reading a book while eating a bit cumbersome. In this case, your best tool is a glass of house wine. Wine is a tool to assist the steak, isn't it? Let's think of steak and wine as notes, like we're in music class. Should I explain this musically? We eat in two-four time. The downbeat is the main course, so steak. The upbeat is a sidepiece, so wine, or something like the potatoes or asparagus here. Yes, that's right. On the downbeat, cut off a mouthful of steak and eat it, and on the upbeat take a bite of something else, and now you're eating with a rhythm. One-two, one-two, one-two, one-two! Right! Steak is simple, but you're wondering what to eat on the upbeat? You can drink your wine, or eat some potatoes or asparagus: anything is fine. The important thing to remember is one-two. It's the count for a measure in two-four time. After finishing this phrase, your eyes fall away from the plate. You look ahead and pull out a newspaper or something, and your one-measure meal is finished! Oh, you're looking down too much. If you stare down at your plate like that, you look miserable."

I looked up a little bit, like the instructor had suggested. As I moved my gaze from my plate to the chalkboard, from the chalkboard to corners of the classroom, my line of sight widened. The instructor counted while walking between tables. One-two, one-two, one-two, one-two. Among the masses moving their forks and knives to and fro with the beat, someone suddenly raised her hand.

"Teacher! This isn't one beat, is it? That would be more like dun, dun, dun, dun, right?"

The instructor stopped his conducting.

"This isn't some sort of class for music majors," he said. "I'm just making a comparison. If dun, dun, dun, dun really were how you counted individual beats, then you'd give yourself an upset stomach eating along to it, wouldn't you? All that matters is that you decide on a beat that matches your digestive abilities and follow it. It's okay if your one beat is more of a *duuuuuuunnnnn*. Remember, everyone, what's the time signature for steak?"

"Two-four time!"

On Monday, we learned how to eat steak in two-four time; on Wednesday, black bean noodles in three-four time; and on Friday, a traditional Korean meal in six-eight time. On days I didn't have class, I practiced two-four and three-four. When it was time to practice six-eight, I called ahead and made a reservation at a nice Korean restaurant. Making a reservation was a pretty good method. If I just said my name at the entrance, I could listen casually to the employees' direction. And when I went to my seat, my table was no longer an active boxing ring. The table was set up like a musical score, a nice musical score that just needed to be played. My pulse raced like a metronome. Six-eight time. *One*-two-three-*four*-five-six. Rice on the downbeat, vegetables on the upbeat, soup on the middle beat. *One*-two-three-*four*-five-six. If I finished a measure, I let my eyes pierce the open air for a moment, and once again—*one*-two-three-*four*-five-six. *Rice*-vegetables-vegetables-*soup*-vegetables-vegetables. *One*-two-three-*four*-five-six.

Rice-vegetables-vegetables-*soup*-vegetables-vegetables. Circling through those measures, the score, and my meal, were finished.

On class days, I learned by rote in the classroom, and on other days, I reviewed what I'd learned at restaurants near my job. The first place I went after plucking up a bit of courage was an Italian restaurant. As usual, it was more than five hundred meters from my office, but it was popular among young couples and friends, which was why I'd ignored it until now. I thought about the right beat to match a bowl of pasta and enthusiastically entered the restaurant. It was clean and cozy. *How many people with you today? Just me*. Answering this question was no longer a big deal. I was shown to a seat appropriate for a solo diner, a seat surrounded on all sides by couples. I wanted to somehow give up the seat, but it would be difficult to find another that wasn't also surrounded. I tried to chat with the waiter like I'd learned. Talking about things like the food, restaurant interior, or the weather wasn't a problem. And in a restaurant like this, where the inside and outside were both covered with a layer of wood, interior decorating was clearly a good conversation topic.

"Is this all pine?" I asked.

"Yes. Our building is pine, too, ma'am."

The waiter responded in a calm voice after refilling my water. I skillfully kept the conversation going.

"I see. There are bits of sap scattered on the wall, too."

The waiter looked to where my finger was pointed and tilted his head.

"There—isn't that sap?"

"That's . . . varnish stains, I think. Shall I check, ma'am?"

My face reddened despite the restaurant being almost empty. I'd definitely ordered spaghetti carbonara, but the scent of varnish seemed to waft out from between the noodles. I quickly pulled a book out of my bag and placed it on the table.

With each new step, my instructor's voice grew louder and louder. And the distance between office and restaurant grew steadily shorter. In the past, there had been times when I'd walked a whole kilometer without finding a restaurant worth entering, but now I could choose a place to eat without going half that distance.

"Now let's talk about tools," the instructor said. "I told you about them as a sort of tip in step two, but go ahead and forget what I said. At a fast-food joint or a cafeteria, of course, you can stick earphones in your ears and listen to music while eating. You can also open up a book and read that during your meal. But in a wedding hall or at a first-birthday party, you'd be a fool to do something of that sort, wouldn't you? All of you who've read a book to act as if you weren't lonely, who've listened to music to act as if you weren't forlorn, who've called someone to act as if you weren't alone, who've busily scribbled something into a notebook to act as if eating was just a break from whatever else you were doing—you're going to need to face the issue head-on."

Books, MP3s, pens and notebooks, laptops, media players, cameras—our instructor had cleared these tools from our arsenal at lightning speed. My initial opportunity to practice the skills in step three came that weekend. This was the first time I'd thought of eating like this—without any tools to help—as an opportunity. I was going to a business client's wedding, to make a brief appearance and hand over a gift. I'd initially thought gift giving was the kind of job assigned to a recent hire, but even after I was no longer the newest worker, I was still forced to attend events like this. Doing such work barely got me anything more than a free meal, which I didn't even take advantage of. I was never with anyone, and I didn't know beforehand if acquaintances from the client's company would be attending. At these events, I always worried much more about whether or not I should stay to eat than I did about what to wear.

The night before the wedding, I turned to the internet, looking for people with the same worries. *Eating alone at wedding.* These were the four words I typed into the search bar. Posts from other people who'd searched "eating alone at wedding" quickly came up on my screen. One comment, that eating alone at a wedding buffet was better than attending a first-birthday party alone, gave me hope, but the thought that I'd have to attend a first-birthday party next made me even more uneasy.

That weekend, after entering the wedding hall, I congratulated the bride's family and handed over a gift, then immediately headed to the buffet. Finally, my meal ticket was going to be useful. The event had just begun, but I could already spot several people eating by themselves. I looked for guests who seemed not to have company and moved to sit near them. I took off my jacket, hung it on the chair opposite me, and then pushed my drink and fruit plate in the same direction. Soon after, a woman came over carrying a plate. She sat down in the seat next to the one covered with my jacket. The woman, sitting diagonally from me, got up at almost the exact same moment I did, but we spent the entire meal without making eye contact even once. This was because the woman was constantly looking downward. Her eyes and nose and mouth moved only within the bounds of her circular plate. Eating alone wasn't really that difficult. And a lot more people than I'd expected were eating alone. Just like there are islands when there's a mainland, there are also individuals scattered around a crowd. Islands scattered here and there—that and the fact that I didn't know anyone here gave me a sense of relief that eased my digestion. My instructor's words rang in my ears. The only people who need a partner at a wedding are the bride and the groom, that's it.

I hated odd numbers when I was young. The reason I'd hated them was because every so often, crowds would split up into pairs. On the sports field, on the bus during a field trip, on the playground—whenever an odd number of people broke up specifically into twos, someone was left behind. $3 - 2 = 1$; $5 - 2 - 2 = 1$; $7 - 2 - 2 - 2 = 1$—calculated like this, there was always an odd one out. In a class of forty-eight I was at ease, in a class of forty-seven I was nervous. If someone in the class of forty-eight switched schools, or was absent, or left class early, I was nervous then, too.

Back then, I'd thought that the awkwardness of being excluded on the sports field or in the classroom wouldn't extend beyond the school gates, but the real tragedy began when I realized that these problems, so devastating at the time, were nothing more than a miniature version of the real thing. When you're excluded in the real world, without the protective embrace of a campus community, no one cares. You just vanish into the collective disinterest.

But the longer you wallow in that disinterest, the more confused you become about whether it's caused by you or by other people. So when something like lunchtime comes around, it's a bit of an awkward situation. For someone like me trying to eat alone, even more so.

As soon as the clock struck twelve, everyone in the office quickly got up and headed to the scheduled company lunch. I had class, but I couldn't skip an official function just because of that. Our destination was a place barely one hundred meters from the office. It was significantly closer than my usual lunchtime walk, but for some reason those hundred meters felt far too long. I couldn't see the inside of the restaurants we passed on our way. All I saw in the reflection in the windows was myself, moving with the crowd.

The food on the table was plentiful. Beef tenderloin pho, brisket pho, seafood pho, fried rice, egg rolls, Vietnamese spring rolls—it was all there. I chose half tenderloin–half brisket noodles, but I could barely taste them. For me, today's menu didn't consist of noodles but of the words and looks flitting across the table. Holding my chopsticks was awkward. *Have you seen that new TV show? The one that plays on the weekends. He really can't act, but nowadays they're all like that.* The topic of conversation moved from TV shows to serial killings to health insurance and school tuition. Only the beat could save me from the flow of words. One-two-three. One-two-three. For noodles with broth, broth was the downbeat. Broth-noodles-noodles. Broth-noodles-noodles. As I ate the noodles, my eyes naturally turned to the bowl, and after swallowing, I lifted my head, so it was easy to make eye contact. One-two-three. Broth-noodles-noodles. The conversation turned to how so-and-so on the other team was doing. I chimed in on things I knew about and stayed silent on less familiar topics. As a result, I didn't talk much throughout the meal. Instead, I was staring at the table more attentively than anybody else. So when someone added chili pepper and onion to their bowl for a second helping, I saw an empty plate and quickly summoned the appropriate words. I lightly raised my hand and said, "Excuse me. More noodles, please."

"Noodles? Inyeong, have you been eating rice cakes and ramen recently? Those are bean sprouts—bean sprouts!"

Not noodles but bean sprouts. One coworker latched onto my mistake, and the others laughed loudly. I laughed, too. I laughed while admiring how adaptive and how socially aware my face muscles were. I laughed enthusiastically as I tried to hide how startled I was, thinking about how I'd eaten rice cakes for lunch yesterday. The bean sprouts arrived. The coworker who'd needed them grabbed some with chopsticks and placed them in her bowl. Following suit, others added a chopstick's worth of bean sprouts to their own bowls. I lifted my chopsticks as well. The beat had begun again. One-two-three. One-two-three. The topic of conversation moved on to something else. One-two-three. One-two-three.

The next day at lunch, I found myself part of a crowd again. It wasn't a day I had class, so I'd gotten up from my desk chair unhurriedly, but then my coworkers called for me to go eat with them. I hadn't moved any faster than usual—were they moving slower? Just as I hadn't clearly understood why they'd excluded me, now I didn't understand why I was being included. I could only guess that I'd been left out for standing in the wrong line, and now I stood in the right line, whatever that was. As we rode the elevator downstairs, passed the lobby, and came out of the building, I wondered if anyone would call my name if I lagged behind or went in the opposite direction, but I decided not to risk it. Exclusion is a sensitive issue and could be triggered again by such a trivial experiment.

The lunch menu was stew with side dishes. One-two-three-four. My body now counted the beat automatically before I could even think about it. It was four-four time. Rice-omelet-broth-seaweed. Rice-fried pork-broth-chili peppers. Rice-seaweed-broth-. . . .

"Inyeong, you must not watch much reality TV."

My hands faltered as I grabbed a piece of tofu. Was this a question, or was it a statement? The beat got tangled as I thought. I was supposed to be eating a side dish right now, but my chopsticks went toward my rice bowl. My sense of time was a mess, like a broken metronome. My heart beat with wild thuds, generating its own strange rhythm.

After finishing lunch and waiting for people to use the rest-room, we all went to get coffee together. And holding our coffees one by one, we headed back to the office. The smokers among us each pulled out a cigarette before entering the building. Some of the nonsmokers went inside and others lingered. They didn't smoke, but there they stayed, surrounded by the fumes. More people were outside than inside, so I stayed outside, too, without smoking.

The reason people complain about being sleepy in the afternoon is because their minds and bodies are tired from the energy expended eating lunch. After finding people to eat lunch with, I too was growing more and more fatigued. The next day, I counted four-four time, the day after that, nine-eight. Now, if people just talked about what we'd be eating, the beat would echo in my head the entire walk from our office to the restaurant. The third day was two-four time again, and after that, three-four. On the day everyone went to eat chicken ginseng soup, I ate Vietnamese noodle soup again, alone. After skipping class and being blessed with company at meals for almost a week, I could truly appreciate how comfortable it was to eat in solitude. And with the strength of such solitude, I finally felt dignified eating within one hundred meters of the office. I left the crowd like a spring that bounces back harder than ever when stretched out. This time, I was excluding them.

"If mountain climbers have Everest, we have barbecue restaurants," our instructor said. In order to conquer Everest, we learned how to pick a barbecue restaurant for beginners, how to deal with the grill and tongs, how to order and call for a waiter among the din, how to manage sitting between large groups, and how to share or refuse to share a table with someone else. We also had to visit a barbecue restaurant at least five times over a period of two weeks and provide our instructor with receipts proving that we had eaten alone. This was an assignment with a lot of flaws, though. The instructor believed in the diligence of his students, but even so, Everest was Everest. There were cases where students had gone to a barbecue restaurant with a partner, ordered two servings, and turned in the receipt as if they'd ordered those two servings alone. We'd been told to refrain from interaction with classmates as much as possible due to the purpose of the course, but people naturally became friends while eating together in class. There were even students who had begun to have lunch together on Tuesdays and Thursdays, learning to eat alone on Mondays, Wednesdays, and Fridays. Some whispered complaints about whether it was really even necessary to master the barbecue restaurant; others had signed up specifically for this step. Still others hadn't been to class in ages, perhaps because they were taking the exam.

I, too, tried climbing Everest several times, but it wasn't easy. A sushi restaurant was naturally as difficult as barbecue—my attitude toward restaurants like these tended to differ depending on the interior ambience and customers, as well as the time of day. Multiple times, I'd gone to a sushi restaurant only to leave after eating a fish-and-rice bowl. The instructor's number one tip was to try your best. Try and try again, there was no better trick than that.

And as I followed that number one tip—to give it my all—I found myself making unforeseen errors. Payday barbecue joint: the Chinese restaurant next door. Three Hundred Times a Bacon Thief: the snack stall next door. Winner's Ribs: the pasta restaurant next door. Grilling Day: the clay-pot stew place next door. All choices I'd made after standing in front of the aforementioned barbecue restaurants.

Before opening the restaurant door to go inside. When I opened the door and went in. When I flipped open the menu. Facing the person who'd come to take my order. People eating alone can change their minds in a single moment. In order to overcome those trials, I specifically searched out barbecue restaurants for dinner and not for lunch. This was because at lunchtime the chance I'd be able to order from a different, non-barbecue menu was high.

I found a seat in the center of the barbecue restaurant, but before I even started to move toward it, I saw the perfect table in the corner. My legs led me there before I could think, my behind marking the spot with a thud as I sat down. After perusing the menu carefully, I snapped it shut and called for the waiter. Two servings of pork belly, no need to think about it anymore. But at that moment, I saw a crowd of men enter the restaurant, and something else came out of my mouth.

"Beef brisket soup, please."

I placed the menu, as useless as it was, in front of me, and my shoulders seized up. How was beef soup really that different from barbecue? Only after eating a few spoonfuls of soup could I think of a difference. Beef soup had a designated beat, while pork belly barbecue did not. Pork belly was a food to eat confidently and by itself, a food that transcended even the rhythm of eating.

In the past, I wouldn't have been able to come into a place like this, I told myself as I ate the soup. My cheeks, which would have been burning red, were calm. My heart wasn't beating fast, either. But before I dared to imagine the possibility of a future passing score, my chest constricted with pressure. Times like this were the reason I always kept digestive aids in my bag.

A woman with long, straight hair entered the restaurant. *Huh?* She'd come alone, but she didn't head to a corner. She grabbed a chair in the middle of the room and asked, "Is it possible to order just one serving of pork belly?" The woman ordered two servings and began to grill her meat as naturally as if someone were with her. The woman was visible from every seat and every corner of the building. She was sitting in the middle like a round, coal-burning heater from an old-fashioned elementary school classroom, like someone trying to expel heat throughout the entirety of the restaurant. I wasn't the only person amazed by this woman. Couples filling secluded tables, and a group of office workers sitting in a line, also stared at the woman in her oblivious solitude. She really was just like one of those heaters, singular yet surrounded. The woman was exposed. Without giving any hints as to whether or not she was aware of her exposure, she called for the owner. "Give me a bowl of rice here, and a bottle of soju. Make it Chumchurum."

From now on, let's call the woman the Expert. The woman really was an expert at what she was doing. The Expert was, at most, in her early thirties. The Expert was pretty and perfectly groomed. The Expert's grill was hot, and she busily grilled her meat upon it. The Expert pulled a hair tie out of her shoulder bag and twisted it around her long, straight hair to tie it up behind her neck. After tousling her ponytail, she looked at her profile in the mirror. She patted the back of her neck with a wet cloth. Was this woman even aware of anyone staring at her? I wondered, and in that moment, she opened her mouth. "Could you please turn on the air conditioning?" The restaurant owner turned on the air conditioning. "Shall I turn on the fan over there, too?" the owner asked.

As I watched the Expert, the beef stew in front of me slowly cooled without being eaten. The cold soup and hardened rice looked miserable. They were miserable because they weren't the food I'd been preparing for.

"Excuse me, two servings of pork belly, please."

The words flew out of my mouth instantaneously, with a strength I'd gained from watching the Expert. Everyone except the Expert stared at me. Actually, I don't really know. It seemed I was being stared at, and it also seemed like I wasn't. What was certain was that the waiter was looking at me. The waiter asked again. "Two servings of pork belly?"

Why do you have to ask like that?

"Yes, and a bottle of soju, too. Chamisul Fresh."

Oho, so this was how the conversation with the waiter would be. It did feel impressively natural. But after hearing the words I'd spat out so ostentatiously, the waiter clarified once more.

"A whole bottle?"

He indicated a one with his pointer finger. What had I said? I wanted one bottle! Even if I *could* only drink half of it. I showed the waiter with my finger as well, deliberately smiling to myself to stop my face from turning red.

I had to get up before the Expert. Pork belly, which doesn't even have its own beat, is a food to be eaten confidently and by itself. I was going to eat all the food in front of me before the Expert left and took her sense of calm with her. If the Expert, sitting there like a heater, got up, then a brisk cold was sure to set in. I grilled the pork belly hastily, like I was being chased by all the musical notes in the world, and then quickly wrapped it up in lettuce and carried it to my mouth. I also poured myself glass after glass of soju. Soju was as good a tool as wine. And after thirty minutes, I was sitting in front of the Expert. I don't understand how it happened, but there the Expert was, filling my glass with alcohol as she talked. It seemed like we'd already been chatting for a long time. Only now did I feel like I'd snapped back to my senses.

"What class did you say you were?" she asked me. "Ah, the twenty-eighth? Well then, I graduated almost ten terms before you. What step does it go to now? Oh, it's changed a lot since my time. In my day, it was a little bit less systematic, you see."

The Expert went to the cinema alone, went to amusement parks alone, went on hiking trips alone, went to salsa bars alone, went late-night shopping alone, and went on cruises alone. She lived an active and enthusiastic solo life. And this solo life all started with a course to learn to eat alone.

"Restaurants are like bathrooms," she continued. "There are a lot of people who still hold hands and walk all the way to the toilet together, like little girls in kindergarten. One person pisses while the other talks incessantly by his or her side, and after that they switch roles. I really don't understand how someone can do such an inefficient and shameful thing. People say that society wastes a lot of energy, but the way I see it, manpower is the worst kind of waste. That's because it's human energy. There's going to the cafeteria in droves, for one. Have you ever thought about all the things we do in order to eat with others? It takes time, stamina, consideration of your partner's food tastes, the TV and movies you have to watch in order to sustain the conversation, and all sorts of effort besides that, not to mention listening to your partner's personal affairs. If it's that much work, whew."

"There are people starving to death, so isn't it an extravagance to pay money to take a class like this? I've thought about that a lot, recently."

As soon as I finished my question, the Expert put the last piece of meat in her mouth. Then she filled her glass with Chumchurum, mine with Chamisul Fresh.

"In a world where people are starving to death, how extravagant is it that some people can't eat even a bite of food by themselves? It's been said over and over again that the modern man is soft, but not even having the courage to eat the food that's given to you alone, feeling nauseous and just leaving it and purposefully not eating, how shameful is it to make a fuss like that? You have to be able to think about this kind of thing. Try fasting for three or four days. Will you pay attention to the people around you then? You'll just see the plate in front of you—you'll shed that pointless shame like a snake sheds its skin. You have to think a little more deeply, take it all in. The course? Don't quit."

The Expert's glass came toward mine and collided with it. Like a rear-end collision, Chumchurum crashed into Chamisul Fresh. And once more: Chamisul Fresh crashed into Chumchurum. As they collided into a toast, something resounded with a thud. Thud, and my indigestion dissipated entirely. Thud, and the world changed.

We emptied a bottle of soju each. It seemed like the Expert had drunk to her limit, and I'd drunk to twice mine. After the Expert took her bill and disappeared, I purposefully stayed for about five more minutes, sitting quietly. The Expert's rant during our soju-glass collision was ringing in my ears.

"My diploma changed the axis of the world. Now everything revolves around me."

My body faltered. Had the world's axis really changed like the Expert said? I leaned to the left and to the right. *Crack.* My joints let out a stiff groan.

After drinking with the Expert, my grades improved day by day. Restaurant or not, every place in the world looked like a dinner table of a different size. All the worries that had troubled me as I decided where to eat alone consolidated into a single worry: *What kind of food do I want to eat today?*

It was a tabletop revolution, but the aftereffect wasn't limited to the table. It continued during rush hour, on packed subways. I realized that I wasn't one of the many planets circling the solar system. I was in the *spotlight*. Alone at both barbecue restaurants and wedding buffets, I was not lonely but a star in the crowd, and with that thought, I was awash with the feeling that I was the center of the subway, the core of the earth, the nucleus of the universe, the world's innermost layer. Each time the subway door opened, numerous people moved here and there as always, but even as I was swept up into the crowd, I was the protagonist. All I had to do was make sure I didn't stray out of orbit.

As if the world's axis really was changing, some trendy restaurants had started to increase the focus on solo seating. Bar stools and seating divided by partitions were both popping up. In these kinds of spaces, you didn't actually lock eyes with anyone even if you looked around as you fiddled with your spoon. These were spaces where everyone was eating together, but everyone was also eating alone. The people who came to this kind of place, with nothing but solo seating, might be the sort who were so reserved that they couldn't even pass step one. They might be the kind of people who would drag a friend along to a wedding or stop by the butcher rather than go to a barbecue restaurant alone. But here they'd be, eating alone and indifferently, as if they had casually passed all five steps and whatever lay beyond them. People who can't share tables can't crack jokes, and some can't even tell the truth. Office chatter is never meant for them. But no matter what the reason for their exclusion may be, the people sitting here would at least have the view in front of them—their food trays—guaranteed.

Those of us who had passed the sushi restaurant and barbecue restaurant were now receiving video instruction on the unexpected situations that could arise regardless of setting, and we used role-play to learn an adaptive response method. The classroom had multipurpose walls like a studio, so sometimes it became a snack bar filled with high school girls, other times it became the restaurant in front of a terminal filled with soldiers, and still other times it became a barbecue restaurant filled with employees enjoying a company dinner. We pretended that I'd just ordered a higher-level food when I discovered a foreign substance inside my meal, or I had to share a table with another person, or I ran into an old flame while eating alone. We acted out situations where that old flame had a new partner or spouse but I was single, or where I ran into old classmates or coworkers. There were many possible courses of action in these situations, and we tried them all out. We went through each of the five steps like this. But our instructor explained that the real world always has more than five steps, his voice almost an octave higher than it had been at the beginning of the course.

"Now it's time for the real-life test," he told us. "Pick ten restaurants from these sixty and write down the dates and times you're going to visit them. On the corresponding date, simply go to the restaurant and eat as usual. Just one place out of the ten will be the real test site. Judges will be placed here and there, but you all won't notice them. They could be a diner or an employee. Go to each of the ten places, have a meal, and bring the receipts back here. The date and time will be written on the receipts, so they'll count as proof."

I use my lunch hour to visit one restaurant per day, the same as when I had class. I enter the test site and order kimchi soup. I order beef ribs. I order a pizza, eat two slices, and casually take the rest to go; I order cold noodles and even drink the beef broth straight from the bowl. I eat spicy seafood noodle soup squeezed between soldiers on leave, I eat ramen surrounded by high school boys, I eat tripe and soju between coworkers having dinner together. Left hook, right hook: the looks are flying at me, but they can't even reach the surface of my table before they fall to the floor. I mean, I've passed all five steps. I'm taking the final exam now. These dull-witted looks are beneath me—they crash before they can even get close. When I ask for more side dishes or strike up a conversation with the staff, I get extra points. Of course, it's more important not to have points deducted. Is my gaze natural, is my face turning red, is my digestion okay, am I matching the beat? The moment I transcended these fears, an uppercut suddenly flew up from below.

"This is limited since we're looking at the situation through CCTV, but if you compare your appearance here to your typical demeanor at meals, Inyeong, there's something lacking. When you ordered, and for about ten minutes after receiving your food, it seemed like you were fine, but see the screen? Right here, from this point on, your pace began to falter. Don't you agree?"

The instructor pointed at the monitor as he spoke. On the screen, I was eating with difficulty, not following a beat.

"One-two-three-four. This is four-four time, but it's hard to tell the beat here when you're eating, Inyeong. You eat only rice, then you eat only soup, then you just drink water. Did you see the CCTV, perhaps? When you were taking the test, did you realize the CCTV was recording?"

"No."

"Then did you run into someone you knew? An ex, perhaps?"

"No."

"Were you nervous because it was a test?"

I nodded. On the screen, I was holding my chopsticks, but I looked like someone who had no will to eat. The only things moving somewhat energetically were two rows of teeth, constantly chewing. I didn't even put any more food in my mouth, but the two rows of teeth continuously chewed something. And then at some moment I went off-screen. I went somewhere the CCTV couldn't record and returned five minutes later, my face gaunt. During the five minutes the CCTV couldn't capture, I had crouched in front of the bathroom toilet and thrown everything up. What I'd thrown up wasn't just pizza or cold noodles, pork wraps or sausage; it was a mixture of all those and the past ten days of testing.

The screen showed me getting up from my seat, paying, and leaving; then it stopped. The instructor didn't say anything, but I could guess that I'd failed for sure. As soon as he'd left the room, the consultant came up to me.

"This is a typical case, extremely typical," he said. "You had digestion problems, didn't you? I remember that: a typical case. The exam is a bit taxing, isn't it?"

I hadn't passed the exam, but without any desire for a diploma, I had no reason to attend class anymore. Menus no longer caused me fear, and my body had adjusted to eating alone. But a few days later at lunchtime, I found myself walking far, far from the office, looking for a table for one. I wasn't someone who ignored her hunger, nor was I the kind of person who'd make do with a hamburger patty when she wanted real meat, but I was the kind of person who peeked inside restaurants the whole time I was walking to see whether or not there were guests eating alone. I was the kind of person whose face burned red when one of the other customers, or a passerby outside the window, resembled someone from my office. When choosing food, the most important thing was, as always, my own desire, but for some reason the food I wanted to eat was only sold at restaurants with at least one other person eating solo.

And just like that, I went back to square one. For three months, I went to countless restaurants alone under the pretext of review, but even if I went into a restaurant I'd been to before, it somehow felt awkward. The fact that I no longer had any assignments, any tests, any grades, was unfamiliar. On a tabletop more than five hundred meters from the office, in a place I'd barely managed to enter, I relived the five minutes that I'd disappeared from the CCTV. The truth—the weight of the truth—pressed down on my throat.

Only after failing the exam did I understand why a mere 15 percent of students got a diploma in one go. The thing that 85 percent of people were afraid of wasn't the test. It was the real life that came after the test. After completing the course, there was no more reason to attend class, and with that, be part of a group. The dispersion of a crowd united by common interests and goals, people whom they'd sat with at every lunch hour, and just a diploma to show for it; the absence of a reason to come to this place; having to really go out into the world and face eating alone—these were all objects of terror. To them—no, to us—what was necessary was not the diploma but the time to delay reality.

The thing I'd wanted to learn was how to eat alone naturally, but instead I had gotten from the course the comfort that I wasn't the only person eating alone. I was an individual franchise among many in the chain store of solo eaters.

What I had actually learned was that tables could be disguised as tables for one, and what class had forced me to face was reality disguised as reality. The first time, I'd enrolled without knowing this, and the second time I enrolled knowing. Now, the course would start again from the beginning, with a table for me and for all the others who fear the very thing that I do.

"I said that more than half of the 85 percent re-enroll, right? It's already way more than half. And this is, well, a typical case. Okay, before you start the course again, see this empty box? There may have been something new that you felt during the past three months of class, so write one word here."

The consultant grinned as he held out the forms. At the end of his mouthful of straight teeth, a lone gold tooth shone like a star. Eating alone is ____. The blank space looked like an empty restaurant. I picked up a pen and slowly went toward the blank.

Eating alone is <u>enjoyable</u>.

The customer comes in alone. The owner is a bit slow-witted and asks, "How many in your party tonight?" This is a family-style barbecue restaurant, though, so you can't really say she's slow-witted. Two servings of pork belly, a bowl of rice, a bottle of soju. Nothing too unusual, but for the order of a woman who came in alone at 7:00 p.m., it is sort of strange.

The woman drinks half a glass of soju for every three pork wraps, using both of her hands to have a quiet meal. Flipping meat with tongs, cutting it with scissors, grabbing it with chopsticks, putting it in her mouth with her hands—a typical way to eat. In spite of this, the woman is, as always, standing on a square boxing ring. In the fight with spectators, the woman's best defense is attack. Before I can look at the woman, she is already looking at me. As our eyes meet, we open our mouths in sync. On both sides of the mirror, those words that transcend the beat I've so diligently practiced. *Shall we sit together?*

2. SWEET ESCAPE

After the coffee maker was delivered, he brewed coffee every morning. The aroma would slowly travel from the kitchen to the den, and from there to every other room in the house. He had decided to try Ethiopian Yirgacheffe and Indonesian Mandela first. One day, he would drink Yirgacheffe, the next, Mandela. He wasn't yet able to distinguish the subtle differences between the types of coffee, but he soon wanted to taste beans from other countries.

The coffee maker was the first purchase he'd made with his severance pay. He had lost his job, which he'd had for seven years. He hadn't started looking for another one immediately and instead declared the next six months work-free. He wanted to rest for a little bit while his unemployment benefits were coming in. His second purchase was a DSLR camera. He joined a photography club but didn't regularly attend meetings. Still, he did learn how to use the camera from books and the internet. He bought two memory cards, as well as an external hard drive and a netbook. He also bought plane tickets. Two of them. He wanted to leave immediately after his wife, a teacher, began her summer break. They would be heading off on a two-week trip to Europe.

He prepared for those two weeks for two months. After becoming more or less familiar with the camera, he joined a travel club. He bought a guidebook, learned phrases from the languages of the cities they would visit, and read books and watched movies about those cities. Even without work, he had a regular routine. After his wife left for school, he would eat breakfast, brew coffee, and carry a mug over to the computer and sit down. When he turned on the computer, a different world opened up in front of him. Thanks to the travel club, he acquired all kinds of information that didn't show up in the guides. He would jot this information down in his notebook, type it up on the computer, and print it out. He was surprised to realize at one point that bedbugs were mentioned quite often in his printouts.

"Bedbugs, in the twenty-first century? In Europe?" his wife asked. He'd had the same reaction at first. It had been a long time since bedbugs were a part of daily life. He hadn't seen a real one even once. When he was in the military, there had been momentary bedbug scares, but even then, he hadn't actually seen a bedbug or been harmed by one in any way.

"Honey, have you maybe been reading too much? Isn't it enough just to look up the things we need to know?"

His wife smiled as she spoke. She was worried about her husband being unemployed, but at the same time, she looked forward to going to Europe. After three years of marriage, it was their first international vacation since their honeymoon. She was tired, but her fatigue made her even more excited about the trip.

A week passed, and the information he'd collected had been condensed to articles and notes about just a few topics. One of those topics was bedbugs. Information about bedbugs consisted for the most part of personal accounts. He read stories about multiple people. The newlywed couple bitten on a plane, the traveler bitten on a night train—he also read the story of someone who couldn't tell if it was a bedbug or a mosquito that had bitten her but was pestered by an itch that wouldn't go away. There was someone else who, after encountering a bedbug at the end of a trip, returned home and suffered from scars that persisted for over six months. Most people saw bedbugs as something unfamiliar, but if you really thought about it, the chance of encountering bedbugs while traveling was very high. Even if you stayed in a clean place, you couldn't be at ease. Sometimes people at five-star hotels were bitten, too.

Sleep in a place that gets some sunlight. Look at the corners of the bed and the back of the headboard, the seams of the mattress, underneath the baseboard. Search behind frames or calendars or clocks hanging on the wall. Use anti-bedbug tools. This was the strategy he'd worked out. He made a file for things related to bedbugs, and as time went on, that file gradually became thicker. A few days later, anti-bedbug supplies began to arrive at his house, one by one. Lemon, eucalyptus, and mint aroma oils and shower products, cinnamon air freshener, a few sticks of real cinnamon, and even sprays like Tyra-X and Bio Kill.

"You could just smoke instead of doing all this," his wife said. He'd quit smoking a long time ago, but if it could effectively remove bedbugs, he would have gladly started up again.

"Shall we bring mosquito repellant, too? We could bring the kind with replaceable pads," his wife suggested. He shook his head. Mosquitoes and bedbugs were undeniably different. You couldn't put bedbugs in the same category as mosquitoes, lice, or fleas. Bedbugs weren't just creepy-crawlies. They belonged to the order of Hemiptera insects.

"Hemiptera?"

"Uh-huh. There aren't many bloodsucking insects, but they're a special case."

Bedbugs were complicated. Little by little, he was learning more about them. Unlike most bloodsucking insects, bedbugs were not directly parasitic to their hosts. Instead, they lived in the vicinity of their victims and crawled out at night to bite them. So if you wanted to get rid of bedbugs, you first had to defend your territory.

"But are those fragrances effective? Are they fragrances that bedbugs like?"

"What do you mean? Bedbugs hate them," he said. "We have to cover our bodies with things that bedbugs avoid."

His wife, who had been peering intently at the inside of her suitcase, yawned. He was tired as well. He hadn't left the apartment all day, but he was overcome with exhaustion just from packing and looking up travel information. As he grew drowsier, he realized that he hadn't brewed any coffee this morning. Recently, he'd spent more days like this, without coffee. Close to midnight, he brewed some Brazilian Santos.

One day before the trip, he posted in his club's online forum. Like many of the members, his comments were imbued with the excitement and fear of someone leaving the next day for an unknown world. Despite the fact that he might have to face pickpockets, contagious diseases, terrorist threats, and bedbugs, he was still eager to embark, he wrote. He also mentioned that he'd invested one hundred thousand won toward bedbug prevention. The aroma oils, salves, and medicines he'd bought really had cost almost that much. He didn't forget to add that this was all thanks to what he'd learned from the other club members.

The plane carrying the couple finally left the ground, and their regular life disappeared beneath a window the size of a palm. His wife was filled with enthusiasm and ordered glass after glass of wine. He was excited, too, but something he'd read in the airport lounge that morning weighed on his mind. There were twelve responses to his post. Most of the members had praised his preparedness, wished him a good trip, or warned him to be careful. Just one had been different, and that comment alone stayed with him.

"Bedbugs are a crapshoot."

With each change in accommodation, he sprayed their two soft-shell suitcases with bedbug repellant until they were dripping wet. He showered with body wash in a scent that bedbugs hated, applied lotion in a scent that bedbugs hated, and sprayed the pillows, bedsheets, blankets, and more with a scent of aroma oil that bedbugs hated. He didn't forget to check the mattress seams, cracks in the wallpaper, and the backs of picture frames. Around the midpoint of the vacation, his wife spoke up.

"The theme of this trip really has been bedbugs!"

Her fatigue wasn't from bedbugs. It was from a husband who couldn't break free of them. Once they returned to Korea, she would have to go back to work teaching summer school, without much time to rest. He felt sorry that she had to do that.

Thanks to the big fuss he'd made, he didn't actually encounter any bedbugs. Of course, like that person had said, the whole situation was a crapshoot, so he seemed to have gotten lucky, too. If not for the article he saw online before boarding his return flight, he might have at least felt calm on the plane. But he did see it, an article with pictures and text displaying in no uncertain terms what he so vaguely feared. Korea was no longer safe. Since 2006, there had been intermittent cases of people suffering from bedbugs, but now those cases were becoming more common. A dormitory in September 2006, a North Korean labor camp in November 2006, a sports training facility in December 2006, a hotel room in March 2007 . . . The most recent outbreak had been recorded just a few days ago. A woman who'd been living in New York had come back to Korea, and shortly after, her whole body was bitten by an unknown bug. She brought the bug's body and its larvae to the Center for Disease Control and Prevention, which informed her that it wasn't any ordinary bug.

It was a bloodsucking insect—a bedbug. What had happened was that a few New York super-bedbugs had latched onto her bags and traveled back with her. The article was speckled with dot-like pictures of the bodies of a few bedbugs, presumably from New York.

Once the airplane reached an altitude of a few thousand feet, his heart began to race again. He told his wife that tens of thousands of bedbugs were crossing borders unchecked at this very moment. She glared at him in response, so he kept his mouth shut after that. Crossing between the stars, stuck in the sky like bedbugs, they flew back to Korea. A few weeks later, his wife returned to school to teach summer classes. After checking that he was still receiving his unemployment benefits, he returned to his pre-trip life. Thankfully, there weren't any bedbugs stuck to their suitcases. The floor was always clean because he vacuumed every morning, and the aroma of coffee wafted pleasantly through the den. If only his wife, who didn't even spend that much time at home, would stop shedding hair all over the house, his life would have been peaceful.

He opened up the local newspaper. There, he encountered them again. Bedbugs. He read that the studio apartment of the woman who'd returned from New York was in Sinchon. His house was in Sinchon, too. A few days later, he learned that her apartment was not far from his own.

After the incident, the woman moved. The people who lived on the same floor as her and her insectoid guests emptied out, too. What if the bedbugs were sniffing out the blood of their next host? They'd already established themselves by driving someone away. Adult bedbugs could live for a year at room temperature, and they could go hungry for 60 days in the spring and up to 175 in the winter without dying. He pulled out the coffee he'd bought on the trip as he continued to read. The sound of the bag tearing seemed particularly heavy. The inside was filled to the brim with shiny, brown coffee beans. He grabbed a handful of them and thought for the first time about how coffee beans resembled bedbugs. Of course, a round, flat bedbug would have to drink a lot of blood to become as plump as these beans. A hungry bedbug is the size of a grain of rice. Fully grown at five to eight millimeters long, with short forewings and rudimentary hind wings, it's almost like they don't have wings at all.

Short bristles stuck out from the coffee bean, held between thumb and index finger, and it began to shed its outer layer. Bedbug nymphs have to shed their skin five times to become adult bedbugs. The coffee bean shed five times. The females lay five eggs, one millimeter in diameter, per day, and they hatch about ten days later. A week after that, they can drink blood, and after six to eight more weeks, they have matured. When these round, flat vampires suck up blood, their whole bodies are dyed crimson and their abdomens distended. They become as plump as this coffee bean. Bedbugs, coffee, bedbugs, coffee. He spilled the coffee. The fat, brown beans clattered as they fell to the floor. He knelt down and began to pick them up.

He grabbed his mug and went to the computer, but the amount of coffee in the cup didn't decrease even a drop. For the first time, the scent filling the house seemed rancid. He opened the window and poured the cold coffee down the drain. He felt like bedbugs were taking over his mind. He opened up the local newspaper once again. After a short while, he began to search online for other local articles. The world was being contaminated by bedbugs. A few years earlier, New York had declared war on them, at a time when bedbug numbers were the highest they'd been since World War II. New York wasn't the only city to declare a war, or at least take note of them. There had been citywide extermination campaigns, and even whole towns shut down by bedbugs. Every continent was crawling with them.

It only takes one week before a newborn bedbug can drink human blood. As the human birth rate decreases more and more, the number of bedbugs is increasing exponentially each year.

Their fecundity makes our own low birth rate all the more unsettling. Bedbugs were no longer just in the barracks of war zones or the shabby accommodations of some unfamiliar travel destination. Clothing, socks, beds, sofas—they'd latch on and take a ride anywhere. Stuck to bits of clothing, they even boarded trains and planes. They went to five-star hotels, and dorms, too. And now, they'd come here.

The twenty-four-inch soft-shell suitcase made an appearance once again. He took out the travel supplies he'd placed inside, the bedbug repellants like Tyra-X and Bio Kill and the lemon and eucalyptus aroma oils. As he busily moved around in front of the suitcase laid out on the floor, he didn't look much different from when he'd been preparing for travel. But this time, there was no trip. This time was real life.

After his wife left for work, he made breakfast, washed the dishes, and cleaned every corner of the house. His schedule was similar to before the trip, but now it took a lot more time. What had been possible to do in two hours before now took twice as long. When he finished tidying, he was peckish again. He ate lunch and did the dishes, and by then it was almost two in the afternoon. He spent the rest of the day on the internet and reading books and newspapers to learn more about bedbugs. The more he knew about them, the slower he cleaned. Bedbugs were nothing other than a medium by which he could learn about the world. Thanks to bedbugs, he'd learned how to cook. Thanks to bedbugs, he'd learned how to clean. Thanks to bedbugs, he'd learned about real estate. And thanks to bedbugs, he'd gotten to know his neighbors.

The apartment he lived in was within a one-kilometer radius of the studio where the incident had occurred. Most of the ten households in his building, from the basement to the fourth floor, knew about the debacle. Well, maybe not most, but the senior who lived in B102, who distributed the free local newspaper to the building mailboxes each morning—certainly he knew. There was also a good chance that the woman in 102, who dug through the newspaper looking for coupons, knew as well. Same for the college student in 202. Considering how enthusiastic he'd been back when a disinfection company was called to sterilize the whole building, it didn't seem that he'd be insensitive to this issue. The chances that the man next door in 302 also knew were high. They ran into each other quite often. The man in 302 was a bum, too.

The weekly local paper recounted in detail the neighborhood bedbug stories that were left out or abbreviated in the national papers. It relayed the bedbugs' movements. They were closing in, from more than a kilometer away down to nine hundred or even eight hundred meters. Someone from the Center for Disease Control and Prevention said in an interview that an early response was important. That is to say, if you discovered a bedbug in your house, you were to report it to the center rather than just rashly getting rid of it yourself.

He bought paper weather stripping at the grocery store. It may have been weather stripping, but he was going to use it as a bug blocker rather than a wind blocker. He decided to call it "bedbug guard." As he exited the store and walked home, bedbugs were moving toward his house, too. As he neared home, step by step, the bedbugs were also growing centimeter by centimeter closer to their new destination. When he turned his head toward the apartment, the building he'd lived in for three years somehow felt unfamiliar. A strange and awkward energy, unimaginable even two hours earlier when he'd gone out, radiated from the maroon building. War was in the air.

He applied bedbug guard to the windows, bedroom doors, and entryway. He even installed it in the cracks of the windows that looked out onto the third-floor hallway. Just having applied it comforted him. But the day after the next heavy rain, the weather stripping—no, the bedbug guard—had fallen right off.

"It doesn't work like that."

That's what the man in 302, the man he saw so often, said when they ran into each other. He and the man in 302 were sitting side by side on a bench that faced the apartment, both eating popsicles.

"What I'm saying is, just because you lock your doors tight doesn't mean it'll solve the problem. If you read the paper, you'll know that those bastards don't distinguish between apartments. As long as we're sharing the same walls, this is a problem for the whole building. It could go on to become a neighborhood problem, maybe even a national problem, but hopefully there won't be too many other people who get involved."

"Maybe . . ."

"What I'm saying is that we have a common enemy," said 302 while biting into his popsicle with a snap, as if he were breaking something.

The man took a large bite out of his own popsicle and looked at his neighbor from 302. He thought about asking whether he'd seen the most recent bedbug article.

"Hey, a few days ago, did you maybe . . . ?"

"Yeah, it was me."

"What . . . what do you mean?"

"You applied weather stripping to stop the bedbugs, right? The stuff they sell at King Mart. It was me who pulled it off."

"Huh?"

He took another large bite to hide his confusion. 302 continued to speak in a low, scratchy voice.

"I was going to find you and tell you about it at some point. But today we just happened to run into each other. It's been three years since you moved here, right?"

He was flustered by what the man from 302 was saying, unable to ask why he'd removed the bedbug guard. 302 said that they had to approach the situation from more of a macro scale.

"A macro scale?"

"What I mean is that blocking the threshold and crevices in the hall windows won't fix anything. It's because bedbugs crawl between walls. We're already sharing the same wall. The same wall, which means we're sharing an enemy, too! Bedbugs can stick themselves to a human body, or furniture, or the inside of a bag, and then just enter this building. Take the mail that's delivered here every day. The bedbugs can jam themselves in between envelopes and packages and come into our homes. Schools, offices, neighbors' houses, and cafes, too—even riding a taxi just once can bring bedbugs in."

The bedbug guard conversation was petering out. Even so, the man from 302 had piqued his interest. He saw the man finish his popsicle and put the leftover stick on the bench, then he took one last bite himself and put his own popsicle stick on top of the other. Like he was making the sign of the cross with them.

His neighbor looked at him.

"You can't throw that away just anywhere."

He quickly picked up his stick. His neighbor's stick, too.

It was common sense to any resident of multifamily housing that pet owners had to ensure their cats and dogs didn't bother the neighbors. But what about the bedbugs that were crawling between homes, with nothing to stop them? A group strategy was necessary. The street's neighborhood association was being raised from the ashes for this very reason. The more people banded together, the faster the bedbugs moved. According to the newspapers, it wasn't certain whether or not they'd originated in that New Yorker's studio, but the bedbugs were traveling far and wide. Recently, an apartment only five hundred meters away from their own had been overtaken.

A week later, some of the residents of the building formed a bedbug removal group. The name of the group was WWB (World without Bedbugs). The leader was the man from 302.

Afraid that no one else would participate, they made a rule that one person from every household had to attend meetings. More neighbors than expected were aware of bedbugs, though, so the attendance rate was surprisingly high. They were one. They were brought together by the sense of fellowship that people feel when they all live at the same street number, in homes with the exact same layout. These were people whose fridges were all in the same place in their apartments, whose stovetops were in the same place, whose washing machines were in the same place, and who even went to the bathroom in the same place. And more than anything, they had the same enemy.

The first meeting took place in 101, with light refreshments. The senior in B102 talked about his own experiences with bedbugs, and someone told an anecdote about bedbugs and Chung Ju-yung, the founder of Hyundai. There was even a woman who'd ended up fighting with her study-abroad roommate because of bedbugs. The man hadn't suffered from bedbugs himself, but he had a lot to talk about. The further they delved into the topic, the more people began to scratch their bodies. By the time the meeting was over, someone's leg was reddish and swollen. It was the bedbugs. Before any had even entered their building, residents were scratching the places that would be bitten. After the meeting, a few of them headed over to a neighborhood fried chicken joint. They complained about the menaces other than bedbugs that plagued them all. Someone suggested they continue meeting even if the bedbug issue was resolved. Clapping followed, and ideas about how they'd make use of WWB came pouring out. A world without beggars, a world without bias, a world without bullying—they thought of everything the world could do without until late into the night.

WWB usually met once a week, but they didn't always just eat and drink—they also offered bedbug education. They trained residents on the specific scent of bedbugs, something only people who'd personally suffered from them could know.

“Bedbugs give off a certain scent from their chest region,” he said, “and it’s thought that this smell protects them from enemies. Scientists think that in ancient times, bedbugs lived off the blood of bats in caves, and there have been experiments showing that if you apply bedbug secretions to the mealworms that bats eat, the bats won’t touch them.”

A smell would emanate as soon as you opened the door to a room full of bedbugs, he told his neighbors. For that to happen, though, there had to be a lot of bedbugs, and someone who knew what bedbugs smelled like had to open the door. WWB decided that in order to overcome their enemy, they first had to know it. There were just two residents who knew the odor of bedbugs. They were the senior in B102, who’d seen a lot of bedbugs in his youth, and the piano teacher in 402, who had dealt with them while studying abroad. They taught everyone what bedbugs smelled like using cilantro bought at the market. The student in 202 who’d just returned from a trip to Hong Kong sniffed the cilantro and wrinkled her face.

“Ugh, it’s like nail polish! When I was traveling, I specifically asked to have my food made without this. The smell is too strange.”

Each household took a little bit of cilantro home. And exactly one week later, they gathered it all up and threw it away. They didn’t know how familiar they’d become with the scent of bedbugs, but the endeavor had certainly been effective at cultivating a sense of revulsion toward them.

At WWB meetings, they also learned how to look for clues, traces of bedbugs like eggshells, molted skin, and excrement. He used the camera and memory cards he’d bought for the trip to record all this information. The more he recorded, the more widely he had to clean. The house was the same as ever, but the cracks and corners to scrub were ever increasing. He now vacuumed two or three times a day. And each time, he saw fallen hairs tracing his wife’s path of movement and became irritated.

He'd been washing his blankets a little more often, too. He went up to the roof to disinfect his blanket in the sun, and the man from 302 was there, smiling awkwardly. He was holding a few blankets in his hands as well.

The Center for Disease Control and Prevention was no longer in its initial stage of response to the bedbug outbreak. They said that if you found a bedbug in your house, you shouldn't throw it out, you should immediately call the experts and have them deal with it. The bedbugs were now a reality. The woman in 102 had been bitten. At first, they couldn't tell if it was a bedbug or some sort of mosquito that was active through autumn. But the members of WWB pooled their knowledge. On his trip, the man had run into someone who'd been bitten by bedbugs on a night train. The traveler's legs had been bitten in rows of threes and fours. Using his own legs as an example, he'd explained the difference between bedbug bites and non-bedbug bites. The man was now able to use that information at the meeting.

"Bedbugs usually bite to a three-four-three beat. Three bites, four bites, three bites—like this. If you're bitten at specific intervals of several centimeters, it's almost certainly bedbugs. And if you look at the middle of the bite, there will be puncture marks, too."

That was exactly what it looked like. It was clear to anyone who saw the bites that they were from bedbugs. Several people, including the man, nodded in certainty. The woman from 102 scratched her salve-covered parts and wrinkled her nose.

"How did they suddenly go from being five hundred meters away to being here? Does that mean they've spread to the whole neighborhood?"

Someone responded to 102. "Actually, they reached the alley over there last week. Everyone was hush-hush about it."

"Why?"

"Because they're afraid the bedbugs will make the value of their homes go down!"

It was a reason everyone could empathize with. And it meant that the infestation would soon become a secret here as well. The man from 302 spoke.

"Bedbugs don't move much more than three to six feet at a time. You don't really think the bedbugs would cross the road to get here, do you? Bedbugs are smarter than you think, and they use a lot of tools. They can bury themselves in the mail delivered to everyone's house, in secondhand goods and things like tennis shoes or bags. Ultimately, it's people that are transporting bedbugs. Oh, and they can travel on animals, too."

"The dog in 102—we don't know whether or not it's a host, and if it is, that would mean it was a carrier as well. It goes outside a lot, around the whole neighborhood."

Until someone said that, the woman in 102 had been hugging her dog lovingly. But within a few days, she was vacuuming the dog's body all over, and finally she took the nervous creature to a neighborhood a few stations away and returned alone. All the apartment residents were satisfied with what she'd done.

When the bedbugs didn't disappear even after she switched mattresses, the woman decided to call an extermination service. Because it was important to make sure that word didn't get out, she called a company that 202 knew well. When people wearing gas masks showed up in front of the apartment, everyone—not just 102—went downstairs to see the exterminators go through her entryway. The exterminators didn't only disinfect the rooms in which bedbugs had appeared. They decided to disinfect other rooms, too, even the living room. And they rounded up all the household furnishings and put each item outside. It felt like moving day, or the annual kimchi-making day. As the experts were blocking doorways and fighting the bedbugs inside, the man sat on the bench in front of the apartment with his feet off the ground.

Six hours later, the exterminators vacated the unit with a deep breath. They opened the windows, aired the room, and brushed up bedbug corpses alongside dust. They also redid the wallpaper. The method worked. For five days.

In spite of the cleaning operations, 402 was overtaken. There still wasn't anyone in the house who'd been bitten by bedbugs, but the piano teacher in 402 had managed to use a tissue to grab something that looked like a bedbug larva. The fact that there was a larva meant that the bedbugs were settling there. A baby bedbug was even scarier and more horrifying than an adult. Finding hints of such a life, of the emergence of life, on the home front—that was terrifying. Could the bedbugs from the first floor have bypassed the second and third floor to make it to the fourth? Every night, they carried out an expert military operation that was incomprehensible to humans. Now, each time he looked at the ceiling, he was reminded of the fight for survival playing out just one floor above. Clunk, clunk, clunk—clumsy piano scales descended from the floor above, pressing down on the ceiling and slowly squishing his apartment. Into some sort of flat, oval-shaped body. A bedbug.

Bedbugs fed off rumors. 402 now regularly played passionate songs on the piano, like she was trying to deafen them. And 201, who ran a home sewing business, had been sewing particularly frequently. A few days later she discovered the marks of a regular, raised backstitch not just on her fabric but also on her arm. 402 had only been lightly bitten on her limbs, but 201's whole body was a free-for-all. When 201 showed up at a WWB meeting, her fingers were puffy like sausages. It looked like she'd been stuck with a sewing-machine needle, not bitten by bedbugs.

Capture the bedbugs alive. That was WWB's main mission. Their first priority was to catch the bedbugs, take them to the Center for Disease Control and Prevention, and determine exactly what variety they were. But catching them alive wasn't easy, and all they managed to procure was a few larvae and the intact body of a bedbug that had recently died.

WWB grew busier with its activities. But not everyone was so disturbed by the bedbugs. When he came downstairs full of resolve after a WWB meeting, his wife brought up the topic of loans. That quickly devolved into a conversation about his job search. He lied and said that he had a job lined up that he'd start in the spring. It was almost winter, when bedbug infestations were most severe. All he had to do was rid the neighborhood of the little beasts and actually get a new job before spring came around. His wife spoke.

"They say that there are more bedbug outbreaks in the winter."

He washed his body with cold water. If he washed with warm water, the chances of bedbugs clinging to him were higher. In the winter, bedbugs preferred warm bodies. Before being bitten by bedbugs, it was better to rinse your body with cold water, but if you'd already been bitten, hot water was better. The strategy did vary a bit pre- and post-bite, but he was certain that he wouldn't have to use the post-bite strategy.

After washing his body with cold water, he went to the bedroom, still bedbug-free. His wife was lying on the bed and leaned her body against his. His wife's body was hot. The whole room was hot. He stood up to lower the temperature. His wife crossed her arms as if she were annoyed and closed her eyes. When he returned, she reopened them. She began to raise his body temperature again, a temperature that he'd worked so hard to lower. His wife crawled over him. He could hear a Hanon piano exercise from the floor above. The keyboard was moving so furiously tonight that he thought it might collapse. Musical notes tread all over the blanket the man had pulled up to his head. Do-mi-la-sol-ti-la-sol-la. Re-fa-ti-la-do-ti-la-ti. Mi-sol-do-ti-re-do-ti-do . . . the ever-increasing scales were shaky. One by one, the notes went sharp and then flat. The beat began to fall apart as the music got heavier. *Your left ring finger and pinky are too weak—don't put strength in your wrist!* The piano teacher was clapping roughly in front of him. His ring and pinky fingers grew further and further from the score and eventually departed from the music entirely. He worked up a feverish sweat trying to match them to the correct beat. And just when he'd driven all the notes back into the sheet music, he woke up. His wife was looking at him worriedly. Bedbugs had appeared, bedbugs. He stood up with a start, only for his wife to take a deep breath and say, "It's dust—dust."

He didn't make coffee nowadays. As long as parts of the apartment were being invaded by bedbugs, he couldn't afford to casually dull his sense of smell with the scent of coffee. He sniffed, wondering if it was bedbugs he smelled from somewhere inside the room. When he went in and out of the apartment, he was careful not to let his clothes touch the wall, and every time he went to get the mail, he shook it out like laundry. When the basement was overtaken, the building had no choice but to call a mattress-cleaning company. They'd decided to throw away any already-infested mattresses and disinfect the ones that weren't infested yet. The experts entered heroically, carrying all kinds of tools.

"There's an average of twenty million mites, molds, and bacteria crawling around on your mattress," one expert told him. "Dust mites in particular make mattresses their homes and live off human dandruff and skin cells, excreting harmful waste."

"What we want to get rid of isn't mites, it's bedbugs," the man said.

The expert nodded as if he already knew.

"They're all the same, you know."

All the same. The bedbug extermination began. The process finished after several steps that included 150-degree high-pressure steam, UV disinfection, and even the spraying of aromatic scents. A few days later, residents of the apartment realized that the bedbugs had become stronger and more resistant and were not in any way the same as earlier bedbugs or mites. All they'd gotten from inviting the experts into their homes was the realization that there were a lot of pesky little enemies to worry about in addition to bedbugs. That, and the fact that rumors of their fight with bedbugs had spread to the whole neighborhood, even to reporters from the local newspaper.

Clunk.

After returning from a WWB meeting, he was surprised to see that he had locked the front door without thinking. His wife asked why he'd locked it. He shook his head. He didn't know why, either, but locking the door was important.

He spent every night in dutiful pursuit, as if he were the last person on earth. He was in pursuit of the bedbugs drilling into the center of the world. He searched for them the way readers used context clues to decipher unfamiliar vocabulary—word by word, bug by bug. He couldn't fall asleep. Even when he lay down, he couldn't sleep. Still awake after hours in bed, he heard the hazy break between night and dawn. The sounds of a motorbike stopping, of someone running up the stairs, of the paper boy moving around—they ended the night and called forth daybreak. When he opened the door, he saw something about bedbugs on the front page of that day's newspaper. He was slowly becoming nocturnal. It had been three months since he'd returned from his trip, so he couldn't blame it on time zones. The time difference between him and his wife was now so great that at some point, she'd begun to live in a completely different world. When his wife left for work, he went to bed, and when she slept, he awoke.

Whenever his wife came back from work, all she would see of him was the many remnants of his extermination operations, of things he'd installed to block the bedbugs. She was reminded of the existence of bedbugs by the very things he was using to get rid of them. She learned what they looked like from a drawing on a bedbug spray bottle, and she learned about their habits from her husband's printouts. And looking at the labels of the many chemicals he'd bought, she learned what bedbugs liked and disliked. His wife *felt* the existence of bedbugs from his efforts to make them stop existing. She could especially feel them in her husband's eyes. The more space that bedbug-related products took up in their house, the more the bedbug population seemed to be increasing. Their house was becoming some sort of enormous insect encyclopedia.

The man moved their bed slightly so the ceiling light's pull chain would dangle directly above his face when he lay down. This was so that whenever he felt like a bedbug was coming near, he could immediately pull the chain and turn the lights on. His wife looked at the chain as if it were a trap. The two locked eyes in the dark. For some reason, he felt like he was going to turn to stone, so he looked away first.

"Have you all heard of vermin filiality?" the senior in B102 asked. Attendance at WWB meetings had become a bit sparse because the people who'd been bitten most weren't showing up. Everyone understood why their neighbors couldn't come. They had to kill all the bedbugs that might be laying eggs on their bodies. The senior in B102 had been bitten as well, but he continued to regularly attend meetings. Although he did keep a certain level of distance from his neighbors while talking.

"In the past, filially pious children would go into their parents' bedroom and briefly sleep there, letting all the flies, fleas, and bedbugs inside feed off them before their parents went to bed," the senior explained. "That way, the already-sated bedbugs wouldn't want the parents' blood. The children were offering themselves up to the bugs as hosts, so to speak."

He said that this method had been tried successfully in a mountain village a while ago, and some exchange students had exerted great effort to master it as well. The senior's son had lived in Vancouver for four years and in New York for five, so he knew about super-bedbugs better than anyone, he said. If you mixed bedbug bait with a sticky liquid and applied it to your whole body, the bedbugs would smell it and attach themselves to your skin—the host's skin—unable to come off, like an ant falling into a honey pot. Within a week, all the bedbugs in the building would stick themselves to the master host. That way, they could be caught alive. All the master host had to do was draw every bug to their body, go to some destination far away, and remove them all before returning to the home village.

The senior continued to speak.

"One reason it's hard to get rid of bedbugs is because we use bait. Bedbugs drink human blood. You've got to use a method that combines bait with bodies, and that's the master host treatment. The master host is nothing more than a human. You're driving all the bedbugs toward a single person. You might even say that person is human glue."

"So it's like putting a bell on a cat. But who's going to do it?"

After hearing the student in 202 ask this, everyone looked at each other. The man thought about those people he'd occasionally seen on TV who absolutely loved bees, spiders, and scorpions. Their passion was so intense that they'd even let the creatures bite their eyes and tongues. In spite of the pain, they embraced them as soul mates, as if they intended to give up their minds to them, too, not just their bodies.

He was silent, then opened his mouth, afraid of being in the spotlight.

"So does the master host die?"

"Ha-ha, of course not," the senior replied. "You don't have to burn your house down just to catch the bedbugs. But no matter how sticky the liquid that the bedbugs get caught in, no matter how stuck they are, you're bound to get bitten some at first. You'll itch like crazy. You'll also have some scars. So people with sensitive skin aren't really fit to be master hosts."

To save the building, they needed a master host willing to give up their skin for a certain period of time. Qualifications for the master host included:

1. Someone who did not have excessively sensitive skin or allergies.
2. Someone with a strong immune system and stamina, who was not likely to catch a secondary disease.
3. Someone who was bold and had a sense of duty.
4. Someone who could give up at least a week of their time.

Each house was required to nominate one person. People who had to go to work every day were excluded as candidates. This was because once you became the master host, you needed to be away for at least a weeklong incubation period. Going next door and spending the incubation period right there would be a foolish act. They would have to discuss it with the master host, but the further the host went, the better. The apartment residents decided to split up the costs to cover the master host's week away. Of course, the host's family wouldn't have to pay anything. Plans went forward with the assumption that each of the nine households would pay one million won, for a total of nine million.

The master host had to be brave and intrepid. It would be a problem if they screamed at the sight of a single cockroach. Because of this, fearful people were also excluded. The master host would be providing their body as housing for the bedbugs, so tough skin was a requirement as well. Sick or weak people were excluded, too. They decided that families with no one to nominate would pay a little bit more. Out of ten households, there were five candidates, and the remaining five households contributed extra money. After a vote, one of the five was selected. It was 302. He didn't currently have a job, he needed money, and his family lived far away, so he seemed like the most appropriate candidate. Additionally, he had very durable skin.

But a few days later, the man in 302 showed up to a WWB meeting and said the following: "Uh, I got a job. I start the day after tomorrow . . ."

They held another strategy meeting to select a new host. Recently, the bedbugs had spread even further, so they couldn't delay. No one spoke. They all looked in one direction. At him.

He didn't have work to go to, he didn't have a baby to look after, his skin was thick enough, he had free time until the end of winter, and, most importantly, he held a strong animosity toward bedbugs. They gave him a night to think it over. They decided that if he refused, they'd look for an outside person to serve as the host in secret. That night, he thought about the structure of the apartment building.

	X (402)
X (201)	
	X (102)
	X (B102)

(X: infested home)

The bedbugs hadn't been acting in a completely regular manner, but it did seem like it would be the third floor's turn next. If he was going to get bitten anyway, he figured in a moment of rash bravery, he might as well find the bedbugs before they found him. It was better to actually do something rather than stay inside worrying. Let's stop the bedbugs before they can lay eggs in my walls and blankets, he thought. A huge financial benefit would follow if he did this. The nine houses other than his were going to give him 11,500,000 won. With that money, he could ride business class and spend a week at a five-star resort. He would even have money left over. Throwing himself out there for a week, making money while relaxing, would be so much better than his old job. He closed his eyes as he lay down. The walls and ceiling and floor all felt like flimsy wax paper. Sounds crept up the thin walls and reached his ears. Who knew if the bedbugs were somehow crawling up those sounds?

The sewing machine began to thrum at daybreak. There was no way the woman in 201 was sewing at this hour, but he could clearly hear the presser foot plunging over fabric. A reverberation from somewhere facing the wall—the apartment above, or maybe the one below—glued his whole body to the bed. A long breath shivered through the floor, the walls, the ceiling, uprooting the walls of the building. He could now trace which way the presser foot was going just from the hum of the sewing-machine needle turning. He could tell if it was charging precariously, for lack of seam margins, or plodding over tough, thick denim; if the fabric was cotton or a poly blend; and if the machine was wrapping around a sleeve or neckline. In the darkness, the sewing machine lowered the presser foot and its sharp, knifelike edge. The presser foot affixed him to his bed, poking him with a sharp needle at several-second intervals. The apartment residents were stuck in the bobbin case, their nerves coming undone thread by thread, and eventually he was folded in half himself and stitched up from one end to the other.

Bedbugs!

He quickly opened his eyes. Just now, something—something flat, five millimeters long, something that would plump up into a ball if it drank his blood—had crossed his forearm. He quickly snatched the chain in front of his face. Left in the bedbug's path were a few strands of his wife's hair, lying invasively on top of his body. Long, black hairs meandered up and down his forearm. He reached out and tried to remove the tangle. However, as soon as he took hold of the clumps of hair, he dropped them in disgust. The Rapunzel locks that had once called him to bed now seemed like a bedbug hotspot, a breeding ground. He felt like something was taking place in the hairs spread out on his pillow.

He hopped out of bed like a spring and quickly turned on the computer. He had to know about the connection between bedbugs and hair. It was urgent. Within ten minutes, he'd learned that lying on your pillow with wet hair was not good if you were trying to exterminate bedbugs. His wife didn't have time to completely dry her hair before going to bed. Her strands of wet hair looked like Medusa's snakes. A bedbug, or something that wasn't a bedbug, could be hiding in the crevices. If she hung her hair out the window, the bastards might climb up it. Now even things that weren't bedbugs looked like them. That was the problem.

He lay down again. His wife's tresses were like Samson's. Maybe they had become a source of strength for the bedbugs. He wondered if the only way to get some peace would be to take a pair of scissors and cut her hair like Delilah had for Samson. The chain connected to the ceiling light dangled in front of his nose, almost tickling him, like a rescue rope, or maybe a rope on the verge of snapping. He decided to grab it.

The day before becoming the master host, he visited a church, a cathedral, and a temple. He wasn't religious, but some of his neighbors were. Moving busily between houses of worship, he took on their faith traditions as his own. That afternoon, he got a call from a small paper dealing with neighborhood news. If the master host regimen succeeded, they might write a special feature about it, they said. For all they knew, professional master hosts might even start to pop up in the future. Finally the day came. His wife made him seaweed soup. She wasn't particularly sad or disapproving about him being chosen as the master host. She just said, "Let's start over in the spring when this whole thing is done." He didn't know exactly what they'd start over, but he nodded.

The senior came over and handed him a medicine bottle.

"This is a type of pheromone. Males and females both react to it."

"A pheromone that lures bedbugs?"

"A pheromone that seduces them. It's sticky, so if they smell it and attach themselves to the host's body, they won't be able to get free."

Several people took a whiff of the liquid. It didn't have much of an odor. At first it smelled a bit like cilantro, but that wasn't quite it. The only thing you could call it was scentless. Like wind. It smelled like wind.

He washed his body with bedbug pheromones. He washed his hair with bedbug pheromones, and he brushed his teeth with bedbug pheromones. He gave himself a footbath and scrubbed his face with them. He sprinkled the remainder on his thin mattress. He wrapped the bedbugs' future hiding spot around his body, then entered the infested homes. After enveloping himself in the mattress, he felt like he'd become some sort of master bug. Or a master host.

Residents of the infested homes had taken the bare essentials and gone elsewhere. It wasn't strictly necessary, but most of the uninfested households had done the same. He evenly applied pheromones to his body in a space that was suddenly all his own and waited for the bedbugs.

One day passed, then another. In order to attract more bedbugs, he drew the curtains. He rolled around in the sunless interior. Thankfully, there were entertaining shows playing on TV twenty-four hours a day, and his neighbors' fridges were full of tasty snacks. The fact that he didn't have to worry anymore about being bitten by bedbugs made him feel especially carefree. Attracting bedbugs was certainly easier than getting rid of them. This was the first time in the past few months that he'd done nothing but relax. He ate and drank without worry. He slept peacefully, roughly scratched the itches covering his body, and enjoyed the satiety of having nothing else to worry about. He'd found the break he had wanted all this time, and it was with bedbugs. He moved only within a range of three to six feet. Every time he ate, he ordered something sumptuous for delivery. He took pictures of his whole body with the DSLR in order to remember the moment. The camera, netbook, and memory card were very useful in this time of bedbugs. His wife, who had been apathetic about the whole ordeal, even sent a text message of support. That night, he thought about his wife. She was staying in her parents' home near her school.

According to some book he'd read recently, bedbugs have sex more than two hundred times per day. The male pierces the female in the heart with sharp, awl-like genitals. They often don't reach the female's own genitals, but even so, fertilization is possible. The male's semen enters somewhere, be it the back or stomach or genitals, and hides in the female's blood vessels to survive the winter. And in the spring, the sperm that has been hiding throughout her body instinctively begins to look for eggs. He thought about his faraway wife and tried to ejaculate remotely, like bedbugs did. His wife wouldn't know.

He was awakened in the morning not by sunlight or an alarm but by an itch. His forearm was tainted with three equidistant spots. They looked like the stars of the Big Dipper, rising in the dark sky. Each night, more stars appeared on his arm.

Three-four-three. It was the bedbugs.

Four-three-three. Finally, bedbugs.

Three-three-three. Bedbugs, just as he'd expected.

Two-four-three. Three-four-four. Four-three-two. The bedbugs placed their musical notes on his forearms, his thighs, his calves, even his back, neck, and face, as if it were all sheet music. They began to sew his body like fabric. After about a week, he'd managed to collect quite a few bedbugs onto the mattress. As soon as the master host left the room, so did the bedbugs, intoxicated by the pheromones on his body. The pheromones mixed with the scent of his sweat and blood, which made them all the more effective.

The next morning, he set off. In his bag were a week's worth of vacation spending money in crisp bills, a round-trip plane ticket, and a room reservation voucher. The place he'd chosen was an island in the Pacific. He planned to burn his bedbug-infested mattress, wash his body in a freshwater spa, and spend a weeklong incubation period there before returning home. He took a deep breath while wondering what Pacific coffee tasted like.

No one—not even his wife—said goodbye. He picked up a copy of the local paper in front of the door to the apartment. As he stood at the airport bus stop, the street was unusually quiet. All the windows were closed, and not even a solitary cat traversed the road. The airport bus broke through the silence of the street as it arrived, but the bus driver had to make a call before taking him anywhere. Thankfully, the man was able to sit in a bus seat rather than in the cargo storage area. Several passengers turned their heads as he walked by. He opened up the local newspaper he'd gotten that morning to cover his face. It had been a while since he'd read the paper, and there was no news about bedbugs anywhere. He did see his own name, though. It was an obituary. A different person with the same name, but he still felt peculiar.

The bus departed. This was the end. With a whole building's worth of bedbugs clinging to his body, he had nowhere to go but up. He felt a sense of relief that there were no more dreadful events to come. Knowing this put his mind at rest. Finally, after all this time, he'd found it. Peace.

3. INVADER GRAPHIC

When the twentieth-century Austrian writer Peter Altenberg was asked his address, he had the following answer: "Café Central, in Vienna's Innere Stadt."

Another writer, from the twenty-first century, replies this way when asked where she lives: "** Department Store in Seoul."

Altenberg spent all his waking hours in Café Central. Even after he fell asleep for all eternity, he continued to sit in the café, this time as a wax figure. Now some of the café's visitors come specifically to see Altenberg's waxen form, having learned about the café only because of their interest in him.

There's no reason to assume that this other writer, who spends as many of her own waking hours as possible in the department store, couldn't become a wax figure herself in a few centuries. Maybe the store will even make displays out of the writer's favorite destinations within the building, and open them to the public as if they were a musical performance or an exhibition or a puppet show. Over the next few hundred years, as long as the place doesn't collapse, there's no limit to what could be done.

Every morning at 10:30, the writer walks from her home to the department store, a commute equivalent in distance to four stops on the bus. When she arrives, the building's walls and floors and ceilings—from the fourth basement to the seventh story—chorus a greeting.

I, the writer, am neither shopper nor shopkeeper, but going to the department store is a part of my daily routine. The store has undergone several renovations since it was built, slowly evolving into the best possible one-stop creative workroom. It's got sofas and tables on every floor, water dispensers in every corner, soap and tissues in the bathrooms, free mouthwash, foot massagers and sample beverages for anyone to try, food downstairs in the sample corner, internet access, electricity and AC, lights and music, occasional free concerts and art exhibits, even cooking classes sometimes. There are countless ways to take advantage of the venue's offerings.

My first stop is the women's bathroom on the fourth floor. It's near the menswear brands, so the bathroom is less crowded than those on the second or third floors. I prefer to take the elevator there, rather than the escalator. The escalator is in the middle of the building, so I easily become an object of attention when business is slow. If I just want to pop in and out of stores, I prefer staying out of the shopkeepers' sight. When the elevator stops at the fourth floor, I turn right and enter the bathroom. I like this bathroom because it consists of three separate sections: the toilets, the sinks, and the powder room.

All four of the toilets are empty. I go into the first stall and pull an entire roll of toilet paper off its holder. I skip over the second and third stalls and take another roll from the fourth. My bag bulges with the two cylinders. I wash my hands at the sink. After making use of the soap, lotion, and paper towels as I thoroughly clean and dry my hands, I fix my hair with a hairdryer in the powder room. The round brush in my bag comes in handy. I'm finished with everything in three minutes.

Yellow light bathes the gray sofa in the powder room. I slide my laptop out of my bag and plug it into the outlet hidden behind the sofa. The computer is over four years old, and if it's not connected to a power source, it barely lasts an hour. The couch supports the writer's body—my body—with just the right amount of cushioning, and the room's yellowish illumination increases my focus. The rolls of toilet paper function as substitutes for paper. Of course, the pictures hanging on each wall and the gently cascading music also contribute to the room's atmosphere, not to mention the fragrance that's spritzed into the air at regular intervals. The best thing about this space is the generous air conditioning.

Even if you've come to the department store to create rather than to spend, suitable self-presentation is a necessity. The efforts I make for myself include avoiding wearing the same outfit multiple days in a row, reddening my lips with a lively shade of lipstick, and using the hairdryer to tidy my hair as soon as I get to the powder room. It doesn't matter whether or not I'm a consumer. I have to show that I could be one, if I decided to.

The department store doesn't need to worry about my freeloading. The opulent trial creams that I apply on my skin and the sample perfumes I spray on my clothing are expenses already covered by the store. And this isn't the only place that offers free things. There are more ways than you'd think to avoid unnecessary spending. If you take the white envelopes from those automated machines hidden in the corners of banks, you can use them as envelopes like they were intended, or as memo paper. If you pick up a stack of napkins in a café, the paper quality's not bad for note-taking. Books you can just check out at the library. You can also read magazines and newspapers and watch movies there. New books: read them at a large bookstore without buying. If you really want to go to the theater, just enter your name into raffles to watch preview screenings for free. Free internet abounds in public spaces, so if you aren't desperate, you don't really need to install it in your home. As long as you have a laptop—or even if you don't have one—there are lots of places to finish up urgent business. Department store lobbies are equipped with computers for customer use, and plenty of spots offer Wi-Fi. Whenever I turn on my laptop in the fourth-floor bathroom, there's a total of ten wireless networks available, and six or seven of them are open for anyone to use. All I have to do is click "Connect."

I flip open my computer. Using the limitless electricity that the fourth-floor bathroom provides the writer—me—I compose my novel. The title of the book is *Invader Graphic.* It's the story of a man who works for a brokerage firm, except he's about to quit.

"Mr. Gyun Kim: 129th out of 176 employees."

When he starts up his computer, the above caption flashes onscreen for five seconds before disappearing. That one sentence has the force of a starter pistol marking the beginning of a race. The sound of the pistol dissipates quickly, but every one of the runners standing at the starting line hears it. Just like gunfire, the wording on the computer screen also vanishes seconds after it appears, and no employee can ignore it. Today, Gyun will live as number 129. Yesterday, he was 108; the day before, 95. There's a regularity to the numerical changes—each day, Gyun's ranking is a little bit worse than it was before. Tomorrow morning, his performance today will be broadcast with a pistol-like bang as soon as he arrives at work and turns on his monitor.

Gyun is someone who lives by the second. When the stock markets are open, when he's staring at the computer screen, his expression changes on a momentary basis. He smiles for a few seconds, and then he cries for a few more. Only at 3:00 p.m., after the markets have closed, does Gyun escape the boundaries of this cruel quantification. Gyun has worked at the firm for three years, but even now his customers frequently make him anxious. There are those who come into the office carrying vases to give him, and others who bring spirits or neckties, or lye and pesticides, which they threaten to kill themselves with if Gyun doesn't protect their investments. Some brandish family photos and knives as they harass him. Productivity is calculated on an hourly basis, and the results hover behind him like a shadow. The markets operate without even a break for lunch.

From wake-up at five until bedtime after midnight, Gyun's most immediate need is to stay abreast of the issues that affect the stock market. Invader graphics—which never show up in the news—are nothing more than a distant topic of conversation with little relevance to Gyun's life. But that's exactly why he has so quickly grown enamored with them. Every day, when his duties are finished, he logs on to an invader graphic network online. When new posts haven't been uploaded for a few weeks, Gyun begins to reread messages from the first page.

The term "invader graphic" refers to a kind of colorful tile mosaic, a recreation of characters from the video game *Space Invaders* in ceramic form. The phenomenon of decorating walls with images of these invaders, like graffiti, has existed since 1998. Gyun learned about the invaders in 2008. In the ten years since their inception, invader graphics have spread across the world, to a number of major cities. No one knows who is creating them, or exactly how many of these mosaics there are on earth, but the mystery surrounding the invaders is why they've become legendary. An unknown artist turns city spaces—the walls of buildings, slums, and pipes—into canvases, and upon these canvases, he resurrects the once-digital characters.

The artist usually wears a mask as he works. Several photos of him have been made public, but no one is certain if they're of the invader graphics' creator or someone impersonating him. It's not just the artist now—copycats affix their own invader images to surfaces in public spaces everywhere. They're all anonymous. And they all work with tiles. The population of invader graphics increases at a staggering rate with each passing year. Each one varies in size, appearance, and location. It's always surprising when you see an invader on a roof or a sign, somewhere out of the reach of human hands. You wonder how it got there. But that's a question that only people in the know can answer.

At 11:40, I close my laptop. It's time for the cleaning patrol to make their rounds. According to the inspection log on the wall, the bathroom is to be cleaned once every two hours. It's best to avoid sticking around during patrol times if you want to make a habit of writing in the bathroom. That's just a rule of the trade.

The rest spot in front of the elevator isn't far from the bathroom, so I can escape there quickly. Fortunately, there's also a rarely traversed staircase and a public phone booth nearby. If I'm bothered by the elevator, with its constantly opening doors, I go up to the fifth or sixth floor. After waiting upstairs for exactly twenty minutes, I come back down to the fourth-floor bathroom, and the next two hours are once again free of disruption.

Soon after I've dodged two bathroom checks, the morning is over, and both my mind and my belly have grown empty. It's time to go to the underground food court, where the sample corner is open to anyone. Freshly fried pork cutlets, vegetable pancakes grilled golden brown, fat sausages—I grab a skewer of each and chomp on the bite-size morsels. Some days, I come across udon noodles in paper cups, or fruit to cleanse my palette. After I fill my hungry stomach, I head to the basement bathroom. Or to one on the second or third floors—they're not bad options, either. This time, I actually need to use the restroom. I walk into a stall, do what I have to do, nab a roll of toilet paper, wash my hands, and apply hand cream. I brush my teeth, too, and gargle some mouthwash if it's available. Then I step onto the escalator, and it's time to depart for my next destination.

There are three types of people riding the escalator down from the first basement. They're traveling to the second basement to eat in the cafeteria there, or they're going to the underground parking lot, or, like me, they're aiming for the sofa by the side of the second-basement cafeteria. I sit down on the couch and flip open my laptop. I write for forty minutes, until my battery reaches 20 percent. I charged it in the bathroom, but it's nearly depleted already.

"Mr. Gyun Kim, you're 129th out of 176 employees."

When he returns from lunch and turns his monitor on again, the gunfire rings into the air once more. Until tomorrow's rankings come out, the results from yesterday follow his every step. But Gyun is tormented less by these intermittent notifications than he is by all the people ceaselessly looking for him. Everyone wants to talk to him—from the full-time investors, dressed up every day in a suit and tie for their jobs on the trading floor, to Gyun's clients complaining about their rights as customers. There's a limit to Gyun's ability to digest the verbiage around him. Unabsorbed words from his conversations begin to float around the empty air. ㄱ, ㅣ, ㅏ, ㅅ, ㄷ, ㅁ . . . not infrequently, consonants and vowels mix together in front of his eyes and begin a game of *Tetris*, all while his coworker is still talking. Even as Gyun nods appropriately while the speaker talks, he struggles to keep up with the *Tetris* screen hovering before him. If a ㄱ falls atop a ㄴ, or a ㄷ falls on top of a ㄹ, then the row is cleared, but it's always the wrong pieces that pile up. Nothing that can empty out the game's increasingly crowded corners appears before him. Additionally, because of the figures that have already accumulated, there's no time for strategic decisions. Gyun wonders, "How will I—" and is interrupted as a new letter falls with a plop. He hasn't even reached out to move it when yet another shape drops down. *Game over*, the screen says.

Gyun's company lets its workers off relatively early compared to other businesses, but closing time becomes meaningless when there's a late meeting or guests to entertain. On days when there are no conferences or client dinners or overtime, Gyun's coworker suggests that they get a drink together. The two usually go for sake.

The coworker married last year when stock prices were shooting up. Now that prices are in the tank again, he finds both his house and his job to be a burden. As soon as stocks started to fall, his wife developed an unusual interest in his work. He comes home late just as often as he did last year, so he doesn't understand why she questions his occasional tardiness. Even when his wife is just asking what it's like to work in finance, he finds her questions irritating. After he's left for the office at seven in the morning, his wife goes to their computer and types familiar words into the search engine. Broker, branch office, work duties. "Broker," "branch office," "work duties": results with information about all three topics materialize onscreen. Strangers on the internet are kind. Brokers, or people who think they know a lot about them, upload information. His wife pores over what she finds. The posts are endless. At 7:00 a.m., once the man is off to work, his wife turns on the computer to peruse facts about the day-to-day of other women's husbands. She asks questions and receives answers and contemplates even more, and then new information is available online for those with the same worries and frustrations as her. Now, when Gyun's coworker talks about what he's going to do at work that day, his wife sometimes doesn't believe what he says. He doesn't know it, but she's become an expert on his job.

The coworker with a wife who trusts stories on the internet more than she does her own husband tells Gyun not to get married. Instead of replying, Gyun brings up invader graphics. Not long after the topic of conversation changes, they part ways.

On his way home, Gyun discovers that several of the sidewalk blocks beneath his feet are broken. Chunks of concrete are completely gone, like missing pieces in a puzzle. As soon as he takes his eyes off the pavement, he sees loose fragments, ready to fall out of their frames, everywhere he looks. The world transforms into an enormous piece of concrete. According to a story Gyun heard when he was young, a Dutch child once died using his body to block a crevice he'd discovered in a dyke. Perhaps that's how invader graphics originated, too: just like a hand can cover a single hole, maybe the tiles are there to plug the voids in our pockmarked world. As Gyun stares attentively at shattered sidewalks and open manholes in the street, he turns toward his house.

When I exit the department store, it's almost 3:00 p.m. I'm not technically leaving the property. I step through the back door—or maybe it's the front. It's at least the entryway opposite the one I pass through in the morning. Outside is a coffee shop attached to the main building. Recently, a second café was added next door, so my options have widened. Regardless of which shop I choose to patronize, by the time I leave, I'm carrying with me an entire store's worth of three-gram sugar packets and napkins.

I spend three hours in the café, or maybe four. The available seating isn't the only thing I'm making use of. There are also the neatly laid-out packs of white and brown sugar, napkins, ice water with lemon, milk in thermoses, straws, and other freebies available upon request—and everything disappears quickly when I'm around. I typically occupy a seat without ordering, instead filling my bag with the many items available for customers. Truthfully, I have no use for straws or stirring sticks. But even though they're arranged in perfect order, leaving the display intact seems like a loss, so I steal a few. I can't exactly explain it, but the act of taking is a comfort. Sugar is the best thing to take. The more disorganized my life becomes, the more the packets in front of me sparkle. They're just like gold: scintillating, and without an expiration date. If I'm wanting for gold, all I have to do is gather some sugar.

Sometimes groups ask if they can pull one of the chairs at my table over to their own. The small act of giving up one's extra chair can feel very symbolic. Without a barrier to block the emptiness beneath the table like a windshield, my two legs are exposed to the world. If I were holding a coffee, this wouldn't be a big deal, but since I'm not, it's a grave problem. When I first began to frequent coffee shops without buying a drink, I was afraid that customers would stare, so I would place abandoned cups on my table. Not to drink the remaining beverage inside, but so others would see the cups and assume that I, too, was a customer.

Now I know that it's a bit better if I sit in a corner seat, or somewhere on the second floor. I pass the counter confidently, as if I'm meeting someone upstairs. Once I'm on the second floor, I lay my things out on the table and fall into my work. In the morning, the bathroom provides my electricity; in the afternoon, the café keeps me plugged in.

When I attended college and even once I had a job, spaces like this held a slightly different meaning to me. I visited the department store a few times a year, perhaps when spring was turning to summer and summer to fall, and rarely did I spend more than twenty minutes in the bathroom. I had no need to search for electrical outlets, either, and I never filled my bag with straws or napkins.

My reason for preferring the department store to other venues is a very practical matter. Alternative destinations abound: libraries, university campuses, and parks, for example. And on days that I don't make it to my preferred office, I do frequent those other facilities. Sometimes I even pay bus or subway fare to trek out to a distant chain bookstore. Cultural centers are decent places to work, too. On summer nights, parks or the Hangang riverbank become worthwhile studios. Life has an intimate relationship with temperature, and the best place for sleeping out in the open is also the best spot for writing.

But libraries are crammed with patrons, and they're not as comfortable as department stores. Parks lack electrical outlets and air conditioning. Train stations are chaotic. Playgrounds are dangerous. If you're a solitary adult hanging out by the jungle gym, it's only a matter of time before misunderstandings arise. Child disappearances have put the public on edge, and playgrounds are for kids, anyway, not adults. The cheapest place to write is at home, but my house is filled with family members who just want me to leave during the day. So the department store is where I go.

"Vacation?"

When Gyun asks to take a summer holiday, his coworker is surprised.

"Have you seen the new hand dryer in the bathroom?" the coworker asks Gyun. "The managers installed it to save on the cost of paper towels. What about the new bidet? That's to stop spending money on toilet paper. And have you noticed how the water pressure in the toilet is weaker than it used to be? It's to reduce the water bill. Do you understand what I'm saying? We've reached the point where we'll have to turn in our resignation letters on double-sided paper. In a work environment this bleak, going on vacation might mean you'll never come back!"

Gyun's colleague explains to him the correlation between time off and daily rankings. But Gyun decides to purchase a plane ticket anyway, one to Paris. On the day of departure, he boards his plane. Not counting travel time, he has four days to savor fully. All Gyun does the first two days of his trip is walk. He walks and walks, hoping for that moment when an invader graphic tile will serendipitously come into view. But his object of desire doesn't materialize. Surrounded as he is by unfamiliar walls and signs, it would be hard for Gyun to catch sight of an invader even if there were one. On the fourth day, he purchases a map. It's a map marking the locations of invaders spread throughout Paris. The Eiffel Tower may be the city's icon, but to him it's no more than a signpost marking the location of an invader graphic. The Louvre and the Musée d'Orsay and the many bridges along the Seine River are no different. Gyun encounters the first invader graphic of his life on the wall of the Palais de Tokyo. At a glance, the red-and-white tiled alien could easily be mistaken for the flag of an unknown country. On a street corner between the Paris Opera and Place Vendôme, he encounters another: a green body, with red eyes, against a blue backdrop. Gyun doesn't tremble when he sees it, but he is beginning to appreciate why invader aficionados pursue their beloved invaders so relentlessly.

The treasure hunt—reminding him of childhood games—continues. It's not simply a matter of locating a slip of paper in a designated area. Now the whole world is Gyun's playground. He comes across his third and fourth treasures, one after another, in Marais. He pulls out his camera, and the invader graphics fill the viewfinder. The photos function as location markers. Back at the hotel, he boots up his computer and connects to the invader graphic network. But the invaders he's just captured are already old news on the site. While Gyun's camera lens was taking aim at the mosaics, others hunters were on the prowl as well. In fact, there seem to have been several invader marksmen in the area. Gyun shuts his laptop. According to rumors, Paris is speckled with over three hundred invader graphics, and not all of them have been discovered. Gyun is now an archaeologist who's been dropped into a city brimming with relics—except he's leaving town in just two days.

Several years ago, my family probably purchased more copies of the January 1 issue of ** *Newspaper* than anyone else. My father bought about twenty papers and handed them out to acquaintances. My mother bragged that her daughter wasn't only a published writer, she was also a former math champion. My friends from school were jealous. Spending my free time coming up with one story after another wasn't a new development, but only after I won the newspaper contest did people start to call me a writer. Several months later, though, once the awards ceremony was over and summer had begun, my father said the following to me:

"How long are you going to just bask in your own success? You need to get a job."

I couldn't believe what he was telling me. Did my father think that being a novelist was a seasonal event, like the World Cup or the Olympics? I didn't even have a club or team to return to for training. And according to my father's calendar, the deadlines for spring literary contests had already passed.

I may have become a writer, but few people were confident that I'd be able to *live* as a writer. Friends thought that my passion for writing meant I would find work at a publishing company or become a Korean teacher. Maybe they believed that my role wasn't solely writing books, but also making and selling them, and even teaching them.

The only exception among the doubters was the middle schooler I tutored in math twice a week. The child's parents subscribed to ** *Newspaper*, and she said that her entire family had spotted my photo in the paper. The day she told me, our tutoring session devolved from the normal lesson into an hour of chitchat. I then learned for the first time that the child also dreamed of becoming a writer. Of course, her mother didn't approve of her aspiration. After that, I never met with the girl again. I quit tutoring, or more specifically, she quit being tutored by me. I'm sure my selection as the winner of the newspaper's short story contest played a role in the decision. "Miss, I think our child would work better with a teacher who studied math rather than literature. I'm sorry." That's what the text message from the child's mother said. "Good luck with your writing career."

I needed a space where it was truly worthwhile to sit myself down and focus for a few hours. At home, I had my own room, but a safe work environment wasn't guaranteed. By now I'd spent several months without going to school or a job, and my father was growing more and more uneasy. He kept looking at with me with the same kind of gaze he'd had right after my college entrance exams ended, and it made me uneasy, too. Just after I'd finished the tests, he'd suddenly opened the door to my room one night and asked: "Aren't you going to sleep?"

It was four in the morning. Considering that I'd just taken a major exam, why couldn't I stay up until 4:00 a.m.? Thankfully, he didn't barge into my bedroom in the middle of the night to ask about my sleep habits after that. But my father began to inquire more and more about my plans for the future. Whenever we heard about a successful cousin's wedding, or about his friend's daughter getting a job, or if the nine o'clock news was blabbering on about the employment crisis, my father suddenly wanted to know what *I* was doing with my life. His curiosity grew most apparent at the kitchen table, so I began to hate meals.

"Hey, you haven't even experienced the real world," my friends reminded me. "When you do finally start working, it won't be so bad, it really won't."

Hearing them say this made me stubborn. I eventually got into an argument with my friends, about that phrase that seemed stuck to everyone's tongue like it was the chorus to a song: "the real world." They were debating one day whether or not things like offices, employees, and salaries were truly necessary components of "the real world." Could they be unnecessary but still provide structure to society, or did they have no connection to society whatsoever? No one came to any conclusions. After that discussion, no one mentioned the real world in front of me again, so I decided to initiate my own conversation about it.

"I don't know the first thing about the real world, but let me tell you what I think."

That's what I'd said. My friends turned to me in response, but their expressions weren't exactly positive.

"That's not something to be proud of," they admonished.

In order to shake off my doubts that I'd somehow been left behind while my friends charged ahead in life, I finally I got a job to earn spending money. I worked at a publisher for a year and a half, and then for six months at a production company. After me, two new entrants were chosen as winners of ** *Newspaper*'s annual literary prize, and with the coming year, another writer would be selected. Just like that, I was forgotten. While I was working, I didn't write a single new short story. Finally I quit my job. After that, I read novels again and looked up information about writing contests I could enter, and it felt like my passion for books was slowly coming back to me. At the same time, my father grew increasingly concerned.

"Just how many members of our household are unemployed?" he asked one night at dinner.

A housewife who sometimes held part-time jobs, a young man in the midst of military service—in other words, a soldier—and a novelist. There wasn't really anyone you could say was unemployed, but that's what my father had implied. After he'd cleared the dinner table and smoked a cigarette, he worked out possible lotto numbers in his notebook. As he sat there trying to determine winning probabilities, the pages of his book jumbled with digits that taunted him as they grew longer and longer.

The archaeologist's vacation soon ends, and he returns to his duties at the brokerage firm. He's distracted, though, by thoughts of the invader graphics turning round and round inside his head. News of a discovery in Melbourne is uploaded to the invader network. The red and white tiles stand out like a bull's-eye against the gray street corner to which they're clinging. A bull's-eye that's ready to be hit by the stares of passersby instead of arrows.

Korea hasn't yet been used as an invader target. The anonymous artist tends to stick tiles in locations where they're difficult to remove, places unlikely to change over time. But is any place in Korea that impervious to demolition? Pedestrians recently identified an invader graphic on the wall of an underpass in Sinchon, and even though onlookers guaranteed that it wasn't an original, a picture of the mosaic was uploaded to the network. It looked no different from a real invader graphic, and there seemed to be no particular reason to argue against its authenticity. Still, witnesses and even those who'd only heard secondhand accounts assured everyone that it was a counterfeit. This was Korea—it had to be.

To Gyun, invader graphics are like a revolving door. You just push until you start to rotate and are pulled to an entirely new world on the opposite side. Whenever Gyun encounters another invader, the door twirls open before him, but it always deposits him in his original position by the end of the weekend.

Gyun's rank in the company falls continuously, far below that original position: 158th out of 179, 169th out of 177, 174th out of 176, drop after precipitous drop, and finally, just before Gyun plummets beyond the number of employees in the firm, he's fired. Gyun holds his box of possessions and walks out into the street. The multicolored, tile-like buildings around him swell up from the ground and blur as they poke through the clouds. He begins to look for a new job, just like anyone else who's unemployed. But finding a job like anyone else isn't so simple for Gyun. The only times he can quiet his mind are when he connects to the invader graphic network and when he's looking through his notes about invaders. Gyun needs an escape.

I usually bring ten three-gram packets of sugar home with me, sometimes as many as twenty. In a typical month, I take at least one kilogram of sugar. In the same time frame, I accumulate over sixty rolls of the toilet paper—two or three per day—and close to three hundred straws. When I began to compile my collections, though, I didn't suspect that the knickknacks piling up in the kitchen and bedroom would incite my parents' suspicions.

"What are you doing with your time nowadays?" they eventually ask me.

I'm taking advantage of the department store. That's how I should answer, but I can't blurt out the words in front of my father. I'd have to explain exactly what "taking advantage of the department store" really means, and there's a good chance that he won't understand. And I can't simply say that I'm going to the library. That's because we recently heard on the news that Korea's libraries are overflowing with patrons due to the youth unemployment problems, and I don't want to remind my parents of anything to do with joblessness. I feel like the game of *Tetris* that began in Gyun's mind has moved over to mine for a second round.

"Why aren't you answering?" my dad asks. "What's all this sugar and toilet paper?"

"Oh, those are just things I brought home from a café."

I wave my hands at my parents, then hurriedly spit out the following lines to clear the situation, as if it's a piled-up column of *Tetris* pieces: "I've been going to the department store every day."

"The department store—why? To work?"

"Yes."

My parents' expressions grow befuddled as they consider the connection between work that can be done at a department store and the toilet paper rolls and straws piled up in our house. I sample some of the communal side dishes on the dinner table, but they all taste exactly the same.

"What kind of work do you do at the department store?" my father asks.

"I write."

I, *w*, *r*, *i*, *t*, *e*. Now it seems like the *Tetris* shapes are falling on my father's face.

"I've been writing a novel," I explain. "The department store gave me a studio. There's a sofa, and internet—it's a place for writers to concentrate."

That's not a lie. There is a sofa, and internet, and many more things upon which I don't elaborate. And I do write there. It's just that sometimes people enter my workspace for purposes different from my own. I don't explicitly state that the place is a bathroom.

"They're giving you a free studio?" my mother asks.

"Yes," I reply.

"What department store?" This time it's my father.

"Do you want to go see it?"

"I just don't understand what kind of place it is," he says.

"A lot of department stores offer these kinds of amenities for writers nowadays. I mean, most of them already have cultural centers, anyway. But, Dad, you can't come visit. My studio, I mean."

It's not a lie. My father is a man, and the studio is the women's restroom.

I'm not sure what my mother and father think about my confession, but they don't ask about the department store again. I am a little worried about my mom, since she's been learning more and more about computers since her retirement. Who knows what could come up if she typed something like "department store, studio, novel" into a search engine and looked at the results.

My father knocks on my bedroom door, even though it's not four in the morning.

"If you have time, help me run some errands," he calls through the door. "There are a few things I've got to do today."

He sticks out a piece of paper littered with numbers lined up beside one another like the beads on an abacus. Lottery numbers. There are circles drawn around some of the figures, up to four on certain rows.

"Go to the bank and ask them to redeem this," my father says. "It's worth a little more than sixty thousand won."

"You won?"

"Uh-huh." My father is wearing a mysterious expression on his face as he mumbles a response.

"After you get the money, go and buy some black bean noodles," he adds.

"I don't know, black bean noodles are pretty expensive."

I say this as a joke, but my father widens his eyes like I'm being serious.

"Where can you find black bean noodles that cost more than sixty thousand won?"

He leaves me a warning before turning around.

"If you see noodles *anywhere* that cost more than sixty thousand won, they're a rip-off. You're being swindled."

As I listen to my father's advice, unsure if it's sincere or in jest, I stick the paper filled with prizewinning digits in my wallet. Like it's a talisman.

In the department store, there's a cultural center that hosts free classes for potential customers. The metric I use when deciding which classes to attend is not the subject but whether or not there's a materials fee. "Mom's Homemade Brunch," "Beading Conquered in One Hour," Baby's First Organic Cotton Clothing": classes like those cost extra. There are others that don't: "Physiognomy for Good Luck," "A Lawyer's Guide to Law in Daily Life," "Beautify with Face Yoga," "Buying and Selling International and Domestic Funds," and so on. The lecture I choose today will discuss investment strategies and stock market predictions for the second half of the year. To be honest, I'm not remotely interested in stock market predictions or investment strategies, but Gyun might find them necessary. I listen for him. Gyun is currently unemployed, but if he returns to his original position—where he was at the beginning of the story—the brokerage firm will be essential once more.

"Original position?" Gyun asks himself.

My place is now here, he thinks. He may have once held a job at a brokerage firm, but now that his role there has vanished, he has no desire to look for more work in finance. What Gyun searches for instead is airplane tickets and news of invader graphic sightings. The invaders are spinning like a revolving door, and they've already deposited Gyun outside. Gyun heads to New York. Like most other major cities, New York is home to over three hundred invader graphics. It's clear, though, that not all of them remain affixed to their urban canvases. Gyun discovers a green-bodied invader in Brooklyn, but when he returns to see it the day before leaving New York, it's not there. He doesn't know who tore it down; the emptiness where the tiles are missing looks painful, like hunks of flesh have been ripped off of the wall. Upon revisiting mosaics first discovered during prior travels, Gyun realizes some of them no longer exist, and he also runs into invaders in places that were once devoid of them. The orange invader graphic that he encounters on Neal Street in London definitely wasn't there last time he visited. But now it is, skillfully pasted above a street buzzing with passersby. This time, Gyun makes a stop in Bangkok as well. He's not bound by work, so there's no need to insist on a direct flight. With his limitless time, Gyun tends to choose flights with layovers. This allows him to visit two cities, sometimes two continents, on a single leg of his trip. Invader graphic artists are installing new works as industriously as ever, and the world of invaders shows no signs of ending. Gyun and his bank account grow accustomed to frequent plane ticket purchases as he embarks on unfamiliar paths, and it's entirely possible that his balance will reach zero before the proliferation of invaders dies down. It's worth it: how long has it been since he's been on the hunt for something so exciting? This is the kind of work that has actual results. The thing moving Gyun through life isn't digits on a screen anymore. He's not being controlled by his rank. Gyun has transcended numbers; he searches only for invader graphics. Chasing after his tile-adorned prizes, he crosses borders and treks around cities hour upon hour. He spans the world: from Paris to Amsterdam, Amsterdam to Melbourne, Melbourne to Los Angeles, Los Angeles to New York, and finally from New York back to Paris.

Unfortunately, I'm by the register when I run into a college classmate. She's just arrived, and no one's with her. I also just came in, alone. I pull out my wallet, because now I have to. If the rest of my day's going to be like this—punctuated by forced shows of propriety—I'm not going to survive.

"An espresso, please," I tell the cashier.

I order the espresso, of course, because it causes the smallest possible damage to my wallet.

Then I change course. "Actually, I'll have an espresso and a slice of New York cheesecake."

Did those words come out of my mouth? I don't know if it was my lips or my stomach spitting out such thoughtless drivel, but now it's too late. The plate of cake that the attentive employee hands me is mine. When I look to my side, my classmate has already gone up to the second floor.

"How many forks shall I give you, miss?" the cashier asks.

"Three, please," I reply.

I traverse the stairs holding the espresso and the New York cheesecake on a brown tray, along with three disposable forks and a pile of napkins that's expertly hiding my white and brown sugar packets. The heaviest item atop my plentiful platter is the receipt, of course. I patronize this coffee shop every day, but it's been almost a month since I've ordered something and been given a receipt. Something unexpected, like today's encounter, happens at least every thirty days.

My classmate is sitting a slight distance from me. Until she gets up to leave, we meet each other's gaze two or three times per hour, smiling slightly before we return to empty stares. And thanks to our awkward half greetings, I notice something. There's nothing on my classmate's tray save for a single water bottle: a water bottle from a brand that they don't sell here.

I gulp down a sip of espresso. It's bitter. After enduring six hours with the world's bitterest coffee and its smallest slice of cake, I finally rise from my seat. What I've gained over the past few hours is the electricity I used, four piles of napkins, several glasses of ice water, three magazines, three disposable forks, and twenty packets each of white and brown sugar. What the day has cost me is 7,500 won, thanks to the earlier unfair transaction. I stick the two extra forks and the packets of sugar in my purse, but I still feel like I've suffered a loss. I grab ten or so straws and put them in my bag as well, and then I stop by the bathroom to take ten mini paper mouthwash cups. I have an urge to wash my hair and do my laundry in here, too. But no matter how I try to alleviate today's loss, my hunger for the 7,500 missing won isn't going to go away.

Walking home—a distance equivalent in length to four bus stops—expends an unusual amount of energy. The three-gram packets of sugar in my bag, all forty of them, seem to have turned into thirty-kilogram sacks of sand. With each step I take, they crunch against each other. The further I walk from the department store, the brighter the stars in the night sky twinkle. Some of the stars are brown sugar packets, the others white sugar packets—three grams each. Are the stars like sugar, I wonder, available free for anyone who's watching?

The impact of my 7,500-won loss is quite heavy. For the next several days, I don't go to the department store. As long as I seclude myself at home, everything remains peaceful. There's no need to take off from the bathroom before the cleaning crew arrives, I don't have to eat broken-off bits of food with a toothpick, and I'm not carrying around my notebook, half-closed and curved like the blade of a sickle, as I crane my neck in search of a place to sit. I don't get in fights over the outlet, either. Staying at home is cozier than being at the department store, and my belly is fuller. But after a week, I leave my house again, earlier than usual.

Gyun stands on an unfamiliar street, holding a map in one hand and a detector in the other. He bought the detector a while ago at a flea market; it claims to guide the user toward invader graphics more accurately than a map. The shape of the device resembles two divining rods. Compass-like needles stick out from the handles. Just like divining rods pull together into an X shape when the user is close to water, so too does the detector when invaders are near. Gyun's footsteps grow careful. His new tool will be useful in several ways. If he's holding it in his hands as he walks down the street, he might just casually turn his head and find an invader graphic stuck to a building. With the detector, there's no need to look down at a map and continuously check unfamiliar place-names against his surroundings.

The detector points to this alley. The detector points down that alley. Gyun marches forward according to the device's instruction for a long while, but the objects he craves fail to materialize. After a while, the detector's guesses are occasionally accurate—and it does discover invaders—but its success rate is low. Maybe Gyun's detector is a knock-off. The detector frequently leads Gyun in the wrong direction. It pulls him toward gangs of hoodlums, and it draws him into packs of stray dogs. When he holds the map and the detector side by side and compares them, the map and the detector's needle oftentimes point in completely opposite directions. He gives the detector one last chance and begins to follow it. The needle stops moving at the dead end of another alley. All that's in front of Gyun is a huge heap of trash.

As summer sales begin, the number of customers in the bathroom increases. The room now has a thief, whose crime is underway at this very moment. The thief sits on the sofa wearing a flowing dress, unaware of whose property she has stolen. I'm talking about the sofa where I always sit. Of course, it's not unusual that someone else is in my seat when I arrive. It's happened to me a few times before. But it's never happened before 11:00 a.m.

I head toward the stalls, past the thief and the powder room she's occupying, as if that were my original plan. I flush one of the toilets—an innocent bystander to this tragedy—and take a roll of toilet paper. Then I walk to the sinks and turn on the similarly innocent faucet to liberally soap up and wash my hands. I apply more hand cream before sitting down on the sofa opposite the thief, where I look at myself in my portable mirror. Next, I step into the hallway and have a drink of cold water from the cooler in front of the elevator—grabbing ten paper cups while I'm at it—then I return to the bathroom. The thief is still there.

I cut through the menswear section and ride the escalator to the fifth floor. I amble between tableware and bedding, then I leave the fifth floor for the sixth. The cultural center is swarmed with people who've arrived for today's lecture. I skip the sixth-floor bathroom and go back to the fifth floor to use its restroom instead. After about twenty minutes, I retrace my steps to the fourth floor and enter the first bathroom. The thief is sitting in the same place as earlier, like she's become a piece of furniture. Her back scares me. I gradually approach from the side. The thief's left hand holds not a makeup compact but a thick bundle of papers; her right hand clutches a pen in place of lipstick.

That's my seat. I want to speak up, but I can't bring myself to do it, so I settle into a chair across from the thief. The thief resembles me quite a bit. Maybe it's not just that our routines happen to overlap today; it seems like, more generally, our ways of life and values might intersect as well. The thief isn't using an outlet, and she doesn't have a bag on the table. If I weren't paying attention to the fact that someone was sitting in front of me, everything would be normal: I can still charge my laptop. But instead of my computer, I pull a compact out of my purse. As I powder my face for no reason, I stealthily peek in front of me. The woman seated there is definitely the thief. She's snatched my entire morning from me.

The next day, even though I arrive at the bathroom five minutes earlier than usual, my seat has been stolen again. The thief reclines comfortably, writing something on her stack of paper as if this place were her office. With no alternative, I sit across from her. Ten, twenty, thirty minutes pass, and I don't move; the thief turns her head. She glances at me and then swivels her gaze back toward the pile of notes. What the heck is she writing? Could the thief be a writer like me? Maybe she's a poet. Or a novelist or screenwriter. If not one of those, maybe a children's book author. We don't know much about one another, but over the next several days, we naturally come to share our workspace. Without either of us suggesting or agreeing on it, we join together in a tacit symbiotic relationship. Our unity has brought about greater consequences than I expected. No longer do I have to evacuate before the cleaners arrive.

We turn a blind eye to each other's offenses. The thief overlooks the fact that the toilet paper runs out immediately in every stall I enter. I realize that the trashcan in each stall the thief frequents will soon overflow with household waste, but I ignore the mess. While I eat into the department store's supply of toilet paper, the thief consumes the trashcans' emptiness. Today, the thief has thrown away food waste. Yesterday, she threw out a plastic water bottle and a can of tuna. Two days ago, it was a pile of papers. She does at least seem to be separating her waste. And, come to think of it, maybe she's even following the prescribed days for disposing of different types of trash.

The detector is still defective, but Gyun no longer needs his map as an alternative. Now, instead of Gyun following the map, the map is going to follow him. When Gyun moves on from his current location, a violet-colored invader with yellow eyes remains in his place. This time he donned a surgical mask as he worked, not a true face-covering disguise, but, upon his return to Korea, he'll buy a more stylish mask straightaway. He'll have to purchase other colors of tiles as well. Once Gyun has bought his ticket home, and then a mask and new tiles, his bank account will hit rock bottom. Three years' worth of brokerage-firm savings will be all gone, as will the year he spent hunting for invaders after he quit his job.

"Gyun, those little bits of tile are essentially a foreclosure notice. Except instead of your house being foreclosed, it's your life."

That's what Gyun's former coworker told him before he embarked on his journey. Gyun doesn't think of the invaders as a foreclosure notice: to him, they're more like a pain-relief patch or a Band-Aid. But the newest invader graphic artist isn't going to use Band-Aids for his work. Instead, he'll make use of structures like buildings, pipes, and bridges to heal people's wounds. Without knowing where the detector is pointing or whether or not there are rules to invader creation, Gyun eagerly walks up to a spot that's calling out to be marked and affixes his tiles. He applies glue as if it's ointment, and he sticks on tiles like they're bandages. Now he's on his way back to Korea. Following the detector's direction, he boards the plane.

As the department store grows and evolves with time, so do its receipts. The café's receipts are the first to change. A receipt is now an entrance fee. It has overstepped its role as proof of purchase to become cost of entry into the shop's bathroom. Receipts are required for internet use as well. They even serve as the barrier between customers and electrical outlet connection. To put it simply, receipts are what allow customers to enjoy the privileges of the café. Freeloaders dot the establishment, trying to calm their hidden anxiety as their stomachs grumble. The shock of coming into work and learning abruptly that your desk has disappeared, or of receiving a notice to vacate your workspace: that feeling isn't just for office workers. As the value of a receipt increases, my chest trembles with the fear that I'll unexpectedly be asked for one and ordered to leave my table.

"Ma'am, sir, can you please tell me your pin number?" the employees ask customers. "You'll have to read out the number on your receipt in order to use the outlets."

Not long after the café blockades its outlets, so does the fourth-floor bathroom. The cleaning crew begins to show up with greater frequency than before. When patrol arrives and I need to escape quickly, my laptop becomes luggage that weighs me down. I really only need a roll of toilet paper or napkins or paper envelopes to write my novel, anyway. But I grab more of the department store's non-paper freebies to quell my depression about the increasingly grim work environment. I pump soap into a bottle to take home with me, and I'm inclined to fill a few liters with water as well. I'm at least fortunate that the fourth-floor bathroom doesn't require receipts for entry.

I quickly attend to my needs in the bathroom, and on my way back to the powder room, I bump into the thief in the doorway. She speeds off, the hems of her skirt flying up in a wind of her own creation. When I look at the seat from which the thief disappeared, I realize that all of the possessions I left in the room are gone. The novel I left on the table isn't there: my book, written on no less than forty sheets of toilet paper—with letters the size of sesame seeds. I crouch down and investigate the powder room floor, but the tome is gone. The image of the thief hurrying away plays over and over again in my mind. But there's no proof of the crime, nor any traces of it. Leaning over, all I can find is Post-it notes clinging to the bottom of the table. The yellow and pink paper squares are bats, dangling from the inside of their cave. I don't know when they were stuck there, but they've lost their stickiness and begun to warp into something like a squid being cooked. I notice something. Could this be an invader graphic?

There it is—boldly adorned with the artist's handwriting. In order to read the message, I have to lean down until my head is below my knees. I lower my line of sight and peek at the thief's Post-it invader on the bottom of the table. The notes are inscribed with study plans for the level-nine civil servant exam. Several of them flutter to the ground like dead leaves. Maybe the thief isn't a poet. Maybe she isn't a novelist, either. Actually, I don't even know if she's a thief.

The underside of the table parallels recent events in my life. Just like my dad's lotto card functioned as a talisman in my wallet, the thief's sticky notes are her own protective talisman. The thief might not have known it, but what she's left behind is an invader. The shape and material may be atypical, but in its heart, it is an invader graphic.

When I inquire whether or not the cleaner has seen my novel, she shakes her head.

"A notebook?" she asks. "I haven't seen anything like that."

"Not a notebook, just notes on sheets of paper," I reply.

To be specific, toilet paper. My novel, written in thick ballpoint pen on a roll of toilet paper.

"Toilet paper, ma'am," I add. "I wrote some important notes on toilet paper."

"Toilet paper? I might have thrown out something like that when I was cleaning. Do you want to come over here and look?"

I go over to the storage room that's only used by the cleaning team. When I push a door with the label "Employees Only" and step inside, I see the bulky shapes of several large trash bags. The cleaning woman explains: "Here's trash I just brought over from the floor you're talking about. This is trash from the same floor, but it won't contain what you're looking for." When I glance at the bag where my novel is unlikely to be, the contents are familiar. The bag is full of plastic waste the thief threw out this morning. A dark soy sauce bottle, simple syrup, canola oil, soybean paste: it's like looking at the inside of someone's kitchen cupboard. It would be impossible to sort through all this trash. I can't even figure out which sack my novel is in, much less where it is among the rubbish.

"Tissues are here, in this plastic bag," the woman says. "But why are you looking for them?"

The contents of the black trash bag look unfamiliar. Thousands of sheets of tissue are tangled up inside. Part of my novel—Gyun's whereabouts—must be in there. The cleaning woman holds out gloves and tongs for me. I take them and fish through several sheets of paper, but they're not my novel. They're tissues. I can't conceive of finding my novel in here. It's impossible to know what among the mess is Gyun.

The thief stops coming to the bathroom. I don't know why she was storming into the hallway the day I almost bumped into her, but after that day, the trashcans in each stall of the bathroom change. Their new openings are too small to fit large or round containers. In order to throw out more substantial trash, you have to use the bin at the bathroom's entrance. But it would have been too demanding for the thief to use that trashcan. The CCTV camera hangs right in front of the bin.

I hadn't yet typed up the lost forty toilet-paper pages of my novel. I remember the plot, but only roughly. Since the story went missing, Gyun seems to have moved on to further adventures about which I don't yet know. According to the network, leaving an invader at one's workplace is a recent trend among people quitting their jobs. The trend began with some guy in banking who'd exposed an invader graphic left behind by a recently fired coworker. "Exposed": that was the word used, and it was an appropriate one. The fired coworker didn't just mess with his own desk; he rearranged every single desk in the office. More specifically, he put together a bunch of invaders made from mini tiles and stuck them to the inner surfaces and left sides of all the desks. The only people who knew what the invaders meant were the fired employee and the man who discovered them. Those violet and yellow blocks had taken over the desks of everyone in the company, from the boss to the disgruntled man's colleagues to the junior staff. The fired coworker may be gone, but the invader graphics he left behind are still in the building, blinking with their enormous eyes. Maybe they're already sneakily making their way toward other, yet unoccupied offices—using desks and walls and ceilings and floors as temporary hosts in their search for a second home.

If I'm looking for a spot unnoticed by the patrol team and unseen by the vacant lens of a CCTV camera, somewhere there's no need for a receipt, the towering roof garden above the department store is the place to go. The wind blows forcefully up here. Once I'm on the roof, the department store seems like nothing more than a stepping-stone beneath my feet. If you stand atop the stepping-stone and look down, the city center—the part to the city's hairdo—is nakedly visible from above. Keep staring, and at some moment you'll see those multicolored tiles protruding between buildings and roads and people and cars and trees. And on a distant street, there's someone walking, holding a detector in front of him. The detector looks like it could be a pair of fishing rods, fishing rods that you might gladly follow, even if there's no bait. The rods' needles come to a stop. They're pointing at me.

4. HYEONMONG PARK'S HALL OF DREAMS

Five point five meters long and two point one meters wide, the bed was more a stage than a piece of furniture. It was a bed for one: used only by Hyeonmong Park, who couldn't lie down for the night until he had dozens of pairs of pajamas on the mattress with him. I prepared the pajamas, each belonging to a different customer, and when the night began, Hyeonmong changed into one pair after another. None of the many items of clothing actually belonged to him. The pajamas Mr. Park slept in, and the dreams he dreamed while wearing them, were all the possessions of others. Each pair of pajamas was affixed with the number of one of Hyeonmong's customers; instead of paperwork, Hyeonmong had sleepwear. It took barely thirty minutes for him to complete a dream and record its contents. The pajamas and robes he wore were a border that separated each slumber from the next, one dream from another. Just like a CD plays a new song when the first track transitions to the second, Hyeonmong delved into a new dream whenever he put on the next set of nightclothes. In order to dream the first customer's dream, he wore the first customer's pajamas; same for the second customer and each one after. Our clientele proliferated with each passing day, and so did the pajamas. Managing them was my job.

"Pajama coordinator" was the title written on my business card, but in truth, my duties mostly consisted of washing, drying, and folding the nightwear. In one day, I washed more than one hundred sets of pajamas. The washing machine was my desk, and the washboards were my files. The drying rack served as my boss's desk, and I visited it almost hourly. The rack was as overworked as I was. Its stainless steel rods bent beneath damp laundry, most of which was, of course, pajamas. The drying fabric ranged from soft and airy to rough and scratchy, from striped to polka-dotted: a variety of patterns and materials that resembled flags from around the world.

Because the pajamas differentiated our customers from one another, it was important that there were no repeats among the designs, colors, and fabrics populating the drying rack. When hanging the pajamas, I made sure to separate pieces with different washing methods, to avoid confusion. Number 150: wool shampoo. Number 165: dry cleaning. Number 107: front-load washer. Number 96: rinse with fabric softener. As the number of customers increased, subtle differences emerged between the washing instructions for each client's pajamas. Customers 155 and 156 differed in the number of buttons I pressed on the washing machine; other customers' dreams varied depending upon whether the clothing in question was to be dried inside or outside. Regardless of what was in it, the washing machine let out a loud and unceasing snore, and the multiple types of fabric softener I used emitted the unique scent of each dream.

Hyeonmong Park was the type of person who was always selling something. Over the years, he had hawked children's books, water dispensers, and roasted chestnuts. Leftovers that he hadn't sold took up more space in his house than people did. His sales record wasn't good. He was drowsy, thin, and had little drive. Finally, when he could no longer sell physical objects, he'd begun to peddle dreams. Dreams were his most successful sales item to date. They didn't take up space, they didn't require any capital, they didn't grow dusty, and each one brought in a good amount of money. They were the things he sold best.

But each time he introduced this kind of work to someone, he had to explain himself at length. The confusion had begun several years earlier, when he went to the tax office to receive a registration number for his fledgling dream business. The tax employee had given him the appropriate documents, but Hyeonmong found no entry specifying his exact occupation. His business corresponded somewhat to all of the available categories, but it fit into none perfectly. The tax office decided to classify Mr. Park as a psychic, and even now he received phone calls asking him to join the Korean Association of Psychics.

I was confused, too, when I first went into Hyeonmong's hall of dreams to interview for my job. I didn't possess the qualifications listed on the help wanted ad he'd posted. I hadn't majored in clothing, and the phrase "pajama coordinator" was unfamiliar to me. But I was the only male applicant for the job—he wanted a man—and I'd just been released from the military two months earlier. Luckily, Hyeonmong was looking for someone who'd already finished mandatory service, so he hired me. The only two things I knew about my new position at the hall of dreams were that it paid well and that it covered room and board. During my first few days at work, my new boss had needed to explain a plethora of unfamiliar terminology. When I still didn't understand after his explanations, he would use expressive gesticulation to describe what my duties entailed. When that, too, failed, we sat in silence.

"Customers commission dreams that they would like me to provide," Hyeonmong told me. "What I do is dream what the customers ask for and then retell it to them. After a client makes an initial order, it usually takes a week before they can pick up the completed dream."

"Okay," I replied. I tried to rephrase what he'd told me. "You come up with some sort of dream and then people pay you for it. Is that how it works?"

Even though he'd explained clearly, I started to worry. The more he spoke, the more vague it all seemed.

"So you mean that people give you money and ask you to dream a dream for them?" I added to clarify.

"That's right."

A long silence followed. A lullaby, which didn't seem appropriate this early in the day, was trickling out of an inner room. I had only one further question: Why?

"What made you want to do this?" I asked.

Starting the next morning, I saw the answer with my own two eyes. The waiting room opened at 10:00 a.m., swarmed with customers number 1 to 100 and beyond. The room bustled all day with people who'd come to request a new dream, and others who had arrived to hear their completed dreams. They weren't patronizing our business out of desperation or because they had strange interests. Among those seeking Hyeonmong Park's assistance were people with too much free time, busy people, wealthy people, people who'd taken out loans to see to him, people who believed most everything, and people who believed very little.

"Oh, I'm so anxious!" Mrs. Wang exclaimed.

When the door opened, the first customer to come inside was always Mrs. Wang. Mrs. Wang was a regular, a woman who spat out the word "anxious" in every conversation. Hyeonmong's dreams were road signs that helped Mrs. Wang navigate the crisscrossing paths of investment. If gold appeared in a dream, she believed, that suggested she invest in a commodity fund. The truth was, Mrs. Wang's wealth *had* increased significantly since she began to frequent the hall of dreams. But what she had the most of wasn't money: it was fear. The hall was like an anti-anxiety pill she ingested at regular intervals.

Money was what customers most often wished to see in their dreams. Many of them visited us to buy dreams in which they won the lottery. But they overlooked the fact that if demand increases, so does competition. If the chances of winning the lottery were one in 8,140,506, then the chances of purchasing a dream about winning were also one in 8,140,506. As customers' desires increasingly overlapped, the price of dreams made a precipitous jump upward. That was the reason I hadn't been able to buy any of Hyeonmong Park's dreams myself. The cost of just one was significantly more than I earned each month.

Money wasn't the only thing a dream could provide. More covert transactions occurred as well. One of the regulars—Taekman Nam, who visited us twice a week—wrote his name on the sign-in sheet with a flashy upward tilt. As time passed, I noticed the strokes to his signature lengthening to show off his increasing self-satisfaction.

"Do you think an elephant's trunk is really a nose?"

Taekman asked this question each time he ran into me. When I looked at him from my seat without a reply, he couldn't wait any longer before telling me his own thoughts.

"It's probably not a nose," he'd say. "Think of it as a second penis."

According to Taekman's boasts, he'd grown a longer pecker, all thanks to Hyeonmong. For him, Hyeonmong Park's hall of dreams wasn't just a place to buy and sell dreams; it was a place to buy and sell confidence.

"Is my dream still effective if I pay in installments?"

Sometimes people asked this as they stood in front of the cash register to check out. When our clientele learned that purchasing a dream outright and paying in installments were equivalent in efficacy, sales increased. One customer had a daughter about to take college entrance exams: she had paid for her dream of a high score over a period of six months. Another customer, who'd ordered a dream of success for his son in the military, had spent two years of the boy's conscription paying off the dream. It was also common, though, to pay for several months' worth of dreams at once. The tireless register spewed out receipts all day long.

Without producing a single shopping bag, we continued to sell our nebulous wares, and by the time I'd been working at the hall for a month, we had over five hundred pages of patient files. Our customers included scholars and professors; doctors and prosecutors, of course; pastors and missionaries; priests and Buddhist monks; and skilled fortune tellers. The intake forms were simple to fill out. Name and contact information, job, and a description of the desired dream were all that we required. We didn't ask for more detail than that; there was no need to. No one actually believed what people wrote down, anyway. Pseudonyms appeared on the forms out of habit, and depending on the day, customers wrote false occupations as well. In one sense, I knew our regulars very well; in another, I didn't know them at all. There were numerous clients who claimed to be doctors but weren't, and there were also a fair number of doctors who hid their occupation from us. Whatever the case, all found comfort in Hyeonmong Park's dreams.

Originally, his name wasn't Hyeonmong: it was Hyeonbong. Hyeonbong Park was someone who'd spent his life being ignored. The only way he could assert his existence, he'd realized, was by dreaming. After switching out one small letter in his name to become Hyeonmong Park (the same *mong* that means "dream"), his life gradually began to change. Some of our customers had even known Hyeonbong, but most of them didn't realize that Hyeonbong Park and Hyeonmong Park were the same person. This was because he had gained a significant amount of weight after his name change, and now there was a different energy about him. After becoming Hyeonmong, he looked significantly older, too, but because he also appeared notably wealthier than before, it wasn't a complete loss.

Hyeonmong Park slept without distinguishing between day and night, and he ate heartily, indifferent to mealtimes. When his belly was full, he slept; when he was hungry, he ate more. As his daily sleep increased, he continued to gain weight. Considering that he was 160 centimeters tall, the 78 or 79 kilograms between which the scale's needle hovered were a heavy burden to both the scale and his body. But each time he noted a new increase in weight, he laughed with vocal cords larger than his stomach.

"Last month, I was seventy-five kilograms," he exclaimed one day. "Do you know what that means? It means that this month, I worked three kilograms harder than last month."

While he was working three kilograms harder, his customers—and the pajamas—had multiplied. Occasionally, customers even sent Hyeonmong pajamas that they wanted him to wear, instead of letting him choose. Some thrust expensive sleepwear at him, and others made him pajamas from materials that weren't cloth. Longtime customer and writer Chunsam Kim brought in a set of pajamas made from enormous manuscript paper and requested that Hyeonmong wear it each time he dreamed for him. The outfit, emanating a pulpy smell, rustled as soon as Hyeonmong put it on.

"Hey, Mr. Coordinator!" Chunsam shouted at me. "Do you know how much money I pay per word when I buy one of my stories?" Chunsam's stories consisted entirely of dreams he purchased from Hyeonmong.

"Five hundred won," I guessed.

Chunsam Kim nodded with a satisfied smile on his lips.

"They're not at all cheap. Have you by any chance read my story 'Number One Search Term'? No? What about 'Story for a Woman's Handbag'? 'Rebellious Words'? Hmmm . . . Mr. Coordinator, you don't like reading, do you?"

"I do like to read," I told Chunsam.

"But why haven't you read any of my writing?" he asked. "If you're going to read, you have to read something good! 'Number One Search Term' is the longest of my works—it's 23,678 words. How much do you think it cost me to buy? How much did I pay—wait a moment, let's see. Eight, five, forty, let's see, let's . . ."

Chunsam Kim speedily calculated how much he'd paid for "Story for a Woman's Handbag" and "Rebellious Words." Soon he glanced at me with an emotional look.

"Mr. Coordinator, do you know why I can't even imagine buying novels rather than short stories?" he asked. "The royalties I'd earn on a longer piece would be less than the cost of buying the dreams that inspire my writing. Why do I keep doing this kind of work, then, in spite of the losses? It's because of my passion for literature. To tell you the truth, it makes sense that dreams would be more expensive than reality. Mr. Park is like a teacher to me, a literature teacher."

Mrs. Wang, who was eavesdropping on the conversation, butted in.

"A literature teacher? Mr. Park is the real writer of your stories. You're just his patron!"

A vague expression, uncomfortable but conciliatory, came across Chunsam Kim's face. Chunsam spoke again.

"This novel is full of my ideas! Did you think that Mr. Park's dreams appear to him as publishable sentences? I edit everything that appears in my books."

"It's plagiarism," Mrs. Wang said.

"If I'm a plagiarist, does that mean that you're a thief? You use dreams to help you buy stocks!"

Mrs. Wang turned away sharply. Chunsam plopped his body onto the waiting room sofa and started to cool himself with a handheld fan.

"Mr. Coordinator, have you heard of Chagall?" he asked me abruptly. "What about Dalí? You must, of course, know about

Picasso, right? Did you know that all of these artists were inspired by their dreams, just like me? They used painting as a way to work out the meaning of what they'd dreamt. And then there's Mark Twain, Graham Greene, Samuel Taylor Coleridge, Edgar Allan Poe, and Robert Louis Stevenson! They're all said to be dream-influenced writers. Stevenson, in particular, would purposefully recite to himself the plots of novels before going to bed. He wanted the stories to inspire him while he slept. Do you not know who Stevenson is? You must not be familiar with *Dr. Jekyll and Mr. Hyde*, either, are you? Mr. Coordinator, I knew you'd be like this even before our conversation today: your basic knowledge about the world seems to be a little lacking in comparison to your age. You have to read real stories—stories! That's the only way that people like me make a living, if you read."

In order to buy a page's worth of dreams, Chunsam paid ten times more than he earned selling a page from one of his manuscripts. But that didn't make him hesitate. When Hyeonmong Park dreamed up manuscripts for Chunsam, the stories arrived complete, with correct spelling and grammar. These dreams brought Chunsam readers so valuable they really couldn't be bought with money.

The hall of dreams brimmed with top-of-the-line consumer products, but they were nothing but symbols of our customers' desires. There was a golf club, a TV that hung on the wall, a laptop, and a massage machine. They were items given to us by customers who hoped that their gifts would bridge the gap between their requested dreams and reality. Of course, no one actually used the gadgets lying around the building. The brand-new laptop from Chunsam had, until now, been just another untouched gift.

"I've been flooded with manuscript requests recently," he told us. "My business will fail if you copy down the dreams on paper as slowly as you've been doing. When demand increases, I need to speed up production."

Typing out dreams on the laptop certainly was more efficient than writing them by hand. Even if you just turned the laptop on while Hyeonmong was sleeping, he would breathe faster as he dreamed. Dreams that had taken over sixty seconds per sentence could now be finished twice as quickly. As the time required for each dream decreased, Chunsam Kim's dependence upon Hyeonmong grew. At first, Hyeonmong had written individual sentences in exchange for Chunsam's money; after that, it was paragraphs; then pages of a manuscript; then Hyeonmong began to compose the structure of Chunsam's stories; and finally the dream came to write everything. When others in the hall made sarcastic remarks about Chunsam Kim buying his novels, Chunsam grew upset. But he couldn't forget the fact that dreams were the wellspring that provided him inspiration, along with all of his sentences, and even his punctuation marks.

As the number of people coming to Hyeonmong Park increased, so did the amount that he slept. Even if he spent all night dreaming and recording what he'd seen in his sleep, still-incomplete dreams remained, piled high as a mountain. Hyeonmong spent more than half of each day dreaming, and during the remaining time, he dealt with customers. One morning, an unfamiliar advertisement came in through the door like it was challenging Hyeonmong to a duel.

Dream Therapy: Prices Slashed!
29,000 won per procedure
20% discount on ten procedures when paid in cash, 10% discount with card

This wasn't a simple flyer for pizza or fried chicken. But these ads were becoming equally ubiquitous. A few leaflets appeared on top of the takeout Hyeonmong ordered for each meal, and they spread like a carpet across the ground below the front gate.

They came inside hiding among the mail, and occasionally they lay scattered throughout the waiting room, like cushions to sit on. The day Hyeonmong discovered a stack of competitors' advertisements inside a pillow, he stormed outside to the gate carrying a broom. The alley outside was wallpapered with ads. Squares of paper were plastered to each wall; affixed to our mailbox, unsurprisingly; stuck to the windshield of each car parked along the alley; and heaped atop trashcans. Hyeonmong hurled his broom toward each of the inflammatory ads and swept them into a pile. At some point, he found himself in the middle of the main road, still in his pajamas. It was the first time he'd gone out in a long time.

Half of the customers with appointments weren't showing up. Mrs. Wang was thirty minutes late to her own appointment, and when she arrived, she made a big fuss asking if we'd heard about the other dream vendors popping up nearby. Six former fund managers sat in their chairs and dreamed expert dreams about investment, she explained. Mrs. Wang said that they were stealing Hyeonmong's business idea. Chunsam Kim claimed that dreams were a trend.

Whether the emerging competitors were plagiarists or trend followers, Hyeonmong Park was no longer the only dreamer around. The next week, Mrs. Wang's footsteps sounded against our floors with diminished frequency. Without Mrs. Wang around, the hall grew thick with old gossip, but nothing new. She had simultaneously purchased dreams from us and from the price-slashing dream vendors, we were told; and the price slashers had sold her a tremendously successful dream. When Hyeonmong heard this, he snorted.

Stores selling dreams opened up in every other building. Sometimes we even got phone ads from competitors, encouraging us to "converse with our dreams." It seemed like everyone was talking about dreams. Hyeonmong attempted to decrease his creation-to-completion timeframe as much as he could. He'd determined that the impatient modern customer couldn't wait a full week for their dream to be ready. But even though Hyeonmong dreamed diligently, the number of customers decreased. When the loss was no longer deniable, Chunsam told Hyeonmong that he needed to start advertising.

"Think of it as personal development, something like that," Chunsam suggested. "You need to commercialize everything. What you're running right now is a cottage industry—is that going to get you anywhere? Nowadays, even fortune-telling is done online."

Excited by Chunsam's counsel, Hyeonmong wrote the word "commercialization" on a piece of paper and stuck it to the headboard of the bed. Back when he was Hyeonbong, he had attached performance goals for the first half of the year to the wall of his office in a similar manner. After several days of thought, Hyeonmong looked into an automated consultation system, like the ones his competitors were using.

"Medicine, law, and fortune-telling," said the voice on the phone. "These are the three industries that benefit most from interactive voice response. This kind of system is a gem: it's going to make you money."

The person saying this was a communications company employee, and one of Hyeonmong's customers. But before Hyeonmong could polish the gem that was interactive voice response, he learned that he wasn't eligible to buy it. In order to apply for automated consultation, he needed at least five psychics on staff.

"This doesn't mean you can't purchase our system," the woman clarified. "This is a loophole, but you can use the names of other psychics. You just have to pay to borrow their names."

There may have been a loophole around his disqualification, but Hyeonmong Park decided to give up. He didn't want to take any shortcuts with his legally run business. Hyeonmong thought about marketing all week long. His personal development made him lose two kilograms.

A bit later, five hundred glass bottles were delivered to the hall. They were cylinders, about fifteen centimeters wide and twenty centimeters tall. The glass was opaque: you couldn't see what was inside.

"They're bedtime bottles," Hyeonmong clarified.

The bottles were the result of market research. The idea was that after Hyeonmong finished a dream, he would twist off the cap of one of the flasks and blow into it, breathing the dream into physical existence. It didn't matter whether or not the dream really had come to life, or if Hyeonmong's breath just languished inside the bedtime bottle. The important thing was that the bottle provided a tangible product for Hyeonmong's customers. The individually labeled bedtime bottles calmed our customers. Thanks to the glass containers' relaxing powers, even those who'd left us for our competitors slowly came back.

Soon, word arrived that other halls of dreams were offering handwritten paper talismans. In some places, they summarized the contents of a dream with a single Chinese character, or drew a picture of it and tattooed the dream on the customer's body. Tattoos began to cover the bodies of Hyeonmong's customers like they were addicted to ink. Clients marked their skin with winning lottery numbers, secret account numbers, Korean flags—American and Japanese flags, too—crosses, and Olympic banners. Someone even got a tattoo of Hyeonmong Park's face. Taekman Nam's tattoo stood out the most. A lithe gochu pepper—a pepper that likely symbolized his pecker—wrapped two times around Taekman's torso. At first glance, the image looked like a thick worm.

Hyeonmong's personal revolution continued. That weekend, the smell of medicine pulsated throughout his hall of dreams. He boiled fresh ginseng and magnolia berry, jujube, milkwort, grassy-leaved sweet flag, white agaric mushroom, peanuts, walnuts, and medicinal herbs, but the sweat he shed while working was his concoction's main ingredient. The final product was "wisdom soup": a Hyeonmong Park creation. Supposedly, if you drank some of the muddy blend, you could dream your own desired dreams instead of needing to outsource them to a professional. But the soup didn't sell. People were too busy. They loved their dreams, but they also wanted pure and uninterrupted sleep. They preferred the convenience of buying dreams. I was no different: just surviving another day was enough for me. At night, I wanted to fall into a deep dormancy that allowed no room for anything else. Whether or not it was intentional, the pressures of society were pushing us toward sleep.

An invisible game of tug-of-war continued. Hyeonmong seemed to have caught an illness that bubbled up from his soupy mixture. He began to have frequent headaches due to worries about his personal development, and in one sitting he would devour several packs of the soup that sold more poorly than expected.

The side effect of his excessive soup dosage was an overuse of commas. Chunsam Kim's manuscript, several chapters of which he received each week from Hyeonmong, looked like it had been attacked by punctuation marks. Between every two words sat an unnecessary comma, making the content of the story difficult to follow. Chunsam was accustomed to receiving his dreams fastidiously punctuated, and the commas disseminating like a virus were too much. He spread out the papers he'd received from Hyeonmong and held a pen in his hand as if he were a farmer plucking weeds. The tails of the commas got caught under its sharp tip and were crushed into oblivion. But as soon as he crossed out one comma, the head of another would emerge from between two new letters. No matter how much he scribbled over them, he couldn't block the proliferating commas. They grew back stronger than before, using Chunsam Kim's sighs as fertilizer.

"To think that commas could outsmart a person!" Chunsam exclaimed. "I'm going to have a hard time if this continues. I guess I should just leave out the commas when I calculate how much to pay you, right?"

Whether or not Chunsam needed to pay Hyeonmong for the extra punctuation in his story, the commas continued to breed. When Hyeonmong turned on his laptop, they could be heard plunging their roots into a recently finished dream. When he turned the laptop off, he could hear the commas that hadn't taken root evaporating.

"Mr. Park doesn't seem to understand the function of commas," Chunsam mused as he read another page of punctuation.

Each printout that Hyeonmong gave him was rife with the tadpole-like specks. They didn't just make it slightly harder to read the text. Now, you couldn't even understand what words you were reading. The commas no longer burrowed between words: as they multiplied, they erased what remained on the page. Their abundance grew with time, and finally commas were the only thing left of Chunsam's story. The flecks of ink could be connected to draw some sort of pattern, like stars in a constellation.

The commas didn't show up only in Chunsam Kim's novel. They also made an appearance in Taekman Nam's gochu. The pepper that was steadily growing across his body started to bend until it turned *into* a comma. It was exactly like Chunsam's novel; both had curled into submission, unable to grow or expand. The commas that put a stop to Chunsam's novel and Taekman's pepper were searching for their next target. They were an ominous mark and an evil code. Hyeonmong Park tried to erase the commas that now appeared in each of his dreams, but they bred without paying him any mind.

"They're just like bedbugs!" he shouted. "Bedbugs!"

After deciding to deal with the commas the same way he would with bedbugs, Hyeonmong purchased a new bed and changed the wallpaper. He threw out his 5.5-meter bed and ordered another, which was only a bit over one meter wide. Several days later, another one-meter bed arrived, and several days after that, more were delivered, bringing the total to five. No matter what bed he slept on, the commas showed up in his dreams. Hyeonmong roughly scratched his entire body until his spine was curled up like a comma. He fell asleep in that position.

The commas drew Hyeonmong outside the front gate of the hall, as if they were an invitation to a lavish event. When we went for a car ride several days later, Hyeonmong was still facing harassment from the commas. The sedan we were sitting in looked brand-new, but Hyeonmong's driving skills were rusty. He was slightly annoyed to learn that I didn't have a driver's license: he seemed to have a hard time comprehending that I'd returned from military service but couldn't drive. I told him that military service and driving had nothing to do with one another, but he looked unconvinced. Perhaps he was suspicious that I'd lied about my years of service. As soon as he started the car with his trembling hands, the engine let out a stifled noise, like it was suffering from constipation. We headed toward the most successful dream seller in the area: Dream Psychology Laboratory.

Hyeonmong feared that someone would recognize him. He donned enormous sunglasses and pulled a hat over his head, but the disguise just made him stand out more. We wrote fake names on the sign-in sheet and waited for thirty minutes before entering the consultation room. Hyeonmong told me to walk around the hallways until the director came in, to note anything distinctive about the place's interior. When I went out to check, I saw nothing special about its design. After we met with the director, though, I realized it wasn't appearances that we needed to worry about.

"People like you are afraid of change," the director of Dream Psychology Laboratory told us. "Dreams are, of course, a subconscious thing, and in the face of such a lack of consciousness, you experience fear. If they're afraid, our patients don't tell us the whole story; they just speak superficially about their anxiety. From what I see, you're currently doing the same. Dreams aren't something to fear, so little by little, we're going to help you open up the door to your mind."

I realized it while the director spoke. He was operating on a different level. Our commercialization, diligence, personal development, and 1,283 pairs of pajamas couldn't compete. The weapons that the competitors carried weren't interior decorating or gifts for clients. What made these other businesses intimidating was their enormous breadth of knowledge, something Hyeonmong Park couldn't simply copy.

"We consider dreams to be something subconscious, don't we?" the man continued. "But if you think about it, we can use our consciousness to control the subconscious. The technical term for it is 'lucid dream,' and it's a way to manipulate the plot or contents of a dream you're having. Frequently visualizing the desired dream is another method. For example, think about something you regularly come into contact with: a teacup, maybe, or someone's face. If you spend several minutes looking at a picture of this thing before you sleep, the chance of it appearing in your dream increases."

"Is that possible?" Hyeonmong asked. "It just doesn't make sense."

"No one believes it at first. But this method has been used for a long time. Lucid dreaming was discovered in 1913 by a doctor named Willem van Eeden. Even before that, though, both Eastern and Western prophets utilized similar techniques."

Hyeonmong Park's face flushed scarlet like he was ready to explode, but the director smiled comfortably. He pushed a white sheet of paper toward Hyeonmong.

"Now try to draw a picture of something you'd like to dream about," he instructed. "Don't think too hard, just sketch an image that comes to mind. These drawings are messages from the patient's subconscious."

Each time the word "patient" came out of the director's mouth, Hyeonmong's brow twitched. But a moment later, neither Hyeonmong nor I believed our eyes. Hyeonmong's sheet of paper was covered with that ominous mark: a comma. After taking the comma from him and dreaming about it for thirty minutes, the director called us back into the room.

"Mr. Patient, I can tell that you've come to your wits' end. I saw earth-destroying disasters in your dream. Whenever such an angry vision comes to me, I can't help but feel upset myself. Do you drive, by any chance?"

The question was simple, but Hyeonmong's face grew red again.

"Disasters in dreams are—well, they symbolize disgraceful events from our lives. Knives, blood, betrayal, slander: you never know if they'll be in your future. I saw a scene in your dream where you drove the wrong direction down a one-way road and caused a car accident. I'm not saying that this is definitely going to happen to you, but the nightmare I witnessed suggests that you'll at least get something like a traffic ticket."

The director urged Hyeonmong Park to believe the dream. After we returned to the car, Hyeonmong started to shout loudly.

"A patient!" he cried. "What kind of patient does that guy think I am? He thinks acting like a doctor will help him attract customers? They treated me like I was an invalid."

Still, Hyeonmong silently followed the Dream Psychology Laboratory's advice to be careful on the road. We avoided all the one-way streets on the way back, which made the trip an hour longer than it needed to be. Hyeonmong Park rejected the dream he'd been offered, but he did what the director had told him. He seemed uneasy, as if he *had* become the man's patient. I felt just as tense. But when we returned to our own hall of dreams, I had to admit to myself that Hyeonmong's room, filled with multiple beds lined up equidistant from one another, looked like an infirmary. No matter what pajamas he put on, he seemed to be wearing hospital robes. With sleeves and legs hanging low, the pajamas on the drying rack drooped like bandages.

The next morning, it wasn't my alarm clock or ringing phone that woke me up. It was Hyeonmong shrieking. He was standing on top of his bed, tearing pajamas into pieces. The word "disaster" seemed to be plastered across his face. The night before, Hyeonmong hadn't spent a single minute working. Instead, he'd just closed and opened his eyes until morning came. Hyeonmong grabbed at the air with his hands and shouted. Never, since the day he was born, had such severe insomnia befallen him.

It wasn't an exaggeration. His nights always overflowed with dreams, and even after he'd sold all the dreams people wanted to buy, he still had more available. But now the dreams were all gone. At first I didn't understand the implications of their disappearance Most people wouldn't say that one night without dreams was a real problem. Couldn't everyone enjoy a dreamless night once in a while? Wasn't it okay to relax and let sleep come to you, to let sleep press the Fast-Forward button, to let the moon set and the sun rise before you opened your eyes in the morning? Hyeonmong was sitting as vacantly as if he'd been sentenced to death. The pajamas he was supposed to have gone through the night before hung unwrinkled on the drying rack. They looked like inventory that had been lying there for years.

A piece of paper was pasted to the front gate to inform passersby of a death. The fake mourning continued for four days. No one had actually died, but the beds laid out inside the hall of dreams were now coffins. Hyeonmong Park spent the entire time lying inside the coffins, sleeping and sleeping some more. He covered himself with several layers of blankets, he stuffed earplugs in his ears, and he slipped a hat over his head. He hung a second layer of curtains in the windows, and he wore his thickest pajamas. He didn't forget to wear underwear and socks underneath the pajamas. These measures were all taken to stop reality from infringing upon Hyeonmong's life. When his dream drought showed no improvement, he changed course and tried the exact opposite of what he'd been doing. But the dreams continued to dry up until the hall was more parched than ever.

Hyeonmong Park visited the hospital with downcast eyes and underwent several types of examinations. But, considering how much time and money he'd invested to obtain them, the results were cursory and superficial. All he was told was to exercise to get rid of his excess abdominal fat. No one knew why his dreams had disappeared.

"It seems like the disasters they were talking about have begun," he said to me.

Hyeonmong changed his pajamas several times in the hope that sleep would come, but nothing he wore could pull him into the world of rest. Our drying rack stood in the middle of the dreamless hall of dreams, holding up sets of pajamas as a form of punishment. Lying on one of his coffin-mattresses, Hyeonmong thought about his last dream. He remembered only the protagonist's face—nothing else. He had been the main character. It was a dream he'd had on his own, not one for a client.

Three days later, a traditional medicine doctor was the first customer to come inside. He was surprised to see the sunken and disheveled look in Hyeonmong's eyes, but he couldn't give him any advice. That's because he wasn't really a medical practitioner. The doctor had been Hyeonmong's customer for two years, but this was the first time Hyeonmong had heard that he wasn't really a doctor. The man only bought dreams about doctors and their work, so the delayed revelation of truth was awkward for both him and Hyeonmong. When Hyeonmong asked the man why he had lied, he gazed into Hyeonmong's eyes.

"Well, am I not allowed to lie?" he asked.

The doctor and Hyeonmong Park had similar expressions on their faces. If one could buy doctors' dreams without being a doctor, then it also seemed possible to sell dreams without actually dreaming them. Hyeonmong dug into his stockpile of unsold dreams and continued to sell his products like he always had. But each day of business was followed by a series of experiments conducted inside the hall of dreams. Temperature; humidity; diet; exercise; mattress thickness, obviously; even the direction he placed his head—Hyeonmong needed to make slight changes to each element that could affect dreams. After several days of experimentation, he decided on the optimum temperature and humidity for dreaming: 25 degrees, and 75 percent humidity.

He spent several days sleeping in the above conditions, but instead of producing dreams, he got heat rash. The rash formed an ominous constellation of bumps on his dreamless body.

With all of Hyeonmong's dreams evaporated, lies filled the empty space left behind. He had been modifying dreams he'd already sold and was matching them to different customers, but now even those were running low. When he saw advertisements for competitors, ceaselessly pushing their way inside the hall, Hyeonmong's lies grew more desperate and sloppy. Eventually, Hyeonmong discovered the source of the ads relentlessly coming in through the front gate.

"It's a hole!" he exclaimed.

As Hyeonmong ordered, I plugged all the holes in the hall of dreams, to prevent the unwanted flyers from entering. After using the sink in the bathroom, we had to block the tap; same for the kitchen sink. We covered every cup with a lid, and if no lid existed, we turned the cup upside down. Caps for toothpaste and lotion were a given, and we absolutely had to button all the pajamas to ensure that each buttonhole was filled. Even though we checked every possible opening, each day at dawn, Hyeonmong would slam open the door to his bedroom, and I could hear him running around the building in hopes of blocking more holes. A washing machine door that wasn't completely closed, open gas valves, and electrical outlets with nothing plugged into them:

they were chasing after his dreams. They were all potential dangers. Once, Hyeonmong abruptly opened the door to my room while I was sleeping and declared my open mouth to be a problem.

"Just do me a favor, please," he asked, waking me up. "Can you sleep with your mouth closed?"

This was how we found ourselves together in front of every single hole in the hall of dreams. But even though the hole crackdown continued, advertisements flew in like dandelion seeds and put down their roots. The slogans varied: "Do you believe in instant dreams? Dreams in only ten minutes!" and "Full-grown dreams, matured for one week" and "Dreams can change the world." Some companies even offered age-specific dreams: "Twenty dreams for college entrance-exam success"; "Twenty dreams you must buy in your thirties"; "Thirty dreams you must buy in your forties." For the health-conscious consumer: "Organic dreams direct!" One dream delivery service had a 1-800 number. "Delivery within thirty minutes, guaranteed!" When Hyeonmong saw that, he yelped.

"Are dreams fried chicken?" he asked indignantly.

His voice oozed with the inferiority of a man no longer in his prime. The bedtime bottle he was carrying shattered between his fingers. The bottle was labeled with the name of customer number 73, and Hyeonmong Park had been in the middle of blowing empty breath into it. There was no secret flyer hiding inside the bottle, but Hyeonmong's paranoid eyes saw an enemy's dream slogan on the glass, and his ears had heard his competitors jeering at him. I hurried to bring Hyeonmong a new bottle and affix customer 73's name to it before they arrived. The next day, a second bedtime bottle cracked in the middle of the night, and before morning, I put another bottle in its place.

"Mr. Park's writing seems to be getting worse and worse," Chunsam Kim informed me.

Each time Chunsam received a new dream for his writing, his reaction was increasingly inscrutable. Since Hyeonmong's ability to dream disappeared, so had the commas in his dreams, but in spite of that, Chunsam's stories were stranger than ever. The plot was vague, and the sentences were a mess. The biggest problem was that it frequently repeated details from Chunsam's previously purchased work. Chunsam's initial suspicion was that Hyeonmong was so busy, he didn't have time to dream. He had no idea that the dreams had disappeared altogether.

"Has something been going on recently with Mr. Park?" he asked me. "Or does this mean that he's trying to raise his manuscript rates? Is it because I complained about the commas? You must know, Mr. Coordinator."

Chunsam Kim offered to pay one hundred won more per letter, but negotiation was impossible. No matter how much he was willing to give, the dreams weren't going to materialize like they once had. Finally, after Chunsam raised his voice to claim that our business was mistreating regular customers, Hyeonmong confessed that the dreams had disappeared. Upon hearing this, Chunsam's face looked like Hyeonmong's had when he let out a horrible shriek the morning after the first dreamless night. The truth was more heinous than mistreatment of customers. Chunsam worried that readers would say that his stories were becoming less coherent. Hyeonmong worried that rumors of his dreams' lack of efficacy would spread. They decided to join forces.

"You need a narrative for your dreams," Chunsam urged Hyeonmong. "A plot. And figure out how to dream with correct punctuation, for once."

Chunsam Kim and Hyeonmong Park changed roles. If they had one similarity, it was their newfound obsession with narrative. A storyline was needed to retell a dream, and Hyeonmong could no longer use his subconscious to build a narrative. Chunsam chose books that Hyeonmong needed to read and movies that he needed to watch, and he made Hyeonmong copy out his own works, too—by hand. Hyeonmong's lies gradually morphed into something more elegant. But it wasn't enough to grab onto the customers who were leaving us in droves. Selling someone a fabricated dream and handing them an empty bedtime bottle was no problem, but the customers who wanted to foresee winning lotto numbers or predict stocks moved to other dream sellers. The rumor that Hyeonmong's dreams were losing efficacy *had* spread. Chunsam shuddered with the thought that soon readers would also complain about his short stories' lack of coherence.

The person most affected by Hyeonmong's study of narrative was Taekman Nam. Chunsam was a particularly prolific writer of adult novels, and after writing out his books and memorizing parts of them, Hyeonmong could excite Taekman just by quoting a few of Chunsam's lines in his dreams. It wasn't just Taekman, either. Customers with impotence came in and out of the hall of dreams like it was a hospital. When Hyeonmong gave Taekman a dream in which his pecker grew like Pinocchio's nose, until it was the size of a telephone pole, Taekman shouted the following: "All that is flaccid and stumpy, soon you shall grow erect. Hallelujah!"

Chunsam, sitting with a grave expression on his face, quickly wrote down the exclamation. Chunsam was impatient and had grown jealous of the literary phrases flowing from Taekman's mouth. Without his dreams, Hyeonmong couldn't help Chunsam write his stories anymore. But Chunsam continued to pay Hyeonmong for his now-useless services because he had nowhere else to go. He'd tried other halls of dreams, but after running into fellow writers, he didn't dare go back. He'd also attempted to write stories using his own authorial power, but he still couldn't fill a single sheet of manuscript paper. Perhaps his dependence upon the words in dreams had made him forget his mother tongue. Chunsam lay clumsily in his chair. He seemed to have lost his facility for human language. Hyeonmong Park looked just as awkward. The two sat like something had been stolen from them as they conversed about how a story's plot should unfold. They discussed the scenes in a story, its characters, conflict, metaphor, style, perspective, narrator—and narrative, narrative, narrative! Hyeonmong repeated the unfamiliar words like a babbling baby. Once Chunsam left the hall of dreams, he took control of the unused TV, hanging on the wall like a fossil, and watched several movies in a row. He brandished untouched golf clubs—gifts from other customers—pretending they were baseball bats, and then he carefully read the hall's bank statements. Our account was bleeding money, part of which went to Chunsam Kim. It was payment for teaching Hyeonmong about stories.

When the dreams left Hyeonmong, other things had started to leave him as well. The housekeeper, the car salesperson, the woman who sold yogurt, the insurance seller, and the fund manager stopped showing up to their appointments. Taekman Nam, Chunsam Kim, and Mrs. Wang—who made the rounds between every hall of dreams in existence—were the only people left other than ten tenacious regulars. The empty drying rack looked thin, like a tree heading toward winter.

Outside the gate, no one knew about our financial slump. The market for buying and selling dreams grew bigger and bigger, until dream sellers formed a sleep society. Dream discussions and auctions now occurred as periodically as department store sales. Hyeonmong thought *he* was the founder of dream selling, but members of the sleep society created their own list of dreaming forefathers. According to the list, Hyeonmong wasn't the originator; he was vendor number 257. Without acquiescing and becoming member 257, it was going to be difficult to continue selling dreams. To customers, the sleep society was now a guarantor of quality.

When the society planned a public auction of dreams that had never been picked up by their purchasers, Hyeonmong decided to participate as a seller. Three days before the event, the hall of dreams bustled with energy as he prepared. Hyeonmong had grown so thin over the past month that he didn't have a suit that fit him. He discovered a wrinkled suit in the corner of his dresser, but it wasn't his. It was an outfit that had been worn by salesman Hyeonbong Park. The jacket and pants fit Hyeonmong perfectly, but they were so threadbare that they looked like hand-me-downs. Finally, one day before the auction, I went to a department store to buy him a suit worth wearing. Hyeonmong's store of cash had disappeared long ago, so I first had to stop by the bank and take out what remained of our checking account.

But before the sales even started, the back of Hyeonmong's new suit was soaked with so much sweat that the blossoming liquid looked like blood from a gunshot wound. Hyeonmong's fervor over the past three days wasn't just because of his attempt to procure a suit. He needed dreams to sell at the auction. Instead of dreams, Hyeonmong prepared lies. At some point, dreams had merged with lies in Hyeonmong's mind. But it was still difficult for him to speak of dreams with such vulgarity.

As soon as the MC started the auction, the inside of the hall quieted.

"Bachelard stated that the beginning of dreams was concurrent with the beginning of humans," he told the crowd. "But that's not all, is it?"

"It's said that in ancient Greece, one could receive dream therapy at the temple of Asclepius. People are claiming all kinds of things about the dream business nowadays, but do you remember learning in school about general Yusin Kim, whose sister Bohui gave her lucky dream away? Remember what happened to her? All her fortune vanished after that, and Yusin's other sister, Munhui, ended up marrying King Chunchu! Today, after the auction has concluded, we're going to use brain waves to show how dreams have been a part of the human experience through history. You'll even watch a live recording of a dream in action. I'd like to thank the CEO of Very Good Brain, which is sponsoring today's meeting."

Hyeonmong's dream was going to be auctioned last, and as his turn neared, the dampness on his back darkened. Hyeonmong Park's dream finally sold when the back of his shirt was entirely submerged in sweat. The winning bid was 910,000 won. The seller and the winner shook hands, and just as they were about to exchange money and a receipt, a woman rose her hand and interrupted.

"What, exactly, is the criteria for the dreams being sold?" she asked.

Everyone's attention fell upon the speaker.

"I was going to keep my mouth shut and listen," she said, "but no matter how subjective you say dreams are, there's something funny about this one, isn't there? A man wearing sunglasses and a trench coat, who can scale walls like he's flying: Shall I say what everyone is thinking but afraid to say? This dream is just like *The Matrix*! Anyone can see that it's copying *The Matrix*. And you said the man pulls out his eyeballs, because information is stored in them. Can I say what you're all thinking? It's *Minority Report*! This character in your dream is both Keanu Reeves and then Tom Cruise—and then it seems that he travels to Chungmuro, in Seoul, because there's also a Korean movie this dream resembles. There's the line in the dream where he says, 'I went to Ewha Womans University!' Isn't that scene familiar to everyone? I'll say what no one's saying. *The High Rollers*! That's the movie the line is from. Is the main character here supposed to be two different people at once? I could make up this kind of dream myself!"

The High Rollers, *The Matrix*, and *Minority Report* were all movies that Chunsam Kim liked. They were also movies that Hyeonmong had watched one after another, several times in a row. They had been the course materials for his private class on narrative. But now the movies were over, and class had long been dismissed. Silence flowed throughout the room, until someone interjected. "I knew there was something weird about this dream," she said. Someone else spoke: "Fake fortune tellers are being caught left and right; how can dream selling remain pure?" A third person asked a question: "Can dreams really be a lie? Maybe it was the movies that copied this man's dream."

Hyeonmong sat in his chair like he was about to cry as every drop of sweat in his body trickled down his back. All eyes in the event hall were on him. They weren't just eyes; they also looked like holes. Hyeonmong couldn't bring his gaze toward any of the holes. The MC opened his mouth.

"Sit down, everyone. Please, sit down," he instructed. "This is exactly the kind of situation where we need a brain wave measurer. Thankfully, the CEO of Very Good Brain is participating today, so we'll just move straight to our next event, which will illuminate the connection between dreams and brain waves."

A silent gunshot, like the one that had left Hyeonmong's suit plastered with sweat, rang into the air. This second bullet didn't pierce Hyeonmong Park's back or face or heart, it went straight for his hidden pile of lies. Sweat pumped out of his body like it was blood. A researcher appeared carrying a lightweight brain wave measurer and asked Hyeonmong if he consented to an examination. Hyeonmong shook his head, but the word "yes" escaped from his mouth. Such was the situation in which he'd found himself. Hyeonmong's feet were stuck firmly to the ground, but his arms placed themselves on the mattress, ready to climb up onto the bed. The time had come.

The researcher stuck several wirelike lines to Hyeonmong's temples. They didn't look like wires so much as straws sucking the juice out of his body. The doctor used a pointer to draw attention to a large screen, then stepped forward like a conductor. Hyeonmong's body, connected to the screen by the tubes, shivered all over like it was a vibrating string instrument. Audience members held their breath as they waited for the performance about to reverberate from his body.

"Now," the MC exclaimed, "we're going to see Hyeonmong Park's brain go from stage four non-REM sleep to REM sleep, or dream sleep. If you wake someone up during REM sleep, they typically remember their dream. You can then ask the person what they were dreaming in order to verify the dream while it's still fresh. Okay, now Mr. Park is going to fall asleep. The first stage of sleep lasts between thirty seconds and seven minutes. What we see on the screen is a beta wave. See it here? The shape is rather complex, and there's not much rhythm to it, is there? This is a brain wave indicating a state of anxiety. Next comes a slightly slower alpha wave. This is also a wave that we want to see when we're awake, as it's a sign of health. Okay, and now the screen's changed again, see? The wavelength has increased slightly: this is a theta wave. Finally, Mr. Park has reached the sleep stage. Next he'll move on to delta waves."

The researcher wrote a list of symbols on the wall, next to the brain waves being projected onscreen.

"β (beta), α (alpha), θ (theta), δ (delta)," the list read.

This is the order for the cycle we're seeing," he told the room.

The audience wrote the symbols down. Some people even chanted "beta, alpha, theta, delta" to themselves in order to commit the words to memory.

"Okay, so this is one cycle," the researcher continued. "See how the brain waves are moving? Don't just write the stages down: memorize them. Try singing the sleep stages to yourself like they're a lullaby, and use your notes as lyrics. Beta, alpha, theta, delta—repeat after me. Yes, good. Next we move on to REM sleep. A wave shaped like a serrated saw is going to show up on the screen. This one's fast-moving. Women, pay attention: in this phase, men get an erection. Alright, now we're going into the dream."

In that moment, Hyeonmong's brain deviated from the intended musical score. It traced an irregular curve that began to decelerate. The doctor repeated what he'd just said like the voice of a broken GPS system, but the brain wave was heading in a completely different direction than it was supposed to. At one point, we all believed that Hyeonmong had died. The curves of the wave grew dormant, until what we were looking at was almost a stiff, straight line. This was a world of sleep so deep that not even dreams could intrude. I turned away from the screen and surveyed my surroundings. The scene, with everyone focusing on the inside of one person's mind, was tinged with an otherworldly languor. From the unfamiliar crowd, familiar faces came into view. Mrs. Wang was staring at Hyeonmong's brain waves like she was looking at falling stock prices. Taekman Nam grasped at his ever-shrinking penis, and Chunsam Kim was in the midst of a fight against commas. Pajama fabric patterns overlapped with their faces. None of them could hear it, but Hyeonmong was almost certainly crying out "REM! REM! REM! REM!" from his unknowable haven of hibernation. His dreams were escaping to an even more remote place, somewhere between the REMs, hiding amidst this REM and that REM and that REM: somewhere the REMs couldn't reach.

"When you fall into deep sleep, the delta waves appear again—waves of about three hertz," the researcher told us. "If this were REM sleep as planned, the wave would be sixty to seventy hertz. Mr. Hyeonmong has fallen into an unexpected deep sleep. Our bodies are normally in this absolute sleep stage for about fifteen minutes per night. Right now, this man is sleeping so deeply that he can't even dream. And he's been at it for fifty minutes."

"Is he dead?" someone asked.

But Hyeonmong's breathing hadn't stopped, only his dreams had. His musical performance was over. Hyeonmong awoke, and the researcher asked him what he had dreamed about.

Hyeonmong was the only person in the room who didn't know what his brain waves had done. With a messy tangle of wires encircling his head, Hyeonmong spoke to the audience.

"I dreamed about a hall of dreams that was on fire," he said. "My hall of dreams."

The researcher stared at Hyeonmong and asked if he really remembered his dream. Hyeonmong nodded and energetically described a scene in which his business was overtaken by flames. Glints of scorn spread throughout his listeners' eyes. Hyeonmong was being more loquacious than necessary. The longer he talked about his dream, the darker the expressions in the crowd grew. Someone interrupted in an agitated voice.

"The show's over," the person said. "How many dreams did you manage to trick people into buying?"

Hyeonmong stood up awkwardly, like someone who'd been caught in the middle of peeing. The more he talked, the more his words sounded like excuses. Several familiar faces were among those attacking Hyeonmong as a swindler, and they shouted loudly for him to give back their money. After a while, someone spoke.

"We don't actually know if what this man has said is a lie. Doesn't the human mind sometimes do inexplicable things? Brain waves show the electrical activity of the brain—action that comes from the realm of consciousness—but don't sleep and dreams belong to the subconscious? If it's true that this guy dreamed something the brain waves couldn't catch, like he said, then that's way more interesting than a normal dream."

Surprisingly, it was Taekman Nam who said this. Someone shouted "Doctor Nam!" when he finished speaking. Several people in the audience were sympathetic to Taekman's, or Doctor Nam's, idea. Those who wanted to believe Hyeonmong asserted that he must have dreamed a dream that evaded measurement by brain wave. Hyeonmong agreed. He yelled that his dream was unknowable to the brain wave measurer, and that the image of the hall of dreams on fire remained fresh in his mind. Confused uproar continued until the MC grabbed the microphone.

"Mr. Lee, let's move to the next item on the schedule," he said.

The new speaker addressed the audience. "Okay. My name is Very Lee, and I'm the CEO of Very Good Brain. You've seen it in today's experiment: Very Good Brain is an advanced brain wave–measuring instrument that you can easily use at home. It's small and light, so you can bring it with you anytime and anywhere. *Tame your brain waves, and you can conquer the world.*"

Opinions about measuring brain waves flew through the air and collided. Everyone ignored the noise coming out of the loudspeakers. To them, it was nothing but white noise. Someone said that you could go to the police station to see brain wave–measuring lie detectors worth five hundred million won each. If you showed a suspect photos or words related to the crime, the detectors measured brain waves to determine if the person was lying or telling the truth. But lie detectors made no appearance today. Competent dreamers were scattered all over the room, and many among them held the title of doctor or professor. The most brutal and certain method to determine Hyeonmong's validity was simply to allow the marketplace to take over. Busy consumers hungry for dreams would simply avoid Hyeonmong if his product seemed inauthentic. They had many other places to take their business, and shunning Hyeonmong felt only natural.

Hyeonmong returned to his hall of dreams, but no one was waiting for him there. Customers weren't the only thing snatched up by competitors. At some point, Hyeonmong had begun to mumble the advertising slogans of the other dream sellers, as if the competition was encroaching upon his brain. Not even the layers of pajamas enveloping his body, or liters of fabric detergent, could call forth his dreams. Even the drying rack was missing something, like Adam's torso after God took one of his ribs.

At dawn, the building caught on fire. The flames started in the leftmost room, where five hundred bedtime bottles were stored. The blaze licked at the bottles, using their contents as kindling as the fire pushed into the waiting room. When I looked for Hyeonmong in the midst of the fire, he was holding an extinguisher with the safety pin pulled out. But an inferno swirled in his pupils. I looked into his eyes and knew how the fire within them had started. His eyes brimmed with the embers of extinguished dreams. Hyeonmong was panting.

"This is a dream," he told me.

The smell of oil wafted from his hand.

Exactly half of the hall of dreams burned and half survived. The aftermath would have been easier to deal with if the arson was a dream. But it wasn't. We had to face reality. The careless criminal was caught within a day. Many people, including me, first suspected that Hyeonmong had burnt the building, but he hadn't. Yes, he'd poured gasoline on the flames, but someone else had started the fire.

"Fire in a Nonhyeon-dong Hall of Dreams—Customer at Fault" read the headlines.

The news said that it was a customer, but I didn't recognize the face. Not even Hyeonmong remembered who the person was. The name, appearance, and voice were all unfamiliar. It felt strange trying to decide whether we should remember the person as a customer or as a criminal. The article I read about the incident was only a few lines long. What caught my eye more than the story itself was the thick and sizeable lettering on the ad below it.

"Is mistrust blossoming in your life? We use brain waves to prove your suspicions while you dream."

The rumor that an overzealous customer had set the hall on fire spread like flames. Few, however, believed that Hyeonmong's dream on the day of the auction was a prediction of his hall of dream's future. Even after the brain wave examination ended, the image of Hyeonmong's dream description—so different from his idle brain waves—was engraved in people's memories. It was like pulling the plug in a bathtub full of water: the more the water drains out of the tub, the louder it gurgles. The hall was swept away in a similarly raucous whirlpool of disaster.

The hall of dreams, and its ethos of "personal development," may have been an imposing structure, but its impressive physical frame concealed mounds of debt. Phone calls from unknown numbers and visits from unknown guests increased until finally red slips of paper were strewn about the property. Notices were tacked to the wall, TV, laptop, golf clubs, piano, washing machine, and even the charred fence. *Now we're in charge*, the flyers seemed to be saying.

Our former customers were viewed as victims; people said our former regulars needed to be institutionalized. The victims were faceless. The more well-known they were, the more they wanted to hide the fact that they'd frequented a hall of dreams. Many called Hyeonmong Park a swindler, but some who maligned him didn't even know what he'd taken. Others who'd heard that Hyeonmong's dreams had disappeared still didn't believe it. Some of the faithful congregated at the remaining half of the hall. They locked eyes with me, but we didn't recognize each other. Their footsteps and the ruckus they created were enough to make the structure, filled with bedtime bottles, rattle. The sound was similar to an expectant drumbeat, or a pounding heart. Finally, the bedtime bottles gave a boisterous round of applause as they came crashing to the ground. Scattered among the cracked and shattered bottles were several that escaped the disaster intact, nestled in the arms of their owners. Our former customers were, of course, carrying the bottles bearing their own names, and some even carried bottles that bore the names of other customers too.

After the uproarious din passed, Hyeonmong Park was discovered in a pile of pajamas. He wore number 132 on one leg, number 378 on the other, and 201 on his arms; his head was inside customer 24's pajamas. His entire body appeared to have become a drying rack.

"It came," he said from inside the sooty fabric.

"Who? A person?" I asked.

"Something scarier."

Hyeonmong's next utterance sounded less like a word than a groan.

"Reality."

In that moment, the washing machine beeped to indicate the end of the wash cycle. I opened the door to the machine. Dozens of pairs of dreams were tangled up together so that you couldn't distinguish their individual forms. That was the last thing I did.

Was the opposite of dreams reality, or was it lies? Every wall I came across until I exited the property was lined with bedtime bottles. So many bottles had shattered and burned in the fire that I couldn't imagine where these new ones came from. When I reached out to touch one, the cold surface felt odd against my hand. It was almost as if my fingers were brushing over Hyeonmong Park's bumpy name written on the glass in Braille. I picked up one of the bottles and walked out of the gate. My pace unintentionally quickened. When my palpitating heart settled somewhat, I tried opening the bottle. There was nothing inside. And that's how the hall of dreams came to an end.

"Dreams are more expensive than reality—we all know that, right? As dreams become more expensive, the market opens up to sell high-quality pajamas—the kind of pajamas that will help people dream their own dreams. We want to attract the home dreamer as our customer, rather than someone who will buy their experience in a shop. And that's why we need all of you guys! Pajama coordinator is a promising career field, one that will stay relevant not only well into the twenty-first century, but throughout the twenty-second century as well."

The boss at my new job repeated the same spiel to everyone he encountered, whether it was a jobseeker offering him a résumé or a disgruntled employee handing in a resignation letter. Considering how more and more businesses were hiring pajama coordinators, though, he sold me on the job: it really did seem like I had a future here. I hadn't lived in the twenty-second century yet, but I'd been working under my new boss for the past several months of the twenty-first century. In my new job, post-Hyeonmong, I helped customers select their desired sleepwear. To put it simply, I was a salesperson.

"A pajama coordinator is not a salesperson," my new boss said. "They are a cultural evangelist, spreading pajama culture to the people."

According to the boss, miniskirts sold best during economic recessions, and pajamas sold best during times of anxiety. If you could use pajama sales as an index of public anxiety, the world was in the midst of heightening unease.

The work of dealing dreams continued just as it had with Hyeonmong; only the sign outside and method of sales differed. Anxiety was like a shirt button: when it fell off the shirt, people tended to sew it back on straightaway. If they didn't sew the original stressor back on, then a new one took its place. Even with several other halls of dreams falling like bankrupt dominoes after Hyeonmong's breakdown, the dream market flourished. Maybe the cure for anxiety wasn't stability; maybe it was dreams. Could anything be more nerve-wracking than the thought of such anxiety disappearing altogether? I imagined that by now Mrs. Wang was frequenting some sort of venue other than a hall of dreams. She was probably searching for faith in something new. Taekman Nam, I presumed, was still trying to calm his worries about the length of his penis.

The boss tried to partner with businesses that sold dreams to offer joint promotions for their customers, but each business he contacted claimed to be the original vendor of dreams, with no need to resort to such gimmicks. Nowadays, everyone claimed to be the originator of dream selling. My boss claimed determinedly that there was a way to differentiate the real original from the fakes. The place that did the best business, he said, was the original.

Based on the above criterion, the originator of the modern dream market was a place that sold dreams by the pound. A large glass showcase displayed the store's wares, like a butcher shop or a bakery. The dreams existed in powder and occasionally liquid form. Every item was priced at 2,500 won per 100 grams.

You selected each part of your dream like it was food at a self-serve buffet. First the "actions" that might appear in the dream: gathering, carrying, approaching, taking responsibility, receiving applause, drifting apart, moving forward, and stepping backward. Next were "geometric figures" you could add: circle, square, triangle, star, and arch. Dream topics included conflict, restoration, and rendezvous, among others. There were also animals, plants, and a multitude of other categories from which to select. I ladled my desired dream elements onto my tray. The woman at the counter placed it all on a scale. The scale's needle wavered slightly. My dream weighed 515 grams.

"That will be 12,870 won," she said. "One hour before sleeping, mix the powder with water and drink it."

It was the same as Hyeonmong's dream soup, just in a new form. In my dream, I wanted to see what the former occupants of Hyeonmong's hall of dreams were up to now. But that's not what I saw. Reality knew me better than dreams did: several days later, I encountered Chunsam Kim in an article my boss had cut out from the newspaper.

After Hyeonmong's business crumbled, Chunsam Kim had written a two thousand–page manifesto declaring the end of his writing career. He sent it to a publishing company, but the publisher seemed to have thought the manifesto was a novel and published it. The title was *Chunsam Kim's Declaration of the End of His Writing Career*. The words in the book didn't, in fact, bring about the end of Chunsam's career. Instead, they brought him renewed determination. Chunsam took his near end to be a golden opportunity. Even though no one had noticed his fall, he succeeded at a comeback. His novel was so thick that it didn't fit into trendy women's handbags, but many readers considered the thickness to be proof of his literary capacity.

"Who is happier: the laborer who dreams for twelve hours each night about being a king, or the king who dreams for twelve hours each night about being a laborer? Pascal asks this very question in *Pensées*, and he answers that they are almost equally happy.

"If in some world, these two people actually existed—the laborer dreaming of being a king and the king dreaming of being a laborer—then dreams and the revelations they unveil are what would allow them to switch roles. This is a story from the Senoi people, who lived in the primeval forests of Malaysia. These people, called the tribe of dreams, considered dreams to be prophecies, and they lived their lives accordingly. They did only as much work as needed and spent their remaining time subject to the governance of dreams. Their society lacked violence, mental illness, and stress. My book is going to tell the tale of the last remaining group of Senoi."

After reading the beginning of his novel aloud, Chunsam Kim abruptly stopped, looked at his readers, and broke into a completely unrelated monologue.

"Hyeonmong Park may have been a swindler, but he was also the savior of our generation. His dreams that disappeared so suddenly definitely did exist—before they disappeared. Were the dreams lies? Not at the beginning. The dreams simply went extinct. Why did they go? I'll leave that to the imagination of my readers."

Someone in the audience asked a question.

"You said you didn't use commas even once in this book: is there a particular reason why?"

"The answer is in the book," Chunsam replied.

"Do you really think Hyeonmong Park is a swindler?"

It was me who asked that. An ambiguous expression flitted across Chunsam's face.

"My readers have to decide that for themselves," he said.

For a while even after the hall closed, money kept coming into my bank account. Because it was the account tied to our business, I'm sure that someone was still sending payment for dreams. When the deposits stopped after several months, I took the money and went to Hyeonmong Park's hall of dreams. I carried two brand-new sets of pajamas with me.

The hall of dreams was no more. There was just a little house left, its frame shrunken and unable to stand the harsh sunlight. Inside the not-quite-closed front gate lived Hyeonbong Park, who once again spelled his name with a *b*.

Like a curtain pulling back on stage, the gate slowly opened. Only random knickknacks and a few pieces of furniture remained on the property. These remnants hadn't been claimed by reality: the fire had spared them. They now made up a feeble memorial to the former hall of dreams. The items were maimed. I saw a hollow mattress, large pajamas, wisdom soup long past its expiration date, and an old drying rack.

The drying rack stood at one end of the narrow yard as if it were Atlas, bearing the weight of the hall with its two metal arms. The pajamas hanging from Atlas's emaciated biceps were made from bulky and durable fabric: fabric too thick for dreams to pass through. Water drip-drip-dripped from the pajama's seams. The drip-drip-drip sounded like knocking. When the knocks hit the ground, they flowed together into a drain beneath the drying rack.

I wasn't the only person looking at the drain hole. A man as slender as an anchovy, his skin hanging off him like a pair of pajamas, was crouched down to peer inside. Hyeonmong Park and I had run into each other in front of yet another hole. He lay prostrate on the ground, supporting his body with his four limbs like an animal as one hand touched the drain. He breathed into it. He breathed into the passageway through which dreams spread across the inside of the earth; he breathed and breathed and leaned the weight of his body toward the hole. It seemed like he was going to kick his feet up into the empty air. I heard a strange laugh coming out of him as his body squeezed inside the drain.

The sky brightened, and the next few seconds felt like several years. I rinsed my eyes with the dripping water and looked again, but Hyeonmong Park wasn't there. I imagined hearing the sound of waves lapping in some sewer where all the drains in the world converged. It was an image I'd seen somewhere before. I opened up the last chapter of Chunsam Kim's novel. The words on the page seemed to be flying.

"The inside of the hole was dark. I thought that it would be filled with revelations from the dreams, indecipherable though they may be. But I was afraid to look too closely."

5. ROADKILL

Road 436 had no cameras and almost no traffic. There were a few signs here and there that said "Caution: Wildlife Crossing," but that was all. Several years ago, after two tunnels were built nearby, Road 436 had grown quiet. Barring holidays, cars rarely came through. One afternoon, when the rain was falling like April cherry blossoms, a man's truck sped by. Three kilometers away from the motel, all vehicles on the road had the same destination.

The unmanned motel towered high in the hills, the only landmark visible from the road. As soon as the building came into view on the left, the man turned the steering wheel widely with one hand and unbuckled his seatbelt with the other. Next, he pressed down on the power button of his incessantly ringing phone. The cheerful ringtone died. From every direction, silence.

The underground parking lot was filled with dusty cars. He had never spent the night at the motel, but every time he visited, he had to scour the lot to find a place to park. There was a reason why people came to such an isolated place. Motels were like casinos in that they were hard to leave. After finally finding an empty spot and parking, he pulled a box out of the bed of his truck and went inside.

The hallway floor was moving. Vending machines flowed by slowly like conveyor-belt sushi. The floor rotated as relentlessly as the earth orbited—snow or rain, guests or not, it never stopped. If you were a guest here, all you had to do was open the door to your room, come outside, and wait for a vending machine you liked to pass by. You just opened your door, and faceless kiosks abounded. You didn't have to leave the building to buy what you needed. Each floor was plastered with advertisements stating that the conveyor belt was ready to cater to customers' every desire. The man stood in front, watching a familiar vending machine go by, then quickly climbed aboard the conveyor. Fantastic Love. It was a party supply vending machine he'd installed in this motel six months earlier.

Every sort of party imaginable was possible in the motel. If you wanted balloons, there they were; the same for bubbles, ropes, and garter belts. Because of this, the vending machine was filled with all sorts of things that didn't seem to go together. But it wasn't a problem. When you pressed the button for "balloon" or "garter belt" or whatever else you wanted, the object specified was the only thing that would emerge.

The man placed the box at his side and opened the vending machine. Bills and coins for the goods sold were waiting for him in one corner. He liked the way vending machines would spit out change if given too much money, and how they indicated sold-out items with the words "Out of Stock." Filling that space between where the money went in and the product came out made him feel like his life was in order. To him, Fantastic Love was a party in itself. He put the balloons, firecrackers, and ropes in their respective compartments, then closed the door. Fantastic Love was splendid once again.

Since installing Fantastic Love in the motel, he had gotten rid of a few other vending machines he'd set up around the city.

Unlike those other machines, which were always backlogged with inventory and just ran up the electricity bill, Fantastic Love was quite profitable. He had been able to preorder several months of party supplies thanks to its proven sales record. His plan was to buy two more machines in the spring. When he left the motel after polishing the outside of Fantastic Love until it shone, the world was covered in snow. It had piled up in just an hour and a half. He looked at his watch. Five p.m. Time to return to the city.

He got into his truck and pulled the seat forward. The slope leading back down to Road 436 was slippery. The sun had suddenly set, and in the meantime the ground had frozen. As soon as he turned his phone on again, a barrage of text messages poured in. He turned it off. He was definitely waiting for something, but this wasn't it. Maybe if more snow fell, it would be an excuse not to go back, he thought. It was just a fleeting thought, but as if triggered by the idea, wind-driven flurries began to batter the door.

There was only one room left at the motel, which made him feel even more certain that he was destined to spend the night there. The price for a room was one hundred thousand won. He inserted his credit card into the automated rental machine, but in vain. He had exceeded the card's limit this month buying the products he'd placed in Fantastic Love. There wasn't much money left in his wallet, but Fantastic Love's profits were ample. Pooling the cash he had, he inserted one hundred thousand won into the slot, and a card key slid out immediately.

In the morning, the room was filled with traces of his purchases from the night before. Food containers, empty and white; scattered beer cans; cigarette butts; a sports newspaper . . . all from the conveyor belt traveling round and round in the hallway. He stretched his limbs as he looked up at the ceiling, seemingly twice as high as in a regular room, and down at the king-size bed. He felt his bones and muscles growing to fit such a big space.

Outside the window, all was snow. News anchors on the TV rambled on and on about unprecedented storms all over the country. But from atop such a plush bed, the snow looked as calm as a pattern on curtains or wallpaper. It was kind of like packing foam, he thought. A white buffer surrounding the motel, that's what the stuff on the ground was.

Whenever there was a storm, the demand for Fantastic Love increased. Overnight, the number of balloons and butterfly masks had diminished by more than half. Fifty balloons, fifty butterfly masks—numbers as surprising as the snow itself. He hurriedly descended to the parking garage and pulled a box from his truck to refill the machine. As he restocked Fantastic Love, he pocketed the cash from the products that had sold. At this rate, maybe he'd be able to put in a second Fantastic Love before spring. He returned to his truck and whistled as he climbed in. The news said another bout of snow would hit this afternoon. His truck started up with a beastly groan. The radio signal wasn't good, but a cheerful tune was still audible through the static. The truck carefully descended the snowy slope. When he rolled down the window, a harsh windy howl intermingled with the radio tune.

But at some point, all sound stopped—and not just sound. The road that was supposed to be at the bottom of the slope simply wasn't there. Everything had turned pure white. Road 436 was lost in the snow, the distinction between pavement and non-pavement gone. He slowly depressed the brake, and the truck began to slide as fast as balloons and butterfly masks had slid out of Fantastic Love. Its four wheels and headlights were enveloped by a wave of white as it dove into the snow. The truck stopped. Even if it had been able to move, the road had already disappeared.

This was truly a snowstorm among snowstorms, the likes of which he hadn't seen since his military days. He was stranded more than thirty minutes from anywhere, on a road devoid not only of vehicles but also of people and animals. The cell phone that had been ringing so furiously couldn't even send or receive text messages now. Flurries poured onto the sunken truck as if to bury all evidence of its existence. He left the truck where it was and walked back to the motel, slipping several times along the way. The waist-high drifts became shallower closer to the building, and by the time he reached the entrance, they were only underfoot. Whoever had shoveled the snow so thoroughly had to be somewhere inside, but he waited and waited for that person to no avail. The pay phone in the lobby was, of course, dead. Exactly one room left. There was no other choice.

The blizzard continued for a week. The news described it as an "unimaginable storm." Clouds moved around in stagnant circles, and there were snow-ins all over the place. The road froze; the roof of a house caved in from the weight of the ice. The river, the city's lifeline, froze solid. Birds taxidermied in white were found here and there along its course. The flurries gradually became stronger. Thin-branched trees bent sharply wherever the snow pummeled them.

Just as the news had warned, everything outside was still the same color. The color of snow. In all that monochrome, the only place even somewhat interesting was the hallway. All you had to do was open your door and climb onto the conveyor belt, and a dazzlingly fantastic world unfolded. There was nothing that wasn't there. The man had been able to stay at the motel for over a week only because of these vending machines gliding by on the conveyor belt. His Fantastic Love was, of course, selling products left and right, what with the weather. He jotted down the names of items that had lit up in random order. Two boxes of firecrackers, one box each of handcuffs and garter belts, half a box each of balloons and butterfly masks. He cheerfully descended the snow-covered path to the main road, indifferent to his shoes dirtying and sludgy water flecking the cuffs of his pants. Venturing through the drifts of fluffy popcorn snow was as exciting as sledding. He picked out some dry boxes from his truck stuck in the road and carried them back up. He may have been stranded, but at least he was working, and as long as he had money, there was no reason he couldn't survive here. Money from the goods he'd sold paid for each day's lodging and meals. Of course, he couldn't stay in a room with a ceiling twice as high as normal like he had on the first night. That would be a luxury and a waste. Thankfully, slightly more reasonably priced rooms began to open up, and even under a regular-height or low ceiling he slept well.

He discovered an intercom between the hall vending machines one afternoon when a quiet snowfall was again beginning to intensify. The intercom emitted a long, bored dial tone as the storm raged outside.

"For guest inquiries, press 1; for vending machine inquiries, press 2; for service questions, press 3; for parking, press 4; and for all other questions, press 0."

He thought for a moment, then pressed 0.

"The volume of calls is currently high and your call cannot be connected. Please leave your information after the beep and a representative will contact you. Bee—."

"Hello, I manage the Fantastic Love. There's a lot of broken equipment in the motel. The pay phone's out of order, my cell phone doesn't get a signal, and my truck broke down, too, so I'm stuck here. If you could please get in touch and send an employee over . . ."

Several days passed after he left the message. The longer he stayed at the motel, the more unfamiliar it became. He didn't know how many rooms were on each floor or even how many floors the building had. He also had no idea how many kinds of vending machines there were. It seemed like the rooms should be completely full because of the snowstorm, but he hadn't yet seen a single person in the motel. The uncountable array of vending machines was in stark contrast to the absence of people. This array was also why he had already run out of cash.

He charged his cell phone every day inside a charging kiosk. He would peek at the LCD screen at five-minute intervals. When it looked like the signal antenna had grown longer, he'd try pressing the call button. Recently, he'd been hanging around in front of Fantastic Love more often, watching the news on the hall TV. The simple action soothed his anxiety, and he didn't really have anything to do other than check on Fantastic Love and look at his phone, anyway. Fantastic Love was getting empty. As the inventory boxes in his truck bed decreased, so did the ceiling height of the rooms he stayed in. He'd slowly begun to choose cheaper and cheaper rooms, and price and ceiling height were correlated.

When the whips and ropes sold out, he was down to his last box. The bottom of the container had turned mushy with dampness, but it couldn't be helped. The next day, several more items sold out, but there was nothing to replace them with. Thirty days of snow, and an inventory that had been meant to last months was already gone. No profit remained in his pockets.

In this place abandoned by the sun, the frozen motel didn't cast a shadow. When it was time to check out, all noise in the room stopped and the door opened automatically. The room's floor heating cooled instantaneously to a chill. The door opened and he emerged. The conveyor belt in the hall was moving at the same speed as always. It flowed forward as smoothly as an iron, an iron that flattened all noise from the floors above and below. If you stood in the hallway, all you could hear was the vibration of the conveyor belt, no matter how hard you listened. There had certainly been a time when that stillness made him feel peaceful, but now it was unwelcome. He hurried into the elevator, but as soon as he left the building, he realized he had no idea where he should go. The snow was lashing down like a whip.

"For guest inquiries, press 1; for vending machine inquiries, press 2; for service questions . . . for all other . . . The volume of calls is currently high and your call cannot be connected. Please leave your information after the beep and a representative will contact you. Bee—."

After the call ended, unsuccessful for the usual reason, a deep sense of quiet set in again. He'd made this call several days in a row, so it wasn't the first time this had happened. But what was different now was that Fantastic Love was completely empty, any cash from it already gone. He quietly pulled himself together. The voice on the intercom was calm, and so were those vending machines moving endlessly at the same speed. He hid the excitement and irritation he felt in his throat and exhaled evenly. Strangely, the more aloof he was with the voice on the phone, the friendlier that voice became. Whenever he let down his guard, though, even for just a moment, the voice would immediately cool into icy hostility. After taking a deep breath, he decided he'd try being a customer rather than the manager of Fantastic Love, and pretend to have a complaint. He pressed 2 and was connected with a representative all too easily.

"This is about Fantastic Love," he said. "It's out of merchandise, which is very inconvenient. Contact the manager and fill it up again soon, please. And because of the snowstorm . . ."

"Yes, sir. You're calling about the Fantastic Love outage? We'll contact the manager as soon as we can. Can I help you with anything else?"

"Yes, the storm here is really severe, so the road is blocked and I can't . . ."

"Sir, I'm sorry, but questions about anything other than the vending machines go through our automated message system, so can you try our other number? I'll let someone know about your important question. Have a nice day."

The phone disconnected with a series of cacophonous beeps. The man couldn't put the receiver down so quickly after yet another failed call, so he turned round and round on the conveyor belt alongside the intercom. It was at that moment that he discovered a new vending machine. It was the same shape as an ATM, but it wasn't an ATM, strictly speaking. It was a machine that would let you take out a loan using your ID, perhaps something between an ATM and those machines that dispensed documents in government offices. He looked at it carefully.

1. Place ID card in slot.
2. After credit evaluation, withdrawal amount will be displayed on screen. Allowable withdrawal amount varies with individual credit score.
3. Press one-day personal information transfer button, and ID and cash will be released.
4. Limit of one withdrawal per day.
5. May not use ID card for twenty-four hours after cash withdrawal.

A machine that read your ID card and gave you cash! It took your identity as collateral before dispensing the money. For now, he passed it by. Over the last few days, it felt like he'd become a stoplight in the game *Red Light, Green Light*—whenever he called "red light" and looked behind his back, it would seem like somebody had moved, but everyone feigned ignorance. Overdrawn credit card, empty wallet, closed road, immovable truck, and Fantastic Love near death from starvation. He fiddled under his chin with his left hand. His beard was bushy. Considering that this place only took cash, there was no way he could stay in the motel any longer. Of course, he couldn't leave either. At least not as long as snow was falling.

He turned back. Thankfully, the loan machine hadn't gone too far yet and was still nearby. He didn't know why it required him to insert his ID, but even if it didn't return the card, he could always apply for a new one. He put his ID into the machine. After a moment, it came back out with three hundred thousand won. The man stole a glance at the hallway CCTV. While he'd had his eyes closed as the stoplight, others must have been accomplices in the strange doings at this motel.

He chose a room ten thousand won cheaper than the night before, and it was proportionally smaller. It wasn't just narrow—the ceiling was low, too, and the window and door were comparably small. The room was about two-thirds the size of a normal room from floor to ceiling, as tall as he was. Strangely enough, before the storm—before he had spent the night here—he hadn't realized that room height differed on each floor. But as the rooms became cheaper, their ceilings drew closer and closer to his head.

Thunk, thunk, thunk.

Someone knocked on his door while he was sleeping. He got up drowsily and looked through the peephole. He didn't open the door. Through the circle of glass, each end of the hallway was warped. The peephole gave anyone looking through it the odd feeling that they were being watched.

"Mail delivery."

Startled to alertness by the voice, he opened the door, but no one was outside. He went back in his room. Moments later, an envelope flitted in through the crack under the door. In the envelope was a photo of the man's truck, as accusatory as a police sketch. Parking violation, sixty thousand won fine. The truck was being ticketed in the very spot where it had been trapped for the past few days. Really, parking tickets, here? Where everything was so covered in snow that you couldn't even tell the difference between road and sidewalk, asphalt and dirt? Anyhow, maybe this was a good sign. Did it mean that the road was cleared now? He looked at the bill for a long time, then abruptly went back to the door, and turned the handle to open it. But all he saw in the hallway was stillness, the CCTV looking at him with a vacant lens.

"Freeways, airports, and rail lines have been brought to a standstill, and now suicide attempts are occurring one after another in areas that have been cut off by the snowstorm. Last night, the body of an unidentified guest was found in one motel in Gangwon Province. According to the police, no foul play is suspected."

The news played on TV twenty-four hours a day, but it was too depressing. He changed channels.

"A plastic container filled with potassium cyanide and a bottle of alcohol were discovered inside the room. Because no ID card was found, police are holding off from . . ."

He tried to change the channel once more, but the TV continued to broadcast the same story. There was no signal from any other station. He gave the screen a piercing stare. The image he saw was all too familiar. He looked around, then turned toward the screen before looking around again. Red bedding, a bare sort of appearance, the same windows and curtain color, slightly low ceiling, forest green wallpaper. The only thing he didn't see onscreen was his own unease. It doesn't matter where you go, motels all look the same, he said to himself as his chopsticks reached for air instead of food. His insides felt uneasy. A dry belch rose from the bottom of his throat.

Early in the morning, he went down to his truck, but couldn't find it. There was a lot less snow on the road, and it seemed like removal operations were progressing somewhat. Maybe the truck had been towed. He had a nervous sense that he'd been misled in some strange way, as if a garter belt had come out when he'd pressed the button for a balloon, or a whip when he'd wanted firecrackers. He glanced at his phone again. The antenna symbol on his phone screen was short, showing a weak connection that wasn't getting any stronger. When he went back up to the motel, clutching his cell phone tightly, for some reason there was an ID photo machine where Fantastic Love was supposed to be. The order of the vending machines had gotten all mixed up just a few days since he'd last seen them. He walked round and round the motel and went up and down, to every floor, but he couldn't find Fantastic Love anywhere. There were no direction signs in the building, and it was impossible to figure out the layout no matter how far you walked.

"Get your photos, get your photos!"

At some point, the photo machine moved in front of him again. It had a cheerful advertising ditty, but for some reason the device looked like it took funerary portraits rather than ID photos. His legs trembled, even though he was sure that wasn't the case. His vending machine was gone, only a day after being sold out. He turned toward the CCTV. If there was a god, it had to be inside that lens, right? He wanted to believe in something, but nothing would take hold. Finally, when he had waited all afternoon, the intercom looped in front of him again. He grabbed the receiver tightly with both hands. Its signal went out to an unknown recipient and connected with a mosquito sound. After a long while, someone picked up.

"I'm sorry, sir, we don't have a machine by that name in our motel."

"What do you mean? It was definitely here yesterday!"

"Sir, are you talking about the party supply machine? Ah, yes, sir, that machine was taken out of service yesterday, and three new upgraded party supply machines were brought into the motel. You can start using them today."

He fell to his knees in spite of himself. His legs had buckled.

"Look, I was the manager of Fantastic Love. I was—ugh! Do you really think it's okay to deal with this so haphazardly? What? Insufficient stock? Look, it's barely been a day. I'm saying it's barely been a day since everything sold out. And don't you have to tell me when you throw away a machine? Do you even know where I am right now?"

"We called you several times, sir, but because your phone was turned off, we had to remove it on our own. The machine is being stored near the back door of the motel—we kept trying to contact you to tell you this. If you pick up the machine within three days, you won't be fined."

"Uh, okay. Please give me the manager."

"If you leave a message, I can let the manager know."

"Give me the manager now!"

"Sir, I want to help you. According to our policy, if you leave a message, we'll give you a call back."

He flung the receiver, but it didn't break anything as it fell—only the empty air shattered. After a moment, he regretted hanging up first. The intercom phone was already buried between vending machines, and he couldn't see where it had gone. It seemed like the messages he was leaving for motel management were vanishing into the phone, because there was never any response. Parking-ticket reminders continued to infiltrate his room.

He walked to the back door of the motel. His legs felt weak. Even before he saw Fantastic Love, he was ready to collapse. He may have only lost the contract for one of his vending machines, but it was more than that: he no longer had the ability to explain himself. He kept thinking about what the person on the phone had said, about picking up the vending machine within three days. What were they really telling him to pick up—what? The moment he saw neglected Fantastic Love, discarded and unplugged, he knew. His identity was in that rectangular lump of metal.

Fantastic Love had a broken spring, and a single rope that hadn't been dispensed because of it rolled around inside. After pulling out the rope, he carefully repaired the spring. It barely took five minutes to fix, but even after the coil had regained its elasticity, there was nothing but wind to fill the vending machine.

Night fell, and the loan machine began to appear in front of him more and more often. He helplessly inserted his ID card. The room he was staying in now was only half as high as a regular room, so it was impossible to stand up straight. Inside, he had to bend everything. His knees, his head, his spine. The ceiling, ever shorter as the rooms became cheaper, was now lower than his height.

As the ceilings grew lower and the number of guests increased by floor, the decrease in ceiling height started to become even more extreme. If the height difference between a hundred-thousand-won room and a ninety-thousand-won room was worth exactly ten thousand won, then the difference between a ninety-thousand-won room and an eighty-thousand-won room was worth a lot more. As the room price decreased, changes in things like the space between floor and ceiling, window size, and door height grew steadily greater.

His ID card was losing its value, but the fines he had to pay multiplied with the overdue charges assessed. The truck and Fantastic Love—everything he owned—had become a mountain of debt. Recently, when he'd inserted his ID card, only ten thousand won had come out. And one day, when he inserted his card, his information wasn't accepted.

"Limit exceeded."

He wasn't sure if what had exceeded the limit was his card or his life. That night, unable to pay for a room or food, he decided to leave the motel. Fantastic Love may have been emptied of all its contents, but its frame was heavy. He set it on the snow-covered ground like a tombstone and left it behind as he descended the slope, in knee-high snow. After walking a certain distance, he could see Road 436 below. In one spot, the snow was mounded up. Inside the pile was his truck. It was definitely his. Seeing this thing that had been invisible until just a few days before unnerved him more than anything else. Just as the road wasn't really a road anymore, neither was the truck a truck. Covered in snow, it couldn't carry passengers—it couldn't even move on its own. It was just a lump of scrap iron. He took huge steps, one by one, over the snow. He planned to keep going until exhausted, but it turned out that sense of direction was a lot more important than physical strength. He walked and walked, but kept going in circles. Then, at some point, something abandoned in the snow caught his eye. He slowly approached. It was an elderly person. There were traces of dried blood on the snowy ground, as if the person had fallen long ago. Had they been hit by a car? Or maybe fallen from somewhere else? He hesitated a moment, wondering if the person was dead or alive, before hoisting the body onto his back. Even through his thick winter clothes, he could feel warmth radiating from it.

Snow pelted the ground furiously. The only bright thing in sight was light spurting from the motel on the hill, sprinkling the dark road with brightness, like a lighthouse beam. Finally he decided to follow the light. Moving faster than ever, though his body sank deep into the snow banks, he ran without stopping. When he arrived, his back was on fire, but the motel in its sluggish silence had never felt so cold. He left the body outside and then ran down the hallway faster than the conveyor belt, calling for help, but not a single door among the endless rooms opened. His voice was muffled by the drone of the conveyor belt moving horizontally and the elevator moving vertically, by the whoosh of bills entering vending machine slots and items exiting. The red light of the fire alarm on the wall blinked like an emergency exit. He grabbed a decorative flower vase and struck the glass casing. The alarm was a metronome for his flight up the stairway. The fire alarm on the next floor exploded into a similar song. On the next floor, too, and the one after that, the rhythm of the fire alarms going off dictated his own rhythm. The stairs under his nimble feet alternated: white, then black, then white, like piano keys. Before his performance reached the roof, everything inside the motel stopped. The conveyor belt, the elevator, the vending machines, and the silence, too.

The whole time he'd been shattering fire alarm casings, he hadn't run into a single person, hadn't seen the gleam of a single pair of eyes. But the CCTV recording on each floor was also a kind of eye, even if he wasn't aware of it. The CCTV first captured the man as he broke the glass. As sirens went off, the camera turned to surveil the guests pouring out of their rooms en masse like a tide. The people who rushed out of their rooms and the building were relieved that there was no fire but at the same time they seemed annoyed that they'd all been brought together by a false alarm.

"A person's—been hit—by a car. Down there."

The man's breath was ragged as he spoke. To the others, his motions looked like a blazing fire, too rapid to comprehend.

"I just, I picked this person up on the road, and brought them here. An ambulance, quick."

Instead of an ambulance, the motel manager appeared. He was wearing a uniform and looked as cool as ever.

"Did you break the fire alarm panels?"

A cracked piece of vase fell from the man's hand. He had thought that the fire alarms would be interpreted as a call for help—a distress signal in the empty wilderness of this motel—but it looked like the others didn't feel the same way. He explained that there had been no other way to bring everyone together. When he finished speaking, a bystander said, "So, what's the matter?"

"Someone fell on the road. I'm talking about this person here."

As soon as the man indicated the fallen figure by his side, every face in the crowd wore the same expression. Judging from the way they were looking at him, it was clear that he was going to be on his own.

"How'd he hit such an old thing?" someone asked.

The woman next to the man shook her head, and someone else clucked his tongue as he headed back into the motel. The person standing closest to the man looked at him and spoke.

"Wild animals run across that road a lot. Isn't that why it's a wildlife crossing zone?"

The man looked down at the old person again. He couldn't see anything odd, but the other guests saw fur and a tail and claws. They all glared viciously at him. He looked down at the person again and again. No shoes, thick toenails—and was that fur actually part of a human body? In a second, this elderly person had become the most unfamiliar creature on earth. And the man was more of a laughingstock than ever.

"You'll have to take responsibility for the disturbance you've caused. And get rid of the body of that animal somehow—put it back on the road, or bury it, or burn it. If you just throw it out near the motel, it'll be an eyesore, and we'll have to fine you."

Uniform handed the man a hastily written fine as he spoke. The man took the note and immediately crumpled it. Uniform quickly wrote out another.

"Call the police. I'll pay for everything. Just call someone."

"That's not my job. Ask about it on the intercom."

Uniform finished speaking, then turned away before looking back.

"And anyway, think about the weather—think about it. If you were a policeman, would you be able to get here? In this snowstorm, really?"

By ones and twos, the residents returned to the motel, to their floors, to their rooms, to their beds. Once the crowd dispersed, there were only two people left. The man, and a woman who was looking at him. They stared at each other for a long time. They both had a strange appearance. They were severely hunchbacked, and their gazes were uneasy. Almost everything around them melded into the snowy background, which made them stand out even more. As the others squeezed back into the motel's silence, these stragglers couldn't bring themselves to follow the crowd. Now alone, they were able to recognize each other as outsiders. When the man picked up the possible animal/possible human and began to move it, the woman came up to him and lifted it from the other side. The two silently put it inside Fantastic Love. With all its items sold out, the only thing that would emerge if you inserted money was this miserable corpse. Snow flurries were starting to fall again on Fantastic Love. At that moment, the man stared at the woman again. The woman was the only *person* he had met at the motel.

The man and the woman decided to share a room, to cut costs. From floor to ceiling, it was barely one-third the height of a regular room, so if you stretched your back, you couldn't sit up straight. The woman, her back hunched, held her hand out to the man and spoke.

"One thousand won for ten minutes. I can sing, I can dance. I can have a conversation."

The man didn't really understand what she was saying, but he pulled out one thousand won and gave it to the woman. She clasped it in her hands.

"I'm a machine, so press a button. Singing, dancing, conversation—what do you want?"

"Uh . . . can we talk? So, a conversation."

The woman nodded.

"When did you get here?"

"About two months ago? It could be longer."

"Why did you come?"

After the man asked this, he added onto his question.

"I guess I'm wondering if you maybe wanted to leave but haven't been able to."

The woman responded, "That's half-true."

The man leaned toward her.

"Explain a little more specifically," he insisted. "You're the only person in this place that I've been able to talk to, you know."

The woman drew up her knees and covered them with her arms. She buried her head in her lap and, after a moment, began to explain.

"It was the night of the performance after party. The day we tore down the set. I only had a bit part in the play, but even so, as we drank, I kept thinking that I wanted to go back on stage. Not because I loved my role but because I disliked the party. I must have seemed really disconnected from everyone else there. I don't know when I started feeling that way, but mingling with people after the performance had ended, exchanging lines without a script—it was kind of a burden. So finally at two in the morning I grabbed my bag and stood up.

"At that moment, one of the older cast members said something to me. 'Hey, have another drink and just sleep over at my place.' She had played the female lead. I insisted that I had to go home, but she wouldn't have it. 'It's past two, there won't be a later bus. Then just come with me. Who goes home early on a night like this? I have to go home. So do the rest of us. You're the only one with a family? We all have families.' Finally I spoke up. 'No, it's because I have to change my panties!' Upon hearing those words, the older cast member froze. The party atmosphere suddenly became awkward. I'd always been able to create an uncomfortable situation, regardless of what I said. But when I spoke at that moment, I truly felt like I needed to change my panties before dawn. And I didn't want to go to the protagonist's house just to become some temporary prop for her to collect. When I was about to leave, bag in hand, the woman said something behind my back. Like she was improvising, maybe. 'Hey, I have a lot of new panties at my house!' I ran away blindly. It felt like she and her new panties were chasing me. I knew how the conversation about me back at the bar would go. My fellow cast members would be saying, 'What the heck?' and, 'She's definitely the kind of person who would do that sort of thing.' And then, just as quickly, they'd move on to talk about something else. Taxis zipped by on the road. Sort of like, they, well, like they were erasers erasing everything on the road, they were going like that. I hailed an eraser. And I shouted."

The woman's story suddenly stopped.

"What did you shout?"

"It's been ten minutes. My lips are sealed."

The man rummaged through his bag for coins and found one thousand more won. He held it out to the woman, and the story resumed.

"I don't remember what I shouted. I wasn't even that drunk, but when I opened my eyes, I was already in a room here, and I vaguely remembered the taxi dropping me off in front of the motel the night before."

The man remembered his own first night. That night, when all he'd had to do was open his door to find everything he could need stocked in the full vending machines, he couldn't have imagined staying this long.

"Was snow falling?"

"Well, the first few days were so good that I just stayed inside this room, so I don't actually know if it snowed or not."

"Did you buy something from the vending machines?"

"Yeah. When I opened the door and went out into the hallway, I was surprised to see how many vending machines there were. It's like a display window out there. What really startled me, though, wasn't the vending machines, but the fact that the layout of the building was all too familiar. It looked like the backdrop of a stage I'd once performed on. I didn't know how I'd reentered the play, but I realized that here at least I wouldn't have a minor role. I always played minor roles, you know. An underwear vending machine came by, and I selected a pair of three-thousand-won cotton panties. With that pair of panties, my part changed. I was now the main character. I needed a fresh start. I knew the stage, and I had no audience, no one to say anything to me. Thinking those thoughts made me happy."

The motel, marooned by the snowstorm, was the audience-free set the woman had always dreamed of. She said that she'd never played a starring role until now, not even once. The one time that she'd gotten a supporting role to the lead actress, she'd made a mistake. She had said the lines for another part. It was a mistake that she hadn't made during read-through or rehearsal, but there on stage, she faltered. The lines that she blurted out were what the main character was supposed to say seconds later. Something that could easily be edited out in a TV show or movie, but not here, because this was a play. Her mistake trickled down to the audience. There, it rode on the ensuing waves of confusion before snaking back up to her onstage. The lead had handled the situation by improvising lines that weren't in the script. But the woman couldn't do anything, couldn't say lines that were in the script or lines that weren't, and she just stood there. After that day, the woman found it hard to look her coworkers in the eye, or even to have an audience in front of her.

"Did you know that motels have trends, too? When balloons were popular, I would circle the hallways carrying a balloon. Sometimes couples would call me over and ask me to sing a song. One thousand won for ten minutes. Back then, I did it for more, too. I made good money. After that, butterfly masks were a trend. When I wore one and danced, everyone loved it—even the older men and women. Sometimes, if there wasn't anyone in the hallway, I'd light a firecracker to let them know where I was. Since I was wearing a garter belt and holding a whip, business was a little better than it would have been otherwise—by the way, can you hear what I'm saying?"

The man nodded.

"Strange. For a while now, no one in this place has been able to understand me."

The woman had been beaten once before her ten-minute song ended. A customer struck her as if she were a vending machine that had taken his money and delivered nothing in return. He said the woman's song sounded like static.

"I had no money, so I couldn't go back to a room, and as I circled round and round the hallways, I thought that maybe someone could take me to theirs. But no one would look at me."

The woman was one machine of many going down the conveyor belt, and just as no one asks for cola from a coffee machine, no one asks a machine selling performances to sell her body. What the woman really had to worry about wasn't leering customers but a lack of them.

"I was forced to suspend my business," she said. "You can't keep an unprofitable vending machine for long. So I had to quit. I realized then that this place wasn't a stage, it was reality, and reality wasn't dictated by a script. A play was just an hour or so, but I had been going on for who knows how long."

"Those props you used, like the butterfly mask. Do you still have them?" the man asked. The woman pulled a bag from a corner. Out of it came a firecracker, a butterfly mask, an uninflated balloon, a whip, and a garter belt. The only thing she hadn't purchased was a rope. When she went to buy one—any kind, thick or thin—they were already all sold out. The inside of the woman's bag was a sort of second Fantastic Love. The man looked at the fossil-like butterfly mask, whip, and other items for a long time.

The woman stopped telling her story. The stage may not have needed a heater, but real life did. There, she'd been illuminated whenever the lights hit her, but now she had to turn the lights on and off by herself when she needed them. There were good acoustics in the theater, but not here. And when she had performed in the past, she acted in a room with an audience, but here the CCTV recording in the hallway was all there was. This wasn't theater after all, but reality, a tragedy in which she'd thought her entire life was a play. When the man started to root around in his pocket again, the woman held out the two thousand won she had received just a little while ago.

"Today, let's just say I bought time from you."

To be more accurate, they both had bought time from each other. The man lay on the bed. The ceiling was low, so it felt stuffy. The room spanned seventy centimeters all told, and the mattress lay thirty centimeters above the ground. As he lay down, his nose almost touched the plaster above. The woman turned off the lights. Under the cover of darkness, it was difficult to judge how much space there was. The room expanded in the blackness. If you turned the light off and closed your eyes, the ceiling, one-third the regular height, grew to infinity. It was nice to not be alone in the dark.

A few days later, they moved to a room with an even lower ceiling. The height of the room was one-fourth what was normal, so it was a good room to lie down in. If you lay prone, your head wouldn't bump into anything, and there was no need to stoop until your spine warped. But because the room was so good for lying down, some people who went in would come out unable to walk very well. Their bodies had been molded to fit the room. When they moved, they'd crawl on all fours, or they'd stretch their arms out like feelers and sweep the floor with their butts and thighs. The man and woman were now such veterans they could slide their bodies across a bed of gravel. At some point, the man began to stroke the woman's rounded back. Her spine was gone. It didn't look like a back, but rather like the stomach of an expectant mother approaching delivery.

The walls diminished into nonexistence as rooms grew cheaper and higher up. The man and woman were now surrounded on all four sides by partitions as flimsy as a stage set. Here, everyone had to roll their back up like a ball to move even a little. The man and woman overheard some of their neighbors say that it wasn't that the ceiling was too low: their own bodies were too long. Others said the problem was that their backs were too stiff. Of course, this was all just chatter that crept through the walls. One day, though, it sounded as if someone was purposefully sending a signal. They pressed their ears against the wall the sound was coming from. It was a rhythmical ringing.

. .—. /. .—. /. /.

Something like Morse code was coming through the wall, as if someone were trying to send a message. The sound continued for a bit and then stopped. After the first message ended, they continued to hear occasional tapping. Even if it were Morse code, they couldn't decipher it. Still, the act of listening was meaningful, so they enthusiastically leaned toward the wall. They would sometimes bang the wall with a cup, too. Without knowing the meaning of what message they were sending, or even what letters they might be hitting against the wall, they tried to communicate.

One morning, someone flung their body out the window like a shooting star, and after that, there was no Morse code to be heard. They didn't know if that someone, shrieking in midair, was committing suicide or attempting to fly, but the first thing they did after hearing the offbeat thud that followed was firmly close the double-pane windows. After closing all the windows, they got under the covers. They weren't sure if the fallen person was male or female, young or old. But they did know that the moment that person had thrust their body into the air, they were finally able to straighten out a back and knees made crooked by the motel's tiny rooms. Even if only for a second.

The thing they feared more than falling was ascension. Falling left traces on the ground, but when you rose into the heavens, up and up, until you were just a speck in the sky, there was nothing left behind. They were already so far up that they couldn't see the ground from their window. The man wanted to put the woman, and her bag, inside Fantastic Love and carry them out of the motel. And if the snow had melted, and the road was clear, and he could find his truck and drive down Road 436 back to the city? He'd go to a room where he could put his two feet on the ground and stand up straight. Since the man was taller than the woman, the woman would be able to stand up on two feet right beside him.

At that moment, someone knocked on the door.

Thunk, thunk, thunk.

"If you don't remove your vending machine by tomorrow, the motel will dispose of it. Have a wonderful day."

As soon as it was bright the next day, the man went to the back door of the motel. He remembered that he'd placed the old person's corpse inside Fantastic Love. But when he opened the door to the machine, what was curled up in between the springs wasn't the body of an old person but that of an animal, its spine crumbling from decay. The wild beast had slipped to the bottom, like one of the vending machine's products.

The snow flurries lightened up, little by little. When the man and woman ran out of all the money they had with them, a loan machine showed up again. This one was a little different. Its official name was ID Revocation Machine. It processed requests quickly.

1. Place ID card in slot.
2. After credit evaluation, withdrawal amount will be displayed on screen. Allowable withdrawal amount varies with individual credit score.
3. Press button for lifetime personal information transfer, and cash will be released.
4. ID card will not be returned; ID number will be authorized for external use from moment of cash withdrawal.

The man pulled his ID card out of his wallet. "If money comes out," he said, "let's pick the room with the highest ceiling in the whole motel." The woman also pulled her ID out of her wallet. "Let's eat steak and drink wine in the room with the highest ceiling," she added. Considering that she was mortgaging her entire life, she wanted to spend the money on something special. They pushed their ID cards into the machine, and the cards didn't come out again. All they received was eighty thousand won.

A room with a high ceiling would be too expensive. They calculated that they could manage to stay at the motel only for another day, maybe two. And so they paid for a room even better for lying down than any of the rooms before. It was one-fifth sized. They also bought a razor and nail clippers. They'd decided to tame into neatness everything that had grown too long. With the remaining money, they bought pork belly and vitamins. Lying prostrate, they placed the strips of pork belly on a frying pan. They crunched the bumpy bones between thick layers of fat. The whole room was filled with the sound of munching and crunching. It was only two servings, but no matter how much they ate, there was as much meat on the pan as when they'd started. The man and the woman placed several pieces of blackened, fossilized pork in front of them and lay side by side under the low ceiling. The woman pulled out the bottle of vitamins. They put several pills in their mouths as the label directed and gulped them down. A few tablets of hope fell down their long, tubular throats like shooting stars. Or maybe the tablets were more like crashing stars. On that night when shooting stars crashed down their throats, the two looked out their flat window at the moonless, starless sky until they could look no more.

Mail arrived for them. An envelope contained a bill for a card in the woman's name. Someone had now taken her identity. A few days later, another bill came. Someone else had set up a phone number in the man's name. While the man and woman lay in this narrow coffin, their ID cards had sprouted wings and flown out of the motel in a gust of lies. For some reason, every time a bill arrived, the man's and the woman's pulses quickened, their faces etched with a vague expression somewhere between resignation and ecstasy.

They could hear the sound of their bones adapting to the price of each room as they rolled their bodies into balls to avoid the ever-lower ceilings. They didn't know if this was evolution or atrophy. Anyhow, in their one-sixth–sized room, there was no window, so they couldn't even see the sky. All they could do was lie down. Because there was no furniture and no bedding inside, it was the best room of them all for lying down. Unwelcome mail like bills, past-due invoices, car-seizure notices, obituaries, and other such things flew through their firmly closed door and perished like birds hitting an iceberg. Time accumulated in front of the door like layers of dirt, and their room continued to rise higher and higher off the ground. And when it became so high that there was no way to climb down, it stayed up there like a dot in the sky.

One day, when the snow flurries had grown thin, the ice on the road cracked mightily and revealed what was hiding underneath. Layers of months-old moss were tangled between the cracks. The wing from a frozen bird spat out a necrotic groan. Then someone knocked on the door.

They couldn't tell if the words they'd heard were "Leave the room" or "Leave the building." What was clear was that there was no longer a single square foot of the motel in which they could stay. The woman left her stage, the man left his vending machine, and they both exited the motel. Straightening their curved spines once again felt awkward. They crawled on all fours the whole way down the slope. It was more stable that way, and faster. Their hands were roughened like feet. They could see Road 436 laid out below like tape at a finish line. Road 436, which had been at some point fully cleared, was now lacking more than just cameras and traffic. There was no snow, no trucks, no fallen bodies. The road looked like it had been wiped clean with an eraser.

They motioned wildly to stop one of the cars passing by the motel, racing along with no apparent regard for the speed limit. They waved their arms up and down, made hand gestures, and even stomped their feet. But no car stopped. Their horns honking, the cars flashed by in windstorms of their own making. The louder the man spoke, the larger the woman's hand gestures, the faster the cars.

They saw a passing truck and ran to the middle of the road. The two tried to block the vehicle with their bodies, but it didn't slow down. Man and woman, they lurched up into the wind, then fell onto the road like late-autumn leaves. From their point of view, it looked like the motel had flipped upside down. Up became down, down became up, and the mixed-up scene before them winked.

Someone emerged from the truck and checked on them before getting back in. They hadn't died, but they were no longer human. Unbeknownst to them, the truck driver looked back through his rearview mirror as he drove farther and farther away. He was watching two wild animals lying in the middle of the road, their backs round as balloons, legs thin as whips, eyes dangerous as fireworks. And the "Caution: Wildlife Crossing" sign sticking up from the ground behind them.

"Wildlife crossing zone ahead. Wildlife crossing zone ahead."

The GPS in the truck chirped like a cricket as the vehicle drove away.

6. TIME CAPSULE 1994

In 1994, the people of Seoul wrapped up their city and sent it deep underground, below the neighborhood of Namsangol. What they buried was the evidence of an era, to be unveiled four centuries later for Seoul's thousand-year anniversary. But after fourteen short years, the city's residents have decided to unearth it prematurely. The cover to the Namsangol time capsule is now removed, creating the world's largest and most dangerous manhole.

A crane pulls the time capsule up from a hole in the ground—fifteen meters deep. Rotted before its time, the enormous metal receptacle is carried out on a stretcher, like a hospital patient. The truck onto which it is loaded moves as slowly as a hearse, and several cameras focus on the empty spot where the time capsule once lay. As I cover the hole with a blue cloth, I feel like I'm dressing a wound. Two ginkgo trees stand nearby like mourners: the trees are the only things left on the circular plaza now that the time capsule has been carried away. Because of the recent snowstorm, everything is frozen over, even the walkway between the ginkgos. The wind plays a dirge in the air, and the commemorative slogan carved into the wall—something that begins with the words "Citizens of Seoul"—becomes an epitaph.

The city of Seoul has hurriedly called together everyone involved with the time capsule, but scarcely a third of the people contacted can remember the events of fourteen years ago. Some of them have retired, or moved abroad. Others have died. That's what happened to my predecessor—now he can't even attend the time capsule's untimely funeral. And so a new group of "time capsule managers" has been formed: fifteen or so dedicated volunteers. The group ranges from senior citizens who are so old they hardly remember the creation of the capsule to people who are young enough that, until recently, they didn't know it existed.

The rusty vessel heads not to an emergency room but to a morgue. Or maybe a butcher. The technicians don white gowns and slip thin gloves over their hands; over their faces, they wear masks. Working in the aftermath of the storm, they conserve their breath as much as possible to avoid contaminating the wares they're handling.

The time capsule is shaped like the famous Bosingak Bell, filled with four compartments that slide out of the main structure like drawers in a dresser. As soon as we cut its lock, the innards spill from the capsule like peas from a pod. The tops of the four compartments are covered with rust, just like the outside. The capsule has degraded masterfully, not a single part of it left intact. With its four inner components removed, the structure looks like a womb that has lost its child before the due date.

The section chief presents the cause of death. It's corrosion due to humidity. Recent snows covered the slab above the time capsule and permeated fifteen meters below the ground. The siloxylane meant to block out moisture and foreign substances became a sort of poison instead. With all the acidic substances the sealant was up against, it turned into something that accelerated corrosion. Liquid that seeped into the frame of the time capsule quickly penetrated the nozzle on the outside of the first compartment. Several additional layers of protective coating have been rendered useless by the blizzard.

"See this thing shaped like an icicle?" the section chief asks us. "It's a type of tubular stalactite made from hardened limestone. It's hard and gray, you see. Concrete is usually heavily alkaline, but can corrode in acid rain. This snowstorm has been really acidic, to the point that these welded nozzles are rusty enough for water to leak in."

The section chief emphasizes the word "acidic" as he reads the report. Someone asks a question: "So it corroded even though you used special, high-strength steel?" Another time capsule manager asks: "Didn't you guys do tests before burying the time capsule? I was under the impression that you spent two months performing environmental breakdown tests. Why did this happen if you verified the time capsule's environmental limits?"

"This *is* the limit. It's outside the range of breakdown scenarios we imagined. Isn't that a limit—something beyond what experiments can account for?"

The person who answers isn't the section chief, who's sweating despite the cold. It's the man in charge of welding. He's the same man who was the head welder fourteen years ago.

"Nothing can overcome nature," he continues. "What we applied to the time capsule was a kind of preservative. Do you think a simple measure like that can really stop decay? All it does is delay the corrosion."

After welding the Namsangol time capsule in 1994, he spent the rest of the nineties sealing other moments of history. Burying time capsules was a trend in the years before and after the millennium. Today, capsules large and small rest beneath modest plots of land across the country, vowing to stay underground. Indifferent to this vow, the backhoe crouches down and prepares to dig. In a city dotted with underground metal fortresses that have been planted like landmines, one of the grandest has corroded. Maybe now the other capsules will begin to fall, like dominoes.

Perhaps it's a hollow task, stuffing a container with relics to withstand the passing years. Even now, untold numbers of citizens continue to bury history underground. But a perfect seal against the passage of time is nowhere to be found.

They've placed a "Do Not Enter" sign in front of the plaza, now time capsule–free. But every day, visitors come to the site. People dressed in black stand behind the safety barrier and throw white chrysanthemums over it. Flower vendors have flocked to the front of the plaza. It's only two thousand won for a bouquet to ease the pain caused by the time capsule's corrosion. Maybe the flowers drive away bad omens, too. Couples that used to meet at the circular plaza to kiss until their mouths ran out of saliva now throw flowers at their former hangout. Children who once raced enthusiastically across the plaza's stone surface toss flowers, too.

I was a spectator the day the time capsule was unearthed: a mourner, paying my respects. Water filled the crater where the time capsule had been. People who saw the liquid said that the ground was crying. Was I the only person thinking about funerals when the time capsule was pulled out of the ground? It reminded me of my husband's funeral. There are similarities between a premature death and a capsule that is exhumed before its time.

The streets I used to traverse with my husband are mostly gone—already extinct. The city has changed since he was alive. Namsan Botanical Garden is where we first talked about getting married, but now not even a cornerstone of the garden's main building remains. Our favorite movie theater went through three name changes before finally becoming a sushi restaurant. The café owner who always remembered us retired. The city rumbled with constant redevelopment and renovation, but the neighborhoods my husband and I frequented weren't targets for gentrification. We met at an ambiguous time for the city, just as it was beginning to develop. The streets we explored on dates were never particularly noteworthy. During our excursions, we searched out buildings on the brink of extinction. When we heard that a building was going to be torn down, my husband and I began to long for the place, as if our brains had suddenly filled with previously unknown memories of it. But we didn't want to dwell on memories, we wanted to make them—so we explored, and our destinations were always terminally ill. Businesses and buildings on the brink of death shone on our map like gleaming tombstones. A theater about to shut down and a store holding a closeout sale, a gym that was going to turn into a park, an apartment building to be torn down: as we wandered around these spaces, we didn't know our own future. We couldn't have known that soon one of us would be dead, too.

He and I spent four years together. Four years is such an unfairly short time to be married. My husband was twelve years older than me, so the chances were good that he would die first. But I didn't know that the duration granted to us would be only four years. Because we liked to visit places about to disappear, almost no evidence of my life with him remains. Except for one thing: a child.

When I married my husband, the house he was living in had no thresholds under the doors. I don't know if his ex-wife had removed the thresholds, but the lack of privacy made me uncomfortable. There was a gap of one or two centimeters between the doors and the floor. Light and sound escaped through the gaps each night, and every room in the house became one common space connected by the living room. The day I moved in, I plugged up the threshold beneath the bedroom door before unpacking my bags. I purchased the necessary materials and affixed a board of wood to the floor, then I closed the door tightly once I was done.

You couldn't hide that it was the work of an amateur. The door didn't move smoothly. It resisted when you tried to open it, like something was holding it back, and when it was closed, it blocked sound so well that the bedroom and living room felt stuffy. In order to open the door, you had to twist the doorknob with force. If you didn't, it would feel like the whole wall was going to follow the door, ripping away its framework as you pulled. The construction was certainly shoddy, but there was a reason that I liked the excessively tight threshold. It was because of my husband's daughter.

My husband's daughter lived with us from the age of eight to the age of twelve. After we returned from our honeymoon, the adults in my husband's family set the child in front of me and taught her to call me "Mom." The eight-year-old had spent the first four years of her life with a mother, and the next four without one. She must have been confused by the appearance of another maternal figure. "If it's too difficult to call me Mom, you don't have to," I told her. "Call me Mom if you want." The child nodded when I said this. She wasn't moved by my words, but I was. I was satisfied with myself for not pressuring her.

But before a month had passed, I did pressure the child into something. I trained her to knock, which was much more important to me than using the word "mom."

Looking back, I wasn't simply trying to avoid pushing "mom" on her; I was actively postponing her use of the word. "Knocking" was similarly necessary to postpone a real mother-daughter relationship.

The child was an unwelcome guest in the night. She would fall asleep with the fluorescent lights in her room left on, and music playing. She couldn't stand the house's darkness and quiet, and sometime before dawn, she'd tear out of her room yelling the name I feared: "Mom!" And without the child even realizing it, her footsteps would take her to the master bedroom, where she twisted the doorknob with all her strength. This didn't happen every night—it was intermittent. I could never predict the child's nighttime habits.

The child's outbursts were an old problem that had begun before she came to live with us. During the four years we spent together, *she* wasn't the family member most afraid of the night: that was me. The child's sudden trespassing disconcerted me. I told her that if she wanted to open our bedroom door in the middle of the night, she had to knock. When she asked "Why?" with an innocent expression on her face, I had to tell her that it was good manners. This was a difficult answer for an eight-year-old to accept.

The child didn't knock. Manners belonged to the realm of consciousness, and the girl dashed to our room still half-asleep. I figured there was no way to tear down the border between consciousness and unconscious without repeating myself, so I gave her the same instructions for four years. "When you're in front of bedroom doors at night, you have to knock. If you just pull the door open without knocking, that's bad manners, understand? If you call for Mom, you have to give me time to respond."

A few days each week, I ended up locking the bedroom door before sleep. My husband unbolted the lock only after our post-coital panting slowed. The clunk of the door opening again sounded more provocative than the snap of a bra being unhooked. When the lock was no longer engaged, once there was the danger we might reveal ourselves to the child: that was the most exciting moment for me. But I had no opportunity to relish such excitement. Before the stale air above our bed dissipated, the child would walk in holding a pillow and lie down next to her father.

As years passed, the frequency with which my husband and I locked the door to our bedroom diminished. Two bodies would be lying on our bed, and suddenly two became three, then one of the three got up and it would return to two; the situation repeated over and over. Before darkness brightened into day, the person lying in bed with me would transform into someone younger, a little more delicate, fairer skinned. As I looked at my slight bed partner, outstretched on the mattress, I felt uncomfortable. In the morning, when we lay together on the bed with open eyes, we looked less like mother and daughter and more like sisters with a large age gap.

The section chief gives me twelve files to take care of. My assignment is to restore the damaged videos. The first vessel is the one with the most problems; that's where video materials like CDs and microfilms were stored. I put a CD-ROM from compartment 1 into my computer and press Play. Wealthy Apgujeong youths; unwed teen mothers; Daehangno street scenes; traffic at Gwanghwamun; albums by once-popular singers: carefully selected moments are now marred by dried bubbles and organic matter from the murky water that contaminated the CD. The screen cuts off here and there. In some scenes, it only shows half the image. The disc is sending out dated electromagnetic waves, as if the time capsule were a broken radio.

Approximately 20 percent of the materials in the first compartment is damaged, but even the intact items have to be replaced. Duplicates were prepared fourteen years ago in case the time capsule ever needed to be reburied. Even with the wreckage in front of us, the capsule managers haven't adjusted to the reality of the task at hand. Technology has evolved since the time capsule began its hibernation. Cataloging the historical items that were inside it didn't take long, but now we have to refill the time capsule. We're reevaluating the most important historical relics from the entire year 1994: a clumsy and difficult task. No one ordered us to change the contents in the replacement time capsule, but the public seems to want us to. A list of six hundred evocative mid-nineties artifacts is spreading fast across the internet. As internet users discuss those relics one by one, the public forms a courtroom, deciding for us what to add to the time capsule. They discuss what to do with items that are now associated with scandal, like CDs containing songs exposed as works of plagiarism. Some have even curated six hundred entirely new pieces to go in the time capsule. "If what we believed to be the truth in 1994 wasn't actually the truth, don't we have to get rid of it?" That's what they've said. Others have asked what we will do if the truth of 2008 turns out to be a lie, and the truth we knew in 1994 was the *real* truth. There are slight differences between 1994 as we remember it now and 1994 as we lived it. The now-broken time capsule doesn't betray an awareness of the differences.

People hope to discover something magnificent in the grave of this mummy exhumed prematurely from its four-hundred-year entombment. Maybe a video of a test-tube baby, only the baby has transformed into a real infant, its heart beating with energy absorbed fifteen meters below ground. Or an unidentified hair that's grown as long as Rapunzel's and now forms a rope that leads deep into the earth. Or an empty tomb that's already been scavenged and left to implode into dust. But fourteen years isn't enough time for real legends to grow.

It isn't the cry of a baby or Rapunzel's hair, but one unexpected item does surprise us: a CD that plays nothing but a quiet screen for eighteen minutes. The nameless disc isn't among the list of relics, and it's not a copy of something either. No one remembers what the CD originally contained, and no one can explain how an artifact not on the list was put in the capsule. Something that shouldn't have been in the time capsule has come out of it. I play the empty CD again. My computer screen tries hard to process something—anything—but there's nothing for it to read.

The screen plays only darkness for a good while, but I start to make out light and shadow and patterns inside the obscurity. I play the CD for a second time in hopes of something new appearing. Instead of paying attention to the video, though, my mind begins to flip through images on the far side of my own memory.

"What do you think is going to appear?"

The child said that if I turned the light off in her room before she fell asleep, she'd worry something would show up in the dark. She said she was scared. I told her several times, "You are the owner of this room. There's not a single thing in here to be afraid of." Thinking back on what I'd told her, it now seems like I was warning her: "This is your room—don't leave." If I closed the child's bedroom door and moved to walk away, she'd ask me through the door to flip the light on—it was scary, she said. Finally, I would turn on a table lamp that shut off automatically after fifteen minutes, then I'd close the door again. Out of necessity, the child fell asleep before the light disappeared. But she often woke up in a fit of anxiety just before daybreak, crying in distress as she ran out of the room. When I found the child and grabbed her to ask what was wrong, the answer was always the same: it seemed like there was something in the dark.

Even though nothing had appeared, the girl was terrified by the thought that something might. When I asked my husband if he thought she should see a child psychologist, he flinched. "Other than the fact that she can't sleep alone, she's a completely normal child: Why stir up trouble?" As if she'd heard our conversation, the child didn't wake up early for the next few days. The fluorescent lights in her room shone brightly until morning. Underneath them, the child slept, bloodshot eyes hidden beneath her closed eyelids.

The CD with almost nothing on it stops abruptly. How am I supposed to record this unrecorded object, discovered fourteen years after it was buried without a name? The CD may not officially exist, may not have an official label, but here it is. When I tell the section chief that I've come across a CD that doesn't play anything, he asks, "What number is the item?"

There's no way this thing has a serial number, or any other number to record its existence.

"In the documents we have, there's a list detailing the collection, you know. The CD's not there?" The section chief looks at the empty CD, devoid of content and absent from the list, for a long time. "Is there a copy?"

"No," I reply. "But it did come from the dig site."

The unaccounted-for CD is a surprise to the section chief when I tell him about it. But he doesn't nervously shiver in response; he just continues to sweat like always. The section chief drips with sweat even in the cold. "Follow the list," he tells me. "Use that as your guide and get rid of anything that's in the time capsule and not on the list. Only put the recorded items in the time capsule." The chief did multiple interviews with the media after the capsule's corrosion was broadcast to the public. Dogged by the press, he's grown experienced; he knows how people might react to the discovery of this misfit artifact. "The CD's blank—throw it out, and put it somewhere separate from the rest of the garbage, cause if someone rummages through our trash, it's gonna be a real pain."

I nod as I turn around to walk away, and the section chief repeats his instructions. "These documents are our guide, the answers to any questions we might have. Keep what's on the list and throw away anything else, got it?"

The documents contain answers that make me doubt 1994. The papers are their own form of time capsule, linking the present with the fourteen-year-distant past. The empty CD isn't in the records, so it never really existed at all. The CD goes into my drawer. Eighteen minutes of fourteen years—minutes for which our documents cannot account—enter a black hole of darkness.

As the section chief instructs, I place the damaged videos on a red cloth. I take a few photos with my camera. After I record the original relics, they become trash that I can throw away. Copies are now the originals. "It feels like we're taking police pictures of criminal evidence," the section chief says.

After commemorating the final moments of these criminal items on film, we discard them, through a seven-step process. People initially expressed interest in taking items formerly inside the time capsule home with them, but the desire has quickly waned. Fourteen years is too short a time, they think, for something to become valuable.

I take the empty CD out of its case, and it lights up my face with its glittering surface. My expression is reflected on the disc's surface. It shakes when I hold the CD at different angles. Surely, unreadable video material like this must contain a story. We just can't know what.

I still sometimes think about the last weekend my husband and I spent together. I can hear the child turning the doorknob to our room. It sounded like a mouse gnawing on sharp metal. The child grabbed the knob and slowly turned. The locked door squeaked. Why was I the only person who ever heard her? I wrapped my arms around my husband's neck and blocked his ears with my body heat. I heard the child calling, "Mom," in a feeble voice. I pulled my husband inside of me. The child couldn't enter the room. I had to hide my husband somewhere she couldn't knock, somewhere her knocking wouldn't reach. I was struggling to reach such a place when the door opened. The reverberations of the child's thumping broke the vacuum seal inside our room, and everything in the bedroom began to squeeze through the doorway into the living room.

The next morning, only two occupants, both female, remained in the bed. The mattress was stained with blood, but it wasn't mine. As soon as the child woke up, I asked her how the blood had gotten there. Of course, she didn't know. We'd first met when the child was eight: I was supposed to have acted like her mother. But I'd forgotten my role, and that was why the child didn't know what was happening. I hadn't been able to do what other mothers did. I hadn't warned her, "If this kind of thing happens, don't be startled, just tell me—it's only natural." That morning, when my head was a mishmash of confusion, I realized that it wasn't the child who feared the surprise of a first period, it was me. Embarrassment kept me from looking into the child's eyes. My inability to make eye contact alerted me of my embarrassment.

That day, I spent a long time shopping after work, as if I were buying things in preparation for the holidays. I knew I was dealing with the issue belatedly. I started with period panties, then looked at various types of pads, then even checked out aromatics oils and patches to stick on your stomach to alleviate cramps. As I bought items that I'd never used myself, I realized something. If I gave the child her hygiene products without any discussion, I'd probably be conveying the wrong message. I'd be telling her, "Don't make the house smell like your period. Don't *have* a period." When the child took the box full of products from me, she made a face like it was homework. Each month, she used a small number of items, leaving no trace, as if she were a cat.

Women who live in the same house end up syncing hormones. Cycles are highly contagious. If my husband hadn't died, the child and I might have ended up with the same bodily rhythms. But my husband's cancer cells moved faster than the hormones of two women. They say that pancreatic cancer is the one that progresses fastest from diagnosis to death.

My husband was the sole point at which I intersected with the child, and after he died, things became very awkward between us. As soon as the funeral ended, the child's aunt took her away, like I wasn't the only one aware of the awkwardness. But no one in my husband's family acted with any hostility: the many relatives I met at the funeral were sympathetic.

After the funeral was over, I slept for several days in a row. Funerals are more for those still alive than they are for the dead. Those of us left on earth need some sort of gateway where we bid our farewell to the deceased, as they cross over into a new world.

Four days later, I awoke alone in what had once been a bed for two and sometimes three. I didn't sit up; I turned over and held my nose close to my husband's pillow. It emanated the child's scent. I turned the blanket over and saw several of the child's hairs spread across it.

Those four days gave me time to resurrect myself, but little changed afterward. When I got out of bed and went through the doorway, into the hall, I faltered, even though no one was blocking me. The only thing on the floor below my wavering steps was the clumsily installed threshold, lying there impassively.

I hadn't seen it, but I could imagine it well enough. In the scene I envisioned, the child neatly disposes of all evidence of her period: she places the evidence in a black sack, then in another plastic bag, then, because she can't find a trash can at home that's beyond my gaze, she throws it away outside. I couldn't find a place to throw out the empty CD, so I carried it in my bag: it's similar to what I imagine the child did. Maybe, for the child, reaching womanhood meant becoming a criminal who had to destroy the evidence of her crime for one week each month. A first period was a flare signal indicating the start of a lengthy crime, and I'd taught her to feel ashamed of it.

The child threw away her period waste outside the house because she couldn't do it inside. I don't know how to throw things away, either. Instead of ridding myself of unwanted possessions above the earth's surface, I dispose of them beneath the ground. In 1994, when the Namsangol time capsule was under construction, I cried for days, sobbing until my ears hurt as the four compartments inside the vessel were being completed. My ear-paralyzing cries grew louder and louder, and fireworks at the construction site flared above welding metal while a burning smell tinged the air. That was when I began to believe in time capsules. A tight seal relaxes people: credibility is proportional to tightness.

I set the first compartment on my worktable, and in its place I put copies of the original relics. One other person surveys the compartment alongside me. All he does is read the names and serial numbers stuck to the surfaces of the replacement video equipment. Standing on the other side of the table, he gives me a thumbs-up after checking the requisite labels. The first compartment is full. We place it inside a sterilizer and raise the temperature. Fifty degrees Celsius takes care of microorganisms and mold. Inside the metal frame lies the year 1994, fully restored. The discarded empty CD rests between other items held in the compartment. Sterilization isn't going to recover the CD's original contents. The truth is, we don't know what on the disk was damaged, so it's a bit awkward to say that there's anything to "recover" in the first place. I didn't know how to destroy the CD above ground, so I let it linger in my bag for several days before sending it fifteen meters below the earth's surface.

No one is suspicious about the secret addition. No one would imagine that nothing is on the CD. As the section chief has instructed, all we need to worry about is whether or not something's on the list. A serial number has been boldly added to the list's newest addition: an unidentifiable, unfixable CD, labeled "restored."

The time capsule hugs all four of its compartments tight. We fasten the nozzles. As the capsule undergoes dozens of X-rays, invisible light claws at it. Now the time capsule really is restored.

After losing her father at the age of twelve, the child spent two years living with her aunt. The child fit into the family very well during those two years, like she was a piece of furniture that had been a part of their home for a long time. Or maybe she wasn't an especially good match in the aunt's house: maybe the child was like furniture that would have matched the décor in any home. But after two years, the girl ran away, still dressed in her school uniform when she fled.

The child had told her relatives that she was going to find "Mom," so the aunt contacted me. "The child's run away from home—she said she wanted to see her mom." Neither the child's aunt nor I had a clear idea of who that mom was. This was six months ago. The girl must not have found her mother yet. That's because she doesn't know her biological mother's number, nor mine since I changed it.

According to her aunt, the child had no problems sleeping at her new home. She didn't sleep with the lights on, and she didn't cry out at night. Her aunt says that she never came into the master bedroom carrying a pillow, or stepping noiselessly so you couldn't tell if she was really there or not. The child always slept with her bedroom door locked and woke up before her aunt.

I was the person who couldn't fall asleep then. From the day I heard about the child running away, I slept fitfully. The girl was knocking. She knocked at the cracks in my sleep. She squeezed between my dreams, entered them, and took up a corner of my king-size bed. She lay there with her body curled up like a dog at its owner's feet. And before morning, she squeezed herself out of my restless sleep and departed.

Maybe what I needed to do was leave the house. It wasn't easy falling asleep and waking up each day alone, in a house where three people once lived together. Everything looked just like it had before: the structure of the home, and all the furniture, remained unchanged. The only thing that differed now was that the house was under my name, but I still had the feeling that I was freeloading. The fact that my husband's ex-wife had chosen some of the furniture weighed on my mind. The wallpaper felt damp, and the small stains on the floor irritated me. I had the uncomfortable feeling that someone else's fingerprints were on the water faucet and gas valve that I'd touched without issue over the past four years. The discomfort was like SARS: it spread from contact. One day, when I turned the doorknob and felt a mysterious body heat lingering on it, I decided to change everything: the faucet, the toilet seats, and all the light switches.

After throwing away a bunch of household goods—one here, two there—I finally disposed of the king-size bed. When I threw it out, I saw that a huge spring at one corner had collapsed. In the empty lot behind the apartment, sitting between items that had passed their prime, the bed looked shabby. A strange wind blew through the crooked spring.

I went down to the empty lot again a few days later and saw that my furniture was now a part of someone else's home. As night fell, several cats stepped through the door of an old wardrobe that had become their domicile. The discarded cushions around me had absorbed the smell of the street like a sponge. Beds separated into mattress and frame stood stooped, like clumsy walls blocking the wind. I couldn't tell if anything among the rubbish was mine.

There's a bed at home that definitely *is* mine. A bed that's all mine: that no one else has touched. The twin bed still emanates the smell of newness, and it's so narrow that you feel like you're in a coffin when you lie on it. As the night deepens, the mattress loses its plumpness and grows thin as newsprint under the weight of my body. Only after the sun rises does it swell up again. Time passes like it's a musical score. I have countless bars to play even in the dark, and sometimes I'm out of breath as I try to read the notes. Maybe this is the path the child walked alone each night. Maybe she walked and walked until she was swept up in a passionate beat, until she had to push open my door without even a knock—all in order to make it through a single bar of music. This nocturnal path allows for no stops, no braking.

The child began to appear and then disappear all over the place. I didn't know the color or pattern of her uniform, but whenever I saw a middle school student in a school uniform, the child's face was superimposed above the student's body. Holes lingered in the air after the child vanished, holes shaped like the squares of plaid on her uniform skirt. Before I knew it, the threads of the child's uniform were sewing together patches of air all around me.

I lie on my narrow, coffin-like bed and think. Why can I still not leave this house? Why haven't I even changed the code to the front door? One of the three people who knew the password has died, and another has disappeared. I'm still here, the only witness to the past. Being the only earthly witness to our family's history is more than I can handle. Lifting such a burden off my shoulders should be simple. All I have to do is change a few numbers, but for some reason, I keep putting off the task. I don't want to admit it, but I'm waiting for the girl to return home.

The day the circular plaza opens again, several other time capsules throughout the city are revealed to have corroded as well, like land mines exploding one after another. In spite of the news, we bury the replacement time capsule—and a few new ones, too—deep underground. The capsules descend fifteen meters, unaccompanied by music or the traditional parade, a congratulatory speech from the president, commemorative tree plantings, or boisterous cheers. It's just members of the press, clicking their camera shutters. Several people take turns filling a shovel full of dirt and tossing it on top of the time capsule. Once the tomb is sealed, I see someone milling about around the stone above the time capsule. It's another witness, someone who shares a secret with me: the child. The girl slowly fades away until I can't see her anymore. She sparkles somewhere between the many numbers carved into the chunk of stone above the time capsule.

From the outside, the circular plaza looks like a tomb. To get to it, you have to walk through a stone passage that resembles a casket for an enormous snail. At the end of the passage, what appears is a space that looks like a moon crater, with the time capsule buried beneath it. There's no sound inside, no wind, not even gravity. Even time moves slowly here. It's like a crater formed by an ancient meteor, unchanged for millions of years.

The two ginkgo trees on the plaza turn their backs against each other. Or maybe they just happen to be standing back to back, with only air in between. It seems like you could plummet into this place, and the fall would somehow shoot you into the distant future. You might stay here until you become a corpse, an eternal mummy. And maybe timid monologues or uncertain propositions spoken inside this stone depression could become vows, made of letters carved deeply into the surrounding walls.

If I place my ears against the slab, I can hear the child walking toward me. The child wears a middle school uniform; she looks at the slab and tries to read letters that she cannot decipher. The child asks me, "Is this a code?" The fine lettering carved into the stone lists the names of cities that sent Korea notes of congratulations when the time capsule was buried. There are also signatures from important people commemorating the freezing of time. The letters stretch in all four directions—north, south, east, west. The child asks, "How deep is it, the time capsule?" When I tell her that it's fifteen meters below ground, she gasps.

"I, I knocked when I entered," she says.

My chest sinks. There's no need to knock here. This place doesn't have a door.

The girl speaks again. "I knocked because you're here, Mom."

With those words, I'm completely disarmed. The child is watching me.

"I have to knock if you're around, Mom, so you'll have time to answer."

The girl's wrists and ankles are exposed as she says this. Her clothing is now much too short—my heart may have grown still since her disappearance, but the child has continued to grow.

"Aren't you cold?" I ask.

"I'm not cold, but I'm tired. I want to sleep."

I climb onto the stone first and lie down. What I can see of the sky is round, as big as the circular plaza. The child climbs onto the stone after me. We fall asleep separated by a distance, a distance where knocking and thresholds and locks are unnecessary. To the child, this craterlike slab of stone is somehow a comfortable cradle. In this tomb where everything is frozen, only the child grows. The girl ages like she has progeria, until her height exceeds the diameter of the stone. Even so, I still detect the innocent scent of ice cream emanating from her body. We sleep like we aren't going to wake up for four hundred years. When I do wake up, there's nothing but darkness left in the child's place.

The space where we were lying is as quiet as the eye of a hurricane. I lean an ear against the cold slab. My heart thumps. I feel a strange orgasmic pulsation: probably my heartbeat pounding inside me.

7. ICELAND

Guidebooks didn't have plots. What they did have were foreign place-names, littered throughout their pages like puzzle pieces. It was the reader's role to make a story out of the names. That's why I liked guidebooks. Last week, I'd read Japan. It took me one week to go from Fukuoka to Hokkaido. The week before, I'd read Russia. I rode the Trans-Siberian Express between Vladivostok and Moscow. Today, it was time for me to read Iceland. My trip, which took place for one hour each night, required a bookmark instead of a suitcase. Apart from my imaginary vacations, I'd never actually ventured beyond the borders of Korea. I had no real need to.

Iceland was a country of emptiness. Its area was similar to that of South Korea, but little of the land was inhabitable. Because it was so far north, the guide told me, Iceland was sometimes absent from world maps. Iceland: a land casually omitted from the earth, like the invisible words following an ellipsis at the end of a sentence. A country located on a fault line, where volcanoes exploded as if they were fireworks. And lastly, a country with an ill-fitting name, thanks to greedy Vikings who wanted to deter visitors. I imagined that if I traveled to Iceland, I too would vanish, with only my footsteps remaining behind like the periods of an ellipsis.

I set my sights on Iceland after learning about a website. It was a site where users could take a quiz to learn their compatibility with the country of Korea. The website also informed users which other countries might be more suitable for them. After answering 120 questions, I learned that my match with Korea was not good: only 2.3 percent. I don't know what the test's criteria were, but according to its results, I had spent over thirty years living in a country I didn't fit into at all.

Did my poor results indicate a simple problem between me and Korea, or a broader problem between me and the world? There was no need to waste time worrying. The website that judged my Korean-ness—its name was Laundry—had another test in which it assigned participants an alternate nationality, from a more compatible country. Perhaps there were others like me, because Laundry always had a high number of "users online." If you took the second test, the website would select a country for you like a doctor selecting the appropriate treatment for their patient. I answered nearly two hundred more questions and was informed that my country was Iceland.

It was a 42.5 percent match, a greater percentage than I had with any other country on earth. It was twenty times higher than the number for the country in which I was currently living. My body and mind were worn out after years of trying to satisfy the demands of this country. I'd had to jump over hurdle after hurdle, interconnected like the links of a sausage. I'd made it through the unemployment crisis and gotten a job, but I still questioned my quality of life. Considering my constant worry, the answer was clear: "2.3 percent" was nothing more than sheet music that made visible the disharmonious symphony I'd begun to hear long ago.

"Who does this website think it is, telling us whether or not we should leave for another country?" asked my coworker Kim from behind the partition that separated our desks.

Kim quickly found himself just as ensnared by Laundry as I was. Kim was destined for Jamaica. He didn't know if Jamaica was in Africa or America, but after receiving the verdict that Jamaica was his match made in heaven, he noticed connections to the country everywhere. He began to plan his daily life around the assumption that he'd eventually travel there. Perhaps he thought that if he went to this perfect match of a country, everything from his personal relationships to his health would improve. Maybe all test takers attached such hopes to their new countries. If not, there would be no way to explain why people filled out fifty-question application forms to become members of groups like Café Iceland.

Café Iceland was an online meeting place for those who dreamed of Iceland, where Icelandophiles curious about everything from travel to immigration could exchange information. You could see how exclusive a website it was from the moment you first visited. The fifty-question membership application was your first obstacle. The application had several functions. It made the people filling out the form—those intent upon becoming Café members—list their workplace, age, address, car ownership status, the model of any car they owned, their salary, and the type of work they did. They had to share all sorts of personal information, even if the answers they provided were lies. The application also had the function of making prospective members reflect upon their present circumstances. Such an unpleasant and chaotic application procedure made them ask themselves, do I *really* need to join Café Iceland? After completing the questionnaire, each new member of the Café enjoyed the satisfaction of having broken through a barrier, fulfilling the application's third purpose.

Once I'd answered all fifty questions, I received membership approval from the administrator. But all I could see of the exclusive forum was the main page, decorated with a large image of a glacier, and a message board for new members to introduce themselves. I didn't read any of the introductions. To gain permission to read posts on the website, I had to confront a second, hundred-question quiz. The questions in this next quiz were so personal that I felt uncomfortable answering them. They asked about hobbies, marital status, relationship status, what I thought about pets, my taste in food; even the questions that seemed friendly, or were simple to answer, attacked without hesitation. They were a requirement to level up as a Café member. Further questions interrogated me about what kind of music I liked, my hobbies (again), what I would do if I were dropped onto a desert island, my ideal partner, and how I'd describe myself in one word. Only after making it through all the questions could I meet the ten or so other Café members who'd forged down the same path.

The members were a diverse group. Gender, hometown, age, job: none of us were exactly alike, but we all dreamed about the life of the common Icelander. Our sense of kinship began with the fact that we'd all completed Café Iceland's pesky questionnaires. It was proof of our belief in the country. No online forum had ever seemed as necessary to me as Café Iceland did. I already felt closer to Iceland after completing the two-step process to join. The last thing to do was get permission to write posts. For that, I first had to comment at least twenty times on other people's posts.

As I clicked around, I noticed a pop-up box in the corner of the page. I read what it said: "It's easy to go to Iceland, but becoming a citizen is difficult."

Whenever he had time, Kim logged on to Laundry, took the country quiz again, and expressed doubts about his most recent match. His country was no longer Jamaica, as the results changed each time he took the quiz.

"You know what's funny?" he said. "Yesterday I got Tibet, but today I got Malaysia. My results are as unpredictable as the weather."

Kim had been matched with thirty-four distinct nationalities over the past week. All you had to do was answer a few questions differently, and the resulting country wasn't the only thing that would change—you'd find yourself on an entirely new continent. When Kim took Laundry's country quiz, he was essentially twirling a globe and pointing to a random spot with his finger. His nationalities were all over the place. But my taste in countries wasn't as broad, so every time I took the test, I got Iceland.

Our boss was unpredictable, like Kim—as fickle as Icelandic weather. Every day his goals for the team changed, as did his assessment of employee efforts. The boss had one body, but three personalities—and at times four or even five. Sometimes it was the first of these personalities explaining how he would judge our progress, sometimes it was the second, and other times the third. There was even a rumor that the boss was actually a set of quintuplets who took turns coming into work. Like Kim had forecast, today's boss was the third quintuplet, a different one from yesterday. The third quintuplet had the sourest temper. I wanted to leave for Iceland as soon as possible.

The first time I attended an offline Café Iceland meeting, I was surprised by the appearance of the other attendees. Café Iceland members were sophisticated and elegant, notwithstanding their howls on the message board about wanting the world to forget them. They had their problems: some of the members had been questioned by the police when walking around Gwanghwamun, just because of where they were going and the clothing they wore. Others were estranged from their families. Still others had to pretend they weren't aware that they had no friends at work, even though they were more conscious of it than anyone. But it was hard to find a true loser among the attendees in this Buam-dong café. I somewhat regretted how plainly I'd dressed. I did receive the most attention at the meeting, but that was because I was a newbie. The other members asked about my first impression of Iceland. "It's a cold country," I said.

"That's what people usually think, but it's not that cold," someone replied. "Thanks to the Gulf Stream, it's pretty much heaven compared to other countries at the same latitude."

"There's warm water flowing beneath the ground, too," someone else added. "Icelanders use the water for heating. Oh, and Reykjavík was voted the cleanest city in the world. Have you heard that before?"

"Summer is the optimal season to visit," a third member advised. "People say that May to September is the best travel time, but what they mean is that you can't go to Iceland any other time of the year. June is my favorite month in Iceland. The weather's so inconsistent that sometimes you can see all four seasons in one day."

The members took turns speaking. Not many of them had actually been to Iceland, but they knew an awful lot about the country, and they liked to talk about it.

"There's still no Korean guidebook to Iceland," the organizer of the meeting said. "All we've been able to find is an English-language Lonely Planet guide. This is what we'll have to use for now."

The organizer had translated the Lonely Planet guide into Korean. He'd also gotten information from the Norwegian embassy, which represented Icelandic consular interests, and bound it into a book. We had 128 pages of materials. According to the organizer, who'd been to Iceland six times, the country was losing its primitive nature as it developed commercially, but it was still mostly unblemished by humans. Long ago, when the Vikings discovered the virgin land, they'd given it the name

"Iceland" to make it seem like it was a place of snow and ice. The Vikings had circulated lies. Glaciers made up less than 15 percent of the country. The members of Café Iceland discussed the Vikings' greed and decided that we were no less selfish. *Our* exclusiveness and *our* particularity about new members came from a desire to keep Iceland to ourselves. For our next gathering, we decided to meet at Heyri Art Village in Paju.

There was a long, thin gap in the middle of Iceland, a fault line between two tectonic plates. As magma squeezed out of the fault line and hardened, the island nation slowly widened in area. The magma added only 0.6 to 1 centimeter of land per year, but if it continued, Iceland would someday reach the peninsula of Scandinavia. Just like the actual country, the Iceland inside my body was also widening little by little. At first, Iceland hadn't meant anything at all to me. When I learned that I was a 42.5 percent match with the country, Iceland was merely a curiosity. But once I'd answered 150 questions to become a member of Café Iceland, the country's name began to sound like a rallying cry, and as I frequented the Café, that cry grew louder.

Through my study of Iceland, I began to understand why Laundry had assigned me to the country. For someone sensitive to heat like myself, Iceland—with an average summer temperature of eleven degrees Celsius—was paradise. It was the only European country with a birth rate above two, which corresponded with my desire to have lots of kids. I also liked the fact that there wasn't a single McDonald's or Starbucks in the entire country. Iceland had been identified as the nation that read more books than any other, and that was appealing. It wasn't bad, either, that they used the same electrical current and outlets as Korea. And since I feared alkaline water, I found it charmingly comforting that their tap water was safe to drink. In many parts of Iceland, the speed limit was fifty kilometers per hour, so the country needed drivers like me who didn't know how to press down on the accelerator. A country where work wasn't compulsory, but less than 1 percent of the population was unemployed: that was Iceland. There was no need to worry about after-school tutoring for one's children, either. In this beautiful country, citizens invested over 7 percent of their gross national product in education. Pensions for seniors were significantly higher than in Iceland's neighboring countries, Norway and Canada. Medical care was completely free, and all media remained unrestricted by government censorship. As you lived your simple Icelandic life, you'd probably even see glaciers, whisked down from the North Pole on the East Greenland Current. I realized that I hadn't chosen Iceland: Iceland had chosen me. I was the ideal Icelandic citizen—even if I was currently marooned somewhere less appealing.

Iceland hadn't moved: I had. I drifted toward Iceland like a North Pole glacier, like an ocean current. Each time Café Iceland convened, I had to pay fifty thousand won in membership dues, sometimes more, but I didn't feel like I was wasting money. Iceland began to make frequent appearances in my credit card statements. I bought every album by Björk and the famous Icelandic band Sigur Rós, as well as the documentary *Heima*, about Sigur Rós. I purchased the DVD of *The Lord of the Rings*, too, because Tolkien's fictional land of Mordor was modeled after Iceland. I also went online and bought traditional Icelandic snacks and makeup made from hot-springs minerals. I looked for works by artists who were from Iceland, creatively inspired by Iceland, or residents of Iceland. I spent time and money buying their wares and hoped I'd eventually remember their long Icelandic names. Thankfully, my brain was just as addicted to Iceland as my credit card, ready to be activated the moment I heard something related to the country.

The problem wasn't Iceland, it was here. The boss tested my patience with his finicky nature. At some point, everything he said to me started to sound like a foreign language. I had no way to know if this was happening only to me or to everyone in the office. Actually, I was sure Kim still comprehended him. But me—I would listen to what the boss said, but I couldn't understand it. I overlaid Iceland on top of every word that came out of his mouth. Hvannadalshnúkur: that was Iceland's tallest mountain. Vatnajökull: a glacier as wide as all the glaciers on the continent of Europe combined. Þórsá: the longest river in Iceland. Reykjavík: Iceland's beautiful capital. It was a placid city whose only tall building was Hallgrímskirkja, a church that resembled a volcano. As I listened to my incomprehensible boss, I memorized the names of every place listed on a map of Iceland. I knew that if I were there, in Iceland, I wouldn't suffer from the discord I felt here. I'd at least feel 42.5 percent comfortable, instead of 2.3 percent. My boss's utterances sounded like unfamiliar place-names that I had yet to memorize.

On the way home from work, I considered how I'd get around during my trip to Iceland. I would take a Korean airline to the country, and once I was there, I could purchase a bus tour package, buy a bus pass, rent a four-wheel-drive vehicle, or hitchhike. I almost forgot to get off at my subway station as I debated between the tour package and the bus pass. When planning a vacation to Iceland, the timing of the trip—summer or fall—merited serious deliberation, despite what my fellow Café members had told me. Weather was clear and bright in the summer, and the midnight sun meant you could see the ocean in the middle of the night. It was also peak travel season. Once autumn began, Iceland froze over until it felt like a real Northern European country. Almost all the tourist attractions were closed in the fall, but the country was less crowded with visitors, and you could see auroras. I debated between summer's midnight sun and the autumn auroras. I didn't have to make an immediate decision, but I enjoyed pondering my options while I put off a verdict.

Café Iceland's ten initial members had increased twofold, maybe threefold. Even my coworker, Kim, who'd tried out every country from Jamaica to Malaysia, followed me in joining Café Iceland. Kim had simultaneously joined forums for several other countries, but he said that Iceland's exclusivity appealed to him. Kim still mixed up Ireland and Iceland, but it wasn't a big problem. The organizer of our meetings decided to arrange a pop quiz to narrow down the number of members. The quiz took place with thirty participants in a quiet teahouse in Samcheong-dong. The organizer had written almost sixty questions, and we spent an hour answering them. Most of the questions asked general information about Iceland. I got eight wrong—questions about Iceland's climate, pension system, traffic laws, and glacier tours. Thankfully, I was allowed to maintain my membership. Kim also barely made it.

Iceland tended not to welcome immigrants. You could receive permanent residency if you were hired for a job there, worked in an Icelandic branch office of a foreign company, married a local, studied at an Icelandic university, or cohabited with an Icelander, but it wasn't easy. Of course, even though Iceland had fewer than 310,000 *citizens*, anyone with a certain amount of money and time could visit. But Koreans could stay for only ninety days. After those ninety days, you had to pack your bags or find a reason to remain in the country. For this reason, I was surprised to learn that Koreans lived in Iceland. The organizer decided to recruit one such Korean Icelander, who was on a brief trip back home, to talk to us. We had to pay, but we all wanted to hear her speak.

We called her the Expert. She had lived in this realm called Iceland for over ten years. It was decided that the Expert would give several lectures at Café Iceland meetings, on obtaining permanent residency and assimilating to Icelandic culture. When I first saw the Expert's silhouette across the room, I got the feeling that there wasn't just a person sitting in front of me: the Expert was Iceland itself, a magnificent piece of land in human form. The physical incarnation of the nation of ice and snow—the mass of white we were here to see—sat in her chair and chilled the vicinity.

The Expert told us that she was one of the twelve Koreans living in Reykjavík, and one of one hundred thousand city residents. She was also one of Reykjavík's hairdressers. She belonged to multiple groups. And now she was a part of our Café Iceland. Every time the name of one of the twelve Koreans in Reykjavík escaped from her mouth, I felt like I was hearing the name of a saint. I didn't know anything about these twelve people, but they seemed like old acquaintances.

The night after I met the Expert, I stood on top of a trampoline with the other Café members. It was a dream. We ran across the elastic mat swaying below us before starting to bounce into the air. Kim stamped his feet energetically. That made other members—including Lee and Park—fall over. Park quickly stood up and pounded his own feet against the trampoline mat. Lee just fell backward and didn't get up. As Park pounded with increasing vigor and Kim flew higher and higher into the air, Lee curled up into a ball like a squid sizzling on top of a grill. The Expert put her hands around her mouth and started to shout at us. She had a lot to say.

"Even if you try to sit still, you're bound to be pushed around by recoil from everyone else on the trampoline. If you don't want to be knocked all over the place—if you want to maintain some sense of equilibrium—you can't sit quietly. You have to jump harder than the others—harder than them. Higher, and more forcefully. You'll fall behind the competition if you don't jump aggressively. That's a trampoline for you. That's Korea, too. As long as everyone's moving, you can't stop the inertia. People don't climb onto trampolines in order to stay still. What I'm saying is that we've been forced to compete since birth."

Lee stood up in order to regain control. I stood up, too. I set my feet on the mat like they were two awls, and I jumped forcefully. Once I was up in the air, I looked down. What I saw beneath me was neither plaything nor land: it was a black sea. The trampoline looked so small. At some point, after bouncing like springs for quite a while, we all flopped back onto the mat. Only then did the trampoline, the earth, the sea, grow still. The Expert spoke.

"This moment: this is Iceland."

My office and Iceland were like opposite ends of a seesaw. As Iceland rose higher into the air, this place—the office—dropped lower and lower. The more time I spent mesmerized by Iceland, the more my present location—the ground on which my feet currently stood—disintegrated like a motheaten piece of fabric. Iceland was dotted with *geysers*, bubbling puddles that would spout water into the air without warning. The Iceland in my heart was no different: it bubbled somewhere deep inside me, until the moment that it shot skyward, eighty meters or higher. Everything that wasn't Iceland was starting to look pitiful.

My daily reality was growing pitiful as well, thanks to the new office intern, who'd been hired purely out of nepotism. At work, I was like a strainer, filtering communication between the boss and the intern as they relayed messages through me. And when I sat down at my desk at 9:00 a.m., my body and mind were nine hours in the past, on Iceland time. It was around midnight in Iceland, so I felt terribly drowsy all day. I felt the time difference between Korea and Iceland with my entire being. I had nothing to ask of the intern, nothing to teach him or tell him, even though he was hoping to use his school break to try out a whole range of office work. My time for my own assignments dwindled as I curated the intern's experience. He had lots of questions, lots of knowledge, and lots of energy. The intern often called our office practices into question, comparing Korea's and America's business environments with monologues that began, "In the U.S., we . . ." Whenever he did that, I drew the line: this was Korea. When he tried one last time to say this wasn't how things were done in the U.S., I changed the topic.

"Have you been to Iceland?" I asked him.

"Iceland?"

"Yeah," I said. "Not Ireland. Iceland."

"No, I've never been," he replied. "Isn't it a cold country?"

To think that all he could say was "Isn't it a cold country"?! *Iceland is a country that a rookie like you can't understand.* Thoughts of Iceland spun around my head, and my body temperature quickly cooled.

As I leaned over my desk, I realized that only three certainties existed in the world. One, deserts lasted forever, and two, they didn't actually contain oases. Instead of an oasis, all you could expect to find was the occasional mirage. That was the third certainty. Maybe Iceland was my mirage. Now all I could do was visit the country and see for myself.

After Iceland entered my life, I began to spend more time in motion than I did idle. I needed to live my reality more fully: I needed to prepare. Iceland may have had lower healthcare costs than Korea, but until a foreigner was completely assimilated into Icelandic society, they would be limited in daily life, including at the doctor's office. Foreigners had to be healthy, before anything else. They couldn't be sick. Before leaving for Iceland, they needed to prepare for the future, in a place where they could speak the language and were familiar with the culture. The Expert said that it was a good idea to preemptively get rid of time bombs that could explode at any place and any time: things like wisdom teeth and appendices. The next day, I went to the dentist. I had six cavities. The dentist told me it would take two months and two million won to fix them. I immediately got the recommended fillings that I would have put off in the past. It was going be a bit more difficult to have my appendix prophylactically removed, but it wouldn't be impossible.

After the Expert showed up at Café Iceland, our membership fees increased. But the Café fees were for a more effective form of personal care than exercise or massages or learning a foreign language or eating health foods. We were receiving private lessons from a Korean who'd experienced Iceland firsthand. I never thought that I was wasting money. The people who complained that membership fees were too expensive stopped coming to meetings, and that was it. Everyone else happily paid. Until we started to get fed up with the Expert's lectures.

The members asked for recommended restaurants, hotels, and shopping destinations, but the Expert couldn't give us real answers. When she answered our questions, she'd tell us something already printed in the guidebook. For someone who'd lived in Reykjavík until just a few months ago, the Expert didn't know much about the city. The Expert knew as much about Reykjavík as our guidebook did, and the only things she told us that weren't already familiar were incessant stories about her hair salon. The information that the Expert gave us was unclear. If she told us that a slice of pizza from a street vendor cost 150 krónur, a member who'd recently returned from a trip to Iceland would correct her and say that it was 300 krónur, and then the Expert would claim that pizza prices varied by neighborhood. But if asked where to find a 150-krónur pizza joint, the Expert couldn't tell us. The supposed price of a postcard, a bottle of water, and even a haircut differed from what we knew. When the Expert mixed up details about her own life, our suspicions grew. The only time she could give us specific information was when we were talking about the inside of her hair salon. But the members all wanted to know about what was outside the hair salon. The Expert couldn't tell us anything. The Expert had never even eaten shark meat, which she claimed was because she was a picky eater, but that just further amplified suspicion. The Expert didn't know much about Lake Mývatn or Jökulsárgljúfur National Park, either. When she opened her mouth to begin another personal anecdote with the phrase "In my salon . . .," we said that we'd heard the story. Park began to ask her questions to which he already knew the answer.

"What about hrútspungur?" he demanded. "How is it?"

"If you want to go to hrútspungur, you should buy a package tour," the Expert said. "It's hard to get there."

Lee disputed her answer.

"Hrútspungur is a food, isn't it?" he asked.

Park nodded. But the Expert's expression didn't change at all.

"Well, there are tours you can go on to eat it," she said.

Several weeks later, Park disappeared from Café Iceland. Not just from the offline meetings—he left the website, too. He'd been such an active participant in the Café that the remaining members worried he'd undergone a change of heart about Iceland. Some blamed his departure on the inarticulate and suspicious Expert. But the real explanation lay elsewhere.

One of Park's coworkers joined Café Iceland as a new member and told everyone that Park had been fired. Park had frequently repeated that he needed to quit working and head to Iceland, but when he really did leave his job, he couldn't go anywhere—much less Iceland. He walked away from Iceland, although it wasn't because he lacked money or time. We knew Iceland was a place that transcended competition and discord. But in order to maintain such a fantasy, you *needed* competition and discord. The surface of water could be still only if you were relentlessly treading water below. Park realized that, and now that his legs were no longer flailing, he'd abandoned notions of surface tranquility. I couldn't free myself from this setup, either, which was why I couldn't quit my job, or close my savings account, or cancel my insurance, or blindly leave. Because the moment I gave everything up and let myself free, Iceland might disappear.

After the meeting ended, two more members left. Before they could go to Iceland, they had to complete mandatory military service. They told us they were going to fulfill their military duties now so that, afterward, they could leave for Iceland with no strings attached. Two years spent in uniform, they said, might even be additional preparation for the trip. The new soldiers buried Iceland deep inside their uniforms and stepped on the bus to Hwacheon, for boot camp. They stowed thoughts of the red mohawk hairstyles preferred by Icelandic bands in their memories and trimmed their hair to two centimeters. Several weeks later, they posted from the training center. Their comments were imbued with a heartfelt longing for something, but considering the circumstances, it wasn't Iceland.

Those who left left, and the rest of us dreamed. We dreamed that Iceland's growth of a bit less than one centimeter per year would one day lead to an entire earth covered with Iceland.

"We've got an unpredictable boss and the unwanted intern, and now the office is moving. If tragedies come in threes, this is it."

That's what Kim said to me after we learned about the office move. The change of building had just been a rumor, but now it was reality. In a few months, we were to move from Yangjae Station to Susaek Station. I lived by Myeongil Station, and the commute from Myeongil to Susaek was longer than a flight from here to Iceland. Kim lived in the Gyeonggi suburb of Gwangju, and he said he was going to quit his job altogether. After suffering from the ever-changing demands of our boss—who'd come in this morning as the second quintuplet but after lunch transformed back into the first—I had the same impulse. Maybe if I quit my job, I really could leave for Iceland. Iceland glittered on the world map affixed to my desk, like it was sending out an aurora.

Tucked in a corner of Reykjavík: the Expert's twenty-square-meter hair salon. At first, we found her stories of the salon, which frequently mentioned some acquaintance's grandmother and the black cat that lived inside the business, to be exciting. Material on Icelandic hair salons wasn't easy to find in a guidebook or embassy.

But at some point, we caught on. The Iceland we were learning about consisted entirely of the inside of one building. The Expert's stories of Iceland were limited to the twenty-square-meter floor of her hair salon. The Expert had spent ten years within those twenty square meters, and even when she did go outside, she was a long way from getting on a tour bus to explore the center of the island, or driving along the coast, or riding a snowmobile. The Expert's range of motion was defined entirely by people whose hair was a bit too long, people who wanted to wrap their tresses around heated rollers, people who wanted their hair untangled, and those who were in need of scissors: it had no relation to Iceland. The Expert's Iceland was the hair salon—a place from which Iceland was so absent, it was difficult to tell whether or not it was in Iceland at all.

The Expert's stories pulled us inside the hair salon. She had nowhere else to take us, nowhere else to tell us about. The result of her anecdotes was that now, if I thought of Iceland, the first thing that came to me wasn't curiosity, it was a headache. The Expert just had to say the word "Iceland," and I could smell the perm chemicals. I was also fed up with her stories of the black cat that wandered the beauty parlor and of so-and-so's grandmother, who was always visiting. Couldn't I see cats and grandmas in any old alley right here in Korea? To be honest, I didn't know if the Expert had really lived in Iceland for ten years or if she had just spent a very short period of time there. I didn't know if she'd lived in Iceland at all—or if she'd even been to the country. I couldn't tell if she was one of twelve Koreans in Reykjavík or if she'd just named her hair salon Reykjavík. Maybe the Expert only knew Iceland in words: perhaps it was like how I had memorized French bus lines without ever going to France, or how I could recite recommended Japanese restaurants and travel budgets and delicacies without having stepped foot there. But I kept my mouth shut.

"It smells like a sham," Kim said. Maybe that was it. I hadn't thought of the Expert as an expert, but as one of the twelve disciples spreading the gospel of Iceland. Even if the gospel she preached was false, perhaps I'd fallen deep into the church and begun to believe its doctrine—and become a believer who wanted to stand on top of that doctrine, even if it was an illusion, until the earth collapsed beneath me. I believed the words of the Expert as is, more than I believed all the detailed and completely credible information I'd learned about Iceland from books and out in the world. Her twenty-square-meter hair salon, so-and-so's grandma, the group of Korean tourists that the Expert had seen exactly once in Reykjavík, the short-tempered guide who'd been leading the group, and the crying baby who lived next door to the Expert: I believe they all existed.

Café Iceland had once hosted well-attended events at venues throughout Seoul and even in the suburbs—we were always looking for the right ambiance for our meetings—but recently we had dwindled to a pitiful group. The organizer of our meetings was at a loss as members asked him to decrease membership fees or give them individual discounts. If you can't stand the heat, get out of the kitchen, he said. Members who couldn't stand the heat left in droves. Now only three or four people went to meetings regularly.

The Expert was quiet as she pulled a silver pair of scissors out of her bag. She unfurled a pink piece of cloth and wrapped it around my neck. The woman standing behind me, looking down at my part and holding silver scissors in her hands: she wasn't the Expert—she was Iceland. All of Iceland groped my scalp with her fingertips as she said the following: "The back of your head sticks out a lot."

Iceland brandished the scissors. She held my thick, black hair between those cold fingers and spread the silver blades open. *Slap*. I didn't know how cutting scissors could make a slapping noise. But the scissors were definitely slapping. It was like the sound of wind hitting a cheek, or of the sea creeping toward shore. The scissors also seemed to be choo-choo-ing like an old locomotive. Iceland was turning my head in this direction and that direction, as if it were a globe. The scissors rolled over my head like train wheels. Twenty active volcanoes and seven hundred hot springs erupted along the blades' path. I worried the scissors were about to reach their destination. I wanted them to keep on going like this forever. Like a train. On my head that stuck out a lot in the back.

Almost everyone cut their hair. Iceland made all our hairstyles exactly the same. Our head shapes and hair texture and length all differed, but our hair became exactly the same: Iceland style. And then the Expert disappeared from our Iceland. She had left Iceland in our hair, we were sure of it. That was our last class with the Expert. As she left the room, her back gave off a commanding aura. But for some reason, her departing gait was very fast. She looked just like us. I didn't know where the axis to our globe was, but the Expert was there, and I was here. Together, we were like a map of the world being violently pressed against another surface to transfer its image.

That's how the meetings ended. More specifically, we delayed the next meeting without rescheduling. Iceland was an abstract concept. The word "Iceland" couldn't help but be subjective: each of us translated it differently, and it held a unique meaning for each member. That was Iceland. I believed that the way to define an abstract concept was to decide what its antonym was, so I thought about the opposite of Iceland. If I could figure that out, then I'd know roughly where Iceland lay. But try as I might, the opposite of Iceland didn't come to me. I kept walking in circles around the same twenty square meters of Iceland. Like I was lost on the side of a mountain.

When I logged back on to the Café website after a long absence, I saw a new notice. The first Korean-language guidebook to Iceland had been published. The Café was organizing a group purchase of the book, but because few members had agreed to participate, the initiative had foundered. I bought the book, and right before I went to sleep, I lay on my bed and flipped it open. Reading about Iceland page by page, from Reykjavík to the less-known middle of the island, was a thrill. Because it was a recent publication, up-to-date consumer prices were written down in detail. Some of them corresponded to what the Expert had told us and some of them didn't. But I decided I wouldn't dispute the Expert's gospel. The Expert's Iceland and this book's Iceland may have differed slightly, that was true. But it wasn't important.

This was how I lived in Iceland for several days and several nights. I paved roads and constructed buildings on top of the words I was reading. Then I imagined that I was walking on those roads and into those buildings. All you had to do was say "Reykjavík," and the words transformed into structures that sprung up before my eyes: structures that were massive, but not overwhelming. I marched right into them. The surprising thing was that the more I read, the more the Iceland on my bookshelf came to resemble the island nation that I'd learned about from the Expert. Pizza joints appeared, selling slices for 150 krónur, and buses traveled routes the Expert had mentioned. After I'd read about seventy pages, I saw the Expert walking away, through the cityscape of Reykjavík, and when I made it to page one hundred, the beauty parlor with its meandering black cat made an appearance as well. Who knew: maybe if I sat down in one of the salon's three styling chairs, the Expert would brandish a pink cloth like she was a magician, obscuring my view with the fabric. The Expert would cover the area below my neck with the pink cutting cape and say the following as she touched my scalp: "The back of your head sticks out a lot."

The office was busy as we prepared for the move. I placed my personal belongings in a large box. Several coworkers had already quit because of the location change. Kim was hidden behind the partition between our cubicles, looking for another job. A map of the world was laid out under the glass panel covering my desk, like an uninteresting tabletop menu at a restaurant. Train tracks and roads resembled blood vessels as they spread across the map, which teemed with so many place-names that I thought they might crash into each other. Iceland was far from such discord. You had to travel by boat or plane to reach the country, located at latitudes between sixty-three and sixty-six degrees. You had to break away from land. While everyone else was trying to decide if they should follow the company to its new location or quit, I was trying to decide if I should buy a backpack or carry-on bag. I skimmed through search results for airfare to Iceland as well. What arrived at my house several days later wasn't a backpack or a carry-on, but the kind of enormous suitcase used when moving countries. I worried that if I didn't purchase such sizeable luggage, Iceland would evaporate out of my life forever.

The next morning, I discovered the evaporated country at a newspaper kiosk in the subway station.

"Financial Collapse in Iceland," said the headline.

"IMF," "unemployment crisis," "national bankruptcy": words I'd never seen in my guidebook were redefining Iceland. Iceland wasn't just a place sometimes omitted from world maps: thanks to bankruptcy, it had almost disappeared from the face of the earth. The value of a króna was down 50 percent. TV and newspapers showed images of Icelanders panic-buying olive oil and pasta in grocery stores. The news reported that tourists were flocking to Iceland because of the króna's decrease in value. This was how Iceland became famous.

The subway rumbled loudly as it entered the station. "The train to Susaek Station is now approaching," said a voice on the loudspeaker. I took a step back before hurriedly boarding the train. It would have been a long ride from Myeongil to Susaek, but Nokbeon to Susaek wasn't too far. I'd decided to deal with my company's change of office in a way that made things easiest for everyone: I moved. Moving was the trend at work. Most of my coworkers who said they were going to switch jobs ended up finding new homes instead, in order to maintain their commute distances. I'd been able to make use of the enormous suitcase in the move. As I held a newspaper—and the Iceland inside it—between my fingers, I boarded the subway.

8. PIERCING

The dark blue metal tail quivered between the tweezers' pincers. The piercing technician held the shattered, centipede-like fragment with the tweezers before dropping it onto a dry piece of cotton.

"The earring broke in half inside your ear, and now there's an infection," she said. "Don't touch it until it heals."

Moments earlier, she'd removed the whale's vertebra, the length of which had cut a hole through the upper part of my ear. The inside of the piercing was completely filled with bacteria-laden pus. Signs of injury remained in places where the whale's corroding body had touched my skin. Bloody rust that had been hiding beneath the whale, brown as the skin of a bad apple, oozed from my ear. Restless yellow desires that once festered inside the infected protuberance flowed freely now that the bulge had been popped. When an alcohol swab touched my cartilage, my ear rode the wave of encroaching disinfectant like a surfer, and I could hear it hum. The sound was as wretched as two tightly fitting wardrobe doors rasping as they closed. The sea disappeared into the mismatched beat: the discordant whine of grating cartilage. I couldn't smell any ocean waves here. Instead, the painful scent of hydrogen peroxide flooded the room as yet another whale left my body. Once the whale was entirely gone, only a damp hole remained.

It was fun to put holes in my body. An earring post was less than twelve millimeters long, but there was nothing that couldn't hang from the end of it: an agile tail, a sturgeon fin, roaring beasts from an Altaic cave painting, even splendid wreaths and blazing sunspots. It didn't take long to stick the metal in. After two or three seconds, the flesh had an opening in it, and I only needed another thirty seconds to stick an earring in the hole. But it took two weeks to a month for the metal post to lay its roots in my skin—and once again, I was taking the earring out after waiting all that time.

The problem was that the metal hadn't completely taken root. I'd only just learned this, but my skin was prone to keloids. My cartilage around the titanium whale couldn't overcome its natural sensitivity. My body had been surprised by the sudden irritation of a piercing and violently pushed out the earring. The whale, firmly fixed to my cartilage, had broken in two inside my ear, and then a round bump emerged around the area, like my body was a criminal trying to cover up a crime.

I wrapped the pus- and scab-covered whale in tissue paper, put it in my pocket, and went to the doctor. This was my seventh whale. It was also the last whale left in my body, because I'd already removed all the others. The smell of blood followed me as I left the clinic. It was the scent of my guilt about giving up and removing the piercings.

Every time I saw J, we got piercings together. Ultimately, though, my pus-filled wounds were all that remained as evidence of our acquaintance. Every whale stuck in my skin eventually broke into shards and left me. The loss of whales is an important matter, but J doesn't answer the phone when I call to tell her. She hasn't just been unreachable for a day or two. She never answers anymore.

"There's nothing strange about it," J told me. "My body's just gotten used to the piercing. It's part of me now, like fingernails or toenails."

If you classified J by species, she would be a crustacean. A crustacean whose wounds hardened into rocks—nodules stuck to each joint of her body. Illuminated beneath the flashing multicolored lights, sharp daggers stuck out from their burial places across J's body. The pieces of metal, each a different shape and in a different location, made their existence known each time the lights moved. Two in her right ear, one in her left ear, one on the edge of her right eyebrow, one in the middle of her forehead, one in her philtrum, one on her tongue, two on her lip, right above her crooked teeth, and who knew how many more bits of metal were hidden under her clothes. J's ears, bound with rings like a spiral notebook, shook every time she nodded. Bones weren't what supported J's body. Metal was. And the holes didn't just cling to her—J clung to the holes.

"How many piercings do you have?" I asked her.

"I haven't counted, so I don't know," she said. "I feel like I find a new one every day when I wake up."

She stuck her tongue out briefly, and the arrow-shaped piercing sparkled. The arrow's triangular head pointed toward J's vocal cords. Everything J said followed the direction of the arrow and swam back down her throat. So did her breaths. Laughs, sobs, and sighs were all reabsorbed into J's esophagus before they could reach the ground. J never had an expression on her face. She was always composed, maybe smiling, maybe not. The day we first met, I'd given J five thousand won because I wanted to swim up her throat, too. It seemed like I'd be taking a weight off myself if I could drop all my words, all my breaths, and all my time inside her mouth.

"You know what I ate for dinner the day I got the arrow piercing?" she asked. "Ramen. Spicy ramen, boiled with slices of gochu pepper. It was a little uncomfortable because the noodles kept touching my arrow. But the flavor was fantastic—maybe it was because there was a hole in my tongue and oxygen could flow through it. I emptied the entire pot and even smoked an after-dinner cigarette!"

As she talked about getting the inward-pointing arrow, J took off her T-shirt. A bloody stench emanated from her body. It wasn't the pungent smell you come across at a fish market stall. It was a reddish odor, red like the liquid that rusty metal secretes on rainy days.

"I pierced it with a needle," she said. "This one hurt more than the others."

J's nipple looked as mournfully pale and frightened as someone with a pillory around their neck. The silver ring hanging from the middle of her round breast reminded me of a torture device. A small lock dangled from the curved ring. My brow wrinkled as I looked at that point where flesh and metal intersected. J leaned her small body toward me. I took a hesitant step back. My whole body itched.

"What's wrong?" she asked.

I didn't know why I was being so flighty, either. Strangely, I didn't desire her. It was like J's body had given me a metal allergy: the moment I saw her, a sharpness shot through my every nerve.

"You'll get used to it soon," she said. "Even if clients think it's weird at first, they like it later."

J sometimes had bruises on her body. When the deep blue blotches on her skin drifted toward the color of a rotten apple, a new piercing was sure to make an appearance—something like bullhorns or a scorpion or a geometric shape. Whenever she got a bruise, she got a promotion. No, maybe every time she got a promotion she got a bruise. When I said she worked for a "pyramid scheme," she would correct me with the phrase "multilevel marketing," because she hated the desperate aura that "pyramid scheme" gave off. Every time she pulled a new person in, she moved up one level. The hawk beak wedged into her right arm was a piercing J had gotten after one such step up the corporate ladder. Two months later, when J rose to "silver," a starfish appeared on the right side of her forehead. In this strange animal hierarchy, J was moving up.

"If I leave now, it'll all come to nothing. I already have my foot in the door," she said. "Now I have to get to 'diamond.' "

J was trying to get rid of her debt when she met me. Even so, I could only pay her fifty thousand won per night. I was glad that the relationship didn't benefit just one of us.

Her phone number has been deactivated. For several weeks, all I get is a dial tone when I call. I've even questioned whether or not I'm calling the right number. During the three months that I met with J, the kid's number changed something like four times. But because J was always the one to call me, the new numbers evaporated from my mind before I could remember them. All I can do is wait. I walk toward the street where I often met J. It's in a red-light district, down a city alley. J is probably still moonlighting there, and soon we'll be able to see each other.

The trees lining the road strain their necks toward the city din. J's face glimmers through the leaves. The seafood stew restaurant at the end of the road is still here, the restaurant that advertises service "twenty-five hours per day" and whose sign is missing a letter. J easily emptied a bowl of stew at dawn every time we met. From our first meeting until the last time I saw her, we always ate seafood stew together. I felt bad, purchasing J's body for a few small bills, so I'd buy her stew in the early hours of morning.

The street continues until it reaches the intersection outside my wife's animal hospital. My wife typically eats lunch at the restaurant across the street; later, she emerges from the café next door holding an Americano. She swallows an antacid in the pharmacy where she's a regular and buys an afternoon snack in the adjacent bakery. I still know many things about my wife, like the fact that her car is parked in space 2-1 in the underground hospital lot, that after work someone is always waiting for her at the intersection, and that the someone changes every few months, sometimes every few weeks.

It's been a year since I separated from my wife. After moving out, I opened the thirty cardboard boxes I'd used for packing—boxes that formerly contained packs of ramen in bulk and were now filled with thick hardcover books. I piled the books against the wall of my two-hundred-thousand-won rented room like they were a fence. It felt like I'd been transported ten years into the past. The earth had revolved around the sun ten times over the past decade, but I'd only spun around in one place. It wasn't that I hadn't made the occasional attempt to do something unconventional. I'd even gotten a job as a copywriter at an advertising agency and begun to follow a well-trodden career path. I married my wife when that path seemed to be taking me somewhere successful. But not long after the wedding, I realized that I'd just been handed off to another relay race runner. From my single mother to my oldest sister, to my second-oldest sister, to my third-oldest sister, and then to my wife: I was a baton constantly passed between sprinters.

The room was small but had a high ceiling. Above my head was a long window that let in narrow beams of sunlight every morning. As rays came through the window's crossbars, tiny as squares on graph paper, I curled up in the light and read. If the sun shifted, I picked up the small table in front of me and moved to a part of the room that was still bright.

Even though we're separated, my wife's workplace and the apartment where she must still be living are hardly five hundred meters from here. My life didn't change much when we parted. I wake up at the same time and go to sleep at the same time, go grocery shopping once every four days and soak rice for thirty minutes before cooking it. Whether my wife is here or not, I fall asleep in the fetal position, all by myself. Other than when I go outside a few times a month, I eat alone and stay in my room.

But if something *has* changed, it's that I no longer pay attention to what day it is. My wife had an exacting personality, and she made me comply with expiration dates on items in the refrigerator. After four days, still-fresh vegetables and meat and fruits were kicked out of the fridge, and we organized a large-scale fridge cleaning twice a week. But I don't check expiration dates anymore. I know that I've already passed the expiration for my former daily life. I'm decaying, out of orbit from my past sense of normalcy.

I lean my face against the glass of the animal hospital wall. I see a number of canine eyes waiting for treatment by my wife's skilled hands, but I don't see my wife. Across the room, the dog groomer looks furtively in my direction. Since I don't see my wife inside, I know she must be in surgery. Soon she'll be ravenous—for both food and sex. As I think of her white gloves and her white gown, I feel a chill down my back and my chest thumps. I separated from her one year ago, but my memories haven't moved on. They're still renting a home from my wife.

A week before Male died, she fixed two dogs that were in heat. On days like that, she always finished a whole bowl of rice by herself. Our house was thick with the smell of the meat and fish that we were continually flipping on the grill. My wife chattered on as we cooked. "I told you to soak the meat in water—you didn't get all the blood off. Why is it so smelly? And it's pretty tough, too. I asked for sesame leaves, not lettuce. You didn't put ginger in the marinade, did you? How about next time we use a gridiron? The meat will be softer that way."

My wife always ate a sumptuous meal after fixing the growling dogs. It was as if she were trying to recover the sexual desire lost during the procedure. She grabbed bluish vegetables with her chopsticks and wrapped them around several chunks of thick meat. As over a pound of flesh entered her chomping mouth, I sat across from her and ensured that the marinade and vegetables and water didn't run out and hinder her enormous appetite. I choked just smelling the meat, but I couldn't imagine getting up first from the table for two: our twice-monthly ritual. I didn't like it when she raised her voice or glared at me with her wide-open eyes if I tried to avoid our communal meals. But that wasn't the main reason I sat with her: the real reason was slightly more practical.

After she set down her spoon at the end of dinner, I would push a piece of paper toward her, breaking down my living expenses. Then I received my month's allowance, and money for cigarettes. I'd spent two years staying at home doing nothing, but she'd never expressed disappointment. She didn't try to convince me to look for work, and she didn't give me weird looks, either. Even when I'd floundered as a salesperson at a pharmaceutical company, unable to make it three months before giving up, and when I'd been kicked out of my prep classes for the entrance exams at other companies, she didn't care. None of it had to do with her. That also meant that I didn't have the obligation or right to interfere with her life. My wife calmly weathered everything—my long unemployment, the incomprehensible cipher-like poems I wrote, my lack of smarts and inability to relax, even how bad I was in bed. In turn, I had to deal with her frequent nights away, her daring affairs, and her one-sided decisions. Our rule was that the marriage wouldn't break down until one member declared that he or she was giving up.

As long as no one tested this unwritten law, our household stayed calm. The atmosphere was just a little unsympathetic. When she wasn't home, Male was my only family member. Our three-month-old cocker spaniel, Male. According to my wife, Male wasn't a purebred. She readily accepted lost dogs like our new puppy, but you couldn't expect her to show compassion beyond simply taking them in. When I asked what we should name the dog, she'd impassively replied, "Male."

"Do you mean we should make that the dog's name?" I asked. She was indifferent.

"Well, is it male or female?" she asked.

She was an expert: she could tell a dog's breed just by looking at its nose. But honestly, to my wife, there were only two kinds of dogs: dogs that were docile and dogs that weren't. If a once-docile dog entered heat or wanted to mate, it typically became distracted and aggressive. So really, the division was between dogs that had been fixed and dogs that hadn't. My wife was a recognized spay and neuter expert. The customers who put their pets in her care loved dogs, although she didn't really like them herself. There was a difference between knowing dogs and loving dogs, but it didn't really matter.

She got a wound on her arm not long after we took in Male. Male was beginning to show signs of rut, like leaning against the wall and barking loudly. That day, as soon as she entered the doorway, he ran up and rubbed his body against her.

"This idiot is horny," she said.

She pushed Male away. At the same time, she picked up the umbrella she'd set down in the entryway. There was no stopping her. The thick-handled umbrella trembled in the narrow hallway like it was being struck by lightning. Male seemed to be snarling, but because the sound was so brief, it was hard to determine whether what I'd heard was real. Moments later, Male was lying on the floor, immobile. She kneeled and poked Male's throat. For a second, she seemed to have stopped breathing, too. An angry blue riverlike vein protruded from her brow, then it receded. She brushed off her hands and stood up.

"You should have told me beforehand. If I'd performed the surgery, this wouldn't have happened!" she shouted.

Bang. I heard the bathroom door close, but I just sat where I was. Male's eyes were completely closed. No quivering motion hid beneath his eyelids. I strode toward the bathroom and twisted the door's handle. The cold, shrill click of the lock blocked the space between us. I put my ear to the bathroom wall and heard her washing her hands. There was the sound of bubbles lathering, of her clean fingers exposing themselves between the bubbles, of tepid water dissolving the bubbles. She was calm and organized as ever, but caught in a rhythm incompatible with everyday life.

That night, I leaned against her bedroom door like a child and opened my mouth.

"I want to have a funeral. For Male," I said.

"What?" she asked.

"People do that nowadays when dogs die. I want to organize a funeral for Male."

"Dogs are dogs," she said. "I could save three or four others for the cost of a funeral."

"If you lend me money, I'll . . ."

"I'm going to make a phone call. Leave, please," she ordered.

I didn't have any money, but I used what I did have to hold a funeral. I wrapped Male up in a blanket and set him down in my room. He was still warm, and I couldn't bury him before his temperature cooled. My whole body was exhausted, taken by a sudden rush of fatigue. After sleeping for a long time, I woke up the next morning and felt like I could still hear the sound of Male moving around. But the day after that, and the third day, Male still hadn't woken up. On the fourth day, Male's body disappeared. Along with the blanket it was wrapped up in. He evaporated with the blanket. One of two things had happened: either Male had reincarnated and walked away, or someone had thrown him out.

After two days, I discovered Male in one of the apartment complex's public trashcans. He was in the food waste bin. I pushed a trash bag to the side and pulled out Male. Apple peels and gluey paste from the end of a rice scooper clung to his fur. My insides were churning. I felt like I was going to throw up, but it wasn't because of Male's miserable body. It wasn't because of the nasty smell, either. The thing that shook me was the phallic bump coming out from below his midsection. *Is the bastard in heat? Is the bastard in heat?* Her biting voice rolled around in my ears. Everything turned yellow before my eyes. My center of balance rushed to my crotch, and the sky swirled. From far away, I could hear the sound of her feet. Her feet tapped on the ground as she walked toward me, carrying scissors with bluish blades and a knife in her hands. Snip, snip. The moment Male's genitalia was cut off, my legs lost their strength. My pants felt clammy.

For a while after Male's death, I couldn't eat anything at all. I kept dreaming that he was exploding into little pieces right in front of me. In my dream, I sewed together the fragments of Male's blown-up body, and my drooping shoulders trembled as I huddled over the completed patchwork. My wife often appeared as well, wearing her white gown. With her vigorous appetite for food and sex, she demanded even in dreams that my genitalia grow larger. And when they grew, she snipped them off. To avoid being castrated, I spent the entire night wandering around outside, and in the morning, I awoke with my body in a slouched position.

My feet stop at DEAD. They're the first part of me to recognize the piercing parlor's gloomy sign, affixed like a doormat to the ground in front of the entrance. Inside, the walls are packed with pieces of metal, and charts show where on your body you can be pierced. Underneath dim lights, holes are pierced over and over, in all heavenly and earthly directions. Dumbbells, locks, stars, hearts, sunglasses, crosses, *x*'s and letters of the alphabet, unknowable hieroglyphs . . . among all the sparkling metals, my fingers turn to the whale out of habit. Was it J or my wife who told me that whales can get erections that are three meters long? I'm not sure. Anyhow, I liked whales from the beginning, and I put seven of them in my body, like an addict. The whales are a beam holding up my life, a prop against which I can lean. The ones in my body were 1.6 centimeters long. But the dreams they hold inside can expand—to three whole meters, like the erections.

The piercer looks carefully at my ears and tilts her head.

"Did you apply the ointment?" she asks. "It looks infected, doesn't it?"

"Please, don't use any sort of anesthetic," I tell her. "Just pierce it again—I can deal with the pain."

The piercer shakes her head, saying that the inflamed ear can't be repierced. But what good does it do to avoid inflammation when you are piercing a hole in an ear? The thing to fear more than inflammation is loneliness. When I hear that she can't pierce me, my entire body itches, and I feel a crawling sensation on my skin. I'd rather be undergoing withdrawal from some kind of drug than feel like this. I buy a few whales, walk over DEAD again, and leave.

This place never exactly agreed with me; it always made me a bit uncomfortable for some reason. But I paid money for that discomfort. Other than my daily half pack of cigarettes and ingredients for meals, DEAD was my only expense. It was because of J.

"It'll get better with time," J said at the beginning. "If you pierce yourself once, you'll just keep doing it again and again."

What initially caught my eye inside DEAD was a diagram of a body showing where you could get pierced. To me, it looked like a target at a shooting range. A target where invisible points marked each part of the body, and to get a perfect score, you had to hit every dot.

"Personally, I think the tongue is the best place to get a piercing," J said. "Cause then you can play with it in your mouth."

I got a tongue piercing, a thick whale, just like J suggested. I'd sat in a chair and stuck my tongue out far. I hadn't eaten for a while, and the bad breath dormant on my tongue began to awake.

"Chew on your tongue with your teeth," the piercer told me. "If you massage it enough, it will hurt less." I chewed the inside of my mouth as instructed.

"Stick your tongue out," she said.

"Ahhh."

A prick. High-pressure current flowed across my tongue. My mouth hurt, but I couldn't tell exactly how much pain I was in. I closed and opened my eyes, and then there was a cold and sharp rod inside me. It was a durable and dangerous rod, worth using to support my entire body.

The piercer said that two weeks was enough to heal from the piercing, but it took a very long time for me to recognize the whale as part of my body. My tongue was connected to a cold metallic protrusion, from which it couldn't free itself. At first, every morning, I had to wrestle with the burning pain that spread across my body. If I drank hot or warm soup, my tongue jumped suddenly like a surprised eel, and whenever I spoke, my voice sounded a bit harsh. When I brushed my teeth, too, I had to brush carefully, and if I happened to put a cigarette in my mouth, I worried about the tip heating up the metal of the piercing. Finally, I grew neurotic and developed sores all over the inside of my mouth from the stress.

The sharply budding sores caused me to push away all food and drink, and an awful film began to coat my tongue. In order to forget the burning, I tried immersing myself fully in my daily activities, but the more I did that, the more painfully the injury throbbed. It throbbed and throbbed and finally it billowed like a strange desire and solidified into a firm marble—a lump. The metal and the entire area around it hardened and turned red and bloated, and each night I could hear the lump growing.

After several weeks like that, the whale had built a nest for itself. It was stuck in my tongue like a mass of cells that had always been there. There was no more pus coming out of the lump, and my voice didn't sound strange anymore. Sometimes gum stuck to the piercing, or ramen noodles got caught on the whale's tail, but that wasn't a big deal. When the pain grew dull, J contacted me. After not seeing each other for almost a month, we relished our reunion as we walked around the city. And before we parted, we decided to give each other a taste of our respective tongues. Two pieces of deeply rooted metal bumped into each other inside our mouths. I could hear the whale breathing. It seemed, too, like the whale's entire body was erect.

After that, we pierced our skin each time we met. I got seven piercings while we were meeting regularly. Like J had said, only the beginning was difficult. The pleasure that came after, the joy of drilling into flesh, ended in just a moment. Nothing was permanent. I was like an addict: each time I drilled a hole, I was already searching for the next spot. The piercings were a conversation recorded on my skin, and because of them, it seemed like my loneliness was being alleviated a little bit. Just like that, piercings began to mark their domain on my body one by one.

On days that I got a piercing, and the metal pin drove its roots into the hole, we went up somewhere higher, even just a floor higher. A place where, if possible, the world felt a little bit more like a toy: a towering lookout where daily life couldn't follow us. We went up there and looked down at the streets and buildings that were so small, you could hide them with the palm of your hand.

J doesn't contact me today, either. I've walked around places where the kid used to show up a lot, but I don't see her. She hasn't gone this long without contacting me before. I fiddle with the silver whale I bought at DEAD. J planned to put this one in her body when she leveled up to "diamond." J is the new runner in my life, holding me: the old baton that she picked up off the ground.

J understood me: she understood how I could fall into a deep sleep only after daybreak, after tainting myself with cigarettes and alcohol, how I only woke up in a fog of bad breath after the sun was high in the sky. I also understood J, who had to sell smiles to earn a living. Our mutual understanding was definitely something different from the indifference that flowed between my wife and me. When J ran, holding me as her baton, I was as happy as she was. Because we were running toward someplace together, even if that place was the fiery pits of hell, or just somewhere far away from heaven.

The relationship between my wife and me was like an imperfect book, one that contained a printing error. I didn't fit into my wife's life at all. Her life contained exactly one incorrectly inserted page: me. My certainty about our incompatibility reached its peak not long after Male's death.

"I'm pregnant."

My wife spit the words out at me, a bag of meat from the butcher dangling beneath her grip. She confirmed as she took her shoes off. "I said I'm pregnant."

In that moment, someone pushed my wife toward the toilet, but it wasn't me. It wasn't me who struck her back with my rough palms. It wasn't me who shouted, "Throw up! Throw up!" Until I heard the sound of slapping, and her cheeks started to burn like they were on fire, I wasn't myself. When I gathered my wits, the plastic bag she'd dropped came into view. Pork neck dripping with red, bloody water. *That nasty pork neck, that nasty pork neck.* When she brushed off her body and stood up, I hugged the toilet and flopped to the ground.

"Isn't it a good thing?" she asked, unsurprised by my violent outburst. "Since we were talking about adopting."

No. I didn't want a baby. The words came up to my throat, but my mouth was too sore to blurt them out. I knew I wasn't the father. *Which lover's child is it? The guy you were seeing recently?* Best-case scenario, it would be the child of the lover who most resembled me.

"Will the baby recognize me?" I asked.

"Of course," she said. "You're the father."

So she acknowledged that I would raise the child. The household she and I had maintained for five years was based on this trust that she wouldn't leave. She always said it was "fair," the way we did things. She earned money, I ran the house, she'd have a kid, I'd take care of the kid: we were that kind of family, logical and egalitarian. But pregnancy: for some reason, a self-mocking smile escaped from my mouth. I was eager for a cigarette, but the inside of the house was a no-smoking zone. I trudged outside and stepped into the pharmacy to buy iron supplements for pregnant women, then I went to the butcher to pick up oxtail, then I stopped by the fruit seller and bought a sack of creamy-skinned peaches. Lastly, I bought a lottery ticket. I picked the six numbers in today's date. I wanted it to be a losing ticket. *Please.* All I wanted was for it to be a losing ticket.

For three, four months, her stomach didn't grow. Her morning sickness worsened, and her nerves grew more sensitive by the day, but her stomach was unmoving. Six months passed, then nine, and when her false pregnancy came to its last few weeks, the only thing that came out of her bloated belly was a tumor that had festered for ten months.

My wife was infertile, just like me. Even before I knew it wasn't real, I hadn't wanted to be involved with her pregnancy, because the kid wouldn't be mine. But I realized afterward that my ever-meticulous wife hadn't gone to the hospital even once, because she was afraid of the truth. She feared what she didn't want to believe, and knew what she did want to believe. She'd already learned that she was infertile, but she couldn't accept it. Her imagination had resisted, but finally, it too fell into the fires of hell and cut her womb out of her life. Her insides empty, she called my name through her parched lips.

"One of us has no womb, and the other has no sperm," she said. "How fair."

We went through the procedures and formally separated. The moment the documents were stamped with our names, I heard the sound of a baton falling onto the surface of a track. Just like that, the curtains fell on our five years together. It didn't hurt, but the spot where she'd existed in my life swelled into a round lump. A lump that you could poke, and those restless, yellow desires inside would explode.

The alley I walk through on the way home is pitted with craters, like the surface of the moon. Down the road's steep incline lies the precariously tilted multiunit complex where I live. Its windows are arranged on the wall like cubes of radish kimchi, and they always look dangerously close to falling off the side of the building.

The door creaks open as I firmly twist the doorknob. The ceiling, once incredibly high, feels about three feet lower than before. The ashes in the ashtray have grown as large as children's fingers, and the blanket that was damp when I went out is now dry and weightless. The half-crumpled can of beer on the floor lurches to straighten its wrinkled frame, and tiny beams of light fall like graph paper squares onto the room. As the room brightens, it becomes less and less familiar, with one new centimeter of space visible every ten minutes. The light seems to be disinfecting the place.

I sweep up hairs woven together on the ground like fishnets until I have a fistful. Long, rough, wavy hair. No one has come in here other than J, so it's definitely hers, but considering that I have almost no memory of sweeping the floor, they must have fallen long ago. I scrunch up the hairs and place them on the table. There's a red wallet underneath it. J's ID card isn't inside. All I find alongside the many debit cards in the wallet is an expired lottery ticket. The crumpled lotto card is riddled with lifeless numbers.

Has something gone wrong with us? Thinking back, I can't say that we had no problems. The last time I saw J, she found me. After we drank together, I took J to my house. J was drunk. On that particular day, she wore thicker makeup than usual and laughed a lot. Unnecessary laughs mixed with a nasal twang—they didn't fit J. The heavy perfume was just as ill-suited. Like always, I paid her five thousand won to twist her nipple. J shouted that it hurt.

"Nasty!" she'd yelped.

Was it nasty?

J chuckled, then spoke.

"You're just like a kid, really."

Just like a kid. That was something my wife had often said to me. When we were in bed, she always told me I was like a kid. Of course, that was my wife: J didn't say things like that. J wasn't that kind of person. I calmed J down and grabbed her nipple one more time. I wanted to twist and twist, like a mechanic in a movie screwing something tight. J got upset again and pulled herself away, and in that moment I realized the ring was gone. I rubbed my eyes and then rubbed them some more. There was no ring.

"When did you take it out?" I asked.

"What are you talking about?"

"The handcuffs that were hanging from the piercing."

I lunged at J, who was smoking her cigarette silently, and ruthlessly bit her nipple, then bit it again. I bit until I could smell the reddish scent of J's blood under the stench of her disgusting perfume. J's arm pushed my body roughly.

"If you're going to do this, five thousand won isn't enough," she said.

Money wasn't the problem. I had to check J's body. J's chest, arms, and ears didn't have any metal in them. She opened her lips and stuck out her tongue. It was entirely soft. There was no sharp dagger inside her mouth. The arrow that I loved so much had disappeared. Had it fallen into her throat since I'd last looked?

"When the hell did you take them out?" I asked. "Without telling me."

"Don't avoid the subject—tell me if you're going to pay," she said. "Five thousand won's not enough."

J made a stiff cracking noise as she chewed her gum. A regular and definite, sharp crack. Like the sound of my wife's tall heels hitting against the cold hallway floor. "Are you going to pay or not?" As J asked, I hugged her body so tightly I could have broken it. Barely able to push my arms away, J took the loud gum out of her mouth and stuck it against a corner of the wall before hacking up some spit.

"Fine, I'll do it for five thousand won, but be quick," she said. "I'm busy."

Splayed on the floor with her skirt pulled down, J didn't look even a little bit beautiful.

"I told you I'd do it for five thousand, so you have to be fast!"

J unzipped my pants with her nimble fingers. Her cold, smooth hands went toward my crotch, but I wasn't excited. J's coquettish moan seemed hollow. I grabbed J's shoulder and shook it. "Get yourself together, just get yourself together!" I shouted.

Squirming against the rhythm I was creating as I jerked her around, J let out one horrible shriek and then stood up suddenly. She didn't look in my direction as she gathered her clothing and put it back on, her brows furrowed. I couldn't send her off like that. I grabbed J's leg. She fell down as she tried to push me away. I leaned toward J's face and spoke desperately. "Eat seafood stew with me in the morning, and then you can go. And what happened to the arrow in your throat—did you swallow it or something?"

"Perv," she said.

J's furrowed brow smoothed out like it had been ironed or something, and for a very brief moment, a blue vein protruded from her forehead. Something hot brushed against my cheek, but I couldn't tell if it was J or my wife who'd hit me. I stared at J while I held my hand to my burning cheek. J resembled my wife more and more. I reached my arms out to hug her. Instantaneously, my ashtray broke into pieces above my head. I stood vacant for a second as I wondered whose head it was, and all the holes in my body grew warm. It was probably my head that was damaged, not the ashtray. Blood clung to the hand that had been touching my head. It was warm. I was the one bleeding, but J was the one who was afraid. I shook J's body and then shook it more. The problem wasn't that she'd injured my head. All I wanted to know was where the arrow in J's throat had gone. J slowly stepped back. The pile of books behind her looked like a dark expanse.

J pushed her back against the book-covered wall. She clasped her hands together and seemed to be begging for something, but I couldn't hear her. "I'll give the whales an erection, an erection that emanates throughout their entire bodies," I told her, "then it'll all be okay. Just don't say that I seem like a child." And then I could feel the corner of one of the thick hardback books striking my temple. I stood vacant for a second as I thought about whose temple had been hit, and all the holes in my body grew warm. It was probably my temple that was damaged, not the book. Blood clung to the hand that had been touching my temple. It was warm. I was the one bleeding, but J was the one who was afraid. The pile of books behind J looked like a dark expanse.

The arrow was nowhere to be found. Clearly, it had escaped J's throat and evaporated out of her body. J lay on the floor, docile once again. Her hair was matted with blood. I pulled her close and wiped the blood off her wrists and eyes. J had a pained expression on her face, but she didn't get angry with me. *Just hold on for a little bit, just a little bit.* I took out the whales I'd bought at DEAD and stuck them in the holes in her genitals and nipples and forehead and tongue and all over her body. Only then did J smile dimly, like she was remembering the whales.

"Sir, are you in there?"

I must have dozed off not long after sprawling out on the ground. It's the woman who owns the building, banging on the door.

"You've been quiet as a mouse for the past few weeks!" she exclaims. "I need to know if there's a tenant in here or not. I said I was going to call someone to open the door for me if it was still locked today—remember?"

"Why?" I ask.

"What do you mean why, can't you smell it? This rotting smell?"

I sniff the air but don't notice anything.

"Sheesh, it's coming from this room," she says. "This place smells foul! Just let me in."

Cold air comes in from behind the door as it rattles open. The items in the room, scattered as if a typhoon has come through, slowly grow in size. A half-opened dresser, escaped clothing, cigarettes I put out on the floor, books that have fallen on the floor, a thick encyclopedia, old illustrated animal and plant guides, and a black dot lying beneath them. The black dot grows, too. The round thing gets bigger and bigger: it's the black dot, the black circle, then the black skull, with two thin arms sticking out from its sides.

It's a person wrapped up in a blanket. A young woman, flowers of blue and red blood blooming all over her face. A crustacean with whales studding her body. I peer at the woman's face for a long time. It's unfamiliar. It's a face that I know must exist, that I'm sure I'll come across at some point in the future, but right now it's unfamiliar to me. Why is this person here?

And where is J?

9. DON'T CRY, HONGDO

1. ORGANIC HELL

I joined the other hungry fourth-graders, lined up like links of sausage, as we awaited our release from prison. Our nametags identified us by grade, then class, then student number: 40510, 40728, 40834, 40938, 40821, 40118, 41112, 40231, 40106, 40513, 40224, 40916, 40134, 40618, 40129, 40827, 40418, 40228, 40332, 40511. We took off the tags and put them in a bag. Beyond the school gates, there was no need to reveal that I was in grade four, class five, number eleven: 40511.

The dried fish fillets, roasting over a food stall's hot fire on this warm spring afternoon, were so fresh they looked like they might rise from the dead days after being cooked. The lettuce in my hamburger crinkled like cellophane. Children crossed through the school's front gate with rolling backpacks as high as their hips. They dropped their bags and headed to the sugar candy stand, where golden-brown sugary discs were stamped with shapes like stars and hearts. Children took turns making their own candy, their wrists twirling nimbly as they stirred cups of melted sugar. It wasn't so much cooking as it was dancing, less dancing than it was spinning a top. The whirlpool swirling inside the ladle made a black hole, and the day melted into it. Holding the ladle over a flame was as quietly thrilling as using a magnifying glass to burn textbooks in the sun. The kids at the cotton candy stand next to the sugar candy opened their mouths wide like the black hole inside the ladle. They crammed cotton candy into their muzzles, pulling it off the stick like they were gnawing on beef ribs. Other students slurped down bloodred slushies. Like marathon runners guzzling water, the kids quenched their thirst with sugar ice.

"Excuse me, this is junk food, right?" I asked.

The cotton candy seller glanced at me before pulling a large sack of sugar from below his motorcycle. The sugar looked like a sandbag. *Organic. Sustainable. Chemical-free. Sugar.*

"So it isn't junk food?"

"Have you ever seen junk food made with organic sugar?" he demanded.

"It's not junk food?" I asked again. "But it is, isn't it?"

"No."

"It's junk food, right?"

"I said it's organic sugar. Haven't you heard of clean eating? If you're not going to buy anything, go away. Stop blocking the street."

It's not a good selling point to insist that cotton candy is clean eating. For me, junk food was worth buying, but what was the point if it was healthy? My home was already filled with wholesome things to eat.

In April, just after fourth grade started, a love of all things organic had begun to spread like a virus. It rushed past the gates of my school at a frightening speed and soon turned the entire campus into an organic meadow. Thanks to the wind blowing its organic gusts, we kids became hosts to a parasite we called "organic."

Not long after the cafeteria meals went organic, a declaration of war was posted at the school's entrance. A banner declaring "Wholesome food for wholesome children" fluttered over the front doors like one of our mothers' skirts. And then, one after another, our favorite street vendors disappeared. The few that managed to remain sold foods made with ingredients bearing the required label: "organic." The man selling sugar candy claimed to use organic sugar, the slushy man said he ordered ice made from mineral water, and the man selling fish jerky said that he dealt directly with vendors who caught fish from unpolluted waters.

"Hey—are you buying anything or not?" the cotton candy man asked. "Oh, and you know what you're holding?"

"Wooden chopsticks," I said.

"That's a domestic product, kid."

I stared blankly at my utensils. The fervor for not only "organic" but also "local" had overtaken everything from cotton candy to chopsticks. Instead of Chinese chopsticks, we now used domestically produced ones. Because of this, the man's prices had gone up by two hundred won.

Cotton candy that was two hundred won better than before lay on the stand amid a swarm of children, squished against each other like layers of pastry dough. The fluffy concoction twirled around the axis of the cotton candy machine, inflating as strands of sugar sucked up air. Who cared if the chopsticks were made in China or Korea, or even if they were from outer space?

"You're acting like this because you eat all that junk," my mom complained to me.

Mom said that the snacks sold at school were ruining children who ate organic food at home, but I disagreed. I was only able to be myself because I did a certain amount of snacking at school. If not for the street vendors, I would have been a pretty awful kid.

Mom had recently joined an "organic club" and now spent her time memorizing things like "how to prepare a fresh meal with twelve kinds of vegetables." But as far as I could tell, a table covered with twelve kinds of vegetables was a field, not a meal. Mom's obsession with organic had made me start to like pesticides. That's what organic food had *really* done to me.

I was drawn to the flavor of beef stock as soon as I stopped breastfeeding. But even back then, my mom's taste was different from mine. She would always try to serve me unappetizing vegetable gruel.

"Hey, at least two bites," she'd say. "It's your duty!"

Every time she tried to get me to eat cabbage salad when I was little, she said the same thing. I'd bombard her with endless questions before following her orders to open my mouth.

"Mom, what's this?" I'd ask.

"Um, Snow White."

The cabbage salad would come a few inches closer to my mouth. I'd flutter my eyelashes while trying to imagine that the cabbage really was Snow White. After I swallowed a mouthful of Snow White, the next runner in the food relay stood at the ready.

"Mom, what is it now?"

"Cinderella."

Later, when my mom understood my food preferences better, she knew to give the cabbage salad names like "dog poop" or "chicken beak." Nothing had really changed since then. Every day, she pulled together an organic dinner that you might as well call rabbit food. Today, the main course was stuffed spring cabbage rolls. Mom put a little bit of multigrain rice inside the cabbage leaf, garnished it with soybean paste, and held the wrap out to me.

"Junk food is what first-graders eat," she said. "If you keep it up, your insides are going to be a mess. Eat this. It's your duty."

Mom didn't push the spoon at me outright, but the "duties" kept coming. I thought of how my cabbage salad used to turn into a princess and decided to play our old dinnertime game, speaking in a singsong voice.

"Mom, what's this?" I asked.

Mom answered brusquely.

"It's spring cabbage."

"Nooooo. Mom, what is it?"

"I said it's spring cabbage."

Mom was basically a rabbit living off grass, and her powers of imagination had bottomed out. When I asked her what the responsibility on my plate really was, she said it was spring cabbage, and when I asked again, it was still spring cabbage. The third time I asked about my duty, it became "Stop it! It's spring cabbage." Vegetables at our organic dinner table no longer turned into something else. Mom didn't understand why I was hungry again as soon as I finished eating. Eating organic makes people unforgiving. Would I have to move out before I became just as mean? Maybe Mom would get a boyfriend like Jinu's mom had. Jinu's mom was married, but she had a boyfriend anyway. The boyfriend gave her necklaces and one time he bought ice cream for Jinu.

"I decided to keep my mouth shut about the affair until I finished the ice cream," Jinu told me.

Jinu had a big mouth, so he went around bragging about how his mom was having an affair. To be honest, maybe he wasn't bragging. Maybe I was just secretly jealous. I was jealous of Jinu's mom's skill. Jinu's mom—who had a husband and wasn't that pretty—had a boyfriend, and my mom—who wasn't married and *was* pretty—didn't. The difference between them was loneliness. My mom needed to be a little lonelier.

I was no less of a loudmouth than Jinu. I told Mom about Jinu's mother's affair as soon as I heard about it, blurting it out in hopes of getting Mom worked up. She listened while peeling garlic, without much of an expression.

"What kind of cheating is *that*?" she asked. "That's nothing."

"But what about his dad?" I asked.

Mom acted like she was about to say something, then she shut her mouth.

"Jinu's mom isn't the kind of person who throws her family away for another man," she said. "The boyfriend is just a fling."

Mom spoke like she was an expert.

"Mom, you should date, too!" I exclaimed. "I don't mind if you throw away your family."

I was serious, but Mom hit me on the head. Then she pulled me into a hug and rubbed my cheeks.

"Hongdo, you're everything to me!" she exclaimed. "My sweet daughter!"

I hated that expression, and when I struggled to get away, Mom hugged me tighter. In moments like this, I really noticed Dad's absence. I was all Mom had, so I had to play the role of daughter *and* husband. Were other relationships this stressful? Jinu shared his thoughts about my situation, trying to comfort me.

"This is how an only child always feels," he said. "But things change once the second kid is born."

The problem with Jinu was that he always spoke in generalities. Unfortunately, I wasn't getting siblings anytime soon. That meant there was only one way for me to free myself from my mother. Mom needed a boyfriend.

2. THE FIRST BACHELOR IN NINE YEARS

The Hongdo Park whom my mom fed organic food was a completely different daughter from the Hongdo Park who secretly snacked on junk. The organic Hongdo was a lot more pretentious.

After joining the organic club, Mom started to lie, and she lied a lot. Lies and imagination obviously occupied different parts of the brain, considering Mom's lack of creativity.

"Oh, my daughter's nothing special," she'd tell other mothers. "She's just gotten into the habit of studying without me even having to push her."

As recently as last month, Mom had been trying to enroll me in classes at Sparta Tutoring Center, the same place Jinu went to, and I kept shouting that I wouldn't go. Mom was creating a new Hongdo Park. This new Hongdo was going to grow up eating only organic, attend a prestigious university, and become a doctor. That was Mom's dream, and she wasn't afraid to make it public. While Mom was busy turning her child into a college graduate and doctor, I couldn't understand why I had to attend elementary school. Honestly, I didn't have any hopes or dreams.

"There's really nothing you want to be when you grow up?" my homeroom teacher asked me in school one day. "Not even the president?"

My teacher asked me about my ambitions several times during our one-on-one meeting. Was it really such a problem that I didn't want to *become* anything? Ten-year-olds have endless opportunities to tell adults about their goals. But even so, it was rude to keep asking what a kid like me wanted to be when she grew up. Open-ended questions are just stressful.

"The president?" I replied. "I guess it would be nice to be president, but it doesn't seem possible."

"Why not?" my teacher asked. "If you study hard and get along with your friends, you could do it."

"Do you really think that?"

My teacher looked at me like I'd disappointed him and added, "Why not? Do you hate the president?"

"My mother's family sympathized with the Japanese during the occupation. How would it be possible for me to be president?"

My homeroom teacher took my statement as a joke. Or maybe he was just forcing himself to laugh. Then he asked if I knew what it meant to sympathize with the Japanese. He thought I didn't know! It made me angry.

My teacher urgently tried to come up with a career path for me, a child with no interest whatsoever in becoming president. I should have said I wanted to be a CEO or a manager, like everyone else did. Or if not those jobs, then I could have said something like "a celebrity." Seriously, though, I had no ambition. That was it. But adults treated children without aspirations like they were children without thoughts.

"Do you have anything else to tell me?" my teacher asked.

"You're not married, right?"

My teacher shook his head.

"Then are you divorced?" I continued.

"You're making fun of me for being an old bachelor, aren't you?"

My homeroom teacher smiled as he said it. Several days earlier, when he had first started working here, rumors spread that he was the "first unmarried male teacher" at our school in nine years. The first bachelor in nine years was a substitute for our regular homeroom teacher, the Shrew. Now that he was teaching Korean instead of her, I had to find my long-untouched Korean textbook before class started. I could have gone to the bookstore to buy a new one, but it was a hassle, so I just stole a copy from the classroom next door. Lots of kids had the same idea, and there was suddenly a shortage of the formerly unpopular textbook.

When the semester started, I should have paid closer attention to the Shrew's belly. If I knew when she was going on maternity leave, I could have prepared more for her replacement's arrival. I would have actually studied for Korean class, or at least not lost my textbook. Honestly, no one in our class imagined that the Shrew would really have a baby. We thought that her bulging belly was filled with several years' worth of fat. So when the Shrew left to give birth a month after the school year started, we were shocked. There were still rumors in school that she hadn't disappeared to have a baby, but to take a massive dump.

Some of us kids believed it was possible to overcome a certain amount of age difference in a relationship. When I thought of the new homeroom teacher, though, I didn't imagine him taking an interest in me: that was inconceivable. When I saw him, I thought of my mother. Our teacher was thirty-three, and so was Mom. Age-wise, they were perfect for each other. The homeroom teacher was the type of person matchmakers wanted. He had a good job, looked presentable, and most importantly, he was considerate. It would be good for Mom to have a young partner, and if they started dating, my life at school would get easier. Plus, the teacher didn't seem like the cheating type. You got that feeling looking at him. This was extremely important. Dad had been a cheater, so Mom didn't miss him much. The only thing cheaters were good for was dying, and I didn't want Mom to become widowed a second time. This is why her new boyfriend was not allowed to cheat.

"Sir, what kind of food do you like?" I asked the new teacher.

"What kind of food do I like?" he repeated.

I asked about his palate the way people asked about blood type or zodiac sign. When he didn't answer right away, I gave him some choices. One: junk food. Two: health food. My teacher smiled widely and then answered that he preferred health food. Ding-ding, correct! His answer proved he was a good match for my mom. As our one-on-one meeting ended, I asked him another question, like I was trying to hit a second bull's-eye.

"What do you like more, meat or vegetables? Do you eat foods like chicory?"

"I drink green juice every morning," he said.

The blades of his juicer whirred in my ear. They sounded like they were clapping to congratulate these two people—my teacher and my mom—for meeting each other. Goosebumps broke out on my arms, as if my entire body were absorbing the vibrations. I imagined Mom walking next to my homeroom teacher while they drank green juice together. A match made in heaven! If they start dating, Mom wouldn't be so bored, and she'd pay less attention to me.

Jinu said that his dream was to be "above average."

"A person who can play Czerny 30 or higher, who can easily join a game of soccer as midfielder, who can dance—at least techno and break-dance—who earns a bit of money, who's in better health than others, who isn't excluded from the group no matter where they are! Maybe not the best, but better than average. That's my dream. I want to be someone like that."

Hearing him speak, I felt like I knew a lot of similar people.

"I know people like that," I said. "The Hongdo Park my mother gave birth to is supposedly 'above average.'"

"But then how are you not?" Jinu thoughtlessly blurted out before quickly covering his mouth with his hands.

We could hear a faint clatter by the front gate. Considering how the other kids weren't really saying hello to the person making the noise, it had to be the art teacher. Of course: she walked by with her heels clacking in six-eight time. Did everyone have to move through life so quickly? Jinu and I were ambling along in four-four time. As he stepped forward, Jinu's head started to bob as quickly as the art teacher's had, then, after a bit, he returned to our original pace. I opened my mouth.

"My mom is so good at getting refunds that sometimes I wonder if she'll exchange *me* for a refund. Since I'm not the kid she wanted."

Jinu took a bite out of his cotton candy, wearing an ambiguous expression on his face.

"There's no way your mom will return you," he said. "Don't worry."

After Jinu walked away, his face buried in cotton candy, my gait grew even slower than four-four time. If I went home, my tongue would probably be dyed green from vegetables again. It would be a bit shameful to be given back to wherever I came from, but sometimes I did wish Mom would return me. I imagined she'd say something like this: "I watered this plant thinking it was a flower for my greenhouse, but it's turned out to be a weed!"

And then the store employee would look Mom over and ask the following: "Did you purchase the plant with a card or with cash?"

"A card."

"The plant's not dead, is it? We can give you a refund as long as the date specified by the return policy hasn't passed."

"Yes, she's a recent purchase. She's not even old enough to have an ID card yet."

The employee taps on the card reader like it's a piano. Her skills are way beyond playing Czerny 30. The register dances, break-dances, as it spews out a receipt.

"Purchase cancellation," the receipt says.

Mom looks satisfied as she sticks her credit card and the receipt in her wallet and then leaves the store. The employee uses my ear as a handle to pick up my body, and after judging that I can't be recycled, she throws me down the drain. I fall down the pipe and drift into junk food heaven.

"This is your duty," Mom said. "Just eat two bites. It's pickled glasswort: it's good for you."

Dang it—of course Mom would be the gatekeeper to junk food heaven. Once again, she'd prepared a fresh dinner with twelve different kinds of vegetables, and she was staring at me intently. Could I get a refund for this meal?

"Mom, what did you want to be when you were a kid?" I asked.

Mom answered while holding out a chopstick full of pickled glasswort.

"A good wife and a wise mother," she said.

Clearly, not everyone achieves their dreams.

3. ORGANIC CLUB

Change the world with dirt.

That's what was written on the cover of Mom's notebook. The notebook was a blacklist, given to Mom when she joined the organic club. On its first few pages was a list of cancerous ingredients that were going to destroy the earth, written in letters as small as sesame seeds. I'd taken a peek at the notebook once. The words inside were so long that if you told me it was a family tree for a Russian dynasty, I would have believed you. The unwieldy words were like Genesis 1: one name begat another, and another, and another, and the list continued on and on. It was so tedious that even if my own name was somewhere in the middle of the page, I wouldn't have been able to find it.

Whenever Mom bought a product, she checked the ingredients one by one against the blacklist. Because of that, we'd wasted two whole hours at the cosmetics store. Just to buy a bottle of toner. Mom's goal was to find cosmetics that didn't list "parabens" as an ingredient. The news had been reporting on the chemicals: apparently if you used cosmetic products that had parabens in them, your chances of getting skin cancer within thirty years were 0.9 percent. It was horrible news, but the more horrible thing was that there were almost no cosmetics that didn't contain parabens. Parabens were a preservative that made the products last longer. As my fussy mother and I turned the makeup counter upside down looking for the right product, an employee began talking to us faster and faster. It was clear that she was growing anxious. When she saw that we'd selected yet another item and were checking the ingredients, she went into the storeroom, like she couldn't handle it anymore. Soon she emerged and showed us a rare, dust-covered bottle.

"This doesn't have anything in it," she said.

Nothing in it! The rare, natural cosmetic she'd given us did contain sorbic acid, though. Sorbic acid was another substance that triggered cancer. Mom was sensitive to cancer. After Dad had died of cancer—no, even before—Mom's life was a war against the disease. We finally left because she couldn't find a makeup product without any dangerous substances. We went to the drugstore, and Mom bought several bottles of glycerin. She'd decided to make her own toner. My whole body was sore. Considering how many stores we'd gone into, we'd hardly bought anything at all. I was suspicious of why someone as meticulous as Mom had chosen to marry Dad.

My school's front gate was the main venue for the ceaseless blacklist-inspired purge. Nonorganic sugar and wooden chopsticks from China, American corn and pizza cheese—they all disappeared. Elementary school kidnappings became a growing problem, and hats with brims were added to the blacklist. The kidnappers in the news wore hats to cover their faces, so it was decided that no one within three hundred meters of the school could wear a hat or a mask. Children weren't exempted from the new rule. We couldn't wear a hat anymore when going to school or coming home. Every morning during our assembly, those covering their faces were asked to think of the children.

"For the sake of the children, please refrain from wearing hats or masks."

After a banner emblazoned with those words was hung over the gates, the cotton candy man started to act a bit awkward. He was always wearing a baseball cap decorated with three or four studs as he rode around, cotton candy dangling in clusters from his motorcycle. I'd never seen him without his hat. The cotton candy man and his baseball cap were stuck to each other like Siamese twins. Rumors spread that not even our mothers' meddling could separate the two.

A "habitual" hat wearer: this was how the organic club moms designated the cotton candy man. They gently suggested a couple of times that he take off his cap, but the cotton candy man didn't understand why he should. Soon, his status had changed: to an "intentional" hat wearer.

The more you're told to stop doing something, the more you want to do it. That's how it was. Seeing the cotton candy man insist upon wearing his hat even though he was told not to—that excited the salivary glands of us kids. Every afternoon, we bought cotton candy to commemorate our release from prison. One day, I saw my mom out front. She hadn't come to pick her daughter up from school, she'd come to scold the person waiting with treats for the newly released prisoners: the cotton candy man.

The organic club moms sometimes mobilized like they were crime scene investigators. Mostly they were just on the lookout for flashers, who'd try to excite the lower-grade students, or they were cracking down on junk food. The front of the school was like a stage for the moms. They wore green clothing and stood exactly one meter apart from one another, so if you looked at them from a distance, they resembled trees bordering the street. There were a lot of trees. Sometimes trees I'd never even seen would nag at me. Not just me: the trees interrupted everyone passing through the gate.

"Please take your hat off. There are children around."

Someone stepped forward from the organic club crowd. The cotton candy man revved the engine to his motorcycle, his attitude toward the moms nastier than ever. *Vroom vroom.* Drowned out by the sound, the organic club's rallying cry still didn't change.

"This is your duty," they told the cotton candy man. "It's a rule you have to follow."

The next person to step forward was my mom. I didn't have the courage to walk up to her, so I watched from a distance. There was a manhole at my feet. Twenty small, round openings were drilled into the manhole cover. I wanted to go inside one of them and hide.

"If you want to be an ethical businessperson, you can't do this," she scolded him.

"Ethical businessperson?"

The cotton candy man had a vacant expression on his face. The man's head and hat were eventually separated, according to the ethics of business. Without his hat, his forehead showed off a rough-looking scar. He looked like someone who'd been struck by lightning. A few days later, the cotton candy man was back to wearing his hat. Apparently, scars didn't match the school's image. The school began to allow people to wear a specific kind of hat: pink hats, like the one the cotton candy man was now required to wear. Pink was our school's official color, seen everywhere from our gym uniforms to the wall paint.

Another banner was hung above the front gate to commemorate a maternal victory.

"A school without the shade of a hat brim means cheerful children."

When the organic club moms saw the banner, they swelled with pride as if looking at a monument celebrating a victorious battle. The children tilted their heads, confused. So many signs hung from the gate that it was now constantly in shadow, making it hard to accept this place as a shade-free school. All the banners were changed to pink. School was starting to get absurd, even without the hat battle.

"Our field trip is on the nineteenth," our homeroom teacher told us, wearing a pink necktie. "Don't come to school that day: we'll meet at Konkuk University Station, on line 2."

The field trip was a legitimate reason to escape from school, but the destination was terrible. To think—it was a field trip, and we weren't even going to an amusement park or to a mountain for hiking: we were visiting a university. No one was on the campus when we arrived. Some kids thought that meant April 19 was a university holiday and said they wanted to be in college, too. We were lucky that there was no one around to see us, looking silly as we walked around in single file, one after another. We toured the campus and the student cafeteria. The university visit was tolerable.

Our homeroom teacher made an impassioned speech about how we all needed to know why April 19 was an important day. It commemorated students who'd protested for democracy in the 1960s. When he asked, "What day is April 19?," one child who'd been carefully listening to his monologue answered innocently: "Field trip day!"

Our teacher seemed so obsessed with April 19 that some kids began to whisper about whether April 19 might be the teacher's birthday. April 19 was an important day for me, too. It wasn't just the day of our field trip, and it definitely wasn't our teacher's birthday: it was the day my mom and my teacher met for the first time.

Mom shattered all my expectations about their first encounter, though. Mom was going to drive me to our class's meeting place at the subway station, but first she stopped the car briefly at a kimbap store where we were regulars. Honestly, I didn't understand why someone who loved organic and handmade things so much was buying kimbap for her daughter's field trip, and from a twenty-four-hour carryout joint. Mom claimed that it was because the kimbap at this store was made from domestic black rice. But it smelled like excuses to me.

While Mom was packing up her kimbap order, I went to the bathroom on the side of the building and peed. As I was leaving the bathroom, I heard a strange sound. It was Mom's voice. I snuck a glance around the corner and saw Mom getting all worked up in front of the car.

"You didn't pick up your phone!" she shouted. "If you just park your car here, what am I supposed to do?"

A man came running from the end of the alley. He explained that he hadn't heard his phone ringing, that he'd pull out his car quickly. But something about his actions seemed sluggish. The two things Mom hated most were illegal parking and not answering the phone. This man had done both. Now that he'd been caught, his day was ruined, too.

"You have no manners!" Mom continued. "Really, not answering the phone when you've blocked someone else's car!"

The pitiful man had, of all things, lost his keys. As he scrambled to find them, Mom's patience reached its limit. Her shadow traced an imposing shape on the ground. The man's shadow, on the other hand, looked tiny.

"This isn't parking, you were basically trying to abandon your car," Mom said to him.

The man's movements grew a little faster. He checked the front and back of his suit and took off his sunglasses. In that moment, I saw his face. It was my homeroom teacher!

"You don't have a key?" Mom questioned. "Are you sure you're not trying to get rid of your car?"

I ran toward the front of the parked car and pointed to the note on the dashboard.

"He's not throwing it away. Look, it's written right here," I said. " 'Temporarily parked' . . ."

Mom kept repeating the same words, like she was deaf and blind.

"Were you disposing of your car just now?" she asked.

The note said he'd parked his car! Could she not read? Mom didn't pay attention to me. Instead, she shot fire from her eyes at the man. He was flustered by my mom's imposing voice. Then he noticed me, hidden behind this unfamiliar woman. Our eyes met. The sky spun like sugar candy melting inside a ladle.

"Hongdo!" he shouted.

It seemed like an order. With my homeroom teacher calling my name, the atmosphere changed. My teacher stopped moving helter-skelter, and his eyes traveled between Mom and me. Then *Mom* began to act a little frazzled.

"Are you Hongdo's . . . mother?" my teacher asked.

For a second, I could almost see an exclamation point flit across Mom's face, like she was a cartoon character realizing something important. I hadn't known that my teacher and Mom would meet so soon, and I also hadn't known that the encounter would end this quickly. Mom's face grew yellow, like a well-heated piece of sugar candy.

"No!" she yelled.

Mom then hurried into our favorite kimbap place. Only after she disappeared did my homeroom teacher find his car keys in his pants pocket. It was as if people really did emanate auras, and this black-rice kimbap shop was the sole point at which my mom's and my teacher's auras would ever overlap.

His hands still shaking, my teacher started his car's engine. He asked again if the woman was my mother. I was conflicted for a moment. She had already denied her maternity, so could I really say that she was my mom?

"She's my aunt," I explained.

Only after parting with my teacher did I realize that I'd lied pointlessly. Mom . . . aunt . . . what was the difference?

Mom finally took me all the way to the field trip site and then hastily left. Mom said that there was no way she could run into my homeroom teacher again. She couldn't pretend to be my aunt. She told me that someday she'd introduce herself to him properly, but now wasn't the time. She left me and my black-rice kimbap all by ourselves. I didn't like the look of the kimbap, so I ate it up so fast that I hardly breathed until it was gone.

When I came home after the field trip, Mom was still wearing makeup as she pulled dusty organic sweet potatoes out of a box.

"What I did this morning was for your own good," she said.

That was her excuse for lying to my teacher. If my classmates learned that I had a mother like this, I would become even more of a joke. As if everything were my fault, Mom started to complain about being stuck in the kimbap joint for over ten minutes that morning.

"How could I have known he was your teacher?" she asked. "He looks so young, I would have thought he was a college student—ugh."

"He's thirty-three."

Mom didn't reply. Only after I pushed her to ask me questions about my teacher did she ask the following: "How many kids does he have?"

"He's not married," I answered.

"He's thirty-three and doesn't have kids or a wife? Is he dating?"

Mom said it like she didn't understand how someone could be single.

"It's strange not to have anyone in your life at thirty-three," she said. "He must be in a lot of debt."

"He's not in debt!" I argued. "He's not!"

My mom's pessimism made me upset, and I didn't want to finish my dinner. I'd barely sat down when she said, gulping down a spoonful of soup, that my teacher's car looked shoddy. I replied that you couldn't judge someone by appearances.

"Are you admitting that he's attractive?" I asked her grouchily. That was my start as a timid matchmaker. Mom didn't answer and for a while just picked up dried slices of daikon and ate them. She sounded anxious as she chewed on the radishes. Mom found people who asked questions frustrating. She had the tendency to wait until the asker was about to die of curiosity before opening her mouth. Finally Mom spoke.

"He looked like the actor Leslie Cheung."

4. FIRST SEMESTER ART CURRICULUM

My art teacher called me into the staff room and told me to look carefully at my drawing. I looked at it vacantly for a while, and then the art teacher said in a slightly condescending tone: "Here—is it supposed to be night in this picture?"

It wasn't really a question. She was trying to point something out. As soon as I nodded, she asked again.

"Then why did you draw a sun?"

"The sun is in the sky."

"But you can't see it at night."

"It's just our eyes that can't see it," I explained. "It's there."

The art teacher shook her head like that wasn't the right answer. Then she asked about a girl I'd drawn walking down the street.

"Is she going home? Is she going to school?"

"She's going to school."

The art teacher snorted while smiling at me. She repeatedly gathered her black hair behind her as she asked about the girl again.

"Why would you go to school at night?"

I didn't say anything. The art teacher was acting like I had some sort of impure intentions making this drawing. When she asked for a second time why my picture featured a sun instead of a moon, I held my ground.

"The sun and the moon are both in the sky," I said. "They stay where they are—the earth is what moves. Why don't you make us draw any of the things the earth rotates around?"

I shouted like Galileo, burning with conviction. The earth rotated, I was sure of it!

"But in a landscape, you draw what you see. I told you to make landscapes."

My art teacher hit the glass surface of the desk, making a clacking noise. A sheet of paper bearing the words "Fourth Grade First Semester Art Curriculum" lay under the glass panel. I looked at it as I answered.

"You can make things up in a drawing, too."

"This is a landscape drawing. Surrealism is next month."

My art teacher spoke with an annoyed tone in her voice.

"And you couldn't really say this is made-up. If something's made-up, there has to be something special about it, right? Something that isn't possible in our reality. Something like a flying carpet, or a time machine, or a city under the sea."

My art teacher looked down at my picture like a person sitting in front of a bunch of food she couldn't eat.

"Well, then, what category does my painting belong to?" I asked. "What kind of painting is it, exactly?"

"I'm just trying to explain things to you," my art teacher retorted. "What are you doing now?"

"You said that there can't be a sun in the night sky."

I was using a black crayon to erase the sun in my picture.

"Is this okay?" I asked.

The red color of the sun mixed with the black crayon, so it looked like clouds or fog. Now my drawing was very realistic.

The art teacher sent a few of our landscape drawings to the children's art competition being held by the local office of education. A few weeks later, I received yet another call to the faculty office. This time, the art teacher greeted me with a slightly friendlier expression on her face. She didn't tap her desktop with her fingernails, and she didn't pick on me by asking whether I had drawn night or day.

"Hongdo Park, you won the silver medal," she said.

The drawing with an erased sun had won silver in the children's art competition. If you looked at the drawing that had won gold, you could see that its sense of time was very exact. But as for creativity, there wasn't any. To be fair, according to the art teacher's logic, *my* picture wasn't a landscape.

On the day of the exhibition, our house was abuzz with energy all morning. Mom wrestled with her hair dryer for thirty minutes before giving up and exasperatedly going to the hair salon. She also wrapped exactly one scarf around her neck, and that was enough to make her look like the kind of woman who wore a different scarf every day of the week. There was a strange piece of fabric wrapped around my art teacher's neck as well. In order to stop the fabric from falling, she'd clasped a sparkling brooch to her clavicle. The whole way home, Mom kept talking about the brooch.

This time, neither Mom nor my homeroom teacher could avoid a face-to-face encounter. Neither of them brought up the April 19 incident. They artfully ignored the issue. My homeroom teacher welcomed Mom like he was seeing her for the first time, and Mom kept a straight face as well. If my teacher asked about what had happened, I was considering telling him that my mom and my aunt were twins. That made me feel really exhausted.

Afterward, my homeroom teacher walked us to the exit. I was acting shy, but Mom looked excited.

"How was it seeing my teacher for the second time?" I asked her once he was gone.

"Looking at him again, I realized he has a hook nose."

"What's a hook nose?" I asked. Mom took her hands off the steering wheel and pretended to draw an incline over her face. Just then, the car rattled as we went over a speed bump.

"The reason this street is bumpy is because it's like a hook nose. People with hook noses are indecisive."

I wasn't sure what that meant, but it didn't give me a good feeling, so I changed the topic of conversation.

"Mom, my homeroom teacher is really talented," I said. "Think about how he joined us in the middle of the semester."

"That's not talent, that just means he's a short-term employee. Your homeroom teacher is a substitute teacher, you know?"

"What's a substitute teacher?"

"A temporary one."

Mom was bad-mouthing my teacher.

"Mom, my teacher drinks green juice every morning, too. He likes clean living."

"Your homeroom teacher seemed stubborn," she replied.

How did green juice equal stubbornness?

"You just said that he's indecisive. How can indecisive people be stubborn?"

"Cause he's got a hook nose."

Sitting next to a matchmaker whose motivation was fading, Mom continued to reveal her pet theories about hook noses, like a quack physiognomist.

"How is class with the substitute?" she asked.

"The substitute? Mom, the way you're talking about him is offensive!"

"What do you mean, the way I'm talking? Hongdo, you need to learn some manners yourself!"

I saw the cotton candy man's motorcycle out the car window. He was starting the engine with a vroom, getting ready to go home. Food that normally felt like lies, food that was a lot less filling than it looked, suddenly seemed like it would really satisfy my hunger.

"Mom!" I shouted. "Stop for a minute!"

"Why?"

When I pointed to the cotton candy, Mom pressed down on the accelerator. The car left the alley in an instant. As I whined about how I was hungry, the following words flew out of her mouth: "Junk like that is all lies. It's not even food."

In the back mirror, I saw the splendid image of the cotton candy man on his way home. Cotton candies flanked him like ornaments, and he disappeared zigzagging between cars.

Honk honk!

Mom honked the horn and unrolled the car window. There was a man in a trench coat—probably a flasher—loitering to our left. He was always hanging around school, waiting to scare unsuspecting students. Now he was on his way to work, or maybe on his way home. He wasn't wearing a hat, but his scruffy attire put him on Mom's blacklist. She looked out the window and said the following: "The girls' high school is the next block, the next block! Not this street."

In that moment, the flasher looked like he was about to pull his pants down, so Mom pressed on the gas pedal again. I don't know if he really went to the girls' high school, but I didn't see him in front of my school again for a while.

5. LIFE IS A PYRAMID SCHEME

I was an early bloomer. At the end of second grade, my chest began to swell, and I was worried about how big it would grow. I'd opened my mom's dresser and saw how Mom's bras ranged from A to C cup. *How could even her underwear be inconsistent?* I wondered. But the size I saw the most was C. Unless I was an aberration, I'd probably grow to be a C cup, too. Or, since I was a glutton for snacks, maybe I'd be a D cup. I didn't know how I'd feel about it later, but having a voluminous body in fourth grade wasn't very comfortable.

When I started to develop, some of the mean girls in my class would yell, "Mrs. Cow, Hongdo Park!" And sometimes they'd ask, with serious expressions on their faces, whether eating carrots really made your chest big. The boys would brush against the girls' backs as they walked past us. Then they'd shout things like, "She's wearing one!" and "She isn't!" To the girls who were "wearing one," they asked, "What cup size are you?"

Teen bras don't usually close with a hook. Even when I wore one that had a band, though, if my outer clothing was thin and someone touched it, they could feel the fabric traversing my back. I hated that. One day, I went to school wearing my mom's strapless bra that she taped to her chest, and I couldn't sit up straight the entire day. My chest wasn't big enough to wear a sticker bra, and after putting on the C-cup stickers, the breasts that I did have hurt, like the bra was pulling my skin off.

The boys' curiosity reached its peak on the day of our physical examinations. They were somehow trying to figure out the circumference of the girls' chests. A pretty pathetic task. I told one boy that, contrary to expectations, chest circumference consisted of breasts and back measured together, in centimeters. The kid listened to me intently before asking, "So what cup are you?"

"I heard that the art teacher is measuring chest circumference!"

As soon as someone said that, an outburst of student gossip erupted across the room. I wasn't the only person to feel a strange sense of rivalry with the art teacher. The girls were embarrassed about having to lift up our shirts in front of her. Why did the art teacher have to measure our chests, and why with a cold tape measure?

Last time I'd gone with Mom to the doctor, she didn't have to lift up the front of her shirt. The doctor held the stethoscope to her back, or maybe she'd placed the stethoscope on the outside of her clothes. I didn't know why I was remembering that, but I hoped that the art teacher would do the same: measure my chest without making me lift up my shirt, or stand facing my backside. I just wanted her to respect my privacy.

"Are you not going to lift up your shirt?" the art teacher asked.

My privacy was gone in two seconds. I became a meek lamb, just like all the other girls who'd gone before me, and pulled my shirt up. Since it had come to this, I thought it would be nice if the art teacher would see my chest and realize that I wasn't a kid anymore. Maybe the art teacher was flat chested. She'd see my chest and get irritated. *Oh*, she'd say. Since my chest was disproportionally large for someone my age.

"Hey, it's over, kid!" she called out.

In another two seconds, my privacy was obliterated for the second time. The art teacher was already thrusting the tape measure at the girl behind me. I rushed to lower my shirt, my face flustered. We sat like products rolling down a conveyor belt, and the art teacher measured us to see if we met the standards.

"Hey, Hongdo Park!"

It was Minyeong Han. Running into Minyeong in the middle of the long hallway outside the examination room felt like meeting an enemy on a single-log bridge. I'd been in the same class as her in third grade, too, but this year, whenever she was in my presence, she'd just look at me and growl. Minyeong stuck out her sharp lips and spoke. I knew she wouldn't have anything good to say.

"Hey, you stupid rooster! I heard your sitting height was crazy high."

Of course.

"No it wasn't."

As I turned to leave, Minyeong called my name again and stopped me.

"Why, I heard that you had the tallest sitting height in our class? Even though you're short."

I quickly swiveled around.

"Don't talk unless you have something nice to say," I said.

Minyeong giggled noisily. I didn't know what was funny. I couldn't tell if she was laughing to laugh or if something actually was humorous.

"Does our homeroom teacher know about your height?" she taunted me. "Since you like him so much."

I realized why Minyeong was nagging me. Minyeong was another one of the girls who liked the homeroom teacher. Among the girls, bras, periods, and cosmetic procedures were no longer the only subject of conversation: a new secret, our homeroom teacher, was emerging as a favored discussion topic.

"Oh, you're embarrassed, aren't you? I heard that last time in art class, you drew our teacher's face."

"What are you talking about?" I asked.

"Now you're playing innocent! In art we were supposed to draw the face of a family member, but you drew our teacher's face—did you think I didn't know?"

The person I'd drawn in art class wasn't our teacher, it was my dad. I'd realized that there weren't many opportunities to talk about family at school, since we mostly gossiped about celebrities and clothing trends and dance moves. Kids spent the school day as fellow prisoners, and after class, we passed through the gates together, briefly making sugar candy and eating it before parting ways to our respective after-school tutoring programs. The next day, we'd convene at school and talk once again about celebrities and clothing and dances and teachers and the weird kids. At school and at home, I didn't have the chance to talk about my dead father. Mom had once told me that if people were ever talking about fatherless children, I should tell them straightaway about Dad, but since first grade, the topic had never come up. There was no reason to talk about children without fathers, and I had no one to tell my story to. Even the people who had found out, like Jinu, were too busy to care. At least my lack of a father wouldn't cause other kids to tease me. There were other things that made you a target of bullying. Like if you were fat or didn't dress well, or if something you did bothered people. And now Minyeong Han seemed to think that I was an enemy on the front lines of her relationship.

"It's not what you think it is," I told her. "Even if I explain, you won't understand. I'll be wasting my breath."

I turned to walk away as soon as I finished talking, but for some reason my feet wouldn't move. Maybe I really was a rooster, ready to fight. I looked like I was waiting for an excuse to shut Minyeong's trap for good. For better or for worse, she had a personality similar to mine. I figured I'd just leave if I could make it through the next five seconds. But after exactly three seconds, Minyeong starting gabbing again.

"Hey, you! Stop being like this."

Sheesh. As soon as my feet touched the hallway floor, my center of gravity shifted, and I faltered. Two more girls came up and encircled us. They weren't on my side. Minyeong was full of confidence.

"Did you hear?" she asked the other girls. "Hongdo Park said she's in love with the homeroom teacher."

It seemed like there was a fire in my chest, growing red-hot. The girls were giggling. I wanted to grab their long hair, but I controlled myself. I took a step forward, barely lifting my feet off the ground. Then two steps. When I was ten steps away, I could hear Minyeong and the two girls next to her murmuring behind me. I didn't understand exactly what they were saying. But a few words flew at me like an axe and stuck in my back. The axe was an order. *Turn around!*, it said.

I turned and made a screeching noise that rang down the hallway. All my eyes could see was Minyeong Han's talkative mouth. She quieted. Until now, I'd never been proud of having large breasts, and the words that came out of my mouth were an exception to how I normally felt.

"Your chest is tiny!"

Minyeong flinched, dumbfounded by the unexpected attack. One of the friends by her side started laughing. Anyone who saw us could tell that my insult was perfect, absurd as it was. Minyeong started chattering again, just as annoyingly as before.

"I'm going to be a model, so it doesn't matter that I don't have a chest. And I'm way taller than you, you know?"

You could smell the flames coming out the top of her head. She seemed fragile enough that now anyone who came at her for a fight could have won. I'd already hit Minyeong's weak point. I could have turned around and left, but a sense of competition flared inside me. I was filled with a previously unknown pride in my voluptuous figure. The voluptuous bad girl inside me spoke.

"So what? Boys don't care. At least, it's not what our teacher likes."

"What are you saying?" Minyeong asked, a little flustered. I wanted to turn around at this point, but my stupid busty alter ego kept going.

"Our homeroom teacher: he said that a little while ago. He said that women who are skinny and flat chested as chopsticks smell like fish. Anyone who looks at you knows you're flat chested. You can go jump off a cliff, little princess!"

The future model flopped on the ground. She broke into tears. It was silly. Fiery energy was still burning above my head, ready to go, but now I'd barely started and Minyeong Han was already crying. She couldn't even insult me: Why had she bothered attacking?

On the way home, I showed Jinu my sketchbook.

"Hey, who do you think this is?" I asked.

Jinu spoke without looking at it for long. "Is it our teacher?"

I looked at my sketchbook for a long time. Our homeroom teacher's face was familiar, but the memory of my dad's face was muddied, so I couldn't know whether or not they resembled each other. It felt like my white notebook had a black ribbon wrapped around it, like it was a funerary portrait, and I quickly closed it.

As he switched repeatedly from hat to scars and then back to hat, the cotton candy man's popularity fell. The pink baseball cap was a symbol of defeat and degradation. The cotton candy man, who'd apparently worked full-time in front of our school for the past twenty years, tried various promotions to recover lost business. One of them was a special deal: bring two friends with you and one eats for free. A sign attached to the front of his cart read: "2 + 1 Free."

He showed lightweight bunches of cotton candy to passing children, advertising his wares.

"If you three come for cotton candy, one of you will eat free."

Hearing those words, some of the children began to talk among themselves.

"Doesn't that make it like a pyramid scheme, since we have to bring our friends?" one asked.

"All of life is a pyramid scheme. Everything's word of mouth."

As the man said that, he twirled the tufts of cotton candy. The pyramid scheme of life made us divide ourselves into groups of three, and the cotton candy man was able to sell a little more cotton candy. Splitting into groups of three didn't lead to fights. Otherwise, Jinu, Minyeong, and I never would have bought cotton candy together.

When I got home, the organic club moms were using my house as a hideout, holding an organic strategy meeting there. I decided to take one of the moms' dogs for a walk and went to find the cotton candy man. With one hand, I pulled Marie, from France, and with the other hand, I pulled Mary, from Australia, until we were standing in front of the cotton candy man's motorcycle. Marie was three years old, and Mary was five. Marie was white, and Mary was black.

According to what I'd heard from the moms, you had to ease into an organic lifestyle step by step. Beginners started by changing what they ate. Next was makeup, and after that, clothing and bed linens, and then there was home décor. If you were a real master, you even dreamed organic dreams. Marie and Mary were supposedly born after their owner had dreamed organic dreams about them. I didn't know if it was because they were raised

Western style or because they were raised organic, but Marie and Mary were wild. Maybe the problem was that they couldn't understand me. They seemed to be spouting curses at me in dog language. Marie and Mary were just animals, but they watched me like they were on edge.

"Sir, do animals count as people?" I asked.

The cotton candy man glanced at me and nodded.

"Marie, Mary," I told the dogs. "This is an order. You each have to eat one."

I took the two organic dogs and enjoyed the pyramid scheme. When she caught a whiff of the cotton candy's fantastic scent, Marie's eyes glittered. Mary wagged her tail like she wanted more. From what I could see, liking junk food was instinctive, regardless of nationality or age.

"Are they your dogs?" the cotton candy man asked.

"No," I said. "They belong to someone else. This one's from France and that one's from Australia. They're foreign dogs."

The cotton candy man looked at Marie and asked: "You're from France? Do French people really think that Koreans cook dogs in the microwave?"

Marie didn't have any thoughts about the matter. She didn't bark and didn't wag her tail. She just stared intently at Mary, and then she licked the remains of sugar left on Mary's lips. As it moved to taste the sugar, Marie's tongue looked like a thin slice of ham.

"These guys aren't used to the time difference, so they're a little out of it," I explained.

Cotton candy is a food that leaves traces on your mouth the way black bean noodles and Jaws bars do, so before returning home, I had to use water to wipe away the evil remnants from Marie's and Mary's lips. If I didn't, maybe the magic that had created my junk food heaven would be broken, and everything would go back to being stupid and organic. The formerly frantic dogs beamed at me. Marie and Mary were proof that junk food transformed personalities. *Good girls*. We became accomplices. I was going to teach Marie and Mary how to avoid becoming a host to the organic plague. Welcome to junk food!

6. COTTON CANDY MAN IN PRISON

"Seoul, Daejeon, Daegu, Busan, Incheon."

I asked Mom where Korea's five biggest cities were, and that's what she told me. I wrote down the names of the cities, and before class started, Jinu saw my list and starting laughing crazily. Incheon was the problem. As soon as class ended, I hurried out the front gate. The organic club moms were wearing their green hats and standing in a line from the front of the school to the nearby apartment complexes, like trees on the side of the road. I barely managed to spot Mom among them.

"I was really embarrassed because of you!" I shouted. "Why'd you say Incheon is a big city? Incheon!"

"Why are you so upset? When I was a kid, Incheon was important."

Mom raised her voice. The more she insisted that Incheon was a major city, the more my trust in her faded. I was now at the age where teach-yourself books were a necessity.

"Incheon? What do you mean, Incheon! Now it's just part of Pangyo."

The woman standing next to Mom chipped in. The five biggest cities were Seoul, Daejeon, Daegu, Busan, and Pangyo, she said. The woman next to *her* said you had to take out Daejeon and add Bundang. Someone then went on a tangent about the island of Dokdo, and said that since it wasn't even a suburb, you couldn't really include it in the list of Korea's five biggest cities. We were in Hanam—a medium-sized suburb at best—but the trees planted in the ground stood so confidently, it seemed like they were adorning one of Korea's five most important cities.

Without guidebooks telling them how to farm, the organic club members brainstormed which five local neighborhoods would be best for weekend farming. They wrote down possibilities on the back of the blacklist notebook. There were a lot of places that I didn't know well or had never even heard of. The back of the blacklist grew like an online shopping list.

When some of the mothers began to actually spend their weekends farming, Mom's interest was aroused. She decided to start cultivating her own plot, and one day, we bought some land in Paju. Mom prepared multiple types of seeds, including a bunch of things you couldn't eat, like flowers and trees.

"What's so great about weekend farming?" I asked. "Why do you have to go all the way to Paju to do it?"

"They say that the land there is good," she explained.

After preparing her Paju plot, Mom spent every other Saturday going there with her friends. She worked two Saturdays each month and farmed the other two. That meant I got to spend at least one day every two weeks enjoying the luxury of junk food. Before leaving the house, Mom prepared prickly multigrain rice with greens and leaves for me. With her gone, though, I could eat what I wanted. I wrapped exactly two scoops of multigrain rice in a trash bag and threw it away outside. Then I ordered black bean noodles, pizza, and sometimes fried chicken, savoring my short-term junk food heaven.

Once, I joined Mom on her farming excursion, and I saw that her plot of land was almost empty. There were just a few heads of lettuce, wilted like curled-up cats. Mom was better at buying blacklist-approved products than she was at farming.

Change the world with dirt.

That was, of course, still the organic club's slogan.

"Hey, have you heard?" Jinu asked the next day at school, looking sad. "The cotton candy man is in the teachers' room right now."

When I said that he was in trouble because of stupid organic, trying to destroy everything for us, Jinu tilted his head.

"No, that's not it," he said. "Apparently it's because of the pyramid scheme? He's being imprisoned because of his pyramid scheme sales!"

According to the organic generation, it wasn't okay to eat snacks, and when the adults who *did* encourage us to eat snacks said something weird, we were supposed to report it quickly. When I asked what that meant, I learned that several rule-following classmates had gone to their moms and reported the cotton candy man. They'd probably made weird facial expressions and said something like the following: "Mom, that man is strange. He tells us to join his pyramid scheme."

I wouldn't have been so upset if those same kids could put their hands on their chests and swear that they'd never eaten at the cotton candy man's stall. But they definitely had. They ratted him out before they could even digest the cotton candy that they'd bought because it looked so good. You might not like the cotton candy man, I thought, but what he said about life being a pyramid scheme was pretty profound. The dim-witted kids didn't understand the meaning of his words, so they snitched?

The stupid girls were glued to the faculty room window, trying to see what was happening to the man they'd outed. The angle at which they had to tilt their head to see into the window suggested that they were in one of the lower grades. I wasn't like those kids, but I still pulled Jinu with me to see what was going on, and we peeked through the faculty room window, too.

"Well, that's what the rumors said about the guy. People were saying that he told them to bring three friends and he'd give you one cotton candy for free. It seems like this happened because of those rumors."

Even without Jinu's voiceover, the scene visible through the office window was strange enough. The cotton candy man was sitting with several teachers, maybe the principal and the vice principal. They were talking with serious expressions. There were also two middle-aged women wearing green hats. The cotton candy man kept bowing his head.

After that, we didn't see the cotton candy man in front of the school gates for a while. I didn't eat cotton candy often, but something felt off now that the cotton candy man—who'd survived the initial gusts of the organic windstorm—was gone. When he disappeared, we felt collective pain. We shook our anxious legs to the same beat, we had diarrhea one after another, and we lowered our heads at the same angles to doze in class. These were our collective withdrawal symptoms after the cotton candy man's disappearance.

As children passed through the school gates from which the cotton candy man had vanished, lies ascended in thick, cotton candy–like clouds. The lies' plots varied, from the cotton candy man having to write an apology letter on his pink hat to him causing a brawl in the faculty room. There was also the story that the cotton candy man had thrown a punch, knocking out either the principal or the vice principal's front tooth. The cotton candy that I'd stuffed into my mouth until I had sugary breath was now gone. Obviously, I was hungry.

The cotton candy man had been the target. But just because the target disappeared, that didn't mean other bad snacks would be left in peace. The organic club moms picked a fight with everything. "Why is the sugar candy color like that? Isn't it too hard? The fish fillets are burnt. If you burn them too much, you'll give the kids cancer. Take care with the slushy ice—if the coloring is really bright, don't use it. Please use natural coloring—not natural coloring stamped on in a factory, but homemade dye made with ingredients from nature—Oh! Why are you wearing a hat? This is a school zone, you can't wear hats. Look, it's written here!"

The more the mothers spoke, the more I dreamed of hats appearing. It would be great if a kidnapper in an unfamiliar hat showed up and caused a ruckus, I thought. If a kidnapper hiding his face with a hat appeared, Jinu said he'd say the following: "Sir, our moms are sad people. They've already been through enough."

I wouldn't let Jinu get the last word. I'd tell the kidnapper: "Our moms haven't been through anything!"

After class, when I'd escaped the school zone, I sometimes ran into the targets of our mothers' ire: people wearing hats. But they didn't fit the stereotype. One hat-wearing man I ran into spoke in a gentle voice, like a teacher.

"You all go home and when your parents arrive, show them this," he said, handing us flyers. "Try bugging them. If you sign up, you'll get a free gift."

The forms that the kidnappers left us, purchase forms for home study materials, weren't leaflets advertising what I longed for. The next morning, the trashcans in my classroom were heaped so high with the flyers that it seemed like they might reach the ceiling.

The homeroom teacher was the common denominator for us girls. We were all numerators, forming fractions as we stood on top of our teacher. 40510, 40834, 40821 . . . as the other teachers acted inappropriately, more girls became numerators, and the value of *our* teacher increased. My situation was a little different from everyone else's, but I still hit on him. It wasn't really important whether I was doing it for myself or for my mom. Even though I didn't feel great about flirting, I stood above the fraction line, with our teacher below it. But one day, in an instant, our classroom fractions were reduced to nothing.

It was because of the art teacher, who clicked as she walked. According to the other kids, there was something going on between the art teacher and our homeroom teacher. Several Korean textbooks were discovered torn up in the trashcan. The covers had our homeroom teacher's name written all over. The boys, who weren't intoxicated by our teacher like the girls were, were shocked. They kept repeating the same hackneyed phrase "How could this have happened behind our backs?"

"Hey, our homeroom teacher is dating the art teacher."

Jinu was one step behind me. I had ears too: I had already heard the news. Apparently, our homeroom teacher had graduated from the same university as the art teacher, and they'd been dating for a long time and were going to get married next spring. Decisive information supporting the rumor continued to leak out. There was a kid who'd spotted them going to the theater together last weekend, and other kids had seen our homeroom teacher's picture on the art teacher's personal blog. The fact that we'd also never seen our homeroom teacher with the art teacher in school was tangible proof. They knew they had to be careful, so they purposefully kept a distance. It was like office dating. What would happen to my mom? She hadn't even started making her move! Was this how my teacher would be stolen from me? There weren't many other eligible bachelors in school.

Men from school were the only people I could enlist to spruce up Mom's love life. A bachelor teacher would be great, but why couldn't I just introduce a friend's dad? The problem wasn't just that Mom hated men who had wives. I also didn't want my friends to pity me after I introduced their dads to my mom. I'd have to wait a whole year before getting a new teacher. In addition, there was no guarantee that next year's teacher would be a man, and even if he was a man, there was no guarantee he'd be a bachelor. This year wasn't necessarily my last chance to have an unmarried male teacher, and maybe in the future I'd meet a superior bachelor teacher, but by then Mom would be older.

The homeroom teacher entered. Because everyone had been talking about how he and the art teacher met, when we saw his face, we had nothing else to ask him about his supposed lover. It felt like we knew more than he did about his relationship. The teacher thought our unusual quiet strange, and he told us several bland jokes. But no one laughed. The kids who usually broke into laughter as soon as he opened his mouth were lukewarm today. The teacher fiddled with his tie, an awkward expression on his face. That empty gesture really did make him look like Leslie Cheung. I didn't know how Leslie Cheung looked, but in that moment, my homeroom teacher somehow resembled him.

"If Leslie Cheung hadn't died, I'd just introduce *him* to my mom," I told Jinu.

"Leslie Cheung?" Jinu asked. "I heard he lives in Las Vegas."

"What are you saying?"

When I said that Leslie Cheung had committed suicide, Jinu answered: "I know. But I heard that's not actually true."

"Then what is true?"

According to Jinu, Leslie Cheung was currently living in Las Vegas. To be specific, he didn't live in Las Vegas, he lived in a town nearby. And one of his neighbors was Elvis Presley. Elvis Presley had died quite a while ago, too. His death was a well-known fact. Was Las Vegas a town where everyone had risen from the dead? If I went to visit, would Dad be there, too?

"Mom, my homeroom teacher is supposedly getting married."

After I repeated the news three times, Mom finally replied. Just barely, as she was squeezing lettuce leaves into her mouth.

"Well, he does have everything. No kids, no debt: he needs a wife."

Mom looked like she thought nothing of it. *I* was the one whose insides were twisting. Men who were in relationships but acted like they weren't needed to be buried. I'd never felt this sort of betrayal from my dad, and he had cheated on my mom. But I couldn't forgive my teacher. I wanted to shift all the blame from my dad to my homeroom teacher, and have him arrested. I ate dinner and crawled under my blankets early, but because of the disgust I felt toward my homeroom teacher, I couldn't sleep at all. Finally I took a pillow and went to Mom's room. Her breath smelled like grass.

"Mom, did Leslie Cheung have a hook nose?" I asked.

"What are you talking about, a hook nose?" she replied. "His nose was perfect, nothing embarrassing, not even a spot."

Mom spoke like she was remembering Leslie Cheung fondly.

"Is a hook nose an embarrassing nose?"

"You're asking if a hook nose is an embarrassing nose?"

Mom answered after I'd asked twice.

"They're not all like that, but the hook noses I've known were. They're a little embarrassing."

"A little embarrassing?"

"Yeah."

Mom was falling asleep.

"Was Dad embarrassing, too?"

There was no answer. I was lying on my side, but I turned to look at the ceiling. The sky wasn't that much higher. I thought about Dad, who must be up there somewhere, and fluttered my eyes open and closed. Mom had looked at my homeroom teacher and said he resembled Leslie Cheung. Minyeong Han and Jinu had looked at Dad and said he resembled our teacher. So then, did Dad look like Leslie Cheung? All night, I sped down an uneven road that felt like it had been embossed with a pattern. Speed bumps were scattered across the road, mixed among the figures of my homeroom teacher, Dad, and Leslie Cheung. Leslie Cheung had a vague appearance, my teacher looked disgraceful, and Dad was—well, I missed him.

In the morning, the speed bumps I'd been driving over all night turned into something vague, like cotton candy. Sitting at the breakfast table—the meadow—Mom said that, come to think of it, the art teacher looked like Anita Mui.

"Who's that?" I asked.

"Leslie Cheung's lover."

Mom really seemed to have accepted my homeroom teacher as Leslie Cheung. And in turn, the art teacher had become Anita Mui. Mom was really open-minded. If I just saw the art teacher and homeroom teacher walking together, my insides twisted, but

Mom was turning our school into a little Hong Kong, filled with Cantonese actors.

"Timid types like your homeroom teacher need to date someone more outgoing. With the art teacher's bluntness, she seemed like she'd be alright for him."

Mom was, once again, explaining things like she was an expert. When I imagined the two teachers as Leslie Cheung and Anita Mui, for some strange reason I was even more unable to forgive my homeroom teacher. Whenever I saw him, I got worked up. And so I glared at him, secretly peeking through the window of the faculty room. One day, we made eye contact as I was glaring, and he asked me if I wanted some ice cream. Of course, I said. I had to take what I could get from my teacher, especially if it meant I could eat for free.

My teacher took us to McDonald's, like a dork. McDonald's was the store closest to the school gates. I grabbed my teacher's shirt and said: "There's nothing to eat here but burgers."

My teacher asked if I didn't like hamburgers. I answered without looking at him.

"Hamburgers are beside the point. Today you said you'd buy me ice cream."

Distinguishing between hamburgers and ice cream reminded me of my art teacher pointing out the differences between landscape drawings and made-up drawings. Annoyance surged inside me. I pulled my teacher out of McDonald's and took us to an organic ice cream store. Worried that Jinu might be following us, I hurried inside. I stared at him—no, glared at him—the whole time I was eating ice cream, observing my teacher's fingers with a piercing gaze. He had no ring. Being in a relationship and not even wearing a couple ring to commemorate it is a crime. It's small, but a crime nonetheless. Anyway, maybe what Mom had said was true: maybe my teacher was lacking something.

"Sir, do you have debt?" I asked him.

"Do I have a pet?" He had misheard.

"No, I'm wondering if you owe money."

My homeroom teacher smiled like he was at a loss for words. In that moment, his face really did look like Leslie Cheung. I didn't know how Leslie Cheung looked, but my teacher really resembled him. I stopped glaring at my teacher and continued my questions while staring at the pattern on my napkin.

"Sir, do you like Leslie Cheung?" I questioned.

"Leslie Cheung? Well, I did like him in the movie *A Better Tomorrow*. But, Hongdo, do you even know who Leslie Cheung is? Leslie Cheung is from *my* generation. *A Better Tomorrow* was the peak of his fame. Back then every middle schooler in the country was wearing a trench coat like Chow Yun-fat did in that movie."

When my homeroom teacher said this, Leslie Cheung suddenly seemed like the most dislikable person in the world.

"I hate him," I said. "My friend says he's still alive. But obviously he died, and I hate it when people go around spreading rumors like that. People should always be clear. If someone died, they should act like they're dead! If they're married, they should act like they're married!"

If they're in a relationship, they should act like they're in a relationship! I was going to say that, too, but I couldn't.

"The cotton candy man—do you like him?" I asked.

"Cotton candy? Hmm. I don't really like sweet things. Do you, Hongdo?"

"All kids like sweet things."

"Well, cotton candy is a snack for kids. I bought it a lot, too, when I was younger. Cotton candy and sugar candy!"

"Oh! Those are the two things I hate more than anything. I like other food, but cotton candy and sugar candy are too cheap. I don't know why people buy them."

"Cheap?"

My homeroom teacher stared at me for a while. A few more of my questions flew at him like axes. When we'd finished the ice cream, my homeroom teacher threw a boomerang of a question back at me.

"Hongdo, are you mad at me for some reason?"

My teacher had a very pleasant expression on his face as he asked. The person asking wasn't just a substitute teacher for the Shrew, or the boyfriend of our art teacher: he was Leslie Cheung, and only Leslie Cheung. I swiveled my head to the side like an idiot.

I couldn't help it: after a few days, the truth about my hastily made-up taste in snacks came out. Jinu and I were eating sugar candy in front of the school when the homeroom teacher walked past. He passed by smiling, and I made a feeble excuse.

"We have to have *something* to eat outside school."

The homeroom teacher briefly rubbed my head and then left. That action influenced my entire day. I didn't hear any of Jinu's chatter the entire way home. Jinu didn't like being ignored, so he let me stroll a few steps ahead and then stopped walking completely.

"Hongdo!" he shouted. "Why are you being like this today?"

When I looked at Jinu with rounded eyes, he was bouncing up and down for some reason.

"I know why you're upset. But don't let it bother you. It's because our teacher just rubbed your head, right?"

I was surprised and couldn't say anything.

"I know you hate our teacher, but school is just like this sometimes."

Jinu patted me on the back twice and then skipped off.

That guy still didn't know anything about girls.

Even after I got home, I kept thinking about how our teacher had rubbed my head, twice. I made a resolution that tomorrow, as soon as school ended, I'd go straight to a hair salon and shave all my hair off. If only the teacher hadn't complimented my hair-pin the next day, I probably would have gone through with the plan. But our teacher saw the pink pins Mom had put in my hair and smiled as he said, “How pretty!” I returned home after school a complete wreck. I couldn’t control my feelings: I wanted to inject Botox or something into my emotions. So I could paralyze my feelings. I didn’t care if there were side effects. As long as something was different from now, that was all that mattered.

7. HANAM: GANGNAM STYLE

The classroom romance died. According to Mom, there was a time when North Korean planes had dropped flyers from the sky, declaring the DPRK’s greatness, and when the boys got whipped instead of the girls. I felt like I had been born in the wrong era. I should have attended school back when you could pick up flyers off the ground and exchange them for mechanical pencils, when the boys chivalrously stepped up to be punished instead of the girls. There were, of course, no longer any of the flyers Mom had described, but it wasn’t just that: nowadays, it was even hard to find kids willing to sacrifice themselves for others. Even if there was some romantic kid willing to be punished for someone else, there was no way that his probably fanatical mother would stay quiet about it. I didn’t need to go far to find proof. Jinu Kim was a typical case of someone who’d been overtaken by his mother’s fanaticism. When I mentioned how things had been in the past, Jinu’s answer was what I expected.

“I’m sorry. I want to be hit instead of you, but I should listen to my mom.”

Jinu said that if he got hit instead of someone else, his mom would be upset. Huh. I guess he was worried that people would think he didn’t care about his family. Jinu didn’t have much else to say today. After mixing three ladles of sugar candy in a row, Jinu finally opened his mouth again.

"My mom and dad are getting divorced."

Jinu cooked the sugar until the ladle burned. Then he started to make his fourth candy disc.

"And starting next month, I have to go to another tutoring center. Maybe then I won't have time to make sugar candy."

Jinu threw the ladle aside as he stood up. He said: "I think there's some connection between their divorce and tutoring. So I don't really like it, how they're getting divorced."

I thought of what Mom had said, that Jinu's mom's boyfriend was a passing fancy. Mom was always saying things like this. She acted like she was an expert, but her men kept getting stolen by other women. Like Leslie Cheung, who was eventually abandoned by Anita Mui! I could hear the clacking noise of the art teacher's shoes, so I hurried away from school.

"Gone to the weekend farm—Mom."

That message was all she left for me at home. After joining the organic club—even though of course she said she'd joined it for me—Mom was way too busy. According to my calculations, Mom had been in love with Leslie Cheung when Anita Mui appeared. That broke her heart, but now she felt better. I don't know, then, why she'd paid so much attention to the art teacher's brooch. It was late when Mom returned.

"Why do you always just look at your land and not even do any actual farming?" I asked.

"Do you understand how wonderful dirt is?"

Mom opened the fridge as she said this. She didn't say anything, even though I clearly hadn't eaten what she'd prepared for me. It seemed like she hadn't noticed.

Mom was leaving the house a lot. The field of grass that she'd prepared for dinner waited on the table. When the sun set, I would look out the window blankly, like I was the grubby flag hanging limp on the veranda. A few days later, I saw Mom outside with some man. They greeted each other, leaning forward at a ninety-degree angle like a new bride and groom bowing to each other. My heart pounded loudly. The man wasn't my dead father, and it wasn't my teacher, who was in a relationship. So it was a man I didn't know. Could Mom have a boyfriend?

"Did you go see the land again?" I asked when she got home.

"What do you mean?" she said. "It's called weekend farming for a reason."

As Mom said that, she pulled out a bunch of tutoring flyers, for some reason. Since I was getting older, I needed to attend tutoring, she said.

"Why?" I asked.

"What do you mean, why? Everyone else has to study, and you're the only one who gets to play? I'm not home much nowadays, and I need to make sure you study enough. If you don't want to do Korean or English or math tutoring, let's sign you up for art. Anyway, you have to go to tutoring."

"Why are you sending me to tutoring all of a sudden?"

My head felt empty, and what Jinu had said earlier flew around inside me, buzzing like flies. The buzzing sound intensified at the end of my nose. I frowned, worried that I'd start crying. I purposefully coughed, loudly—until my irritated throat started to regurgitate food.

My homeroom teacher and Mom had ended their relationship before it even started, but that didn't mean I wanted her to look for other men. When I thought about Mom getting into a relationship with someone else, I could hear that buzzing sound at the edge of my nose. I thought about my homeroom teacher with another woman—like the art teacher—and that made me feel just as suffocated. It was like I was stuck between my mom and my teacher, or maybe two people who didn't know each other at all, but *I* was the one suffering from heartbreak.

After he started to attend more tutoring, Jinu didn't hang out in front of school anymore. Even after being let out of prison, it felt like I was still in jail. The organic field of greens that Mom left on the table was waiting for me when I got home, but Mom wasn't there. The tutoring flyers were spread out by subject. Just like Mom threw out the flyers for black bean noodles, spicy noodle soup, pizza, and fried chicken when they were stuck to our front entryway, I threw away the tutoring flyers. And when I grabbed a carton of milk from the fridge, I took out Mom's soju as well. I stuck a straw in the bottle. I drank some, and my insides burned like I was drilling a manhole into my stomach. It hurt, like going down the waterfall on a log ride, but it wasn't bad.

"Oh my god, my daughter is crazy!"

Those are the last words I remember hearing. Something flitted through my mind, and then I opened my eyes and it was morning. If my memories were correct, the day before, I'd stuck a straw in a bottle of soju and drunk it down to the last drop.

The morning after I drank alcohol for the first time, there was no dried pollack soup on the breakfast table, waiting for me as a hangover cure. There was no bean sprout soup, either. I just sat at the table, stomach full of grass as always, and if anything was different, it was that Mom gave me warm milk with honey. That was my hangover remedy. I drank it in one gulp and then sighed loudly like an old man. To be honest, my insides didn't feel too weird. Since I'd gotten drunk so fast and sprawled out on the ground almost immediately, I didn't even really remember the taste of the soju. I felt fine—I wasn't sure I'd even *drunk* any soju. To sum up, I felt a little anxious.

The whole way to school, I kept thinking about ski lessons. Soju was like skiing. In my rush to make it down the slopes, I didn't bother learning how to stop, so I'd tumbled down the mountain in a straight line, at a very fast pace. In my hurry to drink soju, I hadn't learned how to enjoy it: I'd blacked out straightaway. It was a good metaphor, but when I told the story to Jinu, he suddenly said that I smelled like alcohol. It was strange that he'd had no response until then, although I didn't hate what he'd said. The smell of alcohol was more intense than any perfume. It was the best perfume.

Since I liked art better than Korean, English, or math, I'd been drawing in art class with the intensity of someone writing their will. Several days later, the art teacher called me up to her desk.

"Hongdo," she said. "Your drawing is good. The composition is great, and the colors are good, too. I'm thinking about making you the school representative for the next education department art competition, but there's a problem."

Was there ever *not* a problem?

"This isn't our school. As you know, the prompt for the competition is to make a landscape drawing of your school."

"It looks the same as the front gate, though."

The fish jerky man was here, the hot dog man was there, the slushy man was there, the cotton candy man was here, the sugar candy man was here: I pointed to each vendor like I was looking for the answers to a hidden pictures puzzle. The art teacher tapped the glass on the desk with her pointer finger and said: "Well, that's the problem. We decided in a faculty meeting that this isn't what our school looks like."

"Why?"

"If this picture is shown in the competition, it's not just your talents being made public, Hongdo, it's our school. The reason I don't feel great about the way you drew the front of our school is because of our policy. Our school isn't some cafeteria or flea market. The Gangnam schools aren't like this."

The more she talked, the more inscrutable her expression became.

"Aren't we in Hanam?" I asked.

"Of course. But the principal wants to promote the Gangnam lifestyle, and there's no reason why not. The words she said in the school meeting were, 'This is a drawing that hasn't adjusted to the time change.' Or was it 'a drawing that hadn't adjusted to changing times'? Anyhow."

This was the opinion made official in the school meeting: the fish man and the flasher, and the sugar candy man, were to be erased from fourth-grader Hongdo Park's painting, replaced by flowers and trees.

"Like this."

The art teacher pulled a sheet from a thick heap of drawing paper and showed me, but it didn't look like she was sketching anything. There was really nothing in her drawing. The school gates were okay, and there was a fence, and in front of it, there were beautifully blooming flowers. Children were laughing with their heads turned to the side, and they were all the same height. I scrutinized this drawing with nothing in it for a while. I wanted to ask the same thing I did when Mom pushed a salad made of lettuce in a muddle of sauce at me. "What is this?"

Our homeroom teacher told us that he'd planned to get married next spring, but he was pushing the wedding date forward. Of course, he didn't say that to us directly, it was information we had figured out. The news yielded interest, like all rumors do, and the story spread that his fiancée wasn't really the art teacher: it was another woman. A little while later, rumors spread that the other woman was the Shrew. Apparently, our homeroom teacher was actually the Shrew's fiancé.

"So soon the Shrew will come back. Since the kid's been born, she'll change places again with the substitute homeroom teacher."

A rumbling sound came out of Jinu's belly as he said that. He suffered from a hunger that couldn't be satisfied with food. The bad snacks had disappeared from the front of our school, moving faster than rumors. They'd disappeared, then reappeared briefly, then disappeared again. Students calmed their snack withdrawal symptoms with rumors about our homeroom teacher. The words swirling around our school floated out the main gate and onto the streets, over several speed bumps.

8. A HOLE IN THE SKETCHBOOK

The fish fillet man disappeared. The next day,
The ice cream man disappeared. The day after that,
The hamburger man disappeared,
then we found him by the school's side entrance. Next,
the sugar candy man disappeared,
but thankfully he survived. The criminal to blame
was *organic.*

The men who'd made the front of our school so sweet were essential ingredients in the lives of us kids, but to the adults, they were ingredients worthy of a blacklist. With black paint, I erased the problem people by ones and twos. From the fish fillet man to the sugar candy man: I flecked paint over these vanished people until their forms were unrecognizable. Finally, all that was left in my painting was murky blackness.

Before the paint could dry, I pierced a hole in my sketchbook. The inside of the hole was dark as the paint. The flasher, the cotton candy man, the kidnapper, the fish man: they were all melting into the murky smears. The men became one. They were like a face on a wanted sign, someone guilty of kidnapping. The kidnapper twirled sugar into cotton candy on a ladle from the sugar candy stand. The ladle was heated by the fish fillet man's butane gas canister. The kidnapper held several sacks of ingredients and said: "The world's actually round. That's how it is, right?"

The packages were all different. Organic sugar, nonorganic sugar, organic sugar, nonorganic sugar. The kidnapper scooped up a heap of sugar with a ladle and poured it into the different sacks. The packages varied in price and shape, but they all held the same sugar inside. And each was labeled differently. The kidnapper scooped up water with the same ladle and poured it into the sacks. The packages varied in price and shape, but they all held the same water inside. And each was labeled differently. The kidnapper scooped up dye with the same ladle and poured it into the sacks. The packages varied in price and shape, but they all held the same dye inside . . .

"What's that? Hey, you!"

The kidnapper looked at me. He was wearing a hat, so I couldn't see his eyes. I gulped down the spit in my mouth.

"You, what are you doing? Come in! I said come in."

The kidnapper gestured for me to enter the hole. The hole in the sketchbook grew larger and larger until it was big enough for me to fall inside it. The kidnapper began to take steps toward me. I mumbled the words from my conversation with Jinu, words I'd memorized like they were the Lord's Prayer.

"You know, my mom, she's never really done anything with her life."

"But she looks like she has a lot of money!"

"No, that's not true. Not really. She can't—can't—get a job."

The kidnapper was distracted. He'd come one step closer to me and then draw two steps back. He lifted the trench coat he was wearing, he twirled cotton candy, and he crouched like he was going to punch a shape out of the sugar candy. The smell of fish emanated from his body.

"You, do you know who I am?" he asked.

Who are you? But the words didn't come out of my mouth. The kidnapper's nose flashed briefly under his hat. It was a nose with no speed bump. It was a nose you could run down at full speed.

"Number 40511, Hongdo Park!"

The kidnapper's voice echoed down the long alley. Someone grabbed me by the back of my neck, and I could feel myself being pulled.

"Hongdo, what are you doing there?"

It was my homeroom teacher. His face twirled in front of my eyes. Even though the kidnapper was wearing a hat, I felt like I could already see the scars hiding underneath. The kidnapper wasn't the flasher from earlier, but it seemed like I could draw what was inside the kidnapper's coat. All the things that had disappeared from my school hung from the man's body in clusters, and they fell out of the sketchbook.

"Hongdo, are you alright? Why are you sweating like that?"

My homeroom teacher wiped my forehead with a tissue. His face shook in front of my eyes. A speed bump took its place firmly in the middle of his sharp nose. Maybe to my mom that hook nose was a blacklisted ingredient, but it wasn't to me.

"Hongdo, is something upsetting you?" he asked.

"Sir, I wish my mind were like flour. I wish I could make it into dough and shape it like I want."

As I said that, my face burned like a fish fillet being cooked over a fire. My eyes twirled like a ladle of sugar candy. A burning smell emanated from my tongue. My homeroom teacher rubbed my shoulder comfortingly. I dried my eyes, blew my nose, and wiped off my sweat, and at some moment, when I looked around at my surroundings, I saw a whole lot of tissues at my feet, like flowers.

A week later, the art teacher called me in again.

"Did you draw a new picture?" she asked.

"I just painted over the old one."

"On top of the old picture?"

"Yes. But the Gangnam trees and flowers the principal said to include—there was no space, so I couldn't draw them."

I opened my sketchbook. The entire image was just black. Here and there, the depth of color and the texture varied. There were paler grayish sections and other parts with holes punched out of them, big enough for fingers to go in and out of. I'd painted so many layers on the paper that it had been punctured by my brush. In my painting, there were the pink school gate and several holes—that was it.

A look of confusion showed itself on the art teacher's face. She closed my sketchbook and said: "Hongdo, if your mind is made out of flour, why is this painting so black?"

"Flour?"

The art teacher gathered up her hair, starting at her forehead, until she reached her part. I closed the door to the faculty room and went out into the hallway. Suddenly my homeroom teacher's face looked like an enormous ball of dough. I wanted to hurl his mouth down the hallway. He'd told the flour story to the art teacher! That was the first confession I'd made to him.

I walked, skipped, ran down the hallway. The hall's length seemed to be commanding me to run. No matter how fast I ran, my feet didn't make any clicking noises. The hallway continued without end. I was drifting between Hanam and Gangnam. There were countless valleys between the two places: valleys where the subway didn't go, and holes where busses didn't stop.

The cotton candy man returned. Jinu, who was still suffering from withdrawal, tingled with excitement. The cotton candy man wore red clothing like Santa Claus and twirled white, sugary beards in the middle of a round machine that resembled a washbasin. Lumps of sugar spun like millstones, like tops, and soon they bloomed into mottled blossoms of cotton candy.

"Sir, this is junk food, isn't it?" I asked.

The cotton candy man still didn't know how to market his products, but business was brisk. As soon as the kids escaped from prison, they hurriedly searched for the cotton candy man for their post-prison meal. The cotton candy man wasn't wearing a hat. Instead, he hid his forehead scars with a bandana made from a Korean flag. He sold over one hundred cotton candies per day, and as soon as he was done with work, he took out his sunglasses and put them on. He started up his motorcycle with a vroom, and the dangling cotton candies wobbled like balloons. The cotton candy man left for home as if he were flying into the heavens, his merchandise swollen like balloons.

And at some point, the man in the trench coat started to appear again. Men on the street wearing coats over exercise pants seemed as ubiquitous as telephone poles. It wasn't just in front of the school: they also lurked in nearby alley corners, standing pole-like before suddenly unfurling their jackets. Their huge penises dangled heavily inside. Come to think of it, cotton candy dangled, too, open and exposed. It seemed like my homeroom teacher's face would appear in the midst of everything. But the trench coat men didn't give us much of their time. They closed their coats again an instant after revealing themselves.

I wasn't able to represent my school in the art competition. The principal chose the landscape painting that portrayed the front of the school like it was in Gangnam, but it didn't win a prize in the competition. There was a clear difference between real Gangnam and real Hanam, and no one paid attention to what lay in between.

My picture served another purpose, though. When the thickly applied black paint dried, the drawing started to give off a strange mood. The organic club moms who'd made our house their hideout saw the picture and were mysteriously entranced by it.

Change the World with Dirt.

With this title, the black drawing passed back through the school gates. Several hundred copies of it were affixed to the surrounding walls. The school zone in front of campus was being wallpapered with the drawing. Volcano eruption, fire, earthquake, tsunami . . . if you saw my drawing, a tangle of words like those came to mind. It seemed like, sometime, the inside of the manhole I'd peeked into would come back to life. The note that I'd written was included alongside the drawing, although in an edited version. One of the moms in the organic club claimed to be a poet.

The fish fillet man disappeared. The next day,
The ice cream man disappeared. The day after that,
The hamburger man disappeared,
then we found him by the school's side entrance. Next,
the sugar candy man disappeared,
but thankfully he survived. The criminal to blame
was *E. coli*.

After finishing my painting, I set down my brush.

Around the time when I gave up my creative pursuits, the organic club moms began to call me an artistic genius.

9. HONGDO, DON'T CRY

News spread that at the end of the month, the homeroom teacher would be leaving our school. The students believed that he was switching schools because he had talent, but Mom said it was because his job was only temporary.

"Do you not like my homeroom teacher?"

When I asked that, Mom looked at me blankly and answered: "What does it matter, if I like him or not?"

"He's not your style?"

"He has a hook nose."

"But why did you like Dad? He had a hook nose."

Mom didn't answer. She probably didn't know the answer.

I paced up and down the hallway several times, hoping to see my teacher. After the school day ended, I went back to his classroom. I couldn't explain why I was acting like this. Only when I saw his face through the window, from the hallway, did I feel relieved.

"Unfortunately—"

That's what our teacher said to us the day he left. "Unfortunately, I will be leaving." My heart pounded furiously. For a while, I hadn't been able to see the teacher's face correctly. In my mind, for a long time, our teacher had slowly been losing his hair, locks vanishing like they were being eaten up by a grain thresher. So when I looked at him properly for the first time in a while, he actually looked a little handsome. I seemed to have been aging him too fast in my dreams. As the teacher gave a long speech about the beauty of endings, he looked cool, and I felt confused. I thought of his face in my dreams. *Sir, stop it—bald head, come back!*

The teacher said he was going to America. That was all we knew.

"Everyone, do you remember the poem I talked about once? Kim Chunsu's 'Flowers.' When someone says your name, you become the most meaningful being in the world."

The kids went up to the podium one by one, starting with those by the window. The teacher hugged us while saying our names. He gently patted our backs and shoulders. I stared at the spectacle, but felt strange. As each child went forward, my heart beat a little faster. Finally, when all the kids in row one had gone, and it was time for row two, my stomach made a rumbling noise and began to hurt—it was like my heart was exhausted. As my stomach pained me, the kids in row three received hugs from our teacher. And finally row four! The kids in front of me went up one by one to get hugs from the teacher. My stomach rumbled turbulently. It felt like I needed to run to the bathroom. I stood up carefully so I wouldn't let out an embarrassing noise. Everything went by sluggishly, as if in slow motion. My teacher saw me, he extended his arms toward me, he wrapped his two arms around me, and with one hand he patted my back twice. I was surprised, because it seemed like some part of his fingers was going to touch my bra hook. That day, I'd worn my size 65AA bra that had a hook rather than a band, for the first time, and before the idiot boys could run their fingers over it, my homeroom teacher had patted it. My teacher hit my back with a tapping, or maybe a flicking, or maybe a rapping noise, or did it sound more like dripping? Anyway, as he knocked on my back, I was so overwhelmed that I almost farted. I just barely held it in. And after he said my name, I couldn't hear a single one of his words of advice. When I finally gathered myself together, everyone in row four had all finished their hugs. My stomach must have been crazy, because it didn't hurt anymore and just felt normal.

"What did our teacher just say to me?" I asked Jinu.

Jinu shrugged. This was how it was. He was too preoccupied to remember what he'd said to *him*, much less other people.

"To me he said, 'Jinu, get a pretty girlfriend.' Something like that?"

If I'd known the homeroom teacher was going to give such a concrete message, I would have paid more attention. It was no use feeling regretful. The teacher had already left for the faculty room. For a moment, I considered going down there and asking the teacher what his advice for me was, but it was a silly idea. If he couldn't remember either, I'd feel even more hurt. What had he said, what had he said? The kids left the classroom in swarms. Jinu pestered me to hurry up. I purposefully packed up my things slowly and left the classroom last. Minyeong Han passed by me.

"You, why did the teacher say that to you?" she asked.

"What?"

"'Hongdo, don't cry.' That. Did you really cry? You do everything to try to catch his eye—ugh."

Once again, the hallway was long enough for me to run down it. I dashed down the hall like the floor was going to fall beneath my feet. Everything around me flew out the windows.

The cotton candy outside was two times bigger than usual. What was usually the size of a child's head was now the size of an adult's head. It looked like an eyelid puffy from crying. I wiped the puffy pink eyelid as if I was wiping away tears. Jinu was taken aback.

"What are you doing with my cotton candy?" he questioned.

I was flattening the puffy eyelids with my hands so no more tears could come out of them. I pulled off a fistful and held it out to Jinu.

"What's this for?" Jinu asked, looking upset.

"Cotton candy is full of lies. Let's each eat a bite—it's our duty."

Jinu pushed the cotton candy forward like he was punching me. I hid my face in the snack he was thrusting toward. Nothing came out of the fluffy bundle until we'd gone over the crosswalk in front of school. Then it somehow seemed like a huge fish bone was sticking out of the cotton candy.

Printed and bound by CPI Group (UK) Ltd, Croydon, CR0 4YY

10/04/2024

14481892-0001